Shadow's Son:

… its finest, be prepared for a late night'
… nyder, *New York Times* bestselling author

… vord-and-sorcery tale, with intriguing characters,
… ves at a quick pace' *Booklist*

… *w's Son* is easily one of my favourite books of 2010'
Fantasy Book Critic

'W… Sprunk gets going, he writes with an energy that has to be … erienced to be believed . . . a thoroughly entertaining rea… *Graeme's Fantasy Book Review*

Also by Jon Sprunk from Gollancz:

Shadow's Son
Shadow's Lure
Shadow's Master

SHADOW'S MASTER

Jon Sprunk

Maps by Ed Bourelle

First published by Pyr®,
an imprint of Prometheus Books,
59 John Glenn Drive, Amherst, NY 14228–2119
www.pyrsf.com

First published in Great Britain in 2012 by
Gollancz
An imprint of the Orion Publishing Group
Orion House, 5 Upper St Martin's Lane, London WC2H 9EA
An Hachette UK Company

This edition published in Great Britain in 2013 by Gollancz

1 3 5 7 9 10 8 6 4 2

A CIP catalogue record for this book is available
from the British Library

ISBN 978 0 575 09612 7

Typeset at The Spartan Press Ltd,
Lymington, Hants

Printed in Great Britain by Clays Ltd, St Ives plc

The Orion Publishing Group's policy is to use papers that are natural, renewable and recyclable products and made from wood grown in sustainable forests. The logging and manufacturing processes are expected to conform to the environmental regulations of the country of origin.

www.jonsprunk.com
www.orionbooks.co.uk
www.gollancz.co.uk

For too many reasons to name,
this book is dedicated to my wife, Jenny.

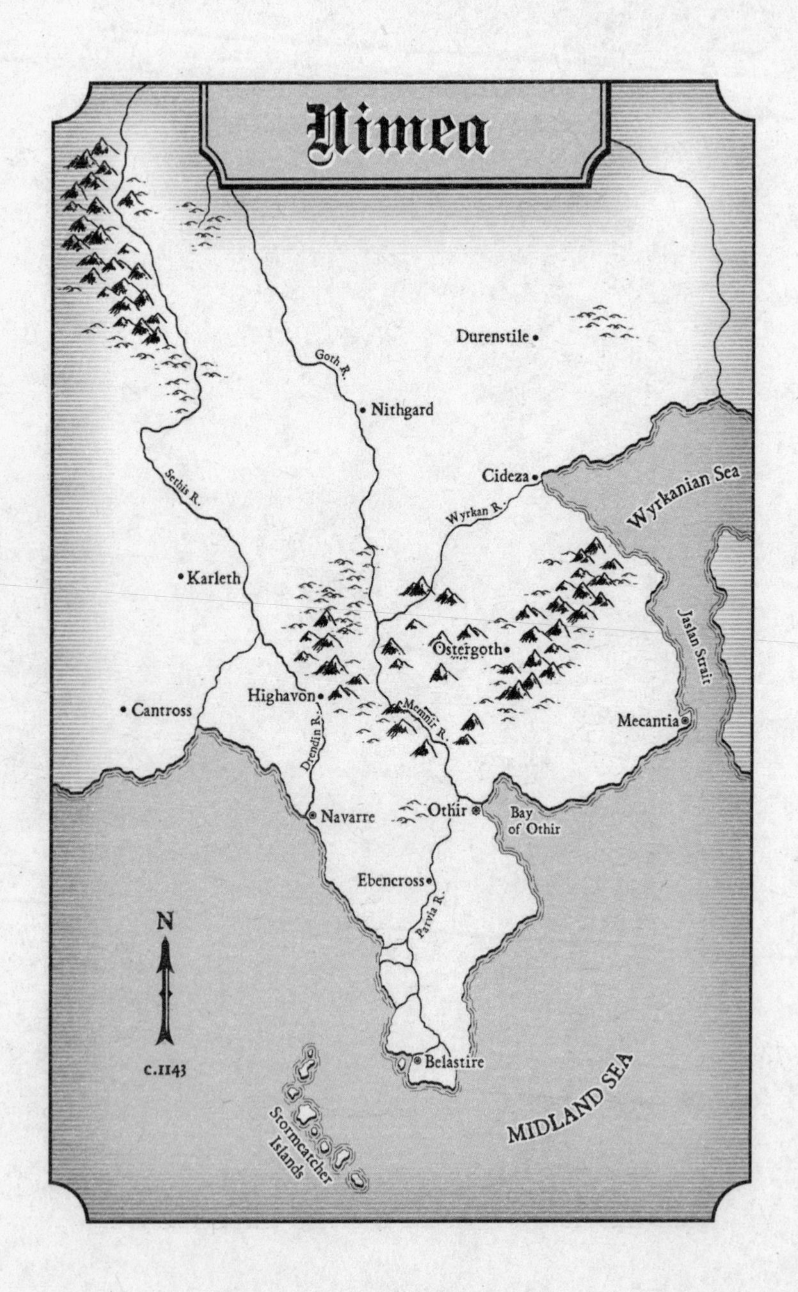
Nimea
Durenstile
Goth R.
Nithgard
Cideza
Wyrkanian Sea
Sethis R.
Wyrkan R.
Karleth
Jaslan Strait
Ostergoth
Highavon
Cantross
Memmir R.
Drendin R.
Mecantia
Navarre
Othir
Bay of Othir
Ebencross
Parvia R.
N
c.1143
Belastire
MIDLAND SEA
Stormcatcher Islands

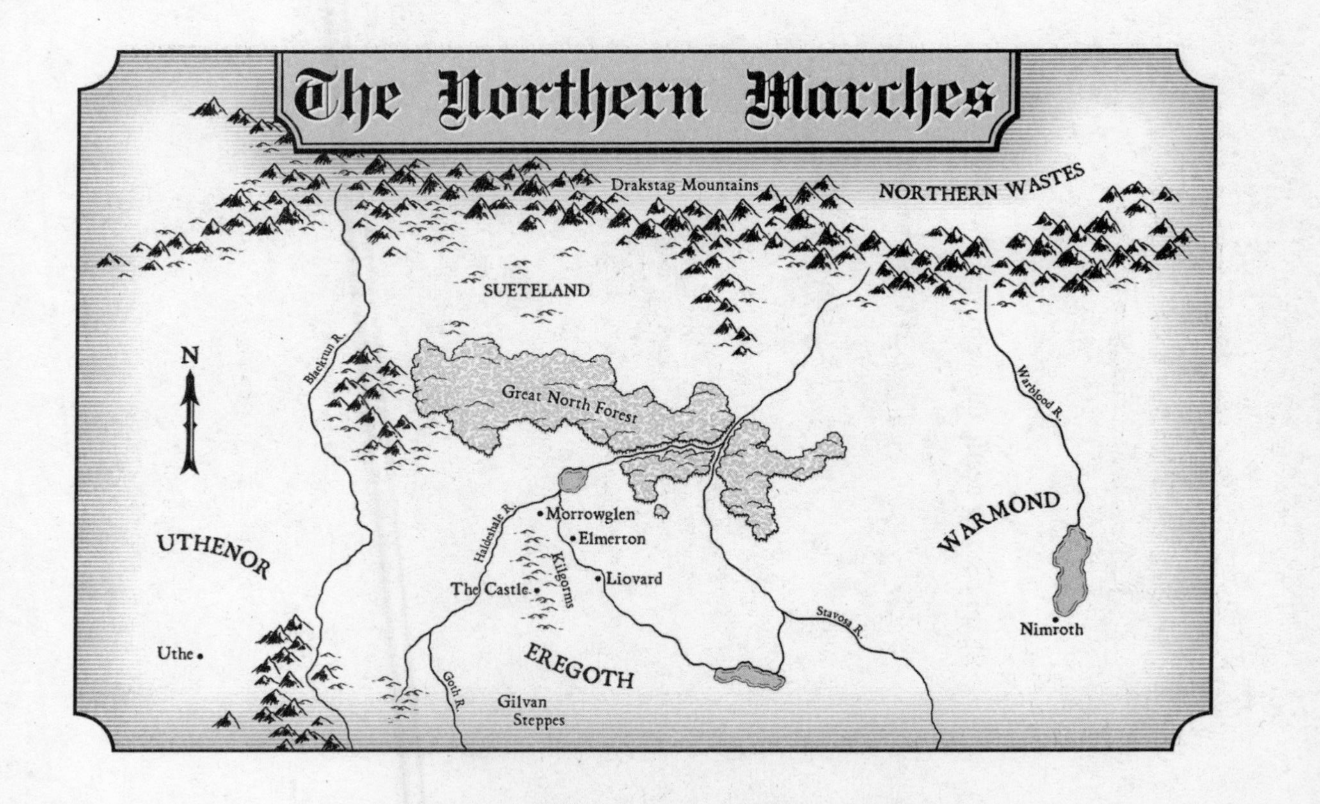
The Northern Marches
Drakstag Mountains
NORTHERN WASTES
SUETELAND
N
Blackrun R.
Great North Forest
Warblood R.
WARMOND
Haldeshale R.
Morrowglen
Elmerton
Liovard
Kilgorms
UTHENOR
The Castle
Stavosa R.
Nimroth
Uthe
EREGOTH
Goth R.
Gilvan
Steppes

I am become death, the destroyer of worlds.

– J. Robert Oppenheimer

CHAPTER ONE

Shadows pooled on the floor of the broken temple and seeped into the cracks between the stones as he stepped out of the portal.

Splintered ends of charred wooden beams protruded from the mounds of shattered masonry, which had fallen from the ceiling and now gaped open to the night sky. Ashes rustled as the gateway closed with a quiet whisper. Outside, chaos reigned over the fallen city. Shouts and despondent cries wafted in from the street along with the stench of burning flesh as Lord Talus's soldiers slaked their lusts on Liovard's hapless survivors. But inside the sanctuary another presence lingered, reeking of death.

Balaam walked around an overturned sarcophagus, its ancient stone surface riddled with cracks. He stopped beside a long smudge on the floor beside a hollow scrying pool. The power he'd felt radiated from the stain. Balaam knelt and traced the spot with his fingers. Here. This was where she had met her end.

He called to the shadows. While they spun a connection between worlds, he stood and took a deep breath. An image formed in the air, a picture of this chamber as it had been on a night two moons ago. In the picture much of the rubble was gone, although some debris littered the floor. The surface of the scrying pool glistened as Lady Sybelle lay against it. Blood streaked her aristocratic features; her black dress was ripped and powdered with dust. A man in southern garb entered the frame. He was not overly large or intimidating, but Lady Sybelle stiffened as he approached.

'Where is she?' the man asked. His voice was low and coarse, like two river stones scraping together.

When she did not answer, the man grabbed her with both hands. 'Tell me where she is!'

Lady Sybelle looked up at him. No, beyond him. Northward. 'You have her eyes,' she whispered.

The man shook her back and forth. 'Where is . . . ?'

Her eyes took on a sudden clarity and focused on his face. 'Find Erebus. Your moth—'

The man jerked back as streamers of smoke rose from her body. Flames lit up the sanctum, highlighting the cracks running through the walls. Lady Sybelle was burning, but Balaam studied her foe. *So this is the scion.*

There was nothing remarkable about the man on the surface. But Balaam looked into the man's eyes and saw his own reflection in their flat surfaces.

Balaam brushed the detritus from his gloves. Lady Sybelle's demise was unfortunate, but far worse was her infidelity at the end. She had betrayed her liege, her people, and her family. He couldn't understand why she would do such a thing. It went against everything he lived for: there was no self, only duty. Balaam glanced around at the destruction. So much potential lost. So much time wasted.

A sliding footstep stirred the dust behind him. Balaam turned to meet his contact. The man was short. Loose folds of skin around his eyes and under his chin hinted he had once been pudgier, but no doubt the last few weeks had been hard on him. After Sybelle's fall, her favored priests found few allies in the new regime. But they had reemerged from the shadows since Lord Talus's victory like maggots spilling from a rotten corpse.

'I am Willich, second archaract of the high fane.' His pale lips twitched as he nodded. 'What message has the Master for me?'

His tone was sharp, almost insolent. Balaam made no movement, except to touch the pommel of his *kalishi* sword with the small finger of his right hand. The gesture was enough to make the priest gulp. His tiny eyes retreated farther into their nests of puckered skin.

'How did this happen?' Balaam didn't look down, but he made it clear what he meant.

The priest licked his lips, which continued to wriggle like two albino worms. 'The Dark Mother was overcome by a stranger who came in the night. He made some trouble with the duke's son, and then the people rose up. My brothers and I tried to help—'

'Tried? Where were you when the scion came for her? Where were your brothers? You who swore to give your lives at her whim. No. You ran.'

'No!'

'You hid in some dank hole like a rat.'

'No!' The priest clutched the robe at his chest where the black amulet of his faith swung. 'How dare you question me, Talon? I have met the new Master. Lord Talus has every confidence in my loyalty.'

A sad statement of these times. Talus had a reputation for expediency. As ruthless as he was successful, he had been waging a winning campaign in the west before this. Now he was shoring up the losses from Lady Sybelle's failure, and who knew what delays that would mean.

The priest was still blustering. 'I shall be on the council that rules Liovard when the new Master departs.'

Balaam curled his fingers around the sword hilt. The warlord's plans were none of his concern. Unfortunately, the priest kept talking, faster with every word as if to prove his value.

'He has announced he will punish those responsible. Everyone knows this menace came from the south. From Nimea, the old whore. The new Master will punish her—'

The priest gasped and put a hand to his loose belly. Balaam held himself rigid, arm extended. 'You failed Lady Sybelle,' he said. 'And failed the one and *only* Master.'

Balaam retracted his sword. The priest sighed as the black blade left his body; then he toppled to the floor. Balaam swept the *kalishi* sword in a half-circle to clear the gore, wiped it on the priest's wide back, and slid it back into the scabbard. The blood called to him, but he resisted, sickened by the idea of feeding from this slug.

Finished here, Balaam left the temple through a fissure in the leaning walls. The sky was laden with heavy black clouds, but the city was awash in darting yellow-and-red light as the fires spread. Bodies sprawled on the cobblestones seeped in blood and ash. None escaped the wrath of Lord Talus, none except the city's former ruler, whom Balaam heard had escaped during the assault. Now entire wards of Liovard burned while soldiers searched for the missing sovereign.

This is how the world will be remade. By fire and shadow. The Master foresaw it, and now it comes to pass.

A shadow floated down to settle on his shoulder. Balaam listened to its message before sending it off. The trail in Liovard was cold. If he had been summoned sooner . . . but there was no use dwelling on that.

Calling upon the darkness, he turned his back on Lady Sybelle's failed experiment and stepped though the forming portal.

CHAPTER TWO

The snow-clad tops of the Drakstag Mountains chewed at the underbelly of a dreary sky as the caravan made torturous progress up the narrow pass. Caim watched a line of thunderclouds approach from the east, crowding out the horizon. The sun's fading rays reflected off sheets of ice on the canyon walls. It wouldn't be long now.

Up ahead, the caravaneer, Teromich, peered back from his seat on the first wagon, wearing his customary frown. *You feel them, too? Watching us. You should've brought more men. Teromich.*

Caim reached under his wool cloak to loosen his knives. They were twenty-seven days out of Gerak's Rock and the last known point of civilization south of the Drakstags. The caravan consisted of three wagons loaded with trade goods, mostly bronzewares, and seven guards on horseback. Aemon and Dray rode near the middle of the pack, talking together. Or more likely arguing. Malig rode point ahead of them, his wide shoulders wrapped in a bearskin. Caim shrugged against his cloak, wishing he'd brought a thicker one. The cold, which had been bad enough in Eregoth, had worsened the farther north they went. He could barely feel the tips of his fingers through his gloves. And the days were becoming shorter.

He straightened up in the saddle of his sturdy piebald gelding as a chill touched the back of his neck, but instead of Kit's whisper in his ear, he was treated to a picture in his head of six swarthy men in buckskin coats crouched behind a shelf of rock. Another shadow caressed his ankle through his boot and showed him seven more men in similar garb moving out from the cover of an outcropping. Caim let out a slow breath. He had expected it to start with arrows, or maybe a cascade of rocks. Instead, they approached boldly on foot, slouched low with long knives extended like silver tongues in the dying light. Familiar knives.

Caim sent the shadows out to keep watch. Where was Kit? He hadn't seen her since last night. But he didn't have time to ponder her whereabouts as a high-pitched yell echoed down the pass, and the men he'd spied appeared both in front of and behind the caravan. Only thirteen, but the Suete were renowned for their violent disposition. They didn't wait on pretense.

The driver in the lead wagon fell out of his seat with a throwing blade buried in his neck before he could set the brake. Teromich jumped off as the wagon kept rolling, horses neighing, and a Suete – a swarthy young man with smooth cheeks and bright blue eyes – came up behind the merchant. A spear thrust forced the young Suete to jump back before he could make the kill. Aemon swung his steed between them, giving Teromich a chance to scramble away. Then the rest of the guards arrived. The three armsmen had the awkward look of overgrown farm boys who had decided wearing a sword was more interesting than shoveling manure. Two of them went down in the first pass. Caim's crew fared better. Malig kept a hillman at bay with his broadaxe while Dray and Aemon took on a Suete together and nearly rode him into the ground as they galloped past. Dray came around quicker and slid from his steed to meet the Suete on foot. The hillman closed with frightening speed. Dray barely fended off the lightning-quick attacks. One stumble would have spelled his end, but Aemon's spear hurtled over his shoulder and slammed into the Suete. Side by side, the brothers moved around the caravan looking for another foe.

Caim wheeled his horse around with a kick and a jerk of the reins. The seven Suete behind the caravan spread out as they approached. They seemed to be taking their time, sizing up the defenses. Caim spotted some gray hair among the men and understood. These were the old hands, the veteran warriors of the tribe. They weren't prone to the recklessness of youth, and that made them especially dangerous.

As he slid from the saddle and drew his knives, the hillmen eyed his *suete* blade. A look passed among the Suete, and one of them came forward alone to meet him. Caim waited on the balls of his feet, his weight balanced, until the hillman came within arm's reach. The shrill cries of striking steel echoed from the stony walls of the pass as their knives arced and collided. The warrior had rows of small white scars across his forehead and down his cheeks. His long hair whipped loose in the wind. He was good, but he couldn't match Caim's speed. After a pair of quick strikes, the hillman fell to his knees, bleeding from his armpit and lower abdomen.

Caim started to deliver the mercy blow when a silvery blur zipped in the corner of his vision. Caim knocked the throwing blade away with his seax knife and turned to a pair of Suete warriors advancing from his flank at a rapid trot. As he settled into a defensive stance, the hillmen separated to come at him from opposite sides.

Both warriors had the same fierce eyes. Eyes like hunting cats. One hillman darted in with a low attack, and Caim pivoted, moving so fast with the power of the shadows flowing through his limbs that he almost tripped over his own feet in the rush to deflect and counter. The warrior's comrade rushed in with an attempted rescue, but Caim wove around the extended knife point. His own *suete* blade flashed once, and the second warrior staggered back. His blood looked like rich red wine dripping down his hide shirt.

A howl alerted Caim as the rest of the hillmen charged him. Caim spun away, but took a shallow cut across the back of his wrist through the cuff of his glove. He deflected a broad, horizontal slash, and then another, and a third. Their knives connected with sharp rings and sprang away, only to return again, but Caim was always a step ahead. He was halfway into a blocking thrust when a tremor ran up through his legs and his vision dimmed. He almost stumbled, but righted himself before the Suete on either side could connect with vicious slashes. His eyesight returned in time to reveal two warriors charging at him, their knives held low for disemboweling cuts. Caim reached out to the shadows clustered in the crevices of the canyon walls as he moved his knives in position to parry. An instant before the hillmen reached him, an avalanche of darkness poured down over them. Caim retreated as the Suete spun about and hacked at the shadows tearing into their skin, and he was reminded of Lord Arion Eviskine, the duke's son; how he and his men had tried to battle the shadows and lost, though their deaths had not been his doing.

Spots of blood appeared on the dry rock of the canyon floor under the hillmen as they rolled on the ground trying to dislodge the darknesses that had infiltrated their clothing. Dizziness washed over Caim, and he forced himself to look away. Farther up the pass, the fighting was over. Dray and Aemon were helping Teromich out from under a wagon while the merchant made frantic gestures.

Caim took a breath. His pulse pounded in his eardrums. The sick feeling was fading, but the weakness, the dizziness – they were too much like the spells he used to suffer. And the shadows. He could hear them feasting on the cooling blood as he cleaned his knives. The sun's last rays caught the wavy temper lines along the seax blade. Keegan had given him this knife the day he left Liovard. It had belonged to the young man's father. It was good steel, more valuable than gold up here in the middle of nowhere. Caim slid the seax back into its sheath and knelt down to pick up a knife from the hand of a dead warrior. It was heavier than his *suete*, the metal of the blade less refined, the horn hilt smooth from use. Nothing elegant about it. He dropped it in the dirt.

'Hey!' Malig shambled over. He had a face that looked like it had been hacked from old pinewood with a hatchet. His wide-set eyes gave him a thoughtful appearance, but Caim hadn't seen much evidence of that in the headstrong clansman. Still, he was reliable in a fight, and bigger than some two men put together. He had a host of scars on his hands and arms, a couple on his face, and he'd picked up a few fresh ones since they'd left Eregoth.

It had taken the four of them – him, Malig, and the brothers Dray and Aemon – almost a month to cross the Great North Forest, which was as wild and savage a place as Caim ever wanted to see again. North of the forest, they had hooked up with Teromich's caravan, posing as experienced guards down on their luck. The meager pay hadn't mattered to Caim as long as the merchant was going north. As it turned out, Teromich was one of the few traders who dared to venture over these mountains to deal with the Northmen on the other side.

Malig snatched up the fallen knife and added it to the three on his belt. 'I can get a fair bit of coin for these pig-stickers.'

The brothers walked up behind him, both covered in spatters of blood with a few cuts and scrapes, but nothing that looked too serious. Dray was a few inches taller than Caim and the murkiest of the three in complexion and mood. His black hair was hacked off above his bushy eyebrows, but hung long in the back. 'Yeah,' he said. 'And you can get your throat cut if a Suete sees you carrying them.'

Aemon nodded. A little taller than his brother and blond-haired, he walked with a bit of a limp. 'It ain't worth it, Mal.'

Malig shrugged as he looked over his collection. 'Caim walks around with one.'

Caim tugged his gloves on tighter. Malig wasn't happy unless he was bitching, and Dray wasn't much better. Aemon was the only one of them with a dram of sense.

'How many dead?' Caim asked.

'All three of those sheep-lovers,' Dray said, referring to the other caravan guards.

'Two drovers, too,' Aemon added. 'And Teromich is shook up.'

At the forefront of the halted caravan, Teromich talked to one of his men while looking back at Caim. The other teamsters were busy seeing to their animals. From behind one of the wagons came the harsh squeal of a horse being put down.

Malig laughed. It was an ugly sound. 'He's just afraid we'll squeeze him for more silver now that we're the only thing standing between him and a cold grave.'

'We should,' Dray said. 'It would serve him right.'

'And he wants to get back on the trail without laying the bodies to rest,' Aemon said. It was clear from his tone that the blond Eregoth didn't hold with this idea.

Caim scanned the cliffs above the pass. What little he knew of the Drakstags he'd learned from Kas, from stories about his days as a soldier in the empire's crusade against the northern wastes. The stories, full of battles and casualties, were exciting to a young boy, especially since Kas had served under Caim's father, Baron Du'Vartha. Now Caim wished the old man had been more forthcoming. He didn't see anyone above, but that meant nothing. Without his shadow spies, he never would have spotted the Suetes coming. As he started to glance away, he caught a hint of movement high up on the rocks. When he looked back, it was gone.

'Fine,' he said. 'Go tell our boss to get moving.'

Malig and Dray walked back up the line of wagons, swapping brags about their fighting prowess, but Aemon hung back. He leaned on his spear. Blood stained the shaft nearly to its midpoint. 'More trouble?'

'I don't know.' Caim looked ahead, beyond the mountain peaks to something he couldn't see, but felt pushing at the back of his skull. 'Keep your eyes open.'

'Aye. That's one thing about you, Caim. Things are never boring when you're around.'

As Aemon went to rejoin the caravan, Caim found his horse. While he gathered up the reins and checked the saddle's cinch strap, a soft tickle caressed the back of his neck.

'Hey there, cutie,' she whispered in his ear. 'Can you give a girl a ride?'

Kit was wearing a short lapis dress. A *painfully* short dress, fitted so tight it left nothing to the imagination.

'That depends,' Caim said under his breath. 'Which way you headed?'

Kit laid her head on his shoulder. 'Anywhere with you. Surprise me.'

'You like surprises?' Caim held up his bleeding wrist. 'That ambush was a nice one.'

'Oh!' Kit spun around him to get a better look at the wound. 'That looks painful. Why haven't you bandaged it up yet?'

'I've been busy staying alive. You couldn't warn me they were coming?'

Her fine eyebrows almost touched above the slim bridge of her nose. 'I did!'

'When was that exactly?'

'Three nights ago. Don't you remember? You were sitting with Aemon by the fire, eating something disgusting with beans in it, and I told you there were wolves in these mountains.'

He stared at her. 'Wolves? You call that a warning?'

Kit walked her fingers up his chest. Her ethereal touch went right through his clothes as if he weren't wearing any. The top of her head barely came up to his chin, even though her feet levitated several inches off the ground. Her long, silver hair bounced as she moved, but never in response to the wind. 'I thought you'd know what I meant. Brigands. Wolves.'

'Dammit, Kit. People died.'

She stuck out her bottom lip. '*You* didn't. You're fine. Just a little cut on the hand. You'll be—'

'You should have told me they were coming, Kit.'

'Well, you've been acting all—' She waved her hands above her head. 'Moody. I thought you'd enjoy a little excitement. And anyway, you've got your little pets to keep you apprised.'

He put his foot into a stirrup and climbed into the saddle. 'Any more surprises waiting ahead for us?'

'No. You aren't angry, are you?'

'I'll get over it.'

Kit rose up to hover beside him. 'You know, Caim, you don't look so good. And I know you haven't been sleeping well. Something's been bothering you since . . .'

He knew what she meant. Since Liovard and the encounter with the witch. Something had changed in him that night. He couldn't say what it was, but he felt different, like he was a stranger in his own skin. 'It's just a cold,' he replied. 'I've been thinking, though, about what's ahead.'

'I told you. No more surprises.'

'No, I mean about . . .' Caim looked to make sure no one was nearby. 'What my mother said to you.'

She floated back a couple feet. 'What about it?'

'I want to hear it again.'

'I told you. I don't remember much. I was all mixed up after being chased through the Barrier. I only talked to her for a moment, and then I was catapulted across the sky.'

Horses whinnied as the first wagons pulled away. Dray and Malig rode in the vanguard. Aemon was about halfway back where the rest of the drivers were getting situated. 'Her words. Tell me again. It might be important.'

'It was mostly about how much she loved you and wanted to know if you were all right. That's all I remember.'

'You told me more before.'

'I was confused.' She huffed. 'I don't want to talk about it, okay? You always get upset.'

He started to curse, but stopped himself. 'I won't this time. Did she say anything about a place called Erebus?'

Kit batted a stray lock of hair from her eyes. 'She didn't speak. Not exactly. It was more like pictures and feelings. Like I was dreaming it.'

'You said you talked to her.' He swung his horse around closer. 'That it was real.'

'It *was* real, but it's just hard to explain. I could try to go back. Maybe find her again.'

'No.' Caim chewed on his lip. The pulling in his head nagged at him all the time. North, always north. It was most of the reason he couldn't sleep. That, and his dreams, which were getting worse. 'This thing in my head. I think it's coming from her.'

Kit came up beside him. Her eyes had turned deeper purple, which meant she was serious. Or pissed off. 'It could be. Or maybe not.'

Caim gritted his teeth. Why did she have to make everything so damned difficult? 'You said she was a powerful sorceress, right?'

'She was,' Kit agreed. 'But when I was talking to her, or *thinking* to her, to put it more accurately . . . I don't know. I got the impression she wanted you to stay away.'

'That's what she wanted? Or what you want?'

Kit crossed her arms. 'Why else didn't she just tell me to fetch you?'

Caim looked into the steel-gray sky. It was going to snow again. 'I don't know. But I mean to find out.'

She lifted her chin toward the departing Eregoths. 'And how do you think they'll take it? They don't have any idea what you're planning.'

'They can do what they like.'

Kit sidled up to his shoulder, tickling his skin through his cloak, jacket, and three layers of shirts. 'What about me?'

'I'd appreciate it if you went and sniffed out any more

surprises along the way before some mountain man puts a knife through my chest.'

'Maybe I will.' She smiled, a little smirk like she didn't think he could imagine the thoughts in her head. 'After you say it.'

He shook his head.

She shrugged. 'I'm not leaving until you say it.'

Caim growled under his breath. 'I love you. All right? Now get going.'

She leaned over and whispered in his ear, 'Love you, too.'

Then, with a swift, ethereal kiss to his neck, she was gone. Caim looked at the others, but everyone was focused on the way ahead as the caravan got under way. The bodies of the Suete were laid out beside the dead guards. Already their faces and hands had begun to pale, or maybe that was his imagination. The wind had picked up. Iron-headed clouds were gathering at the top of the pass.

Caim clucked to his horse and pulled his cloak tighter as he followed the last wagon.

CHAPTER THREE

Josey sat up on the cot and groaned. Knots of soreness ached in every part of her body from weeks of riding. Her back. Her thighs. Even her hair hurt. And sleeping on a sheet of stiff fabric strung across a wooden frame wasn't helping matters. *Why didn't I insist upon bringing a proper bed?*

Despite the protests from her muscles, she swung her legs over the side and stood up to meet another day. Several large trunks served as her wardrobe and vanity. She pulled out a riding dress and sighed. It had once been a lovely turquoise, but now the skirt was mottled brown and gray like the rest of her clothes. There was no time for proper laundering traveling with an army, so they had to make do with quick dunkings in the local stream and a few passes with a cake of lye soap. Shivering in the early-morning chill, she shrugged out of her sleeping shift and pulled the gown over her head. It fit a little loose around her middle. *All* her dresses had been purposely made overlarge in that area. She smoothed the fabric over her stomach to feel the soft rounded bump. Did it show? No, she was fine. She would just go without a belt.

As always, thinking about the baby turned her mind toward Caim. Was he all right? Was he even alive? *Don't think like that!* He *was* alive, and she was going north to find him. And hopefully bring him home.

The cloth door-flap was pushed aside, and a young girl waited in the opening. Josey pulled her hands away from her middle as a frigid breeze blew into the tent and puffed out the canvas sides. It was Iola. When Josey had departed Othir, she decided to leave her maids behind, intending to 'rough it.' But after a few days one of her staff officers, Colonel Klovus, introduced her to his daughter Iola, and Josey had taken an immediate shine to the girl, who was quiet and good-natured, not to mention industrious. Every morning Iola brought her breakfast, which Josey ate while reading the morning dispatches. 'Come in, come in!' she said, waving the girl inside.

'I have your breakfast, Majesty.'

'What is it today? Not more oat porridge with nuts, I hope.'

'No, milady.' Iola set down the covered bowl and whisked off the cloth. 'Oat porridge with *bacon*.'

Josey's nose wrinkled as she leaned over the bowl. She despised porridge, and the cooks' attempts to enliven the dish with flourishes like bacon only made it all the more appalling. She considered waiting to eat until the midday meal, but her stomach started rumbling. *Oh, baby. You can't be serious.*

With a sigh, Josey picked up a spoon and took a bite. It wasn't good, but it wasn't horrible either. Before she knew it, she was scraping the bottom of the bowl and wishing for more. With a sigh, she wiped her mouth with a napkin and gave thanks her morning sickness had waned after the first month of pregnancy. 'Is there anyone waiting outside?'

'Not when I came in, milady.' Iola stripped the cot and folded the blankets. 'I mean, the captain was out there, but he looked to be standing guard. Not waiting, exactly.'

Josey leafed through a small stack of reports on her camp table while she nibbled on her spoon. Over the past two months she had learned much about the logistics involved in transporting an army, even one as small as hers. Four hundred and twenty-eight soldiers ate a great deal more than she had expected. The quartermasters compiled daily lists of everything that was used, from food and beer rations to uniforms and boots.

Several of the papers were letters from Hubert. He kept her

informed of the happenings in the capital. From what she read, it seemed that the city was once again under control. The protests had ceased, and repairs to damaged neighborhoods were under way. There was even a note about Lord Walthorn, whom she had sent west to deal with the banditry problem. The field reports indicated he was doing an excellent job, having freed a town under siege and captured some outlaws. There was no further news from the north, but she tried not to let that disturb her.

The border between Eregoth and Nimea had been a trouble spot since the marchland broke free of Nimean rule a generation ago. The last dispatches, months old, had described a sharp spike in the number of raids from the north, and then the messages stopped. Privately, Josey feared the worst.

Invasion.

But what she'd hoped would be a swift trek to the north had proved both longer and more arduous than expected. The farther north they traveled, the worse the roads became as the empire's paved highways gave way to dirt tracks, made more treacherous by the thawing snow. She'd been disheartened at first to hear how the commons scavenged stone from the roads wherever they could. However, as the army passed villages with meager fields and wretched people, she could not hold such thefts against them. Theirs was a difficult lot, and one she wanted to change for the better if she was able. But she had other worries on her mind. Lady Philomena had accompanied – *without* imperial sanction – the official envoy to Mecantia to engage in negotiations regarding the free status of that city after Hubert's agents reported that their eastern neighbor, Arnos, was making overtures to annex the wealthy trading port. *Philomena! Why didn't I have her imprisoned before I left Othir?*

Josey sighed. While she didn't like the idea of Lady Philomena interfering with state business, it was probably better that the devious woman was out of the capital for a while.

Shuffling through the reports, Josey shrieked when she spied a letter from her dear friend Anastasia. She tore open the seal and unfolded the short note.

Dearest Josey (it feels naughty addressing our Imperial Matron so candidly),

Well, he finally did it. I'm looking at a sparkling diamond sitting on my ring finger, courtesy of your good regent. Hubert asked for my hand! I wish you could have been here, Josey. He invited me over for a private supper on Hale Saints Day and got down on his knee after the soup course. He was so nervous he almost tipped over the table!

Anyway, we're waiting for your triumphant return so you can help me plan the wedding. Come home soon!

Your Loving Servant, Anastasia

Josey kicked her feet under the table. She couldn't believe it. Hubert and 'Stasia! They were simply perfect for each other.

She put the letter aside as a man in a crumpled, oversized brown coat entered the tent. His profile was craggy, with a high brow, full nose, and a block of a chin under his short beard. Fresh snow dusted the brim of his dingy hat. Josey smiled and got up to embrace him. 'Master Hirsch. When did you get back?'

'Just this morning.'

Passing through the ducal seat of Ostergoth three weeks ago, they had found it in the grip of starvation. The problem had been there was no liege lord to tend to the people. Josey recalled hearing something about the old duke and his family being murdered a few months back, but she and Hubert had missed it in the rushed transition to her new government. Once the winter stores were depleted – or stolen, as some suggested – there was no way for the commons to get more. It was a problem all across the country. Years of drought and lack of foresight by the previous prelate when he reigned over Nimea had caused widespread famine. Josey had stayed in the town for a sennight attempting to help, but finally her urgency to get north compelled her to go, leaving Hirsch to manage the problem.

The adept winked at Iola as she left the tent. 'The province is back to some semblance of normal. A shipment of grain arrived from Othir in time to stave off complete disaster. And I found a distant relative of the late duke to take the reins for the time being. I'm not sure he's a long-term solution, but he will serve for now. I wrote to the lord regent with the details.'

Josey let out a deep breath. 'Thank you.'

'Thank me in the spring. If more food doesn't reach the province before then, those people won't wait around to starve.'

She knew what he meant. Rebellion. Before, it had been just a word, something out of the history books, but now it was her worst fear. Well, one of them. She had other, more personal concerns, too.

Josey ran her hands through her hair, which hadn't been properly styled since they left Othir. 'I know. Hubert says the grain barges are on the way, but this being winter—'

'—the Midland Sea is notorious for bad weather,' he finished for her.

'Doesn't it ever get easier being empress?'

'I'm not sure.' He started to sit in a cloth-backed chair, but then got back up and paced across the carpets. 'History tends to skim over the details of rulership in favor of honors and accolades. As far as I can tell, your efforts have been entirely adequate.'

Josey laughed. 'Well, that's a rousing endorsement, Master Hirsch. Thank you. Are the troops ready to march?'

'When I came in it looked like the bulk had already departed, lass. You'd know that if you weren't lazing ab—'

Josey rushed to the entryway and threw back the flap. She

blinked as sunlight dazzled her eyes. As her vision cleared, she saw a column of footmen marching away. Smoke rose from dozens of empty campfires in the muddy field behind them. Every morning it was her custom to ride at the head of the soldiers. Why would they start without her? She looked for someone she could shout at and spotted the back of a familiar head.

'Captain!'

Drathan turned and gave her a firm salute. He had somehow managed to keep up his immaculate appearance all through their journey. Not a speck of grit marred his uniform, and his boots gleamed with a fresh shine. 'Majesty, good morning. Your bodyguard is ready for review.'

On the other side of her tent, a company of soldiers stood at attention in the traditional blue and gold of the Imperial Guard. Josey pointed to the departing troops. 'Why is the army leaving already?'

'Pardon me, Majesty. The lord general ordered an early start.'

'And he didn't think to tell me? Nor you?'

The captain winced as if she'd slapped him. 'Yes, Majesty. But I only command Your Majesty's bodyguard. I didn't think it was my place to—'

Josey sighed. 'No, you're right, Captain. You're not the one I'm angry at. Where is—?'

'Your Highness.'

She turned to the sound of approaching boots. Lord General Argentus was roughly twice her age, with wavy, gray hair and a strong chin. His steel breastplate was polished to a shine. She hadn't known Argentus before they departed on this mission. Hubert had chosen him from among the army's command staff, citing his sterling reputation and complete lack of political aspirations, but Josey still wasn't sure how he felt about her ascension to the throne, and that made her uneasy.

'Good morning, Lord General,' she said. 'I was on my way to see you. Why is my army marching before I am ready to depart?'

The lord general bowed. 'I apologize, Highness. I received a report from our scouts last night after you had retired. There may be trouble ahead. I sent the column onward to ensure that the road remains clear.'

'What kind of trouble?'

'We're unsure as yet, Highness. But I expect we'll hear soon. Would you prefer to remain here until we ascertain the problem?'

'No. Let's be on our way. I don't want our army divided.'

'Very good, Highness.' With a nod, Argentus left them and headed toward the remaining troops.

Hirsch walked out into the morning light holding a half-eaten yellow apple. 'Our general seems like a reliable fellow, though a little dour for my liking.'

Josey looked at him out of the sides of her eyes. 'Yes. I'm hoping his better qualities are contagious.'

The adept snorted, and a piece of apple flew from his mouth. 'Perish the thought.'

A groom brought Lightning and helped Josey to mount. Hirsch fetched his own steed, and they rode off into the cold, misty morning. Riding at a slow walk, Josey mused that the road to Durenstile was a swamp masquerading as a highway. The army's pace was maddeningly sluggish. Sometimes she longed to gallop ahead. Somewhere over the far horizon, Caim waited. *But is he waiting for you?* She could admit to herself, when she was alone in her tent, that she was disappointed Caim hadn't sent word. She didn't expect love letters pleading his eternal devotion – not exactly – but an occasional post to let her know he was all right would have gone far to ease her mind.

Josey tried to stretch in the saddle. Sometimes she imagined she might have been more comfortable in a carriage with thick, padded seats and a blanket to ward off the chill, but riding out in the open air, surrounded by her soldiers, made her feel like she was more a part of this endeavor, and not just a passenger.

Hirsch came up beside her, guiding his diminutive mare. She'd been surprised to hear he didn't have a name for his white mare and took it upon herself to rectify that.

'Snowflake looks to be in fine spirits today,' she said, and grinned sideways at him.

The adept raised an eyebrow under the wrinkled brim of his hat. 'She's tired and cold, like her master. And we're both reconsidering our decision to join this ill-conceived venture.'

'As I recall,' Josey said, 'you didn't volunteer. You're here by imperial decree to help secure our northern border.'

Hirsch settled deeper into his mud-spattered cloak. 'In that case, we're honored to accompany Your Majesty across this depressing morass you call a country.'

'Don't sound so bitter. It's your country, too, Master Hirsch.'

'Only by adoption.'

'I didn't know that. Where are you from? Wait, let me guess. Abyssia? You almost look like something that just crawled out of a tomb in that old coat.'

'Hestria,' he answered, and coughed into his sleeve.

'Hestria? That's so . . .' She didn't finish. Hestria was a wild land of roving horsemen, or that's what she'd been taught by her tutors. 'Do they have many magicians there?'

'None that I've ever met. Then again, I didn't know I was a magician when I lived there, either.'

Josey wasn't sure what to take from that. 'Is that where you came by your sobriquet? Hirsch Red-Hand?'

He looked ahead. 'No, I got that name much later, and I'm not sure it's a topic for discussion on such a fine day as this.'

She heard the distance in his voice, like an old hurt, and would have given him some space, but her thoughts had latched onto another idea. 'Hirsch, is your magic able to find things far away? Like a person?'

He studied her for a long moment, and then shrugged. 'There are ways. Some are more difficult than others. It helps to have something bound to the body you're seeking. Blood and hair are the best, especially if the blood is fresh.'

Josey didn't have either of them, but she thought of the child growing inside her. 'And would you be able to see the person you're seeking? See where they are? Who they're with?'

'You're talking about scrying.'

Josey pulled tight on the frayed ends of her reins, making Lightning look back at her with reproach. 'Is it possible?'

'I've seen it done,' Hirsch said. 'But my talents lay along other paths.'

She looked down at her gloved hands, her fingers wrapped around the leather cords, and tried not to show her disappointment. 'So, what kinds of talents *do* you have?'

Hirsch's mouth twisted up in a quirky grin. 'Well, lass, let's just say—'

They were interrupted by a messenger from the forward units, who saluted as he came near. 'Your Majesty! Lord General Argentus sends word that the bridge over the river before us is out.'

'Out?'

'Yes, Majesty. Collapsed.'

She looked to Hirsch. 'Does the general think it was deliberate?'

The young soldier's eyebrows rose. 'Pardon?'

'The bridge, boy,' Hirsch said. 'Was it sabotage?'

'I don't know, my lord. The lord general did not say. But he is searching for another way across. There may be a ford we can use.'

'And if not?' Josey asked.

'The next nearest bridge is at Clavering Cross, Majesty. About twenty leagues southwest.'

Twenty leagues! The army only managed eight to ten miles on good days, and that was on an established road.

'Very well,' she said. 'Please tell Lord General Argentus we will stop here while he conducts his search. And bid him to be quick!'

The soldier made a parting salute and galloped away. The order to halt was passed down the line as swift as wildfire on an open plain, and everywhere soldiers fell out of ranks. They laughed as they sat down in the mud, some managing to find a bit of grass to stretch out on. She couldn't appreciate their good humor. It wasn't even midday yet. *Half a day wasted.*

She glanced to the north. Something inside told her she needed to get to Caim or she would lose him forever. It was a foolish thought, she knew, but it burrowed into the back of her mind as she climbed down from the saddle.

CHAPTER FOUR

The wind's icy fingers infiltrated Caim's jacket as he pulled his mount to a stop, but the shiver perched at the nape of his neck had nothing to do with the cold. The foothills of the Drakstag Mountains rolled out before him, tumbling down onto the hard plains of the northern wastes. It was barely a candlemark past midday, but the sky was a gray-black sheet of iron. Behind him, the mountain peaks glowed fiery orange like the world's last sunset.

'Un-fucking-natural,' Dray said as he reined up beside him.

'Is it always like this?' Malig asked, staring out over the dusky plains.

'Day and night,' Teromich said as his wagon pulled up. A lantern swung on a pole beside his seat, creating an island of light within the gloom. 'It's always dark as a witch's twat up here. Been that way for as long as I've been coming over these mountains. My da spoke of it being light at least some of the time, but that was years and years back. Myself, I try not to stay any longer in this country than I need to.'

The merchant eyed them as if saying they'd do well to do the same. Caim scanned the far horizon, which was vague and nebulous even to his enhanced night vision. His comrades probably couldn't see much at all. To him, the plains were broken and gray with few defining features. No trees, a few scattered stones with bare faces. Even the grass was stunted and colorless, peeking up through the dirt. According to Teromich the wastes extended for hundreds of leagues without break, perhaps all the way to the edge of the world. And there was something else about the landscape that bothered him. The shadows. Without a light in the sky, there shouldn't have been any, but they pooled around every imperfection in the ground as if cast by an invisible sun.

There were a few buildings situated at the foot of the hills. Points of light shone between them, perhaps torches, but it was hard to say from this distance.

'Where's Aemon?' he asked.

As Dray shouted for his brother, Teromich beckoned to Caim. 'So you're intent then, I take it?'

Since the ambush, the merchant had hounded Caim about his plans. Their agreement was to provide protection on the trip to the wastes, but it ended there. Now, with his other guards dead, he wanted Caim and the Eregoths to make the return trip with him, even offering double wages.

'We're moving on,' Caim said.

He clucked to his mount and preceded the caravan down to the cluster of buildings at the bottom of the pass. The trading center wasn't much of a town, even by northern standards. The outer shacks were little better than hovels. Inside them was a ring of slightly larger, more permanent-looking structures built with a resinous black wood. The shaggy sod roofs made them look like a herd of bison. Wooden beams carved with animal likenesses protruded from the eaves of the larger buildings. The lights he had seen came from flaming lamps suspended on chains from the mouths of these wooden beasts. There were no real streets within the trading post, just snow-packed lanes of varying widths, criss-crossed by wheel ruts and frozen excrement.

Teromich directed them to a wide paddock on the western edge of the settlement. While the wagons rolled in, Caim spotted a pair of men walking parallel to the fenced enclosure. By their size and pale, milk-white skin, he took them for Northmen, but both wore rust-red robes. Their hair was long and wild, giving them a feral appearance. Black medallions hung on their chests.

When his wagons were parked and unhitched, the merchant came over carrying a lantern. He paid out their wages, even adding a generous bonus before putting away his money purse. When Caim indicated the robed men, Teromich shook his head. 'Northern priests. You'll stay clear of them iffen you have any sense. They're worse than the holy men we got down south.'

He looked long at Caim. 'I don't know what you're looking to find in this forsaken land, but I'll be here at least a sennight before I head back.'

They shook hands. Then the merchant took up his lantern and started off toward the center of town with a few of his drovers, leaving the rest behind to guard his wares.

Dray leaned backward, stretching his back. 'So what's next, Caim? All this time you've been dragging us farther and farther north. Well, this is about as far fucking north as you can get.'

The men watched him, waiting for answers, but they would have to keep waiting. 'We'll find a place to stay for the next couple days,' he said. 'And look for a guide to take us up-country.'

'Hell's balls, Caim.' Malig waved his hand back and forth. 'I can barely see my nose in front of my face! Let's head back south with the caravan. There's got to be a war brewing somewhere in the marches. We could check out Uthenor.'

Caim urged his tired horse down the dirt street. 'You do what you want.'

Dray and Malig looked at each other, but kept any further demands to themselves as they followed. Heavily bundled men tromped past, their torches throwing shadows against the weather-beaten walls. Teromich had told him about a hostel where he might find what he needed. Caim located the place without much trouble. He hitched his steed to a post in front and went down a short flight of wooden steps to the front door below street level. Pulling on the iron handle, he unleashed a flood of light and noise.

Square timber pillars supported the low ceiling. The walls were paneled in wooden planks, same as the floor. The wind whistled from around the sheets of rawhide battening the small windows. Men sat shoulder to shoulder around the underground room. About half of them looked to be southerners. Dressed in hides and raw wool, the crowd didn't sport much color save for a group of Illmynish swordsmen in vermilion dueling jackets on the other side of the room. Two women stood behind the long bar, pulling drafts from a row of barrels and shuttling them to a small army of servers.

As the rest of his crew entered, shaking the cold from their cloaks, and went to find a table, Caim headed to the bar. He held up a silver penny to get the attention of a tap-puller.

'*Enka barush?*' she asked as she plucked the coin from his fingers.

'We need rooms,' Caim said, hoping she spoke Nimean.

But the woman stared at him with a blank expression. Caim pointed to the ceiling and moved his fingers to mimic walking up stairs. The woman shouted something over her shoulder. A few moments later, an enormous man shambled out of a doorway behind the bar. Red-faced and stomach jiggling, he came over while the barmaid nodded to Caim.

'What you have?' the fat man said, 'Eat? Drink?'

'Are you the owner?'

'Yes. What you want?'

'I need four rooms,' Caim said. 'And a hot bath.'

The owner said something to a passing server, who babbled a response before plunging back into the crowd. While he waited, Caim gestured for a drink. As he was paying, a voice erupted next to him.

'*Slavka!*'

Caim turned to see a man gulping from a large horn. He

was short for a Northman, standing almost even with Caim, and rather well-groomed in a brown wool suit under a rabbit-fur coat. He had a broad, fleshy nose and plump cheeks covered with scraggly black hair. He appeared to be alone.

'I drink to your health,' the Northman said with a brusque accent. 'You are Hvek-lund?'

'No,' Caim answered. 'From Eregoth.'

That's the story they had agreed upon on the road. They were all clansmen from Eregoth. Caim didn't really look the part, but the clans were diverse enough that the story should pass.

The man smacked his wet lips. 'I am Svart.' When Caim gave his name, adding the surname of a minor clan, he asked, 'You buy? Sell?'

'We're looking for a guide.' When Svart frowned as if he didn't understand, Caim added, 'To go north.'

'Ah!' Svart tapped his chest. 'Guide. Yes, I can do this.'

Caim reevaluated the man. Although Svart appeared to be in decent health, he didn't look like an outdoorsman. Caim started to leave the bar, but Svart hurried to step in front of him. 'No, no. I introduce guide. For a price. You understand?'

Caim paused, now understanding. Svart was a sharper, a middleman with connections in this little hamlet. Precisely the sort of man he needed. 'You know someone who can take us north?'

'Of course. I know everyone. I have right men for you.'

A serving woman came over with a foaming mug of ale. Caim accepted it and paid her. 'Not men,' he said. 'Just one guide. Someone who knows the land.' He took a sip. The malt ale was red and frothy, but better than he assumed it would be, considering the rustic atmosphere. 'And he has to speak Nimean.'

Svart made a big smile that showed his ivory-yellow teeth and pitted gums. 'He speak very good. You give me ten gold.'

Caim almost spit out his ale. 'Did you say ten gold?'

'Yes! You give me. Guide come to you, take you anywhere.'

Caim considered punching the man in the face and calling it a day. If they were anyplace else, he might have. But he didn't want to get lynched his first day here. Svart was oblivious, smiling as if he were doing Caim a favor.

'I'll give you five,' Caim said. And when Svart's smile widened, he added, 'In silver.'

Svart's face collapsed. 'No! This will not do. This guide is the best! You won't find a better man in all Scyalla.'

'Five for you to introduce us. If that's not enough, I'll find someone on my own.'

Caim made as if to leave with his drink, but Svart's smile returned. 'No, five is good. Yes! Five silver is good. You give to me, and I bring guide here to you.'

'I'll pay you when I meet this guide of yours.'

Svart gave him a sideways look. 'You are very cautious, my friend. For you, I will do this. But don't cheat me, eh? That would be very bad.'

'When can you have him here? We want to leave as soon as possible.'

'Early I will bring him.'

As Svart slipped away through the crowd, Caim wondered how he would know the time when there was no sunrise. The serving man reappeared and beckoned. Caim put down his cup and followed him through the crowd to a decrepit wooden staircase at the back of the room. The man showed Caim a room on the upper floor. It was small and dusty, with the sod roof only inches above his head, but after more than a month on the road, it looked like paradise. It had actual beds with sturdy wooden frames.

Caim tossed his pack in a corner and began peeling off numerous layers of clothing. His cloak and jacket were battered and worn. His shirts were stiff with sweat, food stains, and grime. Two men entered with a large, sloshing tub. Caim found his belt pouch and flipped them each a copper halfpenny before he eased into the steaming water. He sighed as the heat seeped into his bones. The journey had been more arduous than he had expected. Eregoth seemed like years ago.

Caim closed his eyes and let the tension drift out of his muscles. *Now if I just had a thick steak and something cold to wash it down. . . .*

Electric tingles across his left nipple made Caim open his eyes. Kit kissed his nose and sighed. She was straddling him, tracing the tattoo of interlocking circles over his heart with her fingertips. Caim sat up straight as some part of her lower body brushed against his lap. His mouth went dry as he looked her up and down. She wasn't wearing anything.

'Kit!'

She planted a kiss on his lips, and the feathery touch shut him up. It was like kissing the breeze, a very amorous breeze, but he couldn't deny that his body was responding. A warm flush flowed through him and pooled between his legs.

'I've been waiting until we could be alone.' She ran her fingers down his chest. 'It's been agony.'

Caim reached out to stop her, but his hands passed right through her. He opened his mouth, and received a tiny shock as his tongue touched her glowing lips. For a moment, she almost seemed real, like an armful of water before it sluiced out of your grip. His heart beat faster.

Caim jerked his head back. 'Whoa, Kit. Slow down.'

She kissed his neck and down to his collarbone. Her hands were wandering again. 'Can you feel me, Caim? Am I real enough for you?'

'Kit, I'm not sure this is the best—'

She chuckled. 'I'm sure. I want to.'

There wasn't much he could do to stop her. He was on the verge of just lying back and seeing where she took things when the door banged open. Candlelight and singing poured into the room ahead of three very drunk Eregoths.

'*Slavka!*' Malig shouted.

Beer dripped from Dray's beard. 'What are you doing up here, Caim? You're missing all the fun.'

Kit giggled and tickled Caim's stomach. With a wink, she ran her hands lower.

Caim drew up his legs in the water. 'I needed to wash off the road.'

Dray knocked back the rest of his cup and belched. 'There's these girls downstairs. You won't believe the size of their—'

Aemon staggered against his brother, nearly knocking them both onto a bed. As he struggled to get loose from Dray's one-armed hug, he lifted his candle higher. 'Quiet down, you two. Can't you see Caim's tired? Don't worry, Caim. We'll let you bathe in peace.'

'Fuck peace.' Dray turned his empty mug upside down. 'I need a woman.'

Malig laughed. 'Fuck sheep? I always knew there was something odd about you, Dray. Aemon, you brother says—'

'Shhh!' Aemon hissed as he tried to shoo the others out the door. 'Sorry, Caim. You want . . . you want us to get you some food?'

Caim ran a wet hand through his hair. 'I'm fine. I'll be down.'

As the men stumbled out, and Aemon tried three times to shut the door before it latched, Caim leaned back and sighed. Kit was gone. It was just like her to get him all worked up and then vanish. *What did you expect? It was never going anywhere in the first place.*

What was he going to do about her? He'd asked himself that every day since they left Liovard, but now it was weeks later and he was no closer to an answer. How could they have a relationship if he couldn't touch her, couldn't even kiss her properly? It was impossible, maybe even more impossible than his brief liaison with Josey. Two women in his life, each unattainable in her own way.

Caim sat there until the bathwater got cold. Then he got

out, scrounged something half-clean from his pack, and started to dress. He was bending down for his boots when he decided to skip the meal. He crawled into a bed instead, not even minding the scratchy straw poking through the thin mattress cover as he laid down his head. He drooped one arm over the side, fingers within easy reach of his knives.

Caim was eating a bowl of bean soup in the inn's common room when Svart walked in. The room was otherwise empty except for an old woman in a gray smock wiping down tables.

'Ah, my friend!' the Northman said as he stamped his boots by the door and came across the room.

'You're here.' Caim put down his spoon. 'I wasn't sure you were going to show up.'

'Me? No, no. I am good for my word. You are ready?'

'Where's the guide?'

'I take you to him. Not far from here.'

Caim hooked a thumb in his belt. 'That wasn't the deal. You were supposed to bring him here.'

'Is not far. Come, my friend. A short walk. You will see.'

'All right. Let me go up and wake my friends.'

Svart held out his hands. 'Better to go now. Guide is very busy. Won't take long.'

Caim turned away as he swung his cloak around his shoulders and pulled on his gloves. The shadows whispered in the corners, watching it all. Svart just smiled and nodded several times as they walked to the door.

Outside, it was dark even though the time was about a candlemark past what should have been dawn. Not completely dark. The sky was more gray-black than midnight dark, but still it felt strange not to see the sun coming up. The streets were deserted except for a few people slugging through the muddy snow. Svart lit a torch from a firepot by the door and started down the lane.

'How you like our northern weather?' the Northman asked with a chuckle. His breath filled the air with jets of steam.

Caim pulled up his collar. 'Does it ever get warm up here?'

'This is very warm for us. Two moon ago, a man froze to death in these street.' He shrugged. 'South man like you. Not used to the cold.'

Caim stepped around an ice puddle in the middle of the street. 'Is it true the sun never comes out in this land?'

The Northman shook his head and made his short beard wiggle back and forth. 'No. No sun. Always dark.'

'But it wasn't always like that, huh?'

Svart's voice dropped to a confidential murmur. 'Best not to talk of such things, my friend. We have a saying here: "The Dark has eyes." '

Caim scanned the buildings lining the street. He hadn't expected a real answer, but the Northman's hushed admonition surprised him. Perhaps it shouldn't have. *The Eregoths lived in fear, too, and they weren't living under a constant reminder of the Shadow's influence.*

At first, Caim thought Svart was taking him to the one of the larger buildings at the village center, but the Northman led him around a collection of fenced pastures filled with livestock and carts, into an area of narrower streets. Caim could tell they'd entered the lower section of the settlement by the condition of the shacks they passed and the general atmosphere. Every town and city had a slum, even if they didn't call it such, a place where the dregs could eke out their lives away from the palaces of the mighty.

Svart turned down a narrow alley between two long, low buildings that looked like storehouses. There weren't many people around this far from the trading paddocks. Caim caught up with the Northman beside a closed door.

'Hell of a place for a meeting,' Caim said.

'He does not like crowds.' Svart lifted the handle. 'This is more quiet. You understand?'

I think I do. Caim resisted the urge to reach for his knives as Svart opened the door. This whole escapade had seemed too convenient from the start. He'd been through similar situations before. All the predators came sniffing around when you're new in town. He wasn't eager to go through it again, but the impatient look on Svart's face convinced him to play his part for a little longer.

Caim got a glimpse of a long, empty interior before Svart extinguished his torch into a snowbank, plunging them into near-absolute darkness. Or so the Northman must have assumed as he muttered for Caim to watch his step, but Caim's night vision adjusted quick enough. The building was some kind of storage house, mostly vacant now except for a few wooden crates. A musty odor rose from the scuffed floorboards. Caim discerned a figure standing near the center of the floor. He was a 'proper' Northman, as tall as Dray or Aemon, wearing a hide jerkin over a thick woolen shirt. Caim couldn't tell if the man was armed. He waited to see how they were going to run the game. Would they play their roles for a little longer, or go right to making threats?

'Granmar,' Svart called out. '*Cuvo der skipa?*'

'*Ja.*' The stranger lifted his arm and opened the shutter of a lantern. Caim blinked as a shaft of bright light struck his eyes.

'Ah. There you are.' Svart turned to Caim. 'This is guide. Very good.'

The man nodded, but didn't come any closer. 'I am Granmar.'

His accent was so thick Caim barely understood even those simple words. And it was hard to get a good look at him with the lantern shining in his eyes. Caim handed Svart his fee, and caught a hint of movement on the far side of the room near a stack of crates. 'Can you take me north?'

'North. East. West,' the man replied. 'I can take.'

Kit appeared beside Caim and wrapped her immaterial

hands around his upper arm. 'So you know there's eight of them. Right, love?'

Caim swallowed the smile that had been threatening to play across his lips. He'd only counted four. He was losing his touch. 'Care to point them out?' he whispered under his breath.

She didn't have to bother as seven lanky shapes emerged from their hiding places. All big men, two of them bigger than Malig. That was a concern. He told his muscles to relax. With the light shining in his eyes, they had to assume he couldn't see them yet. He didn't do anything to disabuse them of that notion.

Kit floated around to his other side. 'The second one from the right has a bad knee.'

Caim looked, but didn't move his head. 'Which one?'

'The second from the—'

'Which *knee?*'

Granmar held the lantern a little higher. 'You bring silver?'

Caim looked over his shoulder as the door creaked behind him. Svart was gone. He sighed. Enough games. He had two options, fight or capitulate. He untied his purse and held it up. 'Right here.'

Granmar approached with lumbering strides. Caim waited in a casual stance, feet spread shoulder-width apart, right arm down by his side, head tilted slightly to the left as if bored. He was almost convinced the Northman meant to deal honestly, but then he spotted a gleam of metal in the guide's off-hand. A knife held against his thigh. At least an eight-inch blade, probably single-edged with a triangular point. Caim shifted his weight a little more onto his left foot. When Granmar started to raise the hidden knife, Caim twisted at the hips while drawing his seax and slashing upward in the same movement. Granmar stepped back, his eyes wide under scraggly brows. The lantern dropped as he pressed his hand to the deep cut slicing him open from navel to collarbone. Glass shattered, but Caim was already moving as darkness smothered the room. The Northman with the bad knee was the next to fall, kicked so he would topple sideways, and then cut across his abdomen.

Another Northman swung a long club that looked like a sheared-off fence post. Caim dipped in behind the swing and stabbed the Northman in the thigh before he could bring the cudgel back around. Instead of falling back, the man stepped up closer. It would have been a simple thing for Caim to plunge both knives into the northerner's unprotected belly and rip him open, but he hesitated. Big hands grabbed him around the neck from behind. The wooden post crashed into his stomach, and Caim gasped as the breath rushed from his lungs. A sharp point dug into the back of his shoulder. Caim dipped his chin and spun out of the grasp of the rough fingers gouging his throat. His knives lashed out, and the Northman behind him fell to his knees, his slippery entrails spilling to the floor.

Caim crouched under another swing of a club. The Northmen could see better in the dark than he anticipated, but just like the fight against the Suete, he moved too fast for them to catch. A vicious, rusty shank stabbed at him. Caim knocked the thrust aside and ran the tip of his *suete* knife up the Northman's arm, splitting the sleeve of his wooly coat and tearing a deep gouge in the skin underneath. As his enemy retreated, making room for the others, Caim maneuvered back toward the exit.

He was almost to the door when a burst of light exploded behind his eyes, accompanied by a blinding headache. Caim put out his left hand as his balance wavered. It felt like he'd taken a blow to the head, but he didn't recall the impact.

Caim reversed his grip on both knives as his vision cleared. Pushing away from the wall, he moved like black quicksilver through the warehouse. Blood dripped from his blades, coated his gloves. Twice he evaded blows that he had been certain would connect. The Northmen fell back from his onslaught. He felt the shadows creeping along the ceiling, huddled in the eaves, hungry to get into the action. Finally he gave in. *Come on, you little bastards. Get a taste.*

An ice-cold pain ripped through Caim's chest. His breath froze in his lungs. Unable to move, Caim watched the advancing Northmen. Their weapons rose up. Just another couple steps would bring them within range. Caim fought to break through the sudden paralysis. *Answer me, damn you! Come and—*

Caim gasped as the pain drained out of him as quick as it had come. Suddenly he could move again, and almost tripped over his own feet backing away. But he needn't have bothered. The shadows rained down from the rafters. His ambushers batted at them, their efforts becoming frantic as the shadows covered them in growing numbers. Grunts and curses turned to yells, and then to hoarse screams. Wood crackled as one man tried to dive through a boarded window and became stuck in the half-broken boards, driving the splintered edges deeper as he thrashed. His cries became choked, gasping, and then he fell silent.

Two men made for the exit. The door crashed open, and three men appeared. Malig's familiar bellow filled the frigid air as he entered in front of Aemon and Dray. Caim reined in the shadows. It was harder than ever before. His arms and legs shook, and a sharp throbbing took up residence over his eyes, but they slowly retreated to the room's dim corners.

As Caim took a deep breath and wiped his brow with the back of a sleeve, he saw his crew had matters well in hand. The last Northmen were dead. Malig shook the blood from his axe while Dray peered about the room. Aemon stood back, breathing hard, his weapon clean. They gathered as Caim approached.

'Looks like you were right,' Dray said. 'You figure them for thieves?'

Caim looked down at the gore-streaked faces. 'What else? We don't know anyone here.'

He hoped that was true. They'd taken pains to appear like caravan guards, beneath anyone's notice.

Malig hiked a thumb toward the door. 'We got your friend outside trussed up like a Yuletide goat. You want to gut him and see what spills out?'

'No.' Caim put his knives away and left his hands behind his back to hide their trembling. 'Let's get back to the hostel. We're leaving.'

'What about finding a guide?' Aemon asked.

The shadows waited. Caim felt them watching from the edges of the room, felt their hunger. 'We'll get directions to the next town and pick up someone there.'

Malig exchanged a look with Dray, but it was Aemon who spoke up. 'Where *are* we headed, Caim? You haven't said nothing since we crossed the mountains.'

Caim started toward the door, ignoring the gazes of his crew and the newly dead alike. 'North.'

CHAPTER FIVE

Darkness reached down from the chamber's high ceiling and distant walls to enfold Balaam as he stepped out onto the receiving platform. The sensation was both familiar and disconcerting to one who had been born under the ebon skies of the Shadowlands, a bitter remembrance of a home he would never see again. Wrapping himself in his cloak, he descended the long, winding steps to the floor far below.

He left the chamber through a mammoth doorway and passed into a corridor sheathed in polished onyx. His footsteps echoed as he navigated the empty halls and passed by windows of frosted glass looking down on the citadel below, a vast, empty city of glittering black stone.

Six Northmen, armed with poleaxes, stood before the entrance to the Grand Hall. As he approached, the bronze valve doors opened, and a slim figure wrapped in a long cloak emerged. Wisps of brown hair poked from under the deep cowl. A mortal. He paused to let her go by, and then entered the chamber.

Curving walls of alabaster enclosed the great hall. Black pillars carved from obsidian reached to the arched ceiling. Accents of wrought iron and black diamond glistened in the luminance of smoky braziers. Elegant women and men in somber dress stood about the room. Their faces were impassive, as if they were watching a pageant, while slaves in a variety of skin shades, from pale white to deepest ebony, passed among them offering libations and whatever else the lords and ladies desired. Here and there a noble supped on the sweet liquor of blood and agony from an accommodating vessel. Despite the languorous heat radiating from the feedings, Balaam's gaze was drawn to the colossal basalt throne at the far end. A powerful presence seized him as he stepped across the threshold, like an iron fist closing around his throat. The Master reclined in a swathe of shadow, hidden from sight, though his power dominated the hall.

Balaam moved behind the crowd and found a vantage point where he could see the dais. Two of his brother Talons, their features concealed behind steely visors, stood at the bottom of the steps. Members of the Shadow Lord's elite cadre of enforcers, only they were permitted to bear arms in the Master's presence.

Six mortals clad in animal furs – their faces obscured behind great, bushy beards and long locks of hair in strange hues of orange, yellow, and brown – stood before the assemblage. One of them, a stout man with strands of gray shot through his ruddy hair and a stuffed bear head perched on his shoulder, addressed the court in the brusque tongue of the humans.

'O Great Lord, defender of the north, bringer of the grasses which feed and sustain us. For all the gifts you have given to us, we pay you this homage.'

While he spoke, his kinsmen laid objects on the floor – bundles of cloth from the Southlands, tusks of ivory, cedar chests filled with incense, and a stack of silver ingots.

'And one hundred new slaves,' the Northman said, 'captured in raids against your enemies. All this we give to you, Great Lord.'

The Northman finished with a deep bow. As he and his men backed away, a voice from atop the dais spoke. 'You and your people honor us, Chief Vanar.' It was not the Master, but a robed figure standing beside the throne. Lord Malphas, the Master's majordomo. His voice clipped each word with precise inflection. 'In his infinite generosity, the Master grants the

Bear tribe additional hunting lands in the west and permission to collect tithes in the Jurengaard region.'

As Balaam listened, a female in black armor migrated toward him through the crowd. A coiled chain whip hung on her belt.

'I greet you, *shalifar*,' she said.

'I see you, Deumas.'

'It is good to have you back. There were whispers that you may have encountered difficulty in the south.'

Balaam looked back to the front of the hall. As the Northmen filed out of the hall, trailing their fur cloaks, a side door opened to admit a squadron of soldiers with a prisoner. 'There was no difficulty.'

Balaam squinted, not sure he could believe his eyes. The man under guard was Lord Oriax, commander of the eastern armies. Balaam had served with him, albeit briefly, years ago during the first stage of the northern conquest. Oriax was from an old bloodline and was known for the high regard in which his men held him.

The guards brought Oriax before the dais and forced him to kneel. Balaam moved closer as Lord Malphas addressed the prisoner. 'Lord Oriax of House Umberal, you have been summoned before this court to answer for your treasons.'

Oriax lifted his gaze. 'I have committed no treasons against our Great Lord. I swear it upon the Mother and my family's sacred name.'

Lord Malphas reached into his sleeve and produced a rolled parchment from which he read. 'Twelve thousand human soldiers. Four thousand draft animals. Sixteen tons of timber. Seven tons of iron. Two coteries of imperial knights . . .'

'This is not well done,' Deumas said. 'Kobal and I were the ones sent to retrieve him from Sirion. I tell you, *shalifar*, this is not the empire we once knew.'

Balaam turned his head slightly. No one was close enough

to overhear their words, but the shadows were everywhere. 'I was not aware of this operation.'

Deumas nodded toward the dais. 'Lord Malphas now directs the Talons.' She lowered her voice. 'Be wary, *shalifar*. That serpent has long fangs.'

With a nod, Deumas turned and left the hall. Balaam returned his attention to the audience. The Talons were the Master's instruments, to be used as he desired. It should not have rankled him that the majordomo was given control over his team, and yet . . .

'Enough!' Oriax shouted as Malphas continued to read from a long list of goods and materials. 'I do not understand. What does this have to do with treason?'

Lord Malphas rolled up the parchment. 'This is a list of the resources that have been placed under your command. Resources that have been squandered and wasted in a fruitless campaign.'

'Wasted?' Oriax tried to rise to his feet, but the soldiers held him down. 'I have won dozens of victories, captured many towns and fortresses. Virtually the whole of Einar is under my—'

Lord Malphas began to answer, but movement stirred on the throne. The crowd murmured as the Lord of Shadow leaned forward in his stony seat. The hall's ruddy light played across his oiled scalp and the long bridge of his nose. Bony shoulders shifted under his mantle of burgundy chased with silver and gold thread.

'Towns and fortresses?' The Shadow Lord's voice was measured, but it resounded through the hall. 'You were charged with subjugating the human nations of Arnos and Hestria.'

'Master, I—'

Oriax flew back onto the floor and rolled over. A titter passed though the assembly, but no one spoke. Even Malphas stood silently, hands folded within his sleeves, but Balaam thought he saw a look of satisfaction cross the majordomo's face.

The Shadow Lord extended a finger. 'You have failed, Lord Oriax. And the cost of your failure is death.'

Oriax climbed to his knees and dared to meet the Master's gaze. 'I would gladly die for my empire and my Master. But grant me the final honor of a proper death as befits my station.'

'You dare to—,' Lord Malphas started to berate.

But the Shadow Lord nodded. 'It is granted. Choose your executioner.'

Oriax craned his head, but none of the nobles would meet his gaze. The hall was silent. Then Balaam found himself stepping forward. 'I will serve as your second, my lord.'

Eyes followed him as he crossed the floor. Balaam stopped before the dais and bowed. Then he drew his sword and turned to the kneeling lord. The soldiers stepped away.

Oriax closed his eyes, head bowed, as the *kalishi* sword lifted above his head. Balaam inhaled a deep breath and held it. His mind was still, his nerves calm. Yet, Deumas's words haunted him. *This is not the empire we once knew.*

Oriax nodded, and the blade fell.

Balaam stepped back. He used his cloak to clean his sword and returned it to the scabbard. Then he laid the cloak over the general's headless body. He stood there for a time as the body discorporated into fine gray ash.

'Balaam.'

He looked up. The hall was empty save for the two figures on the dais. Abraxus, the last Shadow Lord, stood up slowly and beckoned with a veiny hand. 'Come. We have been waiting.'

As Balaam strode forward, he hoped Malphas would depart, but the majordomo remained at the Shadow Lord's side. Balaam concealed his disappointment as he went to one knee at the bottom of the steps. 'Master.'

'Rise and tell me what you found in Liovard. Is my daughter dead?'

'Yes. The temple was in shambles.'

'It is as I feared, but I had to be sure. I cannot trust all that I hear anymore. How did she die?'

'It was the scion's doing, Master.'

Balaam obeyed with a full account of his investigation in Liovard. He would have gladly stopped before reporting Lady Sybelle's final moments in this world, but he was bound by duty. As he related her fateful last words, Abraxus slapped his thigh. His face was a gray mask.

Lord Malphas tsked. 'A great loss to our cause, my lord. A tragedy beyond words. Shall I arrange the funereal rites for your beloved daughter?'

'My daughter.' Abraxus pursed his lips together. 'A more wily creature was never born. If she'd had the opportunity, she would have usurped my throne long ago.'

'A lady of many . . . moods,' Malphas ventured. 'Perhaps a muted affair. The city shall mourn her passing in silence, as befits the daughter of your mighty house.'

Balaam ignored the majordomo, understanding what his Master meant. 'We should prepare.'

Abraxus met his eye with a jaundiced gaze. 'Indeed. One who could overcome my beautiful Sybelle, even besotted and weakened as she had become, is a dangerous foe. I want you to find him. Find him and bring him here.'

Balaam exhaled as the command settled over his shoulders like an ill-fitting coat. 'Master, is that the wisest course? An enemy as powerful as this one, it would be better to slay than capture him.'

The Shadow Lord looked up toward the arched ceiling, and Balaam bowed his head. He shouldn't have said anything. A weapon did not ask where it should be pointed; it only served the purpose for which it had been made.

'There are forces moving,' Abraxus said, 'but I cannot see

them. I can only sense them on the edges of my awareness, shadows within shadows . . .'

His voice trailed away, and he stood that way, saying nothing, for a span of many breaths, until Balaam wondered if he should say something. Then he remembered how long it had been since his Master had left this citadel. Years, perhaps decades. Balaam thought back to the early construction of Erebus, the army of slaves toiling on the wastes. Hundreds died each month, only to be replaced by others, and then by their children. But Abraxus had remained here since the laying of the first foundation. And now an entire city had grown up around the palace, even though their people were fewer with every passing year. A city in search of a people. Caught up in his own reverie, Balaam started when the Shadow Lord spoke again.

'We face a terrible question,' Abraxus said. 'The crusade does not progress as we had hoped. We are losing ground on every side. It is no secret there has been trouble in the east, but with the loss of Eregoth . . .'

Not the loss of your daughter, Master?

'Pardon me,' Balaam said. 'But perhaps if you took a hand personally. Just an appearance in the field would bolster—'

'No. My place is here, seeing to the completion of the citadel.'

'A wise policy,' Malphas murmured. 'To control the campaign from a central location.'

Balaam said nothing as Abraxus continued. 'But the Light is strong in this world. Our power diminishes with every passing year. We need the scion alive. Do you understand?'

Balaam bowed his head. He didn't understand, not fully, but he knew his duty. 'It shall be as you command. I will find the scion and bring him here.'

'Good. Go at once.'

When Balaam looked up, the Shadow Lord and Malphas were gone. Balaam considered the black throne, and all the losses their people had suffered since coming to this realm. *This is not the empire we once knew.*

Balaam turned and departed.

CHAPTER SIX

'You okay, boss?' Aemon asked.

Sitting on his bed shirtless, Caim nodded as the needle pushed through the skin of his shoulder, and he tried to think about something else.

Dray came over carrying his gear and bedroll, all bundled up. 'Fuck me! You got more scars than I ever seen.'

Caim looked down at his body. The scars were like a road-map, tracing the violent history of his life. Knife wounds, punctures, burn marks, and enough stitch tracks to sew a fair-sized quilt. He couldn't remember how he'd gotten most of them. The fights and jobs all blended into a crimson fog.

Malig bit into an ice-pepper as he pointed to Caim's side. 'Is that one from a spear?'

That one Caim remembered like it was yesterday. Carrying Josey over the side of the pier, the sudden pain like a mule kick in the back, and then the icy cold of the bay waters closing over them. 'Crossbow.'

'Damn.'

When Aemon finished his amateur doctoring, Caim eased into his shirt and laced his jerkin over the top of it. The back was a little damp from the blood, but it would dry out on the road. 'You three head out to the stables and get the horses,' he said. 'I'll meet you there after I settle our bill.'

Caim buckled on his knives as the clansmen left the room. A touch of the weakness he'd felt at the storehouse still lingered with him. His balance was slightly off, and a chill had settled into his bones. Maybe he was coming down with something. *Just what I need when we've got who-knows-how-many days of travel ahead of us.*

The common room was packed. Servers bustled back and forth between the bar and the tables. A faint haze smelling of rotten leaves hung in the air.

'Wow,' Kit said as she appeared beside him. 'Too bad we're leaving. This place is full of interesting characters.'

'Nice seeing you again,' he muttered under his breath.

She patted his hurt shoulder. 'Poor darling. Good work back there, by the way. I was wondering if you'd be able to pull it off.'

Caim started making his way through the crowd of people. He ground his teeth together when a laughing Northman holding two mugs jostled his shoulder. When he got to the bar, he waved to get the attention of the nearest bartender, but he had to wait a few minutes before someone saw him.

'We're heading out,' he said over the noise. 'I need to pay up.'

While she went to find the owner, Caim put his back to the bar and surveyed the crowd. He didn't see any familiar faces.

Kit eased up beside him, mimicking his pose against the counter. 'He's not here.'

'Who?'

'Svart. Last I checked in, he was laid up in some woman's shack with snow packed around his jaw. Malig thumped him pretty good.'

The innkeeper shuffled over. 'You leaving?'

'Yes. How much for last night?'

The innkeeper put up two thick fingers. 'You pay for two night.'

Caim held his gaze. After several heartbeats, he asked, 'How much?'

'Two big-heads.'

Caim felt a sigh rise from his chest. A big-head was the

northern term for a double-weight golden soldat. It was more than most people in Othir made in a fortnight. Up here, it was a gods-damn fortune. 'You want to try again?'

'Eh? You no pay?' The innkeeper glared under thickset eyebrows.

Caim growled to himself. This whole place was a nightmare. He reached into his pouch and plunked down two large gold coins. He started to leave, but the innkeeper said something in the northern tongue that sounded like a curse and started rattling off to the tap-woman while holding up the coins. Caim started to argue that they weren't counterfeit when he saw the markings on the faces. They were Nimean mint. *Shit. Those are going to stand out around here.*

He turned to go and almost ran into a man blocking his path. Caim started to go around, but the man put up a hand. Caim stopped, his right hand slipping down behind his back. The man was lean, an inch or two shorter than him. He wore a motley collection of scuffed leathers with a pair of rawhide gloves tucked in to one of two belts wrapped around his waist. The only obvious weapon was a long knife on his hip, almost as big as a *suete.*

Caim waited, his legs tensed. Then Kit floated over. 'Oh. You've met Egil.'

'You're Caim?' the man asked.

It took everything Caim had not to reply with the man's name and see how that grabbed him. This guy didn't look like one of Svart's henchmen, but Caim was done with guessing. 'I don't know you.'

'Name's Egil.'

'What do you want?'

'It's more what I heard you want. It's a little thick in here. Want to talk outside?'

Caim looked over Egil's shoulder. Aemon and the others were already outside. He felt the shadows stir. Then Kit's hand passed through his arm. 'Be good!' she said. 'He's a nice guy.'

Another good egg, huh, Kit? Okay. I'll play along.

'All right,' he said. 'After you.'

Egil pushed through the press of bodies. Caim watched for covert nods or signals to anyone else in the room, but didn't see anything suspicious.

Kit hovered in front of him, keeping pace as he headed to the door. 'Teromich sent him. He's a real guide.'

'Now you care?' Caim whispered, and covered it with a cough as he put on his gloves.

She pouted. 'That's not fair. I was trying to find someone like him when you met that Svart. Anyway, I came in time to get you out of that mess.'

He scowled at her description of the fight at the storehouse, and Kit blew him a kiss before she sank into the floor.

The wind hit Caim in the face as he exited. If anything, it felt colder than before. With no sun, he wondered how cold it would get on the wastes, and then he remembered where they were headed. The cold was the least of his problems.

Egil walked a few paces from the door. Light shined from the windows of the surrounding buildings – the brothel next door gave off enough for them to see each other.

'The trader, Teromich, told me you're looking for a guide,' Egil said. 'He said I could find you and your men here.'

'How did you know it was me at the bar?'

Egil smiled. He was missing an upper front tooth. 'He gave me a description. Not too tall, long scar on the cheek, and the meanest eyes he'd ever seen. You fit the bill.'

The man had a quiet, almost cautious, way about him, but he also sounded confident.

'We're going north.' Caim rolled his shoulders and felt the sutures pull. He didn't know anything about the wastes beyond what little he'd learned from Kas, but he had a suspicion that the farther north they went, the more dangerous it would get.

Egil made a small shrug. 'All right.'

'You know these lands pretty well?'

'Been hunting and trapping them all my life. Hunting's slow this season, so I thought taking you all for a walk would be a nice change.'

A smile tugged at Caim's lips. 'Okay. There's only one hitch. We're leaving now.'

'If you can wait a bit, I'll get my gear. Or we can stop at my place on the way out. It's not far from here.'

They agreed upon a price, which was less than Caim anticipated, and headed around to the back of the hostel where the Eregoths were leading the horses out of the stable. Caim made introductions as he swung into his saddle.

After shaking Egil's hand, Aemon said, 'I wish we could have stayed longer. For the animals' sake. They're still a little thin.'

'That can't be helped,' Caim said.

They left the yard. Ice crackled under their steeds' hooves as they rode through the dark streets. Caim kept a sharp watch as they rode past rows of taverns and flophouses. A dog barked a few blocks away. Egil's house was small, little more than a wooden shack with a peaked roof. Caim and the others waited in the lane while he went inside.

'What's this guy's story?' Malig asked.

'Teromich sent him.' Caim looked over his shoulder. 'He knows the Northlands, and we can afford him.'

'I hope he doesn't turn out to be another fucking setup.'

Caim nodded. The shadows were quiet, which he took for a good sign. And there was always Kit. She was *probably* looking over them. At least, he wanted to think so. She'd certainly been more attentive since they left Liovard, for better and worse.

The door opened, and Egil came out with a pack over his shoulder. A girl wrapped in a woolen housecoat stood in the doorway. She kissed him good-bye and closed the door as Egil walked over to them.

'Do you have a mount?' Caim asked.

'No,' Egil replied. 'But I'll keep up.'

He led them through the dim streets past the outlying buildings and onto a wide, snow-packed road. Once they were beyond the town, Caim wanted to dig his heels into his mount's sides and take off, but he kept it to a steady walking pace. A wind blew down from the north, searing the insides of his nose and mouth.

They rode for several candlemarks, and the sky darkened from slate gray to charcoal. The wastes spread before them, a magnificent desolation bereft of even an occasional hill or wood to break up the monotony. The others couldn't see much beyond the light of the two lanterns they carried, but they weren't missing anything. They traveled on what passed for a road, an ice-encrusted trail broad enough for a pair of riders abreast. Egil walked at the head of the small company with one of the lanterns. Good to his word, he managed to keep up. In fact, from time to time he would range ahead of them. While Caim rode, fighting the urge to yawn, he studied their guide. Egil's coat was patched together from a variety of animal skins, the hood flapping on his back. He also had stiff hide gauntlets that came up nearly to his elbows and furry pants tucked into his boots. His only gear was his belt knife and the rucksack, yet he moved with the practiced ease of someone at home in his environment.

Caim was rubbing his gloves to work some warmth into his extremities when an amazing thing happened. Crimson pin-pricks appeared in the sky. At first it was just a handful peeking through the inky veil of the night sky, but then more appeared until they covered the firmament like an array of twinkling rubies.

'Saronna's ivory teats!' Dray swore.

The others stopped and admired the view. Something bothered Caim about them, but he couldn't say what.

Then Aemon said, 'They're all wrong.'

The familiar constellations were gone. This time of year the

Sickle should have been right over their heads, but that space was empty save for a few red stars in a different pattern. Caim saw something that sort of resembled the Hind, but it was much too far north and its brightest stars were in the wrong position. A superstitious dread crept into his chest.

'How can the stars be wrong?' Malig asked. 'By the Dark, Caim. Where in the seven hells did you bring us?'

Caim shook his head. *I wish I knew.*

'How much longer do you want to keep going tonight?' Egil asked, coming back to meet them.

Caim looked to the horses. 'I suppose this is far enough. I don't figure we'll find much shelter out here.'

'Not much,' Egil said. 'There's a few places where hunters hole up when the weather gets bad, but most of them are off the road.'

'What cities lay north of here?'

Egil shook his head. 'Aren't any cities on the wastes. A few villages, but you can go days out here without seeing another person.'

That didn't make sense. Caim remembered his last moments with Sybelle in her sanctum. As her life bled out on the floor, his aunt had mentioned a name. Erebus. He hadn't learned anything more in the months since to explain what she'd meant. Where was this Erebus? He wanted to come right out and ask, but held back.

It started to snow as they bedded down. While their mounts huddled under tarps, the men slept on the ground huddled around a fire that did little to ward off the bitter cold. Caim listened to the soft fall of flakes on the snow. When the others had closed their eyes and drifted off, he held out his arm. The shoulder was stiff where he'd been wounded. Caim went to the place in his mind where his power resided and called for a shadow to aid in his healing. Moments passed without an appearance, but he could sense them beyond the firelight, watching him with invisible eyes. Sweat formed on his upper lip. *What's wrong? You lost your taste for my blood?*

Finally, he dropped his arm and gave up. Maybe the shadows were acting strange because of this place. He hadn't felt like himself since crossing the mountains. Sighing, Caim closed his eyes. He had just drifted into the first, light throes of sleep when a gentle touch caressed his temple.

'You awake, darling?' Kit asked.

He opened his eyes to find her lying on his chest, her chin propped in one hand as her other hand teased his upper lip. In the dim firelight, he could almost believe she was real. It made his blood quicken. She was more than beautiful. He knew every inch of her face. He could close his eyes and see the exact shade of her violet eyes.

'Let's sneak away,' she said.

'You're crazy,' he whispered. 'It's freezing.'

'I'll keep you warm.'

'You're not—'

She levitated up a few inches and frowned. 'Not what?'

Caim stifled a groan. This was the last thing he wanted right now, an argument with a spirit in the middle of the night after a long day, and with a longer day ahead of him tomorrow. 'I'm just tired, Kit. Let me sleep and we'll talk tomorrow.'

She sunk back to press against him, but the frown didn't move. 'There's a place up ahead if you stay on this path.'

'What kind of place?' He lowered his voice as Aemon rolled over in his sleep. 'A town?'

'Not quite. But there's people.'

'Is it safe?'

She shrugged. 'I was thinking we could stay the night.' Her fingers walked up his chest, making goose bumps on his flesh. 'Get a room to ourselves.'

Caim closed his eyes. 'All right. If you let me sleep, we'll do that.'

'Really?' Her lips made buzzing tingles on his cheek. 'Sleep tight, love. I'll keep watch.'

He drifted back into the pull of slumber with the snow falling around him, into a series of interesting dreams.

CHAPTER SEVEN

Josey leaned back in the wobbly camp chair as she shoved the papers away. Another dispatch had arrived from the capital this morning. *Hubert must be keeping the court scribes working day and night to keep up, not to mention the messenger service.*

It was gratifying to know she'd left the empire in such diligent hands, but the lord regent evidently failed to realize she didn't need to know every aspect of the court's activities while she was away. She'd left him in charge for a reason, but from reading his letters it was apparent that he felt the need to justify every decision.

The door flap moved aside, and Iola entered carrying a basket of laundry. Josey smiled, glad for a distraction, however brief. When she got up to help, Iola shook her head. 'Please, milady. You're busy. Let me do this.'

Josey went over and picked up a kirtle, stiff from drying in the cold air. 'Nonsense. I need a break. My eyes are about to fall out of my head.'

The girl's hands were quick and deft as she folded each article with precision and tucked it away in the large trunks. 'Has there been any word about when we'll be moving again?'

Josey shook her head. She'd gone to see the fallen bridge the previous day. What had once been an impressive wooden span over twenty ells long was now reduced to a few broken pilings sticking up from the river's icy waters. There was no sign of how it had happened, but whatever the cause, the bridge's collapse had put her journey on hold.

'You know,' Iola said. 'I've heard there is a village not far from here. We could go if you like. Maybe we'll find something more edible than gruel.'

'I like that idea. I'll call for Captain Drathan.'

'I can do it, milady.'

Josey regarded the girl. 'Oh?'

She had never seen Iola blush before, but bright spots of red appeared on the girl's cheeks. It was quite fetching.

'Or you could,' Iola said. 'I didn't mean I had to. I mean, you're perfectly capable of—'

'Iola.' Josey couldn't resist smiling. 'Is there something I should know?'

'I'm sure I don't know what you're referring to, milady,' Iola replied, and left the tent before Josey could comment.

Captain Drathan was summoned and preparations made, and a short time later Josey was riding over flat, brown plains. Islands of snow decorated the ground in some places, but mostly what she saw in every direction was mud. *Heavens, I've seen enough mud to last the rest of my life.*

The sun was almost at its zenith, burning away the cloud cover that had lent such a wintry pall to the past couple weeks. Lightning picked his way along, his hooves sinking deep into the saturated earth and coming out with sucking pops.

Iola rode beside her on a beautiful sorrel mare with a flaxen mane. The girl was lively, looking all around, everywhere except the front of her escorting company of bodyguards where Captain Drathan rode. Josey spotted several peaked shapes to the west. Rooftops.

'Is that it, do you think?' she asked.

Iola stood up in her stirrups. 'I think so, Majesty. My father said it wasn't far from camp.'

Her bodyguard had seen it, too. At Captain Drathan's direction, a dozen soldiers cantered ahead. The rest formed up around her. But rather than safe, Josey felt cloistered. The whole point of this jaunt was to get away from the stuffy routines of the camp.

It wasn't long before they reached the village. Josey was dismayed at its ramshackle appearance. She was used to seeing the small homes that the commons of her country lived in, but these buildings were nothing more than shacks. Hovels, really. There were more at the middle of the village, huddled close together, but they were in even worse repair, their walls streaked with ash and soot. A shanty of tents and dilapidated shelters extended out into the surrounding fields.

As they entered the village center, people emerged from the buildings and tents. Josey expected a few dozen, but apprehension stirred in her belly as more and more arrived. Soon the square was surrounded. *There must more than three hundred people here. Where did they all come from?*

Josey stopped inside her cordon of bodyguards, feeling all the eyes suddenly fixed upon her. When Captain Drathan shouted her name and title, a few of the people bowed or curtsied. Others looked away, which made Josey feel even worse. But a number of the villagers simply stared.

Three men exited the largest of the standing structures. They were older, all white-haired and thin. Everyone here was painfully thin, Josey noticed. As the men approached, she dismounted. Captain Drathan likewise got down from his warhorse and came over to stand with her, one hand on the pommel of his sword.

The shortest of the three old men walked before the others. His face was lined and craggy with a large nose, but he smiled as he stopped before her and bowed his head. 'I'm Elser,' he said. 'What brings you out to us, Your Grace?'

Josey found herself smiling back at the old man. There was something comforting about him. Her throat became dry as she remembered this was how her foster father had made her feel. 'We were traveling north, but the bridge is down. While we wait for another route to be found, I thought we would see . . .'

The old man seemed to understand. 'Not what you expected to find, Your Grace?'

'No.' Josey fought the knot forming in her throat. Looking at these people, some of them with hardly anything warm to wear, women holding their rag-swaddled children, was heartbreaking. 'What happened here?'

'War, Your Grace. The oldest story there is.'

Josey pursed her lips. She'd heard the reports of nobles fighting in the heartlands. She never thought it was so devastating. *These people are suffering, and I have failed them.*

'It's been going on for as long as any of us can remember, Your Grace,' the old man said. 'But these past few years it's gotten worse. Spring raids turned into summer campaigns that lasted through the autumn. And now the fighting goes on all winter, too. We haven't been able to bring in a good harvest in years. All the young men were taken away. They've only left those of us too old to fight. Our women have no husbands, our children no fathers. We've been holding on as best we can, waiting for things to get better. Now people from other villages have come here, but we can hardly provide for ourselves. In another season or two, we'll be gone.'

Josey wanted to turn away as pricks of moisture gathered in her eyes, but she forced herself to face the old man. 'How can I help?'

The smile he gave her was like a warm ray of sunshine. 'Our stores are gone. We could use something to eat, Your Grace.'

Josey looked to Drathan. 'Captain, send someone back to the camp. I want wagons here with food, warm clothing, and blankets. Anything these people need. And send for Doctor Krav, too.'

With a salute, Captain Drathan went about following her orders. Some of her bodyguards gave up their cloaks to the people in the crowd and broke out packages of rations from their saddlebags. Like water over a dam, the villagers surged forward, accepting these gifts and thanking the soldiers. Children laughed as they bit into rolls of hard tack and drank from waterskins. Watching Iola hold a small girl of three or four, Josey trembled at the rush of emotions running through her.

She turned back to Elser. 'Who is your liege lord, Elser?'

Josey watched with a child balanced on her hip as the frame of a new barn went up. Ropes creaked and men grunted as the wooden lattice rose to meet the three sides already in place. Villagers with hammers climbed across the framework, pounding in nails to secure it in place.

'What do you think?' Josey asked the child. 'Isn't it big?'

Marian, who was only three, smiled shyly around the candy stick in her mouth and buried her face in Josey's shoulder.

'Marian!' her mother cried as peppermint goo smeared across Josey's gown. 'I'm sorry, Your Majesty.'

Josey laughed. 'It's all right, Tara. Nothing that won't wash out.' She kissed the child's head. 'And who could be cross with such a little angel?'

Her mother shook her head. 'Angel, is she? Tell me that when she's up before the sun.'

They watched as the men, her soldiers and the villagers together, worked on the barn. In two days, they had rebuilt most of the homes in the village. Without any thatch for the roofs, a squad of her army was carving tiles from excess timber. When they were done, this would be the best-looking village in the empire. A line of people waited in a queue outside the tent Doctor Krav had set up in the square. Josey had been appalled to learn they had no medicine except what they could find for themselves in the wild.

'We can't thank you enough, Majesty,' Tara said as she teased the candy from between Marian's teeth. 'If you hadn't come by . . .' A shadow passed over her face, which was far too worn and tired for a woman barely past twenty. 'You've saved us.'

Josey buried her nose in Marian's hair and swallowed the lump in her throat. How many more villages like this one were out there, just weeks or days from starvation? How could she save them all?

A rider maneuvered around the piles of fresh-hewn lumber, coming in her direction. Josey handed the child back to Tara. She'd been expecting word from Lord General Argentus, but she wasn't sure what she wanted to hear anymore. Two days ago she'd been hell-bent for racing north. Now, things looked different. *No. I need to find Caim. He needs to know about his child. And . . .* What? Couldn't she admit her selfish motives for this trip? She missed him. Was that a sin?

The rider was one of her officer corps. As he got closer, she recognized his distinctive sleek, blond mustache that flowed down into his goatee.

'Lieutenant Butus. Good afternoon. What news?'

The lieutenant slid down and took off his helmet. Making a quick bow, he said, 'Majesty, I've just come from the outer patrols. The fourth squad has spotted a party of armed men to the south, riding hard.'

Armed men on horseback. That sounded exactly like the kind of trouble that had caused the people of this village so much misery. Not again, if she had anything to say about it. 'Were they flying a banner?'

'None that the squad could see.'

Josey started to turn. 'Cap—!'

Captain Drathan was right behind her. Sweat matted his hair, which actually made him look more attractive. No wonder Iola seemed smitten with him.

'Yes, Majesty.'

'Lieutenant Butus has a report of a band of men riding in the area. How far did you say, Lieutenant?'

'About half a league, Majesty.'

'We're going to find them before they cause any more damage. Please have Lightning brought over from the pasture.'

Captain Drathan saluted and jogged away, shouting orders. The villagers watched as the soldiers assembled in their little square. Elser walked over from the barn raising.

'Trouble, Majesty?' he asked.

'I don't know yet. We're going to find out.'

Josey looked down at her clothes. Though she wasn't dressed for riding, she couldn't take the time to change. They needed to catch these riders before they slipped away. The village headman backed away as a soldier led Josey's horse over. She put her foot in the stirrup and climbed up, relieved to see her bodyguard was likewise mounting.

Captain Drathan rode over. 'We have thirty-seven men here, Majesty. I could send for more.'

'No. We'll ride with what we have. Elser, can you send someone to the camp and tell them where we've gone?'

As Elser went to find a runner, they rode out at a swift canter, Lieutenant Butus leading the way. They followed a dirt path to the end of the adjacent fields, but then it was a bumpy ride across – of course – more mud. Riding more east than south, they came upon a line of trees running perpendicular to their course and found a raised road running along the arbor. Beyond were more mud flats that extended to the foot of some low hills in the distance.

Lieutenant Butus pointed to a stand of trees bordering the flats. 'That's where they were seen, Majesty. They would have had to cross this ground. So if we—'

'There!' Captain Drathan flung up his hand.

Josey saw them, too, a party of ten horsemen making their way across the eastern edge of the flats. Like Butus had reported, they flew no colors, but she could pick out the gleam of armor even from this distance. 'I want them stopped!' she shouted, and urged Lightning into a gallop.

The clamor of hoofbeats and jangling chainmail filled

Josey's ears as she crouched over Lightning's neck. For a moment, she considered the wisdom of her actions. She had little idea what they were riding into, whether the men ahead had friends in the area. Months ago she had fended off multiple attempts on her life, but after the long, slow journey from Othir she longed for some excitement. *Just a little.*

They approached the end of the arbor, and suddenly the path vanished in a wide patch of frozen mud. Josey tried to pull up, but Lightning had too much momentum to stop. As her steed's hooves struck the slick ice, Josey was hit by the sickening feeling of weightlessness. Lightning floundered, and they would have fallen over except that the horse slid into a patch of knee-deep snow. Josey gulped as the world righted itself, hardly believing she had kept her seat. The others, seeing her folly, rode around the icy patch.

Captain Drathan's face went white as the snow as he reined in close to her. 'Majesty! Are you—?'

Josey took a breath. 'I'm fine. Really.' She bent over to see if Lightning was all right. The stallion's legs quivered, but otherwise he appeared hale and healthy. *That's what I get for not thinking.*

Josey climbed down from her horse, not wanting to risk an injury to him. One of her soldiers dismounted and gave up his steed. While Josey climbed up, her bodyguard continued forward. She rode at the rear across the ground, which was a mash of mud and ice. The stirrups were too long for her, forcing her to cling to the horse's belly with her thighs. She couldn't see the armed riders anywhere. Just as she started cursing in her head, Captain Drathan shouted.

'In the name of Josephine, Empress of Nimea, halt where you stand!'

Josey couldn't see anything through the crowd of tall soldiers, but as they slowed she was able to wend through their ranks. The armed riders had gathered across a small meadow. She could see right away by their gleaming mail and the quality of their steeds that they were men of means and not brigands. All wore great helms that hid their features. Josey imagined what they must look like to the defenseless villagers, riding in with swords swinging. Like monsters. She kneed her mount forward as her bodyguard spread out to surround the men.

The armed riders watched them warily. One of the men in chainmail urged his mount forward, and thirty-six swords cleared their scabbards. The riders started for their weapons, too, but the man who had come forward stopped them with an upraised fist.

'Whoever you are,' he said, 'you had better have a good reason for stopping us.'

'We do.' Captain Drathan nodded to Josey. 'Your empress demands it. Now get down off your horses before we are forced to lay hands upon you.'

Josey swallowed as all the riders turned their heads to look at her. Then their leader slid down from his mount. He reached up and pulled off his helmet to reveal a tan, weathered face. His sweaty gray hair was matted to his pate. Holding his helmet under his arm, he lowered himself to one knee, and his men did likewise.

'Who are you?' Josey asked. 'Where are you from?'

The leader looked at her and frowned. His eyes were steel-blue under bushy black brows. 'I am Gerak Therbold, lord of Aquos.'

Josey had heard of that territory, but knew almost nothing about it. 'Where are you going with these men, Lord Therbold? You're armed as if for battle.'

'I am going to defend my lands, Highness,' he replied without hesitation.

Josey's borrowed horse pranced in a circle, and she had to turn around to keep facing the lord. 'Defend them from whom, my lord?'

'It is a private matter, Highness. I would prefer to deal with it on my own.'

Josey clamped her legs around the horse and jerked the reins sharply to get it to stand still, but with little effect. 'Like you and your ilk have dealt with the local villagers? I have seen the devastation wrought by your private little war, my lord. I aim to put an end to it. Now tell me. Who were you going to fight?'

Lord Therbold's mouth twitched, and Josey thought he wasn't going to answer, but then he said, 'Count Sarrow of Farridon. His men have been pillaging our eastern border since last spring. Two days ago we received a message from Hafsax, one of my larger fiefs, that Sarrow was moving there in force. My son took a party of men to prevent this, but I haven't had word from him since.'

Josey took a deep breath. Her anger was dwindling, against her will. 'And you are going to find your son, my lord?'

'I am, Highness. By the grace of the Prophet.'

'Stand up, Lord Therbold. How far is Hafsax?'

The man climbed to his feet. 'Three leagues from here, Highness. As the crow flies.'

Josey nodded to Captain Drathan. 'We will accompany Lord Therbold on his mission. Send someone back to the lord general for additional men. And have Master Hirsch come with them.'

While the captain selected a messenger, Lord Therbold and his men remounted with Josey's permission. Therbold looked unsure, but surrounded by her bodyguard, he didn't have much choice in the matter. *If he's lying to me . . .*

'Lead the way, my lord,' she said, and flinched at the steel in her own voice.

With a bark to his retainers, the nobleman kicked his steed and took off through the cold mud. They rode for the better part of a candlemark, over countryside that became rougher and hillier as they progressed. The road was little more than a dirt path riddled with ruts and frozen puddles. Josey shifted back and forth trying to find a comfortable position in this saddle, but it was proving a futile endeavor. The borrowed seat was killing her.

'Are you aware,' she said to Lord Therbold, who had deigned to ride beside her, though he hardly spoke at all, 'that my army has been traveling through your lands for more than a sennight?'

'From what I've heard, Highness, it isn't much of an army.'

Ouch. 'Perhaps not, my lord. But it is a sad day when an empress is not welcomed by her vassals when she arrives in their dominion.'

He bent his stiff neck. 'My apologies, Highness. If I have been remiss in my hospitality, pray excuse me.'

'Of course. Tell me about your grievance with Count Sarrow. What started this feud?'

'Sarrow is a swine. He thinks he can intimidate me into rolling back our border from its traditional placement, but I will not yield. And so he provokes me at his pleasure, by which I mean constantly.'

'Why Hafsax? What is its significance?'

Lord Therbold glanced at her out of the corner of his eye. 'As I said, it is one of my larger holdings in the east. It provides much-needed wheat and corn, and wool that I trade in exchange for the things my lands require.'

'That's it? It has no strategic value?'

'Highness, I don't know what you're—'

'I find it difficult to believe that this Count Sarrow would risk open conflict over corn and wool.'

The nobleman rode silently, looking straight ahead. Josey waited, but he said no more. She was about to ask about his son in the hopes of getting him to lower his guard when a shout from the front of the party reached back to them. Josey peered ahead to see what was going on. Clouds of black smoke rose from over the next rise.

Lord Therbold put on his helmet. 'That would be Hafsax. Men of Kistol, to me!'

As the nobleman rode off with his soldiers, Captain Drathan ordered four soldiers to remain with Josey. He didn't give her time to argue before he slammed down his visor and galloped forward, kicking up clods of mud. Josey urged her steed to pick up the pace as well.

She reached the top of the rise, and a patchwork of fields lay before her, at the end of which was a small village. The wattle-and-daub homes huddled together on the banks of a wide stream. Smoke poured from a couple of thatch roofs as men on horseback rode around the village brandishing torches and weapons. A group of villagers stood behind crude barricades – overturned wagons and household furniture. She didn't see any bodies. *Thank heavens. Perhaps we're not too late.*

'Majesty?' Captain Drathan asked.

Josey considered the situation. 'Separate the two sides, Captain. I want a barrier between the soldiers and the village.'

Whatever he thought of her plan, Drathan kept it to himself as he saluted and led her soldiers down toward the conflict. Lord Therbold, meanwhile, had taken his men straight for the village. Josey almost called her guards back. If Therbold did something foolish, this entire situation could explode. But she held her tongue.

Most of the villagers possessed little in the way of weaponry – just farm tools and sticks – but one man wore a shirt of steel scales and carried a sword as he ran back and forth between the barricades wherever Count Sarrow's men advanced. More fires were set, but there was no clash of arms. For the time being, the lone swordsman was holding off the attackers. Shouts arose from Sarrow's men as her bodyguard approached. For one awful moment, Josey thought a real battle would erupt, but then the attackers withdrew to a large field on the far side of the hamlet. Josey breathed easier when Captain Drathan set up a defensive position around the homes. By that time, Therbold and his men had been permitted inside the barricades.

Josey urged her horse down the hill. Captain Drathan rode out to meet her on the trampled field. 'I was going to send a detachment to escort you, Majesty.'

'I was quite safe, Captain. Do you think we can enter the village?'

'I would suggest sending an envoy first. To ascertain their intentions.'

'Ascertain their . . . ?' Josey shook her head. 'Captain, they are my subjects. I can clearly see them from here. All I'm suggesting is that we talk with them.'

Captain Drathan made a tight smile. 'As you wish, Majesty. But I believe that imperial law states that the townships under a lord's control are considered his property, above and beyond the Crown. In effect, you would need Lord Therbold's permission to enter.'

Josey fought the urge to growl something obscene. 'Fine, Captain. Please send a delegation to the village to ask if we may enter. And while you are at it, remind them that their situation could deteriorate quickly if we simply withdrew our presence to, say, over that hill.'

'Aye, Majesty. With pleasure.'

She stopped the captain with a raised hand before he could ride away. 'And send someone to the other side, too. Find out who is in charge and tell them I want to see them. Right away.'

Captain Drathan saluted and hurried away. Josey brushed a gloved hand down her chest and over her skirt, both of which were spattered in tiny dots of mud. *They're never going to come out.*

After several minutes, while she sat on her horse like a grimy statue, a pair of her bodyguards came over and informed her that permission to enter had been given.

'Have we heard a reply from the other force yet?' she asked.

'Yes, Majesty,' one of the soldiers answered. 'Count Sarrow has agreed to a parley if you will guarantee his safety.'

She sent them off with assurances for Sarrow's welfare and started toward the village. A barricade had been moved aside to allow her and a detachment of her soldiers to enter. Captain Drathan met them inside.

'Count Sarrow is on his way, Majesty.'

'Very good. I hope we can clear up this trouble.'

Captain Drathan escorted her to the village square, where the population had gathered. There were over a hundred people in sight, many of them in the same shape as Elser's village. Lord Therbold stood beside the man in scale armor, who was taller than the lord, with a rangy build. *That must be his son.*

As she approached, the swordsman removed his helmet, revealing a younger face than she anticipated. He looked to be about her age. He watched her with eyes like blue ice as Lord Therbold spoke in his ear.

Captain Drathan cleared his throat. 'I present Empress—'

'Josephine.' The swordsman knelt on one knee. 'We thank you, Majesty, with all of our hearts. Your arrival is most welcome.'

Josey bit her tongue as the villagers knelt as one, and even Lord Therbold and his men knelt again. 'Please,' she said. 'Stand up. My Lord Therbold, this is your son?'

The nobleman put a hand on the swordsman's shoulder. 'This is Brian, my heir.' He looked around the village. 'He held off the count's entire band until we could arrive.'

'Not just me.' Brian shrugged off his father's hand. 'Every man here stood bravely.'

'Aye,' Therbold agreed. 'But it was you who put the steel in their backbones.'

Hoofbeats sounded from behind, and Josey turned to see three men ride into the village. The center figure was a man with receding gray hair and sharp hazel eyes half-hidden beneath heavy bags. His sword had a silver handle topped with a polished green tourmaline as big as a quail's egg. A squad of Captain Drathan's men followed the trio at a respectful distance.

'Sarrow!' Therbold shouted. 'You will pay for the damages you've caused here, and I will not forget this insult.'

The older rider regarded Therbold with a perturbed frown. 'It is I who have suffered your insults for too long. I will not suffer them any longer! If not for this interruption, I would have taken back what is mine by rights.'

Interruption? Josey suppressed a curse. She would not be ignored on her own soil. She caught Drathan's eye and nodded firmly.

'Dismount at once,' he called out, 'in the presence of Her Imperial Majesty!'

Count Sarrow pursed his thin lips and, taking his time, got down from his massive warhorse with the help of his aides. He did not kneel, however, but made only a nod in her direction. 'Highness,' he said without emphasis.

Josey contemplated pressing the point, but decided to invoke her better nature. 'I greet you, Count Sarrow, although I wish it could be under other circumstances.'

'Do you mean the circumstance,' Sarrow said, 'by which you stand with the man who has stolen my property, abused my villains, and spit upon my family's honor?'

'Take out your sword!' Therbold roared. 'We'll settle this right now!'

As the nobles reached for their weapons, Captain Drathan moved between them. 'The man who draws a blade in Her Majesty's presence will suffer for it.'

Both men backed off, but they glared at each other with evident hatred.

'My lords,' Josey said. 'I am calling for a halt to all hostilities between your fiefs.'

Lord Therbold snorted. 'That would be my greatest pleasure, Highness. *If* this pig would keep his men off my lands.'

'Lands you stole from me!' Sarrow retorted. 'After you burned down two of my mills.'

'I had nothing to do with it.'

'You lie!'

Josey tried to stand up in the stirrups, but couldn't find purchase even on her tiptoes. Frustrated, she shouted, 'Shut up both of you!'

Sarrow and Therbold glowered at each other, but they remained silent. Brian had a hand on his father's arm.

Josey cleared her throat and tried to ignore the villagers staring at her. 'Now, it is growing late, and my camp is far away.'

Sarrow looked to his rival. 'I would be happy to provide an escort for you—'

'Thank you, my lord, but that will not be necessary.' She smiled. 'You and I will both be guesting with Lord Therbold this evening.'

Therbold's mouth hung open. 'Highness, that would be—'

'That is a command, my lord.' Josey looked to Count Sarrow. 'For both of you. Therbold will play host and we shall sit down like level-headed men and women and solve this problem. Together.'

Lord Therbold muttered something under his breath, and then said, 'I will not allow this mongrel in my house, Highness. I would rather—'

Josey glanced over Count Sarrow's shoulders. Lord Therbold's words died away as Hirsch approached on his small mare, followed by a company of crossbowmen. The soldiers' arrival had a profound effect on both noblemen. After a quiet conference with his officers, Sarrow announced he would be glad for a chance to settle their differences. Therbold was not so effusive, but he bent his stiff neck and mumbled a half-hearted welcome.

As the two sides set out on the road, leaving the villagers in peace, Josey rode up beside Hirsch. The adept smiled beneath the crumpled brim of his hat. 'Making new friends, lass?'

'Not so much.' She leaned closer. 'Your timing is excellent, Master Hirsch.'

'So I've been told, but it looked like you had things well in hand.'

It didn't feel like it. 'Thank you. Any news from Argentus?'

'About finding a crossing? Nothing new. He has scouts on both sides of the river, but my guess is we'll be stuck here at least another couple days.'

'Just what I didn't need to hear. Can't you' – Josey wiggled her fingers in front of her – 'wizard up some way for us to cross?'

He looked at her out of the sides of his eyes with one brow arched.

'All right.' Josey puffed out her cheeks. 'Send a message back to camp, telling them where we'll be. In the meantime, I'll see if I can get these two old bulls talking.'

'I think browbeating them was an auspicious start.'

Josey glared until Hirsch winked, and they both started laughing as they rode down the muddy path.

CHAPTER EIGHT

'What the fuck is that?'

Caim steered his steed around Dray for a closer look. A low structure sat off to the side of the road amid the clumps of colorless grass – an oblong, semi-flat stone about eight feet long laid across two plinths like a crude table. Brown stains marred the surface of the long stone, and three severed heads were displayed on leaning pikes behind it.

Caim's horse shied away when they got within a pace of the display. He held the animal steady while he studied the heads. The victims had been Northmen, judging by the wisps of wheat-colored hair blowing in the wind. Their skin was blackened and ripped. The eyeballs shone in the lantern light like orbs of ice.

'What's it supposed to mean?' Malig asked.

'It means stay the hell away,' Dray answered.

Caim swung his steed around. Egil caught his nod and took off down the trail again. Caim rode up in front with him while the others filed behind. The road was harder to pick out, having shrunk over the past two days to a narrow dirt path little more than a hunting trail. They'd been riding over a monotonous plain of snow and pale grass, past menhirs and over bone-white creeks.

'You see a lot of those shrines out here?' Caim asked.

'Some. Mostly up north.'

'Who puts them up? Priests?' Caim had guessed the table

was an altar, although to what deity he could hardly guess. The stains certainly looked like blood . . .

Egil shrugged. 'I suppose. People don't talk about them. It's best that way.'

'Seems like people don't talk about a lot of things up in these parts.'

Egil pulled something out of a pocket – it looked like a stick with the bark shaved off – and started chewing on it. 'Back when I was a boy, I remember seeing the sun in the sky. It would rise and fall every day. The warmth of it was like an oven on my face. They say the sun still shines in the south beyond the mountains. That true?'

'Sure.' Caim studied the guide's face.

'I was five years old when the Dark came to these lands.' Egil snapped his fingers. 'And all of sudden the light was gone. That was near twenty years ago, and I ain't seen the sun since.'

Caim did the math. That was about the same time his family had been attacked. Were they connected?

'I've got a question,' Dray said. 'How does anything grow up here in the dark?'

'Not much does.' Egil kicked a tuft of grass sticking up through the snow. 'Except for this stuff. We never saw it when I was little, but now it's everywhere. The priests say . . .'

'What?' Dray asked.

'Doesn't matter. I don't listen to them. What are y'all hunting? There's lynxes out here, though they're hard to spot.'

'We're not hunting for game,' Caim answered.

The guide nodded. 'Yeah. I didn't think so. You aren't outfitted for shit.'

Caim inhaled through his nose, pondering his options. He decided to take a chance. 'We're looking for a place.'

'What kind of place? I'll tell you right now there ain't much to find up here. And we'll be entering Bear tribe territory soon.'

'Is that a problem?'

'Not really. We probably won't see anyone unless we go near one of their winter villages. But if we do, they might want a tax for crossing their lands.'

Caim shifted in the saddle. 'I guess we'll handle that when it comes.'

With a nod, Egil jogged ahead, leaving Caim alone in the dark. Caim looked across the plains in search of a landmark he could use to judge their progress, but everywhere was the same dull, gray-black wasteland. Kit had said there was a town up ahead, but he had forgotten to ask how far. Knowing her, it could be days, or even weeks, away.

Electric fingertips ran down his spine. 'Isn't it a beautiful day?'

Caim swallowed a smart retort because, in a way, it *was* beautiful. There was something pure about the lay of the snow on the plains. Virginal. If not for the glow of the lanterns ahead and behind, he could have believed they were the only people in the whole world. 'How much longer till we reach that town?'

'Not too far.' Kit came around to straddle the horse, facing him, her legs wrapped around his waist. 'Remember what you promised.'

'I haven't forgotten.' He tried to imagine exactly what she had planned. He was flesh; she was spirit. They couldn't touch, not even to kiss, but she continued to act as if they were lovers in deed as much as in word. He loved her. He could admit that now, but he didn't know what kind of future they could have together.

Egil came back, his lantern bobbing with his strides. 'We're making good time. We should reach Jarnflein before next rest.'

Caim tried to look through Kit. She kissed him and disappeared. 'Is that a settlement?'

'Yes, somewhat. It's a meeting place. The tribes stop there when passing through following the herds. It can get a bit wild, which is why the hunters like it. It's also a good place to restock.'

Caim nodded. They needed supplies, especially oil for the lanterns. He hadn't thought much of it until they were on the road, surrounded by darkness and leagues of ice and snow.

Malig called out from the back of the line. 'They got girls there, right?'

Egil grinned through his short beard. 'Aye, northern women with hearty appetites. Don't say I didn't warn you.'

'Bring them on!' Malig laughed. 'I've got a big appetite myself.'

'What else can you tell us about this area?' Caim asked.

Egil pointed along the path they followed. 'This is Luca's Run, and it goes all the way to Grippenheimr, which is about as far north as anybody wants to go.'

Caim gazed ahead, trying to imagine what lay beyond the horizon. 'Who controls it?'

'No one anymore. It used to be Snow Owl land, but they moved out west some years back.'

'What?' Dray looked around like he was just seeing the wastes for the first time. 'And leave all *this* behind?'

'It's the Bear tribe,' Egil said. 'They've been expanding their territories. None of the other tribes can stand against them.'

Malig ran gloved fingers through his frozen beard, breaking off small icicles. 'Then you should all band together. That's what we did in Eregoth. Kicked that Eviskine bastard and his witch—'

'Malig.' Caim raised his voice. 'Take the point for a while.'

Malig glared at him, but then clucked his horse and cantered ahead. Everyone else fell quiet, and Caim was glad for it.

The leagues passed by with awful monotony. The wastes were awash in shades of gray and black. Even the few streams and creeks they crossed were gray, with pale fish darting in their currents. An ache developed behind Caim's temples, dull at first, but it grew in strength as the day stretched on. With his hood pulled down and his eyes half-closed, he didn't see the town until they were almost upon it. Egil's whistle made him look up. Cloaked in snow, the town's outer houses were all but invisible against the wastes. There was no outer wall, not even a palisade. Huge, humpbacked animals wandered outside the town without shepherds or watchers, grazing on the pale grass. They looked like buffalo, but with pale, silver fleece and curled horns.

As they passed through the outskirts, the door of a long-house swung open, and five men spilled out in a pool of orange light. They rolled around on the ground like a pack of dogs, punching and kicking each other. Eventually, one of the Northmen rose to his feet. Wobbling, with blood running from his mouth and snow in his beard, he growled something at them and staggered back inside the house. A moment later, shouts and sounds of breakage could be heard within.

Traffic increased as they rode deeper into the town. Unlike the trade settlement where they'd left Teromich, there were no southerners to be seen. Caim kept his hood up, but the Eregoths fit in better, all being large and rawboned themselves. Inside the town proper, there were torches and bowls of burning dung to light the way. The streets teemed with Northmen, powerful warriors dressed in furs and hides, running children, old men, and yellow-haired women who watched the Eregoths with frank, curious gazes. Dogs roamed among the people. Not skinny curs like the ones found in southern cities, but shaggy mastiffs with thick shoulders and long fangs.

Caim steered clear of both men and wolf-dogs, finally stopping in front of a tall building sporting a rack of antlers over its door. Across the way, an old Northman pounded on a piece of iron with a massive hammer, the light from the forge reflecting off his huge, sweaty shoulders.

'Where can we hole up?' Caim asked as the others gathered around. The noise and the smells were making his headache worse. All he wanted to do was get off the street.

'There's places that hire out rooms.' Egil pointed farther down the street, toward the town center.

'Is there some sort of market area?'

'Just follow the hollering. You can't miss it.'

Caim looked to Dray. 'I'll find a place to stay while you three go with Egil. Get everything we'll need for an extended journey.'

'For how many days?'

'Extended,' Caim repeated. 'I'll find you at the market. Try to stay out of trouble.'

Aemon kneed his steed closer to Caim. 'I'll go with you.'

'No—'

But the others were already following Egil through the crowd, and Caim was too tired to argue. His head felt ripe to explode. He clucked to his mount and headed down the street. At least Aemon rode quietly without asking questions.

Kit appeared above him, hanging upside down. 'There's a nice place up ahead. The rooms are a little small, but the beds look comfortable and cleaner than most places. Oh, and the owner's wife makes fresh bread all day long. It smells incredible.'

Caim looked at her, trying to figure out if she was serious. What the hell did she care if the bread was fresh? With Kit floating by his shoulder, he guided his horse past a knot of Northmen with cloaks made from long, white feathers. They had just entered a narrow street flanked by narrow wooden houses when a sharp pain punched through the center of Caim's chest. He bent forward, unable to breathe. It felt like an arrow had rammed right through him. He looked down expecting to see blood spilled down his front, but there was nothing.

Kit hovered in front of him. 'Caim? What's wrong? Caim?'

He couldn't help wheezing as fresh air dribbled into his lungs. Shivers racked his body, and he felt light-headed.

'You all right, Caim?' Aemon asked. 'You don't look so good.'

The clansman took the reins and guided both their mounts out of the flow of people. Caim shook and gasped for breath under a wooden archway hung with icicles while Aemon watched with a concerned gaze. Kit's fingers ran up and down his arm.

'I'm okay,' Caim finally managed to say when he could breathe again. But he felt wrung out. 'Caught a touch of something.'

'You need to get out of this cold,' Kit said.

At the same time, Aemon said, 'You should get someplace warm.'

Caim nodded. 'First place we see.'

Aemon returned his reins but took the lead, pushing through the crowd. They stopped at a boarding house sandwiched between two alehouses. Caim slid out of his saddle and managed to stay upright even as the rest of the world swayed. He didn't complain as Aemon tied up the horses.

'Come on, Caim,' Kit whispered in his ear. 'Just a few more steps to the door.'

Caim pushed off from his horse. Putting one foot in front of the other, he passed Aemon, who held open the door, and staggered inside. His boots scuffed along the bare floor of a tight hallway. The air was stuffy with warmth and woodsmoke, clogging in his throat. Shaggy cloaks hung from pegs on the wall. Caim heard Aemon's voice, followed by a woman's, and then the Eregoth was beside him again. 'Got us a couple rooms upstairs, Caim. You think you can make it?'

Caim let himself be helped up a flight of high steps and around a couple turns. A door opened, and then Aemon was lowering him onto a bed. The mattress was lumpy and stiff, but Caim collapsed without bothering with his boots or clothes and shut his eyes. The light dimmed as footsteps receded. There was talking, but it was miles and miles away in the fog that had set up in his head.

Then a soft voice whispered to him. 'Rest easy, Caim. I'm here.'

He smiled as Kit rubbed his shoulders with a touch that felt almost real.

Caim woke up feeling a world better. He had slept all night and through most of the next day. Sitting up, his head didn't hurt as much, and the hollow pain in his chest was gone, but mainly he was famished.

'See who's finally awake.' Kit settled down on the mattress beside him. 'You look better. I guess you really needed a rest. You've been pushing yourself too hard.'

Caim ran a hand through his stiff hair. 'I guess so. Where's everyone?'

'Dray and Malig went out after noonday. I think they're in a tavern on the east side of town. Horrible place. Egil's shopping for those supplies you wanted.'

'That figures.'

'What?' she asked.

'Nothing. What about Aemon? I think he's the one who brought me here, but my head's all stuffed up. I can hardly remember where I am.'

Kit pointed to the wall. 'He's in the next room. He's been checking in on you every once in a while. I think he was afraid you might die.'

'The way I was feeling, I might have welcomed a quick end.'

She batted at his chest. 'Don't say that!'

As her fingers passed through him, something tickled in the back of Caim's brain. A half-formed memory, but it slipped away. 'Well, I feel like a new man. Where's my clothes?'

Kit trailed her fingers up his stomach. 'I like you better without them.'

'Kit, you just got done telling me I need to take things easy.'

She poked him in the breastbone. Hard.

'Hey!' Caim rubbed the spot. He'd felt her finger. 'That—'

The door pushed open, and Aemon poked his head in. 'Hey, Caim! You're awake!'

Caim glanced at Kit. 'So it would seem. Can I have my clothes?'

Aemon tossed Caim a package. Inside were his garments, cleaned and neatly folded. Even the holes had been mended. Aemon talked, mostly about the townsfolk, while Caim cleaned up in a washbasin and got dressed.

'And you wouldn't believe some of the things these northern gals say,' Aemon said with a shake of his head. 'It's enough to put the steel in your sword, if you know what I mean.'

Feeling almost human, Caim strapped on his knives. 'Don't get too comfortable with them. They're still Northmen, same as the ones who killed your kin in Eregoth.'

Aemon lowered his gaze. 'I know, Caim. I know why we're here.'

Do you? Because I'm starting to doubt whether I *know anymore.* 'Good. I could do with a drink and something warm to eat.'

'Now you're talking.'

They left the small room and went down a narrow flight of steps to a tight foyer. None of it was familiar to Caim. *I must have been sicker than I realized.*

Once outside, Aemon took the lead. Caim breathed in the chill air, letting it wash the sleep from his brain as he followed through the sparse crowd.

'Maybe you should go see one of those mud-men doctors, Caim.' Kit floated beside him. 'Maybe they can fix whatever's wrong.'

'Here?' He snorted and kept his attention on Aemon's broad back. 'I'll be fine, Kit.'

'You keep saying that, but what if it gets worse?'

'I don't think it's anything a doctor could help with. I think it's tied to . . . you know . . . the shadows.'

He closed his mouth, hoping she would volunteer something, a fresh hint about the mysterious world from which his powers sprang. But she just watched him with large, liquid eyes.

'Are you going to tell me what happened back in the room?'

Kit scrunched her eyes. 'What do you mean?'

'When you poked me, Kit. I felt it. Not a little tickle, either. You really touched me.'

'I have no idea what you're talking about.'

'How can you—?'

Caim shut up as Aemon looked back, eyebrows lifted like he'd heard something. When he turned back around, Kit was gone. Caim growled under his breath as he tugged on his gloves.

They entered a crowded street. Raucous voices echoed off the homes and shops. The town, Caim had already decided, possessed no plan or reason; it was just a pile of buildings built around, next to, and over to each other. Every Northman carried a weapon, usually more than one. Here in their natural element they were a loud, lusty people. He hoped Dray and Malig were behaving themselves, but that was almost too much to ask.

Aemon and Caim jostled their way into a great market. Everything was open to the sky. Stalls and wagons lined the perimeter. The shouts of the hawkers combined into a droning cacophony mixed with braying animals and shrill pipes. People mingled about, but most were gathered at the middle of the plaza around a high platform. A row of people, men and women alike, stood upon the stage. It was hard to tell much about them from this distance, except that they were tied together, hand and foot. Prisoners? No. A sour taste filled the back of Caim's mouth as he looked closer. Slaves. One by one they were cut free and marched down from the platform as money changed hands.

Looking at all the establishments around the plaza, Caim didn't know where to start searching for the others. In the end, it was Dray and Malig who found them. Caim and Aemon had paused at a tavern, thinking they would ask if anyone had seen their comrades, when a shout cut through the noise. Dray pushed through the crowd with Malig right behind him. They carried leather flasks and each had their arms draped around a pair of girls, all of them laughing and drinking. The girls looked about sixteen or seventeen. Maybe. Caim looked past his crew, half expecting to see a gang of angry fathers hot on their trail.

'We thought you were dying,' Dray yelled over the crowd.

'Yeah,' Malig echoed. 'You don't look so bad now.'

'Where's Egil?' Caim asked.

'Who?' Dray asked.

Malig shrugged. 'Haven't seen him since this morning. But look what we found! Eh?' He grabbed a rounded buttock, evoking a squeal and more laughter.

'We got a table,' Dray said. 'Follow me.'

Caim allowed the Eregoths to lead him to an outdoor tavern. Dray and Malig sat down and ordered another round of drinks. Caim spotted an empty chair against the wall and claimed it for himself. Aemon started to follow, but Caim waved for him to join his brother.

A bony scullion with copper braids brought Caim a foaming tankard before he even sat down. He pantomimed putting something in his mouth, and she nodded, going back inside. Caim looked around as he sipped the malty beer. It was clear by the variety of garbs and attitudes that several different tribes of Northmen were represented in the square. Most of the men strode about like lords of creation. The inevitable squabbles this caused were quickly decided by blows or a sharing of drinks at the square's plethora of watering holes.

The women were almost as brazen, and just as quick to start a fight when they thought they'd been wronged.

Of his comrades, only Aemon was paying the crowd any mind. The others were too involved in getting to know their girls better. The serving woman returned with a trencher of brown stew and a steaming bread roll. Spurred on by the ache in his gut, Caim didn't bother waiting until it cooled before he started tearing off hunks of bread and dragging them through the stew. The meat was lean and chewy. If it came from the shaggy bison they'd seen outside town, he decided he liked it.

As he sopped up the last bits, Caim glanced over at his comrades. Malig and Dray were tossing back cups like it was their last night, but Aemon stared into the crowd. His hands were clenched around his cup as if he wanted to crush it. Caim followed his gaze. In the center of the square, the slave auction continued. A rotund man in gray furs was addressing the crowd. Caim couldn't make it out, but he saw a slim girl standing on the stage. The first thing he noticed was the mane of rich, black hair that tumbled down her pale shoulders, and for a moment he saw Josey on the stage, shivering and frightened. He almost knocked his mug off the table before he calmed himself. *Don't be crazy.*

A loud roar rose from the crowd as Northmen thrust their hands in the air. On the stage, the woman's shift had been torn away, leaving her naked before the multitude. She had the smoky eyes and bronze features of a southerner, maybe from Illmyn or Michaia. Caim was digging in his pouch to pay for the food when Aemon stood up.

Caim slapped down a handful of coppers. 'Dray! We're leav—' Vertigo washed over him as he stood. He clenched his jaws and tried to shake it off. *Gods be damned. Not again.*

Dray looked over with a frown. 'Caim?'

As Caim fought to stand up straight, something popped behind him. Before he could turn, a wall of heat struck him in the back, turning the air into a haze of boiling flame. The blast carried him over several tumbling chairs and dumped him hard on the ground against on overturned table. His ears hummed. Then sounds began to filter through the thunder in his head, muted screams and yelling from all sides.

Crawling to his knees, Caim looked around at the market, which had been ripped apart. The southern side of the square was a curtain of fire. Fiery cinders swirled overhead amid a cloud of dense smoke. Northmen ran, trampling anyone who didn't move fast enough. Steel flashed here and there.

Caim stood up as Aemon helped his brother out of a pile of people and furniture. Malig sported a big bruise over his right eye. By his scowl, he was ready to wreak some destruction of his own. The girls picked themselves up and scurried away.

'Mal!' Caim shouted. 'Go get the horses.'

Aemon steadied his brother, who was looking around with wide, glassy eyes. Caim looked out over the crowd. The fire was spreading, and the people trapped in the market were becoming more violent in their attempts to escape. Egil emerged from the river of people, with two heavy sacks slung over his shoulder.

'Let's go!' Caim shouted, but then a flash of red from the crowd caught his eye.

Thirty paces behind Egil, a figure in a russet cloak was striding away through the mob. The Northmen didn't seem to notice him, for the figure flowed through their press as easily as a fish through still water. Caim pushed through a knot of leather-clad warriors after the cloaked individual. *I must be crazy. I don't even know what I'm chasing.*

'Caim!'

He turned his head at Aemon's call. A scuffle had broken out at the outdoor tavern. Four big Northmen were grappling with the brothers. Aemon bled from his nose while Dray was being choked. *Shit!*

Caim glanced into the crowd, but the figure in the red cloak was gone. With a growl, he shoved his way back to the tables.

He drew his knives as he came up behind one assailant and punched him in the kidney with a pommel butt while simultaneously stomping on the back of his ankle, toppling him over with a bellow. Caim hoped to extricate the brothers without bloodshed, but two of the Northmen drew daggers from their belts and came at him. Caim feinted left and slashed high to the right, distracting the foe long enough to get in close and bury his seax in the Northman's armpit. The second Northman stabbed, but Caim deflected the weak underhand thrust and spun away, slicing his *suete* along the ribs of the Northman choking Dray. The strangler released Dray and reached for the short-handled axe at his belt, but Caim rushed in before the man could draw. His knives plunged through hide and up to their guards in soft belly flesh. The Northman yelled and tried to shove him away, but Caim twisted around behind him and cut his throat.

Caim stepped back, knives dripping. The last Northman standing took off through the crowd. Aemon helped Dray to his feet. 'You want we should go after him?'

'No. We're getting out.'

With his knives in hand, Caim made a path through the crowd. They found Malig two streets up from the market. Everyone mounted up, except for Egil. Before Caim could offer him a ride, the guide strode ahead of them, making a path. Caim kneed his steed into the breach, and they rode as fast as the press of angry Northmen would allow.

As they approached the town's outer limits, Caim looked back, wondering what had happened. They had escaped unharmed, but although he tried to convince himself he was being paranoid, he couldn't help feeling the mayhem had been aimed at him. The feeling followed him onto the wastes.

CHAPTER NINE

Caim peered through the freezing rain that had inundated them since they left the northern town. They traveled on what could only graciously be called a hunting trail. The rain had left a thick crust of ice, like a glass cocoon, over everything. It crackled under the hooves of their horses and made footing treacherous. Egil walked a hundred paces or so ahead of them, as was his habit. Perhaps he preferred solitude. Caim could understand that. These lonely plains were made for silence. The horizon was a faint divider between black earth and blacker heavens.

Caim buried his face in the shirt he was using for a scarf, feeling the wool snag on his whiskers. For the better part of two days he had been pondering the explosion that had almost killed them. Yet, even as his thoughts chased themselves around and around, he couldn't make up his mind. Had they been attacked, and had it all been an unfortunate accident? Caim had heard of granaries catching fire like that, but not homes exploding without warning. More than anything it reminded him of the fire that had burned down his apartment building in Othir. Coincidence?

'For fuck sakes!' Dray yelled. 'I can't feel my toes.'

Caim swallowed a sharp retort. Dray and Malig had complained nonstop since leaving the town, about the cold, the rain, the darkness, and the food, but mainly about how they had been forced to leave town before they got to 'know' their lady friends. On the other hand, Aemon hadn't said more than a dozen words since they'd left. Caim looked back at the blond Eregoth riding at the rear of the party by himself. *Probably brooding over that slave girl at the market. The boy's too sensitive for his own good.*

But when Caim closed his eyes, he saw her, too. Defenseless and alone before the ravenous crowd. She'd looked nothing like Josey except the hair, but he couldn't put her out of his head. *Now who's the sensitive one?*

'We should have stayed back there,' Dray said. 'What was the harm in a couple more days? Those girls! Oh gods! We should have stayed.'

'Damn right, we should have,' Malig said. 'The fire wasn't even that bad. Those girls were ready to go, and I ain't had a piece of tail in weeks.'

Dray laughed. 'Hell, Mal. The way you were drooling, I didn't think you'd ever had a piece.'

'Fuck you, Dray. I've had half the girls in Joliet. You remember Marsa?'

Caim steered his horse around a crater in the trail. There were a few tall boulders ahead, lying on the plains like huge snowballs. Maybe they could find a place out of the wind to bed down for a couple hours.

'Hamer's sister?' Dray asked.

'That's right. Say, didn't that girl back there look a little like Marsa?'

'Which girl?'

'The one those guys were trying to buy. You know, in the square.'

'At the market?'

'Yeah—'

'Gods!' Aemon's voice called from the back of the line. 'Don't you talk about anything else?'

Caim turned around. The others had pulled up behind him.

'What's the problem?' Malig laughed. 'You don't like girls?'

Aemon's face was stark white in the cold. 'I never said that, but you don't need to be saying those kinds of—'

'Saying what?' Malig spurred his mount closer to Aemon. 'I'll say what I fucking want.'

'Mal,' Dray said. 'Let it be.'

Malig spat on the ground. 'To hell with that! I want to know what your little brother thinks I shouldn't be saying. Maybe he thinks he's the one to shut me—'

Aemon's right fist connected with the side of Malig's jaw with a hard thud. Malig kicked free of his stirrups and lunged, dragging Aemon off his horse. Caim glanced at Dray, who stayed where he was even though Malig was stronger and meaner than his brother by a fair margin, not to mention Aemon had a bad leg. When Malig rolled on top, Caim wondered if he should intervene, but a sharp smack sent the big man toppling over to the ground. Aemon pushed himself to his feet.

'I told you,' Dray said.

Malig sat up, shaking his head. 'Shut up.'

Aemon got back on his horse and waited, saying nothing. Caim swung his steed back around. *Maybe now they'll be quiet for a while.*

Egil had paused down the trail. When the scuffle was over, he headed off again. *Probably thinks we're all crazy. And I'm starting to think we are, too.*

The stars came out in crystalline points of ruby as the sky deepened from twilight's coal to inky jet. At another time, in another place, they would have been beautiful.

'Hey, lover.' Kit planted a feathery kiss on his forehead as she appeared above him.

'You catch the fireworks?' he asked under his breath.

'Yes!' She giggled. 'Malig should have known better than to mess with Aemon.'

'No. Back at town. The explosion?'

Kit came around in front of him. As he told her what had

happened, her dress, or shirt – it barely came down to the tops of her thighs – changed from turquoise to a somber magenta. 'I should have been there,' she said when he was finished.

'That would have been helpful.'

'I'm sorry. I, er . . . I thought you didn't want me around.'

Caim sighed. This was his fault. He had been acting different lately, more distant. 'Don't worry about it. I'm glad you're back.'

She leaned closer. 'You are? Then say it.'

He mouthed the words Kit wanted to hear, and then she threw herself across his lap and wrapped her arms around his neck. 'That's better. Now there's something up ahead—'

A sharp whistle cut the air, and Egil ran back toward the party. His lantern was extinguished. 'Put out the light!' the guide hissed.

Dray turned down his lantern and shut the hood. 'What is it?'

'Torches ahead,' Egil said, his breath puffing in the frosty air. 'A score or more.'

Caim considered the land around them. It was as flat as a griddle except for a few ripples on the snowy plain and some scattered stones. 'Coming this way?'

'Hard to say, but it looks like they'll cross our path. We should be fine if we're quiet.'

Caim glanced at Kit, but asked Egil, 'Are these Bear tribesmen?'

'Most likely. We're pretty deep into their territory now.'

'That's what I was going to tell you,' Kit said. 'They're White Bears heading west to their spring homes. But they don't know you're here.'

'Yet,' Caim whispered under his breath.

The others rode up. Malig had his broadaxe out as he craned his neck around. 'Trouble?'

'Not sure.' Caim wrapped his reins around the horn of his saddle and climbed down. 'But I'm going to take a look.'

Dray loosened his sword. 'Ill go with you.'

When Malig and Aemon got down from their steeds, too, Caim didn't argue. He pointed to a stand of ice-sheathed rocks just off the trail. 'Take the animals over there out of the wind and cover them up, but keep the saddles on.'

'You've got the eyes of a cat,' Egil said with a shake of his head.

As the guide led the horses off, Caim checked his knives. 'Keep up,' he said. 'If we get split up, meet back here.'

Without waiting for a reply, Caim took off. His boots crunched through the snow's light crust, but the sound was swallowed by the wind.

Kit floated along beside him. 'Caim, this isn't funny. What are you doing?'

'Just a peek,' he whispered back, not sure himself. Since leaving the last town he'd been uneasy. Recent events had him feeling like he was searching for a diamond in a heap of glass shards. The explosion had capped it. There were outside forces at work in his life, and it was time he faced them head-on.

'Just a moment.' Kit darted closer and threw her arms around his shoulders. Her feathery touch made him shiver. 'There. Feel anything . . . different?'

Caim clenched his fists while he walked to keep from trying to push her away in front of the others. She was being more irritating than usual. Except he *did* feel something, a lingering pressure where their skin met. More than the normal tickle, but he didn't have time for her games. 'No. Now cut it out.'

She pulled back, her lips pulled down in a frown. 'Okay. Sorry.'

Caim ducked through her with a shake of his head. As he led the Eregoths away, a familiar feeling of ease settled over him. For a moment, it was just like old times. Then Dray cursed and Malig snickered, and he wanted to kill them both.

'I see something.' Aemon pointed. 'Over there.'

Caim had seen them, too. Several points of light bobbed on

the plains north of their position. Hurrying across the uneven ground, Caim found a short esker and crouched behind it. The others joined him, their boots gouging footholds in the snow. The lights grew into torches, illuminating bearded faces under bestial helms. Two dozen Northmen on massive, hairy steeds. They rode double-file as they headed – thankfully – west. Caim was content to stay and watch until they were out of sight, the better to be sure they were gone, before he returned to the horses. He decided they would ride all night. If this territory was patrolled, he wanted to be through it as soon as possible.

A shout caught Caim's attention. The lead Northmen riders had pulled up. Their torches waved back and forth as if they were searching for something. Then a horse screamed, and one of the torches fell to the ground and went out. Caim squinted as more horsemen appeared from the west, plunging into the Bear tribesmen. By the dim light he could make out the rise and fall of gleaming steel, hear the angry clash of arms and men.

'What's going on?' Malig asked, rising up for a better view.

Caim yanked him back down. 'Quiet! And keep your head down. There's two groups fighting. I can't tell who they are except they're both Northmen.'

Dray snorted. 'That's good for us. They keep themselves busy while we slip in there and clean the pick—'

'You three aren't going anywhere,' Caim said. 'Stay put while I go for a closer look.'

'Why?' Malig asked. 'What's it got to do with us?'

Caim tamped down the urge to strangle him. 'We don't know yet. The rest of you—'

'I want to go with you,' Aemon interjected.

'—stay here,' Caim finished. 'If you see trouble, get back to get the horses.'

'What about you?'

'I'll be fine. You just keep heading north and I'll find you.'

'This is bullshit,' Dray muttered.

Caim ignored the comment as he made his way over the esker and down the other side. What was he doing? This was an unnecessary risk. Or was it? For better or worse, he was following his instincts. He looked around, but Kit was gone.

The original column of Northmen had broken up into small knots of fighters, but they still had the advantage of numbers. As those numbers began to tell, the attackers suddenly broke off. The defenders gave chase, cutting down those who were too slow in retreat, and it looked as though they had turned the tables on their assailants. Then clods of snow erupted from the ground, and men emerged – warriors wielding great axes and hammers. They hit the Bear tribe column from both sides.

Caim slipped behind a clump of thorny brush and got down on his belly. The Bear tribesmen were all down. Howls and groans carried on the breeze. Caim saw more headpieces, and for a moment he envisioned them as wolves with fangs agleam, but then they resolved into feline heads perched on iron caps.

A Northman pulled up near Caim's position. He was brawny, with a thick, black beard down to his chest. Blood dripped from the blade of his long-hafted axe; a round shield of wood was strapped to his other arm. His helm was topped by a tall headpiece made from the head of a great, white cat. It swiveled back and forth as if searching for more prey. Caim gritted his teeth as tiny voices chittered to him from the darkness. Shadows oozed from underneath the brush and touched him, crawled up his arms. Their icy caresses drew deep shivers from his muscles. Their hunger infected him, making him want to join the violence and feel the power of death in his hands.

Blood on my knives, dripping in the snow.

Caim shunted the longing away as he gathered his legs under him. The fighting was over. The cat-men were gathering the loose horses and picking through the remains. Corpses made bloody heaps in the trampled snow. Caim was trying to decide what he wanted to do when something crunched behind him. He spun around, both knives drawn, to see Dray crouched a dozen paces away with Aemon and Malig following him. Before Caim could motion for the clansmen to get back, torchlight washed over them, and a hoarse voice bellowed. Caim almost bit off the tip of his tongue. The axe-man rode up, his horse snorting steam in the cold night air. Caim considered the distance between him to the Northman. If he could drop this one fast enough, they might still make a clean escape.

Thoughts of a quick kill-and-dash ended when more hoofbeats and crackling ice sounded from behind. Caim didn't have to look to know that more barbarians had ridden up, cutting off their escape.

'What do we do, Caim?' Dray asked. He and the others had drawn their weapons and stood with their backs together.

Caim calculated the outcome if he attacked. He could escape, he had no doubt, but the others would be run down and slaughtered. With a sigh, he slid his knives back into their sheaths and held up his hands. 'Put up your weapons,' he said.

'The hell I will!' Malig shouted.

Caim shrugged. 'Then you'll die.'

More Northmen arrived. Their voices shot back and forth in the bitter cold air. He didn't know what they said, but he assumed the worst. Then a deep voice spoke in Nimean.

'You are not of the Tribes.'

Caim located the axe-man. It was difficult to make out much of his features under the heavy helm, except for a pitch-black beard and a long puckered scar down the left side of his face. He wore a chainmail hauberk that came down to his knees, rusted in a few places, and over it a cloak of white fur that reminded Caim of the mantles worn by the clan chiefs in Eregoth.

'No, we're not,' Caim replied.

The speaker nudged his steed to approach to within a couple steps. 'Who are you?'

Caim said his name, and those of his crew. Behind him, he heard someone muttering. *Probably Malig. He's going to get us killed if he isn't careful.* One look at the Northmen had been enough to tell Caim that they were the worst kind of deadly. They enjoyed the slaughter. In fact, they reminded him of Soloroth's Northmen.

'We saw the light of the fires,' Caim said. 'And came to see what it was.'

The speaker laughed, but his men remained silent. 'I am Wulfgrim, son of Grimhild, chief of what is left of the Snow Lions. Our camp is not far. You will come and share our fire.'

There was no question in his invitation, and Caim hadn't expected any. They had two choices: go with them, or try to fight their way out. And not being able to rely on the shadows made that a losing proposition. 'We have horses nearby.'

Wulfgrim signaled, and his men prepared to depart.

Caim kept his face neutral as he turned and led the way back to the rocks. Aemon and the others looked to him, but he didn't have anything to tell them. They'd have to play this one as it came.

The walk seemed shorter on the way back. The Northmen rode around them, gibbering in their harsh tongue. Laughing. When they arrived at the spot, their horses were there, huddled together, but Egil was gone.

'Where's—?' Dray started to say, until Caim caught his eye and made a small headshake. 'Where's my waterskin?' he finished. 'I'm damned parched.'

As they mounted up under the watchful gazes and headed out, Caim peered across the wastes. Egil was well and truly gone.

Caim blew into his cupped hands, but his fingertips felt only the barest warmth. Wulfgrim, the Northman leader, had said their camp was nearby, but they had been riding for more than a candlemark. At least they were heading north, mostly. A little west, too, but he had bigger concerns at the moment. Like staying alive.

'I told you to stay away,' Kit said even before she appeared before him. Worry was etched in her eternally youthful features.

Caim hunched over his hands. With the Eregoths and the Northmen riding all around him, there wasn't much he could say. *At this point, does it really matter if they think I'm insane?* Probably not, but he wasn't ready to go down that route, as much as it might tickle Kit.

'I don't like these ones.' Kit straddled his horse's neck, which made the animal lift its head and snort. 'They aren't like Egil. They're . . . different.'

'Like Soloroth's wildmen,' Caim whispered, so quiet he could hardly hear his own words. But Kit caught them.

'Exactly. So how are you planning to get out of this?'

He wished he knew.

Kit leaned in close. 'You don't have a plan, do you? Caim, these men aren't fooling around. And their leader, that Wulfgrim, is deep-down ugly.'

He knew by her tone that Kit didn't mean physically repulsive. 'I'm always careful.'

She shook her head. 'Not careful enough by half. If you were, we'd be lying on a warm beach right now instead of trudging through this miserable ice-hell.'

He couldn't argue, but he knew in his gut that he'd still have come here, somehow. The pulling in his soul had begun so long ago, he couldn't remember a time when he hadn't felt it. Caim started to say something when the Northmen all whooped aloud, and the entire party advanced at a snow-churning canter. Small points of light appeared ahead, campfires shining between low, ice-covered tors. Tall men with spears waited for them. They shouted something, and Wulfgrim replied with a lusty yell. The riders cheered.

The camp consisted of thirty-some round tents of stitched hide scattered around half a dozen fire pits. A trampled area between two long hills served as the pasture. The Northmen hobbled their steeds to spikes and unloaded them, leaving the animals to stand in the cold. The supplies were opened, and their contents passed around. Kettles and pans appeared, and food was cooking in short order. As Caim dismounted, a young Northman with a scraggly yellow beard came to take their horses. Malig started to growl something until Dray slapped him on the shoulder.

'Southlanders!' Wulfgrim waved them over as he sat by a fire. 'You are my guests!'

Caim looked to the others and nodded, and they made their way over to the leader. There was no place to sit except in the snow. Caim eased down onto his cloak. Wulfgrim took off his helm and laid it beside him. The lion head crowning the headpiece was gigantic; the beast must have been as big as a pony. The chieftain rummaged a tarnished silver cup out of a sack and poured into it some milky drink from a huge skin bladder. After a healthy dose, he passed it to Dray, who sniffed it and then took a swig.

'You.' Wulfgrim pointed at Caim. The long scar down his cheek glowed angry red in the firelight. More scars marked his powerful arms. 'Why are you here? Southlanders do not come to the wastes. Maybe trade down by the mountains, but not so far north.'

Caim waited to take his turn with the drink before he spoke, and almost choked on the thick, clotted stuff that filled his mouth.

'Buffalo milk,' Wulfgrim said as Caim struggled to swallow it. 'Mixed with mare's blood.'

Caim passed it on to Aemon. Despite its nasty taste, the liquor heated his insides and made his hands tingle. 'We've sold our swords all across the Southlands, as you call them. We came north to find better sport.'

Wulfgrim refilled his cup. 'More sport? Ulfric, come hear these southerners who speak of war as if it's a game.'

A big Northman glanced over from another fire, blood wetting his beard as he chewed on a half-cooked hunk of meat. '*Tal hundr skyrf na vurd.*'

Wulfgrim laughed. 'He says you look like a pack of hairless dogs.'

'A dog, am I?' Malig asked, loud enough to be heard throughout the camp.

Malig started reaching for his axe, but Caim yanked his arm down and hissed, 'Keep quiet. This isn't a country fair.'

The chieftain chuckled and took another deep gulp. 'Do not mind Ulfric. He lost his heart to a Southland beauty some years ago and misses her still.'

A woman came over with spits of steaming meat for each of them. Kit sniffed it and shrugged, which Caim took to mean it wasn't poisoned or carrying some infection. He noted there weren't many females with the tribe, and even the young ones looked hard-used. He saw why when a Northman at another fire grabbed a woman passing by and threw her down on the cold ground. He climbed on top of her without preamble and began pumping away. None of the other Northmen paid much mind to their grunting, although Malig watched with a wide grin. 'I could do with a piece of that.'

Dray flicked a piece of gristle into the fire. 'Watch out, Mal. These she-lions are like to bite off your member and cook it in a stew.'

Caim glanced at their host, but Wulfgrim grinned, revealing horizontal furrows carved into the fronts of his teeth. The others set to their meals with gusto, but Caim took small bites of the tough meat. When the milk-skin came around again, he passed it without drinking. Aemon, too, was abstaining, and he didn't touch his food. *At least someone is keeping his head on straight.*

When he finished his meal, Caim wiped his greasy fingers on his pants. 'Wulfgrim, why do you war on the Bear tribe?'

Wulfgrim spat a mouthful of liquor into the fire, making the flames sizzle. 'The Night swallow their souls, every last one of them. We war, yes. We kill every one we find. *Austrivegr bjern foera hel!*'

Caim didn't understand the last part, but the other Northmen responded with laughter and catcalls.

'A blood feud,' Dray said with a belch as he lowered the bladder from his mouth.

'Aye.' Wulfgrim patted the axe by his side. 'When my father was chieftain, our lands could not be crossed in a week's time on horseback. The other tribes feared to test our steel. Then came the Dark. The sky turned black, and the Fates fixed us with an evil weird. Now the Bear tribe rules over the wastes.' He tossed a hunk of gristle into the fire.

Caim considered the Northman over the flames. He wasn't as simple as Kit had made him out to be. Caim could understand Wulfgrim's fight to preserve the power and dignity of his people. 'If we go north,' he said, 'will we encounter more of these Bear tribesmen?'

Wulfgrim's eyes were slits through the smoke. His lips were thick and red amid the greasy curls of his beard. 'Aye. They have grown strong under the Dark One's wing, but that will not protect them when we come.'

Caim frowned. Keegan's father, Hagan, had mentioned a dark lord of the north. And then there was the man he'd seen in Sybelle's vision. But before he could ask more, Wulfgrim stood up. He towered over them like a primeval giant. 'Sleep. In the morning we will talk more.'

And then he walked away into the gloom.

Malig clucked his tongue. 'He's a little off, eh?'

'You could say that,' Dray said as he accepted the bladder

back. 'But fuck, these Wastelanders make good firemead. You taste that little something in there? Maybe cloves. We should get their recipe.' He squirted another long gulp into his mouth.

Caim leaned forward. 'Are you three clear-headed enough to think?'

Aemon looked up from the campfire. 'I haven't touched a drop.'

'I know, but you've been in a fog since we left that last town. I need you here.' Caim's gaze wandered across the tents and other fires. 'I don't know what they're planning to do with us, so keep your wits about you and your weapons at hand. We'll sleep in shifts. If anything happens, stay together and try to get to the horses. Aemon, you have first watch.'

Dray eyed the bladder. 'Hey, what if they poisoned the milk?'

Caim pulled his cloak tight around his shoulders and lay down in the snow. The homebrew had left a nasty aftertaste in his mouth. 'Then die quietly so the rest of us can get some sleep.'

While the others settled down, tossing muffled insults back and forth, Aemon scuttled over to Caim. 'What do you think happened to Egil?'

'I hope he was smart enough to get far away from here.'

Aemon glanced beyond the fire, out onto the frozen plains. 'Yeah.'

Caim wanted to close his eyes, but a sense of unease had settled in his chest, and it refused to let him be. These Northmen looked like ordinary men, but something vicious lurked behind their eyes. Something inhuman.

Kit appeared on top of him. For a moment, Caim could have sworn he felt her weight pressing down on him in a surprising – and very enjoyable – way. But then the sensation was gone and she was floating over him, a small frown flattening her lips. 'What are you going to do, Caim?'

Unsure what she meant, he didn't answer. Kit laid her head on his chest, sending electric tingles through his body. 'Is it ever going to be just the two of us again?'

The urge to hold her close washed over Caim. His hands started to reach up, but then fell back by his sides. Through the ethereal halo of her hair he saw the stars twinkling. 'I don't know,' he whispered into her hair.

He closed his eyes, listening to the crackle of the fire. When he opened them again, she was gone.

CHAPTER TEN

Familiar scents greeted Balaam as he stepped from the portal – thistle and white oleander, lacquer and ebonwood, a faint remnant of her favorite incense. He was home.

He entered through the parlor where a fire crackled in the wide hearth. The warmth felt good after four days spent out in the wilds, sleeping under the open sky as he tracked his quarry. But there had been no sign of the scion since Liovard, and the failure ate at him.

Balaam stopped at his bedchamber, thinking to change into something clean, but the echo of dripping water drew him down the hallway. The bathing room was lit with candles, small and large, sitting on the shelves and the floor. Their wavering flames threw shadows across the amber tile. Sweet-smelling steam rose from the water, cut through by the acrid scent of burning lotus.

Dorcas sat in the bath. Her breasts, still firm and buoyant, pointed toward the ceiling as she reclined, eyes closed, in the arms of the servant girl who washed her with a bristled brush. Her face glowed like polished glass, framed in a tumble of silky black hair. Every time he saw her, it was like the first time again. Balaam watched from the doorway as his wife leaned over the burning brazier beside the tub and inhaled the fragrant smoke. Her eyes gleamed with a blue tinge as she looked up. 'Balaam. How long have you been lurking there?'

The servant girl, Anora, looked over, but did not stop her

ministrations. Balaam folded his arms and tried not to look at the narcotic gray haze spilling from the brazier. 'I just arrived.'

Dorcas laughed. It was a smooth, throaty laugh. Once, it would have set his blood on fire. 'Come join us. You look a fright.'

'I'm fine.'

'Anora, undress my husband.'

Small waves washed against the sides of the tub as the girl stood up. She was also nude, her pale skin glistening in the candlelight. Balaam held up a hand to halt her. His wife's eyes swam with amusement. He could feel her gaze following him as he walked back down the hallway.

Balaam was sitting in his favorite chair near the fire, holding a half-filled glass of Illmynish wine and enjoying the heat, when Dorcas entered. She had wrapped herself in an ivory silk robe. Her wet hair cascaded over her shoulders. She sat down on a low divan near his feet. 'You look tired. When was the last time you fed?'

He waved the question away. He hadn't felt the urge to feed in more than a sennight. Not since leaving Liovard.

'Anora!' she called over her shoulder.

'Dorcas, that's not necessary.'

Her lips smiled, but it did not show in her unfocused eyes. 'It's nothing. You must keep up your strength.'

The girl entered, now dressed in a simple white tunic, and came over to kneel beside them. Balaam looked away as Dorcas slit the girl's wrist with a fingernail.

She held the arm up to him. 'Here.'

The blood ran down Anora's arm, more intoxicating than the finest wine, and all his fatigue and angst departed on a roiling red tide of euphoria. Instead of drinking directly from the vein, he leaned over and inhaled. Thin ribbons of energy rose from the blood, which turned black and formed a crust around the edges as the girl's essence flowed into him. They hadn't been forced to feed this way in the Shadowlands. There, surrounded by the Shadow's power, they had been constantly sustained. He'd hoped things would go back to the old ways when the Master scorched the sky, but that hope proved short-lived as the sun's wrath continued to plague them even in the gray gloom. And so they were forced to depend on livestock, human and animal, to exist.

Balaam sat back as feelings of satisfaction and shame dueled inside him. He remained in that state for a short eternity, riding the ecstasy of the blood. When he roused, the servant girl was leaning against his wife's shoulder. Dorcas watched them both with naked arousal, but she pushed the girl to her feet. 'Well,' she said as the servant stumbled out of the room. 'Did you find her?'

Balaam frowned, guarding his thoughts. 'I found the place where she died. She had . . .' He cleared his throat. Why was this so difficult for him to talk about? 'She had already crossed over.'

'How was the news received?'

Balaam tapped on the arm of the chair.

Dorcas inched forward, not quite touching his knee. 'But the Master could not blame you for her fate. Balaam! You were nowhere near when it happened. The Master must know—'

'I do not need you to tell me what the Master must know.'

She moved back, just a handspan, but it was enough. 'No. You never had a problem knowing his mind.'

Only yours. Right, my lovely?

'How long are you back for?' she asked.

'I must leave tonight. Soon. I just came to see you.'

'Here I am. The same as you left me.'

He winced inwardly, but kept his face still. 'I have new orders.'

She called a shadow to her hand. 'Another mission. Of course.'

'Dorcas, I . . .'

Perhaps she sensed it in his voice, because she looked at

him. Really looked at him, her reddened eyes searching his face. He couldn't recall the last time she'd done that.

'What's wrong, Balaam? Did something happen?'

He looked to the flames in the fireplace. How to tell her about the antipathy he'd been suffering of late, the disloyal thoughts? They must be plain on his face. He turned, but she was gone.

He stood up. Part of him wanted to stay, but he could not. He might have failed as a husband, but he still had his duty.

He opened a portal and departed, jumping far to the south in search of a shadow.

CHAPTER ELEVEN

Josey rubbed her temples as the tirades flew back and forth across the long plank table.

'Absolutely not! I would rather die and have my ashes scattered over a charnel pit!'

'That can be arranged!'

'Cur! Progeny of mongrels! I would cut out—'

Count Sarrow and Lord Therbold had been saying much the same for the last three days, until Josey stopped trying to quell the argument and let it play out in the hopes the two men would exhaust themselves. That didn't seem likely any time soon. Still, the past couple days hadn't been a complete waste of her time. She had gotten some much needed rest – in a real bed! – and the food was better than what was served in camp. The decor was more rustic than she was used to, with lots of natural wood and cast-iron accents, but charming nonetheless. And she had learned that the troubles between Therbold and Sarrow were deep and far-reaching. In fact, their grandfathers had started the feud more than fifty years ago. She had also discovered why both were so intent on possessing Hafsax. Water rights. The little hamlet controlled access to the river, which fed the most arable portions of both their lands, as well as being a vital trade route for the province. Whoever possessed Hafsax held the other in his power.

A sudden pressure pushed against her, and Josey lowered a hand to the swollen bump under her bellybutton. Was that a kick? She looked down. *Come on, little one. Do it again for Mommy.*

She didn't realize the room had quieted until Hirsch cleared his throat. Sarrow and Therbold sat at opposite sides of the table, each surrounded by their advisors. She was situated at the center, with Hirsch at her left hand and Captain Drathan at her right. Brian sat beside his father, but hadn't said much so far. Everyone was watching her.

'Majesty,' Hirsch said. 'Are you unwell?'

She shifted in the wooden chair, which had no cushion or padding. 'Not at all. Forgive me, my lords. You were saying?'

'I was saying,' Count Sarrow said, looking down at his rival, 'what a bloated, foul-tongued—'

Hirsch cut him off. 'We were asking if you would like a recess from these proceedings, Majesty. For tempers to cool.'

'A good idea, Master Adept.' Josey stood up, and everyone at the table rose with her. 'My lords. We shall reconvene after the noon meal.'

She took Hirsch's arm and allowed him to escort her away from the table. Both Sarrow and Therbold looked like they had more to say, but both were too disciplined to do it in front of her. *Nonsense. It's my soldiers they fear. Not me.*

Hirsch led her out of the hall into a side chamber where benches and chairs rested against the walls. Iron braziers filled with hot coals were positioned around the room, offering some relief from the castle's chill. Hirsch indicated a cushioned seat, but Josey declined. She was tired of sitting.

Captain Drathan entered after them. 'Majesty, Lord General Argentus reports he has found a fording approximately twelve leagues east of the old bridge's position. He asks if he should begin the crossing.'

Josey's heart leapt at the news, but then she considered the situation here. She couldn't leave these nobles at each other's throats. How long would it take to bring them around to a peace pact? She sighed. The way things were going, it could be a long time. 'Not yet, Captain. Tell Argentus to make the needed preparations, but not to move the army until I've finished here.'

Josey looked to the doorway as the captain left. Brian stood beyond the shoulders of her bodyguards as if waiting for her. He hadn't spoken much at the meetings these past couple days, nor at the feast his father held in her honor.

'Sir,' she said. 'Was there something you wanted?'

Her guards moved aside, but Brian stopped at the threshold as if unwilling to disturb her privacy. 'Highn – Um, Majesty. I just wanted to compliment you on your handling of the negotiations.'

Hirsch smirked at Josey. 'You think so, lad?'

'No one has drawn weapons,' Brian said. 'That's what ended our last discussion.'

Josey put a hand to her mouth to hold back a laugh. 'I suppose that is an improvement. Perhaps we have some hope.'

'I've been trying to get my father to forget this old feud for a long time, but as you have seen he can be quite . . .'

'Formidable,' she finished for him.

'I was going to say pig-headed. Majesty, I was wondering . . . seeing as we have time before the talks resume, would you like to see more of our lands?' He looked to Hirsch. 'Of course, your men are welcome to accompany us.'

'Very nice of you, lad, but—,' Hirsch started to say.

Is he asking to escort me out? Fighting back the sudden flush of heat that rose to her cheeks, Josey considered the ramifications of her answer. If she accepted, she had no doubt that news of their outing would soon be wagging from every tongue in the castle, and she had enough problems on her plate to add romantic gossip on top of it all. Yet if she declined, she could lose a potential ally in these mediations. And he was rather handsome, in a rawboned kind of way. 'That sounds pleasant. But Master Hirsch will have to remain here.'

Hirsch frowned. 'I will? Ah, yes. I will because . . .'

'Because you are now officially charged with handling these talks,' Josey said.

The adept's frown deepened. 'Excellent. I will, of course, endeavor to follow your fine example.'

Josey crossed the room and took Brian's elbow. 'Yes, see that you do.'

She pulled on Brian's arm, forcing the young lord to keep up with her. She couldn't wait to get out of this dreary place. They rode out of the castle surrounded by thirty men of her bodyguard. The day was warm. The sun shone through gaps in the gray clouds. Once they were on the road, Josey loosened the reins and allowed Lightning to gallop. Brian was at ease on his white gelding. He gazed over at her and smiled. He had a kind smile.

'Come on!' Josey shouted, and turned Lightning off the road into a broad dirt field.

She closed her eyes as the cool air rushed through her hair. Lightning appeared to enjoy it, too, running with abandon. As they neared a low stone wall, she reined him in to a trot. The others caught up with the clank of armor and bouncing weapons.

Sergeant Trenor, who was in charge of this detachment, frowned as he rested the stock of his crossbow against his thigh. 'Majesty, I didn't know you were practicing for a race, or I'd have brought my riding breeches.'

Josey ran her ringers through her hair. 'I'm sorry, Sergeant. It won't happen again.'

Brian didn't look to be out of breath in the least. In fact, a healthy glow flushed his cheeks, which bristled with a fine down of whiskers.

Does be have to be so . . . rugged? 'And I apologize to you, sir. This was supposed to be an official tour, not a free-for-all.'

'I didn't mind.' He patted his horse's muscular neck. 'Manfred and I could use the exercise.'

Josey leaned down. 'Manfred, meet Lightning. Now, my lord, where are you taking me?'

Brian pointed over the wall. 'With your permission, Majesty, I'd like to show you our northern range, but it's a bit of a ride.'

Josey looked to her guard. 'Is that all right with you, Sergeant?'

'As you will, Majesty.'

'Then lead the way, Sir Brian.'

They rode side by side along a wide pasture enclosed by trees. Beyond them, low brown hills ringed the land on all sides except to the west, where the plains ran for miles and miles all the way to a faint green line against the horizon. Brian found a country lane winding northward, and they followed it at a leisurely walk. As they rode, Josey caught herself stealing glances at the young lord. *Stop it before he notices! And what about Caim? Have you forgotten him?* Of course, she hadn't. He crashed through her mind every time she looked at herself in the mirror and saw the growing bulge in her belly, every night when she closed her eyes and wondered how she was going to cope with being a mother. *Damn him for leaving us. This is his fault. If he had stayed . . .* What? They would be a happy couple? Even she didn't believe that, not in her wildest fantasies.

They chatted as the sun drifted across the sky. Unlike most of the men she'd met, Brian didn't spend the time talking about himself. He asked her questions about her life, about Othir and what it was like to become the empress. Soon she found herself telling him about Hubert and Anastasia and the goings-on at court, but she avoided the circumstances under which she had gained her crown, and for no good reason that she could fathom. He was sure to have heard the story by now. But it was Caim again. She shied away from anything that remotely touched on their relationship.

'Majesty,' Brian said after they'd ridden a furlong in silence. 'You've been quiet.'

Josey forced a smile. 'I'm enjoying the peace. This is a lovely place.'

They approached a narrow creek. Beyond the sun-dappled waters, emerald-green meadowlands rose in a gentle slope to the distant hills. The wild grasses waved in the breeze. It was a breathtaking sight.

'These are all your family's lands?'

Brian guided his horse into the creek. 'Yes. They have been for generations. One of my ancestors did a service for an emperor – Klinus, I think – and was given this entire range, all the way to the Wolfork.'

'And where does Count Sarrow's demesne begin?'

Brian pointed east past a low chain of hummocks blanketed in cotton-wood and elm trees. 'Farridon lies beyond those peaks. The river is the property line as my father reckons it. Though the count disputes that, of course.'

Of course. Josey tried to get a sense of the lands they were talking about. It was flat with plenty of sunlight and access to water, but most of it was going unused. 'Your family is blessed. This looks to be good farmland.'

'It's one of the reasons I've brought up to my father. This fighting is pointless. We have more land than we can work already. But he's stubborn, as you might have noticed. He'll die before he lets someone else claim a sliver of his property.'

Looking out over the Therbolds' grand demesne, Josey got an idea, but she kept it to herself. She needed to see more of this region and what it had to offer. If there were more lands such as this in the empire, then they had overlooked a vast opportunity.

While Brian pointed out landmarks and unique features of this land, Josey was content to watch and listen to the love in his voice. Growing up in so many places when she was young – Highavon and Navarre, and then the manor in Othir – she'd never felt such a keen connection to the places she called home.

She was relaxed, gazing to the hilltops, as Brian reined up. Josey turned with a smile, expecting another illuminating detail from him. What she saw punched the air from her lungs.

It had once been a village. The outlines of homes and other structures remained, anchored in the red earth amid tumbled stone blocks and blackened timbers. Josey wanted to turn away, but she forced herself to look. There were no bodies evident – thank the heavens – but in her mind's eye she saw the violence that had caused this devastation.

'This was one of our settlements,' Brian said. His voice was low, almost a whisper, stripped of its earlier vitality. 'Thirty families transplanted from our western lands to tend flocks here. By the time we got the warning that the northerners had come, it was already over. Only a handful survived.'

The pain of the disaster was etched into his face. His gloves creaked as his hands gripped the reins tight. 'Between Sarrow and the northerners, so much blood has been spilt over a parcel of land. This is no way for our people to live. One way or another, these feuds must end.'

Josey nodded, afraid to offer a smile for fear he might misinterpret it. 'Then that's what we'll do.'

The clap of hoofbeats sounded behind them. Sergeant Trenor wheeled his steed around to face the lone horse galloping toward their position. Josey recognized Iola in the saddle by her long auburn hair peeking from under the hood.

The girl stopped smoothly before them. 'Your Majesty, Master Hirsch sent me to ask you back to the castle. There's news from the north.'

Josey's heart thudded hard against her riding corset. Was it about Caim? Sawing on the reins, she kicked Lightning into a gallop. She didn't wait for her guards or Brian and Iola as she raced back.

She slid down from Lightning the moment they entered the

castle's tight courtyard, with the soldiers of her bodyguard rumbling in behind her. A hundred worries crowded her thoughts as she hurried to the oaken doors. Sergeant Trenor and his men had caught up by the time she entered the atrium with its bare stone walls.

'Majesty,' the sergeant whispered. 'Please, allow us to properly conduct you—'

But she was rushing past the suits of archaic armor flanking the entry to the long central hall. Hirsch turned as she entered. Sarrow and Therbold were in attendance as well, all of them standing around a man sitting in a chair.

'What is it?' Josey asked.

The man in the chair jumped to his feet and stood at attention, even though he was clearly exhausted. His army uniform was covered in mud, as were his face and hands.

'This rider's just come from Durenstile,' Hirsch said. 'He has so far refused to say why.'

The messenger saluted and pulled a round tube of wood from his satchel. 'I was commanded to give this directly to Your Majesty and no one else.'

Josey clasped her hands together to keep them from shaking. She had a bad feeling. She nodded to Hirsch, who took the tube with a frown at the messenger. He broke it open and slid out a rolled sleeve of parchment, which he handed to her. Josey steeled herself as she opened it. The writer had been in a hurry, as evidenced by the scribbled handwriting and the omission of a perfunctory introduction.

Majesty,

Our position has been overrun. Enemy forces came without warning from the north. Exact numbers unknown. Colonel Restian is dead.

Captain Leoph Fillion, acting commander.
Durenstile Castle

A hard knot formed in Josey's stomach. How could this have happened? Durenstile was a large town with fortifications and a sizable garrison. For it to be wiped out, the attacking force must have been massive, but Hubert's reports had stated that the border was quiet. That the raiders had withdrawn to the north.

Exact numbers unknown.

'Majesty?' Hirsch asked.

'Everyone out.' Josey swallowed. 'Except for my council and Lords Therbold and Sarrow.'

Hirsch scratched his beard as the servants and soldiers filed out of the hall. Captain Drathan, who had been conferring with Sergeant Trenor, remained at a nod from her. Sarrow and Therbold eyed her with as much suspicion as they did each other. *They have good reason to, though they don't know it yet.*

As she read the message aloud, Josey felt the lump in her stomach clench harder. What was she going to do? The northern army was the empire's main line of defense from threats in that direction. She could send for the other armies, but even under the best conditions it would take weeks for them to arrive. By that time the invaders could be within striking distance of Othir. *Oh, gods. Am I going to lose my realm?*

Hirsch, standing by a window, tapped his chin and remained silent. Captain Drathan frowned at the floor as if he might find an answer in the polished hardwood. Count Sarrow gazed into the hearth fire, looking like he had aged ten years in the last dozen heartbeats.

Lord Therbold rapped his knuckles on the tabletop. 'The Eregoths have been raiding across the border since before I was born. We've beaten them back year after year, and we'll do it again this time.'

Josey held up the message. 'It doesn't mention the Eregoths.'

'Who else would it be?' Therbold asked. 'We'll muster the militias and—'

'They sacked Durenstile, you buffoon,' Count Sarrow said. 'This is no ordinary raiding party. We'll go south. Take everything of value and burn the rest. The invaders will need to eat, but they'll find nothing here. Before spring, they'll be packing back to the hinterlands.'

The nobles would escape, certainly, but Josey kept seeing the faces of the people in Elser's village. How far would they get on foot with nothing to eat? She looked down at the signet ring on her finger. 'No.'

Therbold glanced over. 'Highness, I hate to admit it, but it may be the best solution.'

'No.' She knew what she had to do. 'I am taking your soldiers.'

'What?' Sarrow and Therbold said in unison.

Josey took a deep breath. 'I am hereby commandeering the forces of both your lordships. You will remand every man-at-arms and able-bodied male over the age of sixteen into my custody. And every horse, too. Fully provisioned and equipped. I demand this as your liege lord.'

The noblemen couldn't have looked more terrified if she'd poleaxed them. Sarrow gaped at her as if she were the enemy. 'Highness,' he said. 'I don't know if—'

'This is outrageous!' Therbold shouted.

She waited without expression while they complained and equivocated, not deigning to answer until both had fallen silent, Therbold red-faced and sputtering, Sarrow pale and petulant.

'My lords, this is not a request, but a command. Our combined forces will go north to meet these invaders before they infiltrate farther into our country. I expect full compliance from you both.'

She left unsaid the threat of what would happen if they refused. 'Captain Drathan, please see to the collection of men and materials. And send for a messenger.' She nodded to the nobles. 'My lords.'

As she left the chamber heading to her quarters, Josey felt the knot in her middle loosen. Just a hair, but it was a welcome relief. She only prayed she was making the right decision.

She was so lost in her thoughts she almost bumped into Iola. The girl curtsied and turned to accompany her upstairs. 'Majesty, Doctor Krav is here.'

'In the castle?'

'Yes, ma'am. And he's insisting you must see him for an examination at once.' Iola smiled. 'The way he dotes on you reminds me of my grandfather.'

'Yes, well . . .' Josey thought of all the things she had to do, and tried to imagine when she would find the time to see the doctor.

Once they were back in her quarters, which were little more than a bedroom and a small maid's chamber, Josey found parchment and ink and sat at the small, worn desk. While Iola packed and chattered about the latest in camp gossip, Josey focused on what she wanted to say. When she pressed pen to parchment, her hand was steady.

Hubert,

Forgive me, but I must make this short. We are invaded by an unknown army from the north. Durenstile has been sacked. It is my intention to—

The pen hovered until a drop of ink dripped onto the page and sank into the fibers. Was she sure about this? She bent over the letter.

It is my intention to meet these invaders with what forces I can muster. Gather what reinforcements you can in case our efforts fail and you must defend the capital alone.

Until we speak again.

Your empress and friend, Josephine

Josey folded it up, heated a dollop of wax, and pressed her seal into the stamp. It was done. She had decided her course of action. Standing up, she went to the room's only window, the glass pane warped and pocked with bubbles, and looked out onto the lands of Kistol, lands that would soon be threatened by invasion. Unless she stopped it.

With a sigh, she sat back down at the desk and began composing another letter, the first of many, to her vassal lords and ladies of the northern provinces.

CHAPTER TWELVE

Caim shot upright from a deep sleep, his heart pounding in his chest. Aemon and Dray slumbered beside him, neither stirring. He took deep breaths until his heartbeat returned to its normal rhythm. Fresh snow covered the ground, making everything look new and virginal until he spotted a Northman pissing against a hillside. A few others were moving around the campsite, so he guessed it was morning even though the sky was the same dark shade of gray it had been the evening before. Tendrils of mist twisted across the ground, lending the camp an otherworldly atmosphere.

It had gotten colder overnight. Their fire was out, and Malig sat beside the dead ashes. Tiny clouds of steam emerged from under his hood in time with his deep, laborious snoring. Caim sidled up and jabbed him in the shoulder. Malig pitched backward, almost tipping over.

'Dammit, Caim!' he shouted, righting himself. 'You damn near scared me out of my skin.'

'But you weren't scared enough to stay awake.' Caim rooted around the fire's stone-cold cinders. 'Why don't you go steal us some wood?'

Grumbling, Malig shambled away through the camp. Caim started digging in his pouch for flint and tinder when Kit appeared across from him. Her eyes were red like she'd been crying. 'What have you gotten yourself into, Caim?'

He glanced around, 'A storm of shit. Feel free to rub my nose in it.'

'Caim!'

'I'm sorry. I didn't sleep much. There's something strange about these northerners.'

She wiped her nose with the back of a hand. 'That's the first smart thing I've heard you say in days.'

'So where have you—?'

Caim stood up as a huge figure emerged from the mist. Wulfgrim strode up holding two steaming mugs. He drank from one as he offered the other to Caim.

Kit flitted around to hover behind Caim as he accepted the cup. It smelled a little like tea, but much sharper. He thought he detected alcohol as well. He took a sip, and found it wasn't bad.

'We're moving,' Wulfgrim said.

'I don't like the way he looks at you,' Kit whispered in Caim's ear. 'He wants something, and he doesn't look like the type to take no for an answer.'

Caim just nodded and nursed his drink. Dray and Aemon sat up. Dray stretched and yawned, but Aemon just watched the Northman with narrowed eyes crusted with sleep.

'You are heading north?' the Northman asked. 'We will ride with you. I want to learn more of your homeland. Maybe, if the gods are good, I will see it someday, yes?'

Caim handed back the cup, but didn't say anything. There wasn't anything to say unless he wanted to risk angering their host. And by the frank look in Wulfgrim's gaze, the Northman knew it, too. Maybe he was searching for an excuse to take offense.

'I'll get my men ready,' Caim said.

Kit was gone. Off to find them a way out of this, he hoped. Aemon rolled up his blanket and picked up his spear. 'I had a feeling they weren't going to let us go.'

Dray scooped up a handful of snow and ate it. 'Seven hells, I'm just glad I didn't wake up with a cut throat. What do they want with us?'

'I don't know,' Caim replied. 'So everyone keep your mouth shut. Make sure Malig understands that, too. We want these Northmen out of our hair as soon as possible. Don't mention our plans.'

'That'll be easy,' Dray said. 'Seeing as we don't know them ourselves.'

A Northman brought their horses. While the others got themselves together, he checked the animals. They appeared to be weathering the cold climate with few problems. Their hooves were a little discolored, but there were no cracks in the spongy frogs of their feet. Rubbing his horse's nose, Caim watched the camp break down. For all their savage manner, the Northmen moved with quiet efficiency. In addition to their riding animals, the tribe had a small herd of packhorses. Within a quarter of a candlemark, they were ready to ride. Malig made it back, without the wood, just in time to grab a stick of jerked meat out of his saddlebags and mount up.

Dray yawned. 'What if we just made a run for it?'

Caim glanced around, but there were no Northmen close enough to overhear. Aemon cursed aloud. 'For fuck sakes, Dray. Just shut up, will you?'

Dray scowled like he was going to reply, but Wulfgrim rode over with two of his men, both as big as he was. He raised his voice, shouting in the northern tongue, and the camp moved out in two columns; the women and striplings headed west with the pack animals while the warriors rode north. The large northern horses looked ungainly, but they rumbled to a swift trot without apparent effort. Caim wondered how long their southern horses could keep up the pace, and what would happen if their crew started to fall behind.

Wulfgrim rode near Caim all morning, asking him questions about the lands south of the Drakstag Mountains, which the Northmen called the Svartvedir, or Blackstorms. The chief seemed particularly interested in the great cities like Taralon and Othir. 'I hear the homes of your southern kings are made of gold and ivory,' Wulfgrim said with a laugh. 'Is that true? I think I should like to see an ivory house.'

'The duke's keep at Liovard is plain stone,' Malig said. 'Maybe they got that rich stuff down in the lowlands. Caim, you ever seen a—?'

'No,' Caim said, and left it at that.

Wulfgrim watched him out of the side of his eye for a few moments, and then chuckled. 'I like you, Southlander. A strong man needs to speak very little, yes?'

But the questioning went on for some time, although at certain points Wulfgrim would lapse into song in his native tongue. Skins of fermented buffalo milk were passed up and down the line of riders, which Caim always declined with a shake of his head. The uneasy feeling in his stomach was getting worse.

'Caim.' Kit materialized beside him as the company began the ascent of a long hill. 'You're riding straight for a settlement.'

'Lion tribe?' he asked under his breath.

She shook her head, sending her silver tresses bouncing. 'No. Bear. And it looks like most of their menfolk are out hunting.'

Caim started to ask how far away this settlement was when a sharp shout filtered back from the front of the group. Wulfgrim called for a halt. As the war band gathered, Caim tried to make out what they were saying, but his grasp of the northern tongue was almost nonexistent. The few words he knew constituted 'yes,' 'no,' and a couple different words for snow. Points of light shined in the distance.

Wulfgrim turned to him. 'Ready for some sport, Southlander?'

Not liking the way that sounded, Caim just nodded. 'Always. What have you got?'

'An enemy holdfast straight in our path. What luck, yes? The death gods must be watching over our shoulders this day.'

'Your enemies?'

The chief reached into his chain shirt and drew out a cord strung with dozens of teeth. 'Aye, the great Bear. The only prey worth hunting.'

'We will leave you to it then,' Caim said. 'You have our thanks for—'

'*Sudlundas dar hraedir mikt*,' Wulfgrim said, and his warriors laughed with derision as they unlimbered their swords and axes. Wulfgrim strapped his shield to his left arm. 'You will fight with us, yes?'

Caim measured the distance between himself and Wulfgrim, and the warriors around him. Three were in reach of his knives from where he sat, and two more including their leader if he shifted his steed forward a couple paces. Tiny voices nattered in his ear as he loosened his grip on the reins. 'This isn't our fight.'

Wulfgrim's brows knitted together. 'You say you come north to find battle. Now it is here, but you will not join us?'

'It's not that simple.'

Wulfgrim grinned, showing off the carvings on his teeth, mottled with brown-and-yellow stains. 'We fight or we die. That is the law of the north.'

Caim understood completely. This was what the Northmen had wanted from the start: to incorporate them into their death squad. The choice was simple: fight or die. 'Well fight.'

Wulfgrim called out to his men, and they surged ahead in an avalanche of iron, leather, and flying snow. Caim filtered back to his men, who were being swept forward in the movement.

'What's going on?' Malig asked.

After Caim explained the situation, Dray growled, 'What the hell choice do we have? We'll have to fight with them.'

'Stay together,' Caim said. 'If something goes wrong, ride north as hard as you can.'

The lights ahead were brighter now, a scattering of window

ports glowing from a score of shaggy longhouses. Huge mastiffs bayed, but the Northmen didn't slacken. Two wings split off, left and right, while the middle column led by Wulfgrim plunged straight into the heart of the settlement. The first sounds of combat echoed ahead. Shouts of alarm split the darkness.

Caim didn't draw his knives, even though Malig and Dray drew their weapons. A glance from him kept them close by. He didn't want anyone getting lost in the chaos as people spilled out of the longhouses. Spears flew through the air. One missile passed just a few handbreadths above his head, but most were aimed at Wulfgrim's men, who were killing everything they met. Dogs snarled and whimpered as they were pinned to the ground on long lances. Three warriors on horseback plunged through the side of a home and brought down half the roof. Some villagers tried to flee, but the flanking Northmen cut them off and cut them down.

Caim tugged on his gloves as he watched. This wasn't a battle; it was a massacre. There were few warriors among the defenders. If Kit was right, and the rest were out hunting, this village was an easy plum for Wulfgrim's raiders to pluck. The Snow Lions fought like their namesakes, tearing into the villagers, killing without remorse. Wulfgrim rode wherever the carnage was thickest, his voice rising above the wind and the cries.

A lean man, naked to the waist and holding a spear, rushed out of a burning house. He ran straight at Malig, who lifted his axe to defend himself, but a Northman rode past. One blow from his iron warhammer exploded the villager's face in a burst of red pulp, and the Northman rode onward with a booming laugh.

'Damn!' Dray muttered, his sword drooping by his side, forgotten.

'This ain't right,' Aemon said. 'We shouldn't be here.'

Caim agreed, but extricating themselves wouldn't be easy.

The Northmen were all around them, distracted perhaps, but not blind. If they tried to leave, there would be trouble. But neither could they stay. Caim saw two children cut down with their mother in the middle of the lane. The raiders lit torches and flung them into the houses. While the others in his crew flinched and swore at what they witnessed, the slaughter rolled off of Caim. He'd seen and done terrible things before. This was just one more tragedy to be endured. Yet his throat was dry, and his hands shook as he gripped the reins.

A doorway burst open next to Caim, and a woman ran out. She wore a long tunic of animal skin decorated with tiny beads across the front. She stopped and looked up at him, the whites of her eyes huge and gleaming in the light of the rising fires. Her long, copper-hued hair reminded him of Liana. An image flashed through his mind, of her blood-streaked face, her hair wrapped in Soloroth's armored fist. Caim let out a shallow breath that burned his throat.

Hoofbeats pounded in the snow. Steel flashed, and the woman's legs gave out. As she tumbled to the ground, droplets of her blood spattered on Caim's thigh and across the coat of his steed. His horse snorted and stepped away, and a flush of warmth bubbled up from Caim's chest. His vision dimmed as the blood ran down his leg, the drops melding into a rivulet that dribbled through the creases in his pants. A distant buzz droned in his ears, calling him to . . . to . . .

Caim didn't remember kicking his heels, but suddenly he was hurtling forward. The Northman who'd ridden down the woman loomed ahead of him. Gouts of steam billowed from the killer's bearded lips, perhaps in a lusty shout, but Caim couldn't hear anything. His knives had appeared in his hands. The warrior stiffened as the points of the blades entered his back, one to either side of his spine, and pitched forward.

With the shadows chittering in his ears, Caim withdrew his knives and turned to a knot of raiders setting fire to a longhouse. He plunged into them, taking the first one out with a slash across the throat. The others spun to face him. A torch drove at him from the left side while a two-handed greatsword swept in from the other direction. Caim dove headfirst from the saddle. He landed on his shoulder, but kept rolling, through the forest of stamping horse legs, and came up on the far side of the warriors. His knives slashed, and their shouts turned to cries of fury as steaming blood spilled in the snow.

More Northmen jumped into the fray. Caim never stopped moving. This was his element, the order at the heart of violence. Their spears and axes moved too slowly to catch him. A horse reared, and he ducked beneath its kicking hooves. The rider swayed away to avoid his knives, but Caim switched directions to stab another Northman in the gut with his seax and swept his *suete* across the tendons behind the kneecap. Voices clamored in his ear. Some of them were his Eregoths; they had followed him into the melee, but Caim didn't pause to respond.

As the last Northman in his path fell dead to the bloody ground, the door to the house flew open, and a half-naked man appeared in the doorway with a wood axe in his hands. Caim's knives darted forward, moving almost of their own accord, but stopped inches from the villager's chest. He wanted to kill and keep killing. With a grunt, Caim stepped back, and the man ran off with a wild look in his eyes.

Caim scanned the shadows thrown by the leaping fires. Riders galloped beyond the houses, calling out, but they appeared to have given up their sport for the moment. Then a voice thundered behind him.

'Southlander!'

Wulfgrim dismounted at the end of the snow-packed lane. Blood stained the blade of his battleaxe and ran in smeared lines down his wooden shield. His eyes stared with a feverish glare. Aemon and Dray rode up beside Caim, but he waved them back as the Snow Lion chief approached.

He and Wulfgrim stopped a dozen paces from each other. The rest of the Northmen crowded behind their leader in a loose semicircle. It took Caim back to his days riding with the roughnecks of the Western Territories where fights over money or status were commonplace. His pulse began to pound in his temples in the old, familiar rhythm, and he matched Wulfgrim's lurid grin. With a fierce bellow, the Northman charged.

Caim sunk into a low stance, knives out to his sides. No tactics crowded his thoughts, no subtle stratagems to gain advantage. His mind was gloriously clear as he traced the path of the incoming axe. Caim sidestepped and turned behind Wulfgrim's momentum. His *suete* extended almost delicately and cut a line across the Northman's elbow below the sleeve of his chainmail byrnie. Wulfgrim didn't seem to notice the wound as he brought his axe around at chest height. Caim jumped away, but then lunged back inside after the glittering arc passed by. Wulfgrim caught his seax knife on his shield, but the *suete* got underneath the broad buckler, punching through the links of chain to sink two fingers deep into the Northman's abdomen. But Wulfgrim's smile only deepened. With a jerk, the Northman lunged forward, and Caim reeled back from the head-butt. Lights flashed in front of his eyes. In the fog of his sudden pain, he realized he was vulnerable and threw himself sideways into a roll.

Caim shook his head to clear it as he got back to his feet. Wulfgrim charged again, shield held high and axe sweeping low. Caim spun out of the way, but the shield slammed into his side and drove him back. His feet slipped in the muddy slush, and before he could set his feet another shield bash backed by Wulfgrim's full weight carried them both into the side of a longhouse. Thin beams and hide split apart as they fell through the wall. Caim held onto his balance by a razor's edge. The axe swung for his head, and he ducked away, but Wulfgrim kept coming, driving him back across the hard dirt floor. The interior of the longhouse was narrow and littered with obstacles that could trip or entangle. Caim trod on a blanket and kicked it away. He was preparing a feint when Kit's voice rang in his ears.

'Caim!' Her glow lit up the interior of the house. 'You have to get out of here!'

But he didn't want to hear it as he jumped back from another axe swing. Wulfgrim's tongue lolled from his mouth as he raised his shield and charged. Caim twisted out of the way. His seax blade carved a furrow into the back of Wulfgrim's neck above his mail shirt's collar. The Northman didn't falter.

Kit's head emerged from Wulfgrim's chest, which threw off Caim's timing. 'More wildmen are coming! Lots of them.'

Caim slashed across Kit's face, and she darted away. Wulfgrim advanced behind his shield. Caim gave ground step by step. When Wulfgrim wound up for another strike, Caim waited until the axe reached the apex of its arc, and then drove his shoulder into the Northman's torso. It was like running into an iron-clad tree trunk. The breath left Caim's lungs in a bestial yell as he plunged both knives up under the skirt of the chieftain's mail coat. A heavy blow pummeled the middle of his back, but Caim kept stabbing again and again, blood streaming over his hands, until Wulfgrim toppled backward.

Breathing hard, Caim stood over his foe. Air whistled from Wulfgrim's open mouth in a long sigh as blood welled in a widening pool between his legs. The chieftain had dropped his axe, but his hand sought out the long knife at his belt. Trails of crimson steam rose from the wounds. Caim leaned down. He had never seen such a phenomenon before. Then the steam wafted toward him, and Caim hissed as a burst of energy surged into his hands and up through his arms. It was like being set on fire and drowned in icy water at the same time. The electric currents collided in his chest, swelling his heart with their raw heat. He started to feel light-headed from the rush. The blood sang in his veins. Wulfgrim shuddered and groaned.

Caim, they're almost here!

Caim gritted his teeth and yanked himself away. Bile rose in the back of his throat as he turned away from the fallen chieftain. The influx of energy dribbled to a halt, but what had already entered him remained, and he felt strong. Stronger than he had in weeks.

More Northmen gathered outside the longhouse, watching him from under bestial headdresses, but they retreated as Caim stepped through the hole. Fires burned bright under the black sky. Caim walked over to his crew. Aemon held the reins to his steed. Caim sheathed his knives and climbed into the saddle. Dray and Malig fell in beside them as they rode between the burning homes, picking past the bodies of the fallen.

They plunged onto the snowy plains, heading north. Caim looked back as they passed a craggy menhir outside the village. The flaming rooftops lit up the sky. A handful of Northmen watched them with weapons in hand, but no one followed. Then Caim saw lights approaching from beyond the other side of the village. Torches. Lots of them. A shout went up from the settlement. As much as he wanted to see what happened next, he kicked his horse to a swift canter to put some distance between them and the Northmen. As the animal took off, Caim was hit by a strange feeling. Black spots swirled before his eyes while he held tight to the saddle horn and fought to stay upright.

'You all right, Caim?' Aemon asked, riding up close.

'Go on,' Caim grunted. 'Ride ahead of us. But no light!'

He bent over his horse's neck until the disorientation passed. The new strength thrummed inside him like it wanted out. It felt foreign, and yet now a part of him. He didn't know if that was a good thing. He sensed the shadows around him.

They wanted something. Maybe for him to turn around and revisit the slaughter. But he pushed them away, and to his relief they left him in peace as he followed his comrades into the night.

CHAPTER THIRTEEN

Dray hissed and took another pull from the mead-skin as the needle emerged from his upper arm, dragging a trail of catgut. 'You ever heard of being fucking gentle?'

Aemon chuckled. 'Hold still. I'm almost done.'

'Well, hurry it up!'

'There.' Aemon cut the gut string with his teeth and tied it off. 'Good as new. Caim, you got any wounds that need sewed up while I got the needle out?'

Caim shook his head as he wrapped up the wedge of hard cheese he'd been eating and thrust it back into his satchel. They had ridden all night and into the next day, but he felt good. Rested. Almost like his old self. While they rode, the shadows had come stealing back to him, covering his various injuries with their chilling kisses and taking with them all the pain and all traces of the illness that had plagued him for the last few days. Yet, glad as he was for the assistance, Caim couldn't forget the look on Wulfgrim's face as he lay bleeding on the floor of the longhouse, the expression of horror as the last dregs of his life were drawn out and – for lack of a better word – devoured.

Their camp was set against the lee of a steep hillock. Caim figured they had come about fifteen leagues, but it didn't feel like enough. He imagined the Snow Lions prowling on their trail. *You'd make better time on your own.*

Caim winced at the thought. It wasn't the first time it had occurred to him that this entire endeavor would be easier if he were traveling alone. Like the old days. But it went deeper than that. He didn't like feeling responsible for others, and he had a nasty suspicion that this mission wouldn't end well. For any of them.

Snow crunched beyond the circle of firelight, and the others reached for their weapons, but Caim didn't stir. He'd seen the man coming from three hundred paces off.

'Egil!' Dray barked. 'I almost killed you, you dumb shit.'

Malig laughed and lowered his axe. 'We thought you ran off, boy. Never to be seen again.'

Egil unslung his rucksack and knelt by the fire. 'I got out when I saw them kittens coming across the snow with you.'

Dray sat with his bare sword across his knees. 'Kittens?'

'The Snow Lions. That's what we call them. They were a great tribe back in the day.' He pointed up to the murky sky. 'Before this happened, they controlled most of the central lands. But they resisted when the dark lord came, and now they are all but gone. Anyway, they won't be bothering you again. They had unexpected company.'

Caim took out his seax knife and a whetstone, and worked on the blade's edge. 'The other Northmen approaching the village?'

'Aye. Bear tribe. Near a hundred of them. Old Wulfgrim must've been shitting his breeches. Anyway, the kittens ran off as fast as they could ride, heading west by south.'

Dray spat into the fire. 'They were free with their words when they had us all penned up like lambs for a Godsday feast, but they run out at the first sign of real trouble.'

'I don't know,' Aemon said. 'That Wulfgrim is a canny one. If he survived what Caim done to him, I'd not want to be within fifty miles of him.'

Dray looked to Egil. 'So what tribe are you from?'

'Fox. There aren't too many of us left anymore either.'

'And the Bear people,' Aemon said. 'What are they like?'

'They come from up north.' Egil pulled a greenish-yellow

bulb from his rucksack and took a bite. 'They always had a reputation for being an ornery bunch, but with the coming of the dark lord, it got worse. Now they have their run of the wastes. No tribe will stand against them. Those who dare are crushed and their lands taken.'

'Like the Lion tribe,' Aemon said.

'Aye. Like as not we've seen the last of them.'

Caim held up his knife. The edge gleamed like a ribbon of silver. He slid it back into the sheath. 'What can you tell us about this lord?'

Egil finished his fruit, or whatever it was, and threw the stem into the fire. 'Hard to say. What do you want to know?'

'Have you ever seen him?'

'Nah. I don't know of anyone who has. He don't leave his fastness in the north.'

'Never?' Caim asked.

'Not that I've ever heard. His soldiers swing through the villages about once a season, but if you're right with your tithes and make no trouble, they're no worse than other landlords.'

'Does he rule this entire country?' Caim asked.

'Not sure what you mean by country, but he holds all the wastes in his grasp. From ocean to ocean, people say, though I've never been to the great waters, so I couldn't swear to that. They say he rules a fair bit of the Southlands, too.'

'They lie,' Malig growled. 'Eregoth is free.'

Egil shrugged. 'As you say, but that's what I've heard tell. The dark lord's been in power for most of my life.'

Caim did the figures in his head. By that reckoning, this tyrant had come to power roughly two decades ago. That made for a chilling coincidence, considering his own history. Caim had more questions. How far away was this fastness and what was it like? How many soldiers did the ruler of the wastes employ? But he kept them to himself. Egil was no fool.

Caim stood up. 'Aemon, take first watch. I'll be back.'

No one questioned him. Aemon was the only one to look up, and he just nodded and sat cross-legged by the fire.

A bitter wind swept over Caim as he left the tiny circle of light. Without any real plan of where he was going, he let his feet carry him around the base of the hill until he found a gentling of the slope. He began to climb. It got steeper the higher he went, until he was half climbing, half crawling at the end. The top of the hill was relatively flat and covered in icy snow. Below, the wastes spread out in an ocean of white and black shadows. To the north, the darkness was absolute, denying him a glimpse of what lay ahead, but the calling remained, the droning hum in the back of his head, pulling him in that direction.

The plains to the south were brighter, if just by a hair, but it was enough for him to see to the horizon. Somewhere beyond his sight were the mountains, and then Eregoth and Nimea, stretching all the way down to the Midland Sea. What was Josey doing right now? Did she worry about him?

A soft light showered across his shoulders and pooled around his feet. 'It may not be a fancy hotel, but at least we can be alone up here.'

He braced himself as Kit's ethereal arms wrapped around him. Her lips made little electric jolts on the back of his neck. 'You okay, Caim? You've been quiet lately.'

'I'm just tired. I'll be all right.'

She floated around to face him. 'You always say that, but you never let me in.'

He looked past her. Through her. Seeking something else to focus on. How to explain what he felt inside? He didn't understand it himself. 'Things are changing, Kit. Everything is different. My past. The shadows.'

Her eyebrows came together. 'What about me? Am I different, too?'

'I didn't mean—' He lifted a hand, but she hovered out of

his reach. 'Kit, it's been tough. You and I haven't had a lot of time together since we left Othir.'

'Whose fault is that? I've tried again and again to be with you, to get you alone, but you always have excuses.'

'Well, here I am!' He winced as the words carried louder than he intended. 'I'm here, Kit. And this may be as much privacy as we're ever going to get.'

She tilted her head to the side. 'Well, then. I suppose I'll have to make the most of it.'

'What's that supposed to—?'

Kit grinned at him, and something changed. At first Caim couldn't put his finger on it. Then he realized – he could no longer see through her. She looked almost solid.

'Kit.' He reached out. 'What . . . ? How are you—?'

Just before his fingertips made contact, her smile collapsed, and the light of the distant stars shone through her again. Kit sobbed, and Caim wasn't sure what to say. For a moment it had seemed like she was almost real. He stepped toward her. 'Kit, are you all right?'

She retreated off the side of the hilltop, her face hidden within the silver curtain of her hair. 'Stay away!'

'Kit, I almost thought . . . I mean, it looked like you were . . . Will you please tell me what's happening?'

When she didn't answer, Caim lowered his voice. 'Kit, talk to me. I can't help you if I don't know what's going on.'

She took her hands down from her face. She was wholly ethereal once again. 'Why are you here, Caim? This place is wrong. I know you feel it, too. I see it in your eyes. Let's just leave.'

'I can't, Kit. It's too late for that.'

'What do you mean? What are you planning?'

'I don't know.'

'Caim, if you think I'm going to stay around and watch you do something foolish just to satisfy some manly—'

'No one's asking you to stay if you don't want to.'

Kit drifted closer. 'You said you loved me. And that means you have to tell me things.'

'Then maybe I was wrong.' His tongue clove to the roof of his mouth after he said those words, heavy as an iron clapper.

Kit stared at him. What would come next? Tears? Angry recriminations? *Why did I say that? I'll take it ba—*

Without a word, she vanished from sight.

'Kit? Kit, I didn't mean that. Come back!' He looked around, but her glow was gone, leaving him once again in dark. *Now I've gone and buggered it up good. But what did she expect? Roses and serenades? She knows me better than that.*

Kit and Josey, the two people he cared most about in the world, and he'd wronged them both. But just like with his comrades below, he couldn't push them away for good. And as for Josey, he'd been running from her for too long. He could settle it, if he had the courage.

It didn't start off as a conscious thought, more of a hunch. Or a fantasy. He pictured himself back in Othir with Josey as he had last seen her, dolled up in a gown and jewels that cost more than all the money he'd ever made, her hair piled on top of her head like a silky tower. She was gorgeous. Perfect. There was a connection between them. Perhaps it was because of what they'd gone through together, the trials by blood and fire, but if she called, he knew he would go. It was as simple, and as complex, as that.

The pain started in his chest, a sharp tearing like he had swallowed a mouthful of broken glass. His skin felt like it was being torn from his bones with red-hot pincers. He stepped back, almost tumbling off the hilltop, as a loud snap rent the air. A hole appeared before him. The portal wavered in the darkness, and then an image formed inside, of a long marble corridor lit by flambeaux in bronze cressets.

It was the palace at Othir.

He had run down that same corridor – it seemed like a

lifetime ago – chasing after Josey. Now it was only a step away. Did he dare?

With a shiver, he took a hobbled step. And then another. The skin of the portal was ice-cold as he pushed through.

Caim staggered against the wall, waiting for the blinding pain in his skull to abate. He stood in the stone corridor he'd seen through the portal. He was back in Othir.

It didn't seem possible, to travel such a long way in one step.

Caim doubled over and spewed his dinner onto the floor. The racking heaves didn't stop until his stomach was long past empty. When he stood up, however, his head had cleared. He glanced both ways down the corridor to get his bearings. No soldiers in sight, for once. *Maybe my luck is changing.*

Caim started off toward the northeast wing, avoiding the pools of light cast by the ensconced torches on the walls. The shadows welcomed him, and he slid into their cool embrace.

He climbed three flights of stairs, twice avoiding guard patrols. The hallways on the top floor were wider and more opulent, with golden accents and fine pieces of artwork adorning the walls. Walking through them filled him with a host of memories, many of them quite pleasant, but it also wrapped his guts in knots.

He stopped at the doors to the imperial suite, almost wishing an army of soldiers would arrive just so he would have an excuse to leave. *What am I going to say to her? Time to find out.*

Taking a deep breath, he turned the handle and peered inside. The interior was unlit. He entered. A quick search revealed that the interconnected chambers were empty. In the bedchamber, Caim stood over Josey's big feather bed, recalling the time spent with her. He wanted to reach out and touch the bedspread just to make sure it was real, but his hands remained by his sides.

Not sure whether to be relieved or concerned, Caim left the suite and padded down the corridor. There was someone else he needed to see. Yellow light spilled from under the doorway, Caim put his ear to the wooden panel, but heard nothing. He lifted the latch.

Several hanging oil lamps illuminated the room beyond and lent the large chamber a musky scent. The floor was polished parquet wood with a tasteful burgundy rug in the center. Caim's target sat in a leather-bound chair behind a huge mahogany desk piled with stacks of papers and scrolls. He looked older, probably due to the deep circles under his eyes. There was some new gray in his hair and scattered in the short goatee he sported. His pen stopped scratching as he looked up. 'Who—? Caim? Is that you?'

Caim stepped into the light. 'Hello, Hubert. It looks like you've done well for yourself.'

Hubert chuckled as he stood up, rubbing his lower back. 'Actually, I'm the lord regent now. Some climb from the Duke of the Gutters, huh? When did you get back to Othir?'

'Tonight.'

'You're looking . . . well. Have a seat and tell me about your travels. Would you like a drink?'

Caim went over to a picture on the wall opposite the desk. Josey looked regal sitting on a purple divan, gloved hands folded on her lap. He studied her features, captured so well on the canvas. Their time together seemed like so long ago. 'Where is she?'

'She's gone, Caim. She went north to investigate some problems we've been having on the border, but I suspect she really went to find you. You've not seen or heard from her?'

'No. But I've been . . . moving around. Did she intend to go as far as Eregoth?'

Hubert shuffled through a pile of papers. 'Her last letter was sent from a village just south of the Wyrkan River.'

The interior door opened, and a young woman appeared, a

candle in her hand. Her long, blonde hair fell over the front of her long nightdress. 'Who is it, Bert?'

'It's all right, Ana.' Hubert went over to her. 'Just catching up with an old friend. Go back to sleep.'

But the woman peered around him. 'Won't you introduce us?'

Hubert made a strained smile. 'Of course. Caim, this is my fiancée, Anastasia Farthington. Ana, this is Caim.'

'*The* Caim? I've heard a great deal about you, sir. I wish I could say all of it was good.'

'I wouldn't believe it if you had.'

'You're here for Josey,' Anastasia said. 'But you're too late.'

'Yes,' Hubert said. 'I was just telling him—'

'She's lovesick over you,' Anastasia continued. 'Do you know she cried for days after you left? Do you know about the attempts on her life?'

A rush of red-hot rage filled Caim at the thought of someone trying to hurt Josey. 'Who was behind it?'

Hubert rubbed his hands together. 'A foreign sorcerer and a few locals. They've been taken care of, Caim. Really, it sounds worse than it—'

'Were they working alone?' Caim pressed.

'Well, that seems to be—'

'You're not sure,' Caim said in a lowered voice. He had to stop his hands from reaching for his knives. 'And now Josey is off in the north where she could be targeted again, and without even the protection of the palace. Dammit, Hubert. You were supposed to look after her. Not let her go off on some crusade.'

'Josey is the empress of Nimea,' Anastasia said. 'She can take care of herself.'

Hubert put a hand on the lady's shoulder. 'It's true, Caim. The empress isn't the same girl you took from her foster father's home.'

Hands balled into fists, Caim turned and took a step toward

the door. He stopped before he reached the exit. 'You'd better hope so, Lord Regent. Because if she comes to harm, I'll hold you responsible.'

Caim created a portal in the hallway. The effort was almost more than he could manage, the pain incredible. As footsteps echoed in the room behind him, he stepped through and let the portal close before they could catch up.

CHAPTER FOURTEEN

Kit couldn't see through her tears as Caim disappeared through the shadowy gate. She had followed him back to Othir, hoping she was mistaken, but it was plain to her now that the mud-woman still had a hold on him.

Invisible, Kit floated up through the ceiling. It wasn't fair! She had known Caim for most of his life, long before he met the mud-woman. They shared countless memories. She'd tried to show Caim how much she loved him, how special he was to her, but it was clear she couldn't compete with the flesh. Without the ability to touch and hold him, their love was doomed.

The lights of the city glittered below her feet as she emerged from the palace roof. Kit could only think of one place to go. Swallowing her tears, she focused on a place far away, a place between this world and the Other Side. A quiet place. The world tilted around her to the sound of distant chimes.

The lapping of gentle waves greeted her arrival. Kit blinked against the crystalline sunlight washing over the pearl-white sand beneath her toes. Sapphire waters stretched to the hazy horizon. A little house stood farther up the beach on a sward of grass, shaded by a *mesicante* tree. An old woman wearing a large wicker hat worked in the garden behind the house.

With a hoot of joy, Kit wiped her cheeks dry and ran to the house. When the old woman straightened up from her plants, Kit waved and yelled, 'Ealdmoder!'

Kit laughed. The warm sand felt good under her feet. She

ran up the path of smooth stepping stones around the side of the little house and stopped before the arbor. The old woman squinted at her, and Kit held her breath until the old woman rushed forward and gathered her in her arms. She was taller, even taller than Caim, but slim as a cypress tree.

'Kitrine, child. I've missed you!' Kit's grandmother held her out at arm's length. 'You're even more beautiful than I remember.'

Kit laughed and kissed her grandmother on the cheek. 'Not as beautiful as you, Ealdmoder.'

'Come, dear. Let's sit.'

They went around to the back of the house. Nothing had changed. The garden was as immaculate as she remembered, with beds of flowers in every hue – roses, lavenders, chrysanthemums, orchids, lilies, irises, and more. The temperature was neither too hot nor too cold, but exactly right. The breeze was soothing and fragrant with the scent of growing things. It was a perfect day. Too perfect to be real. And it wasn't. Among Kit's people it was common, when they had lived long enough, to retreat to a personal world of their own making, designed in their own ideal of perfection. This was her grandmother's refuge.

Her grandmother pulled her down onto a wooden bench. 'You've been away so long, I was beginning to think I would never see my favorite grandchild again. But I can see you've been crying.'

Kit rubbed her eyes with the back of a hand. 'I'm sorry. I didn't know where else to go. I was upset and needed someone I could talk to. I thought . . .'

Her grandmother squeezed her hand. 'You are always welcome here, Kitrine. Tell me what is troubling you.'

'It's—' Kit felt guilty all of a sudden. She hadn't bothered to visit since she went to the Brightlands, not once, and now she regretted not being a better granddaughter.

'It's a man,' her grandmother said.

Kit swallowed a sob. 'How did you know?'

'Only a man can cause tears like that, child. Which family does he come from? Don't tell me he's lowborn. Your father would never—'

'He's a mortal,' Kit blurted in a rush, and then held her breath, watching her grandmother for a reaction.

The old woman stared at her for several slow heartbeats as the color drained from her face. 'Kitrine, tell me you're joking. Child! You haven't changed at all. Oh, I don't know why you ever went to that dirty, drab world. It could only bring you sadness.'

The old woman sat back against the back of the bench, shaking her head. Kit exhaled softly. *This was a mistake. I shouldn't have come.*

'I'm sorry, Ealdmoder. I'll leave now.'

Her grandmother held onto her wrist. 'No, stay. You have already disturbed my *kwa*. There's nothing to be done for it. But you can tell me about this . . . man.'

'His name is Caim, and I love him. I think I've loved him since the first time I saw him. But I can't have him because . . .'

'Because he is human and you are Fae.'

'Yes. I've tried to be . . . with him, but it's impossible.'

'Oh, my darling Kitrine. You are so young. You have millennia to find your true mate. You'll soon forget this fleeting obsession.'

Kit sobbed. 'I love him! He's been my best friend, my only real friend, for so long, I would do anything for him.' She took a deep breath. 'Ealdmoder, I want to become human.'

Her grandmother sighed. It was the most awful sound Kit could imagine at that moment, laden with disappointment. 'Child, child. You don't know what you are saying.'

Kit couldn't stop the tears from falling. 'I do! I understand what it means, but I can't live without him.'

'Come with me.'

Kit stood up, struggling to control her emotions. She followed her grandmother into the garden, to a bright yellow bush with clusters of tiny pink berries. The old woman plucked a berry and held it up to her mouth for a moment. Then she offered it to Kit. 'Eat this.'

Kit looked at the fruit. 'Why?'

'You wish to have a future with this human man?'

'Yes.'

'Then taste that life before you choose.'

Kit accepted the berry, which was firm with a velvety skin. Looking to her grandmother, she placed it in her mouth and bit down. The cool juice splashed on her tongue, and then her mind exploded as she was deluged by waves of colors and sounds more complex and beautiful than anything she'd ever known before. They surrounded her and lifted her up to the gleaming sky.

Kit blinked. She stood in a dim hallway. Faint rays of light filtered through the lattice of a high window, casting silver diamonds on the hardwood floor. She looked down to see that she was clothed in a long dress. It was stylish and sleek, though with a higher neckline than she usually wore, but it was somber black with no adornment. She started to concentrate to change the color and shorten the skirt, but then realized she was wearing shoes – stiff, leather things – and she could feel the floor. She was solid again!

Excited and anxious and afraid all at the same time, Kit looked around. Where was she? The hallway gave few clues. There was a door a few steps away, but before she could approach it, a young woman in a simple black smock came around a corner with a steaming cup on a fine porcelain saucer.

'Your tea, madam,' the young woman said as she held out the cup.

Kit started to reach for it – she'd never had human tea before – but something didn't feel right. Her stomach hurt fiercely as if it had been beaten with a stick, and a sour taste rose in the back of her throat. 'No,' she said. 'Where am—?'

The door opened, and a man in a long black coat exited. He carried a leather satchel and a straight walking cane. 'He's resting now. I gave him a tonic of figwort and comfrey root for the pain, but it's only a matter of time. In fact, it's a miracle he's lasted this long. I'll send my man around tomorrow to settle accounts.'

Kit didn't understand anything the man said, but the girl in the smock said, 'This way, Doctor.'

Kit watched them go. Then she leaned toward the door, which stood ajar. Inside was a lofty room. The decor was rather opulent, like some of the rooms she used to spy out back in Othir's mansions when Caim was working. Coffered ceiling, wooden chests against the walls, a tall wardrobe and dresser, and a cheval mirror set in a bright brass frame. And, of course, the bed, which was huge, big enough to sleep three or four people, but there was only one person in it now.

Kit went inside for a better look. Still unsure where she was, or how she had gotten here, she moved around to the side of the bed. The occupant was an old man. His silver hair was full, but cropped close to the scalp. His face was creased with deep lines like old leather. Kit leaned closer, and the breath caught in her throat as she recognized a resemblance through the drooping, wrinkled flesh. She swallowed, afraid to speak.

He opened his eyes. 'Kit?'

Through the hoarseness and the straining, she could hear his old voice, the voice she'd loved for so long. 'I'm here, Caim. How did this—?'

Kit stopped talking as she reached for him and saw her own hands. Instead of smooth and elegant, they were withered, the skin along the backs sunken to where she could see the bones. A large brown spot covered the knob of her left wrist. She pulled the hands – her hands – back and tried to hide them in the laced sleeves of her dress. 'Caim, what's happened? You're so old, and I'm . . .'

She turned to the glass, the movement slow and stiff. The face that looked back at her was ancient. Her violet eyes were hidden within deep pockets of wrinkles. 'I'm horrid!'

'No.' He coughed. 'No, my love. You're as beautiful as the first time I saw you.'

Kit sat on the bed and touched his arm. The firm muscles she'd once fantasized about, wanting to hold her, were shrunken to thin cables. 'How did we get so old, Caim? I'm a mud-woman now, but I don't remember how I got this way.'

He shook his head. 'I'm sorry. I know I promised to never leave you, but I don't know . . .'

His eyes closed as his voice drifted off.

'Mistress?' The girl had returned. She stood at the door. 'Can I get you anything?'

Kit shook her head and looked back to Caim, resolved to wake him for some answers, but he exhaled a long, quiet breath before she could shake him. His chest seemed to shrink in upon itself, falling lower and lower. She waited for it to rise again. One heartbeat extended into a second, but his chest did not move. Kit clamped her teeth shut to hold back the wail that clawed up her throat. The room grew dimmer as the walls closed in around her.

The sun was in the same place in the sky when Kit returned to her grandmother's retreat. The flowers of the garden swayed to the breeze, surrounding her in a thousand heady scents that all smelled of ashes. She looked for her grandmother and heard the door to the cottage close. Tears welled up in her eyes, but they did not spill.

Kit walked back down the stony path to the water's edge. Standing in the sand, she thought about what she'd seen. Was it the future, or just a nightmare? A gust of wind blew through her hair. Small waves capped in white foam scudded across the water's surface as Kit pondered her destiny and the man she loved.

CHAPTER FIFTEEN

Caim groaned as he rolled over. The return journey from Othir had been rougher than he expected. He hurt all over.

Blinking up at the soot-black sky, Caim pushed aside his stiff blanket and sat up. Freezing rain encrusted the ground. Dray, bleary-eyed and slack-jawed, sat beside the campfire from which rose a few tendrils of smoke. Caim scooted closer to the warmth of the coals. 'Do we have any more wood?'

Dray shook his head. 'That's the last of it. And I doubt you'll find much dry timber around today. Been raining since midnight.'

Caim rubbed his hands together. A cold breakfast was the least of his worries. Josey was somewhere on her way north, to find him, of all things. From what Hubert said, she'd been through a lot since her ascension to the throne. Would he even recognize her anymore?

And then there was Kit. He'd been cruel last night. He wished he could say it was an isolated incident, but he'd been distracted for weeks, not giving her the attention he knew she wanted. Things had changed between them during their time in Eregoth. He needed to acknowledge that and make things right between them.

Caim studied the terrain to the north. The tugging in his head was strong this morning, as strong as it had ever been. And it had a strange texture, too. The droning buzz had changed to an insistent whine behind his ears. Why was that?

Maybe it's me. Maybe traveling back to Othir, stretching my powers like that, did something to my head.

As he tried to figure it out, the others crawled from their blankets. They ate as they packed up the meager camp. Caim went to Egil and pointed in the direction of the pulling. 'Keep us heading in that direction.'

The guide scratched his beard, which was flecked with small pieces of ice. 'As you say, but the farther north we go, the better the chance we'll be seen. The Bear tribe is thick all through this region.'

'I understand. Do the best you can to keep us out of their way. Unless you'd rather head back. You didn't sign up for this.'

'Nah. This is a good-paying job. Anyway, I'd feel bad if you got lost up here and froze yourselves to death.'

Caim smiled, though it made his cheeks ache. As they headed out single-file after the guide, Caim stayed to the rear. It wasn't long before he heard Malig complaining again, but then Dray pulled something from his saddlebags. A long-necked bottle. Malig snatched it and popped the cork. 'Damn!'

'I've been saving it. Good, eh?'

The two of them passed the bottle back and forth a few times before offering a swig to Aemon, but he declined with a shake of his head.

'Just have a nip, Aemon,' Dray said. 'Maybe it will yank you out of the rotten fucking mood you've been in.'

'And if not,' Malig said, 'at least it'll make you more interesting company.'

Dray said something Caim didn't catch, and both he and Malig guffawed with laughter. Then they started up a drinking song. While they sang, Aemon plucked the bottle from his brother's hand and took a long pull. Caim squinted ahead into the wind, but there was nothing to see except the stark flatness of the wastes. Then he spotted something far ahead in that distance, a slight darkening on the horizon. Not much to go on, but it was the only landmark in sight.

Caim nudged his steed into a canter that carried him up to the drinking Eregoths. Dray held out the nearly empty bottle to him. 'Want the last bit?'

'Keep your voices down,' Caim said. 'And your eyes open.'

Dray stared at him, but said nothing. They rode onward in silence, battered by the frigid wind and occasional flurries of snow. After Dray and Malig finished their liquid amusement, they both leaned forward in their saddles, eyes closed. After a candlemark of riding, Egil fell back to offer them a break. Everyone dismounted to give the animals a rest, but they kept walking at Caim's insistence.

When Malig complained, Caim said, 'Moving will keep you warm. And we still have a ways to go before nightfall.'

Malig snorted. 'Nightfall? In case you haven't noticed, it's always night in this frozen slice of hell.'

Caim felt the muscles in his arms contract. His fingers itched. Bracing himself as the frozen saddle met his thighs, Caim swung back up on his horse and cantered ahead. When he was a hundred yards ahead, he slowed his pace. He was edgy without knowing why. All he could think of was getting to the forest and finding the source of the sensation in his head. The snow lessened enough for him to see the horizon, where the darkness had resolved into a mass of trees. They appeared normal at first, except that they were the first trees he'd seen in the wastes. Yet, as he led his horse farther, small details emerged that gave him pause. The trees were gargantuan in size, even bigger than the mighty oaks of northern Eregoth. And then there was their hue, which was sable black with ash-gray leaves.

Caim pulled his steed back to a slow walk as they entered the forest. Thin, twisted branches entwined in a canopy over his head. Everything smelled bitter and dead. He waited for the others just inside the tree line. The pulling had grown more insistent, urging him forward.

'This might be the place,' he said when his crew caught up. 'Keep your wits about you and your weapons close at hand.'

Aemon pulled on the hilt of his sword. It took him three hard yanks to loosen the frozen blade. Seeing this, the others looked to their weapons as well. Caim reached behind him, but his knives came free at a touch. He led the party deeper into the woods.

Trees blocked out all but narrow patches of the dark sky. There was no trail or path, so Caim made his own, leading his horse around the massive boles. Egil hiked beside him, navigating the woods with ease.

'You have any idea where we are?' Caim asked.

'Some, but no one I know has ever been this far north. If you get caught hunting up here, you're like to lose your hands, if not your head.'

'Great,' Malig said. 'This place just gets more and more inviting. You thinking of building a little house up here, Caim?'

As Caim opened his mouth to make a terse reply, he saw something through the trees ahead. A plinth of stone rose from the snow fifty paces away. 'There's something up ahead.'

The others squinted in the dark. 'What is it?' Dray asked.

Caim shushed him and slid down from the saddle. He didn't sense danger, but it was all too quiet. The wind had dropped away as if the forest was holding its breath.

Caim tossed his reins to Aemon, 'Follow close and stay quiet.'

Moving across the frozen snow, which crunched under his heels no matter how he tried to be quiet, Caim approached the plinth. It was taller than he first assumed, being about twice the height of a man. It was made of green-gray stone, worn and mottled with lichen. Looking through the trees to either side, Caim saw another, shorter plinth fifty paces to the east, and a pile of tumbled stones beyond that. Their positions lined up almost perfectly. He stepped back with a fresh perspective. These stones had once been part of a wall extending through the forest. Then he saw a building beyond the plinth, half-shrouded by the trees. It was difficult to make out, but he thought there were more structures beyond it. Caim pulled Egil aside.

'I don't know about any towns this far north,' the guide said. 'Not except the dark lord's citadel.'

Caim peered through the trees. Was this his destination? He didn't see any inhabitants. Come to think of it, he hadn't seen any animals since entering the forest either, nor heard their cries. The woods were quieter than a graveyard.

He shook his head to clear away these distracting thoughts. He knew what had to be done. Caim glanced at Aemon and the others. 'I'm going in. Count to fifty and then follow me.'

Caim moved ahead with careful steps, hand on the pommel of his seax knife, as he followed the pull's tether toward the buildings. He reached the outer corner of the first structure without trouble. The roof and two outer walls were collapsed, leaving half a shell made of the same stone as the plinths. Square windows gaped at him. The next nearest building was a score of paces away; three of its walls still stood, along with half of an interior partition. The snow between them was unbroken. Caim was about to cross the distance, but something held him back. He looked out at the expanse of whiteness, and then it hit him.

The shadows.

They were all around, clustered in the trees, in the windows of the shattered buildings. Their voices whispered in his ears. Caim exhaled a cloud of steam as he watched them. Whatever this place used to be, the shadows were very interested in it, and that didn't reassure him. But the others were catching up. He kept moving.

From the cover of the next building, Caim saw more broken

constructions ahead, dozens of them ranging in size from modest homes to sprawling edifices that could have been palaces. The structures were lofty, and the existing stonework was elaborate with scrollwork and other decorative touches, unlike anything else he'd seen in the north. There was an open space farther down from his position with a few broken columns visible through the gloom. The ruins looked centuries old. What had happened here? Plague? War was the most likely answer, but none of the tribes they'd encountered were capable of this level of architecture. Had another people lived in these lands once? In the tales he'd been fed as a child, the Northlands were supposed to be the abode of goblins and spooks, but this city was real enough.

The others caught up to him, all of them holding a weapon. Even Egil had his hunting knife out.

'We're not stopping here for the night, are we?' Malig asked.

'Why?' Dray smiled. 'You scared the spirits of the wood are going to get you, Mal?'

Malig scowled. 'Go sod yourself. I'm not worried about no woods.'

Caim winced as their voices carried over the faint clack of the wind through the branches. Aemon spoke up, 'I feel like there's something breathing down my neck.'

'What are you talking about?' Dray asked. 'There hasn't been anyone living here in a long damned time.'

Aemon rolled his shoulders. 'I don't know, but I feel it. Like we're being watched.'

Caim glanced at the nearest shadows as the same feeling itched at the nape of his neck. 'We'll look around. But stay together and keep the horses saddled for now.'

'Can we make a light?' Dray asked. 'I can't see shit.'

'Just one lantern, and be ready to shutter it if I give the word.'

Caim waited while Aemon dug out a lantern and struck a spark to the wick. He wanted to range ahead on his own, but there was something odd here. The ruins appeared empty, except for the shadows. Caim wished he knew the reason behind their sudden appearance. Was this place somehow connected to the Shadowlands? He didn't know, and that ignorance always found a way to kick him in the head. And he had driven Kit away . . .

Caim pushed away from the safety of the building and approached the open area, which he soon realized was a plaza, perhaps even the ancient city's main square. Each of the plaza's four sides was fronted by a huge structure. They might have been temples, or halls of government. With their broken roofs and leaning columns, he didn't relish the thought of entering them to explore.

As Caim prowled the edge of the square, the tugging in his head intensified to where he could hardly think straight. It beckoned him across the plaza, which was empty except for a vertical stone near the center. Taller and more slender than the plinths outside, it looked like the kind of stele used to commemorate important events. Othir was filled with them, chiseled with the heroics of dead generals and politicians. Caim had started across the snow toward it when the others entered the plaza. The lantern's cold light reflected off icicles hanging from the rooftops. The shadows on the entablature above their heads shifted, looking like nothing so much as a flock of blackbirds. Watching them.

The stele's surface was weathered and covered in ice. Caim was so intent on studying it that he almost didn't see the eight-foot-wide pit yawning before it. Pulling back from the brink, he peered over the side, but couldn't see a bottom to the stone shaft falling down into the darkness.

'What'd you find?' Aemon asked as he walked over. He had left the lantern with the others; Egil held it now, turning it to flash across the building fronts.

Caim was turning to answer when a huge, black shape flew up from the mouth of the pit. At first Caim registered it as a flock of bats disturbed from their lair, but then he caught a glimpse of curled talons raking toward his eyes. Without time to move, he threw an arm over his face and grunted as something heavy rammed into him from the side. A shock of long yellow hair flew across his vision, and then he was on the icy ground.

Caim rolled over in time to see Aemon drop to his knees at the lip of the pit. The clansman's arms shook as he grappled with the rippling form rising from the aperture. It was a shadow as big as a draft horse. Before Caim could jump to his feet, Aemon shuddered, and a fountain of blood erupted from his mouth. Caim drew his knives and ran to Aemon. Revulsion twisted in his gut as the clansman collapsed into the snow. Was this his fault? Had his powers finally torn loose from his control? The sick taste of bile tinged the back of his throat, but Caim swallowed it as he flung himself at the shadow creature.

The thing moved faster than a snapping whip, weaving around his attack and lunging at him sideways. Caim lashed out with his knives, but neither blade scored a hit. He landed on his shoulder, skidding in the snow. Caim climbed to one knee and swiveled around, but the shadow drew back as a ruddy light flashed across the walls of the surrounding buildings. It wasn't coming from the lantern. Caim regained his footing as a hulking man wrapped in a dingy cloak appeared from the other side of the stele, swinging a burning pot on the end of a long chain. The giant grunted, and a shower of red embers sailed through the air. The shadow creature wavered as the burning cinders passed through it, gouging holes in its night-black form wherever they touched.

'Fire!' another voice cried from the far side of the plaza. A woman's voice. 'Use fire against it!'

Dray was already charging at the shadow creature, his face contorted with rage. Egil dashed the lantern on the ground.

Then he and Malig yanked off their cloaks and tore them into long strips, dipping the cloth into the pool of burning oil.

Caim circled around the pit, gathering himself for another rush while the shadow creature was distracted, but something else moved in his peripheral vision, coming from a sheltered doorway to his right. A man stood on the threshold of the northern building. Caim stiffened at the sight of his armor. Fashioned from black scales and fine mail mesh, it was the same style as Sybelle's shadow warriors had worn back in Liovard, the same closed helmet. A long, curved sword like a cavalry saber with a long hilt hung from his belt. The newcomer nodded and vanished.

A sharp pain through Caim's chest drove the air from his lungs. Shouts echoed behind him as his comrades joined the fight against the shadow-thing, but Caim ignored them. The shadow warrior had disappeared without even forming a portal. Caim turned in a slow circle. He was sickened by Aemon's death and would have enjoyed carving into the thing that had killed the man, but he knew what these shadow warriors could do.

The shadow warrior appeared on the other side of the stele. Caim circled around to meet him. Before he could close the distance, the warrior attacked. The sword appeared in his hands faster than Caim could follow. It was a magnificent weapon, pure black from point to guard, the thin blade curved for added cutting power. The swordsman met Caim with a slash and a stop-thrust. Caim flicked his *suete* out to connect with the slashing blade as it passed. *And missed.* The black sword sped past faster than a striking adder and returned in a reverse stroke. In a pair of heartbeats Caim was backpedaling fiercely to avoid the midnight blade that wove and twisted around him, evading half of his blocks. If not for his instincts, he would have been skewered in the first exchange. The swordsman's circular fighting style was familiar. Caim racked his brain until he realized where he'd seen it before.

Levictus.

Only this shadow warrior was faster and stronger than Vassili's pet sorcerer had been, and his technique relied less on trickery and more on sheer mastery. Caim adjusted for his opponent's speed, keeping extra space between them, launching parries a moment earlier, but the swordsman made a feint, just a subtle movement, and when Caim reacted, the black sword sliced across his right forearm, slitting open his jacket sleeve from wrist to elbow with a quick flick. Caim hissed between gritted teeth as he jumped back. The wound burned like wildfire. Blood ran down his hand and soaked his glove. His muscles ached already, and his breath was heavy in his chest. The shadows whispered to him. It wasn't difficult to know what they wanted. Blood and more blood, but he didn't trust them.

Something snarled behind him, and a man – Malig or Dray – yelled like he'd been ripped in half, but Caim couldn't spare a glance for them. The swordsman pushed him back with every attack, and Caim kept weaving in a circle to prevent being backed against a wall, but the snow made for unpredictable footing. A slip could mean death. *A slip . . .*

Caim blocked a cut aimed at his knee and took another step backward. The shadow warrior was better than the ones he had battled in Duke Eviskine's keep. This swordsman fought with precision, varying the speed and angle of his attacks, and his longer reach kept Caim's knives at bay. Yet like most fighters, he had a rhythm. Caim had already picked up on it, but he needed an opening.

As he backed up another step, Caim's heel slid out from under him. His balance faltered, just for an instant, but before he could recover, the black sword rushed in with a high-to-low cross-body slash. Caim threw himself sideways. As he leapt, he lashed out with both knives. The *suete* was deflected, but the seax knife got through, slicing straight for the swordsman's throat. Then the swordsman halted his momentum and stepped away in a movement so smooth and quick it sent a shiver up Caim's spine. *How in the hells am I going to get close enough to hit this guy?*

As Caim rolled to his feet, the swordsman waded at him again for another exchange. A high-pitched screech echoed off the buildings from the other side of the plaza where his crew battled the shadow creature. Torches waved back and forth, and one of the horses was down, its legs kicking feebly on the glittering ice. Caim tried to think of a strategy to help the others, but his attention was wrenched back to his own problems as the swordsman disappeared. Again there was no portal. He just vanished. It was almost like watching Kit evaporate, except without the twinkle of ghostly light.

A sudden tightening in his chest was the only warning he received. Caim leapt into a forward roll, rising as he came out of it just in time to block a downward slash at his head with both knives. The swordsman feinted and disappeared once more. Caim spun around, but a stinging cut sliced across the back of his leg as the swordsman materialized behind him. Dripping blood down his arm and the back of his calf, Caim parried and wove as more attacks came at him, but it was just a matter of time. He had to do something drastic. He reached down inside. Bracing himself for the pain, Caim hopped backward and seized hold of the power.

His breath evaporated before he could shout as razor-sharp agony sliced through his lungs. But he held on, and a black hole yawned beside him. Blocking a thrust aimed at his face, Caim dove through. He appeared at a spot behind where the swordsman had been standing, but his foe was waiting. The only thing that saved him was that he emerged from the portal on his hands and knees. The black sword cut the air above him. Before it could turn in Caim's direction, he was back on his feet. His chest burned, and every breath hurt like a bastard, but he was still alive.

Caim gave ground as the swordsman came at him again.

One of his parries arrived a hair late, and a black point slashed in front of his eyes, close enough to make him blink. Caim embraced the pain again and stepped back into the appearing void. This time he split the portal into two paths, each exiting on opposite sides of his adversary, but once again the black sword was waiting for him. Caim twisted away in a violent turn and evaded a cut that would have disemboweled him. The swordsman pressed forward with subsequent attacks that kept him on the defensive.

Fuck this. Instead of retreating, Caim stepped forward to meet his foe. He kept his knives in close, blocking the barrage of attacks in a furious defense. He and the swordsman were only a pace apart, close enough that Caim could reach his opponent with a long lunge, but he didn't have a moment's pause to go on the offense. Yet. He shuffled forward. It was like stepping into the face of a steel hurricane. The staccato of clashing blades pulsed in his ears. His wrists went numb from the pounding. Most fighters would have retreated at this point, wanting the security of more space where their longer weapon would have the advantage, but the swordsman advanced a half step as well. Caim concentrated on his breathing. This was what he had been hoping for, to bring them close enough that the advantage switched to his knives. Caim anticipated a thrust with an early parry and used the extra fraction of a heartbeat of time to swipe the tip of his seax past his opponent's face. The swordsman didn't flinch. He didn't react at all.

Caim pushed himself to the edge, until his arms and legs ached and his breath whistled between clenched teeth. After every second or third parry, he launched an attack of his own. They weren't complex and none connected, but with every passing heartbeat he felt the momentum of the fight turning. Then a black cloud fell over his eyes. Caim winced as ice-cold tendrils dug into his face. He slashed in front of him with the *suete* knife and jumped back. He scraped at the shadow with the back of his hand, causing frigid pains to erupt across his face, and the shadow slipped away.

Blinking to clear his eyes of the motes that danced in his vision, Caim reached for his powers to open another portal. He was heading farther away, to the other side of the plaza, where he could regroup and maybe come up with a plan. But as he stepped back, a terrible pain speared through the center of his breastbone. It was worse than the time he'd been shot with a crossbow. For an agonizing moment, he couldn't move. Every muscle was locked in a rigid paralysis. When sensation returned, he almost collapsed. But no portal appeared.

The swordsman rushed across the snow. Caim raised his knives, fighting through the pain. Images of his battle with Soloroth flashed through his head, that same hopelessness he'd felt facing the armored giant crashing over him now. Before the black sword landed, a brilliant flash of light burst around the shadow warrior. Caim braced himself for some new attack, but the swordsman was turning away from him, his cloak awash in flames.

Caim lunged, but his knives encountered only swirling air as the swordsman disappeared into nothingness.

The giant stranger stood behind the spot where the swordsman had been standing, an empty brazier dangling in his hands.

Caim had seen his share of death. Not just marks and competitors, but friends, too. Mathias, Oak, Liana, Hagan, Caedman. And now Aemon. The world wasn't a fair place. *If it were, I'd have been dead a long time ago, and they would still be alive.*

Dray stood over his brother's body at the plaza center. Malig and Egil remained behind him, each holding a flaming brand. There was no sign of the shadow creature or the swordsman. Silence draped over the ruins, broken only by the sigh of the wind and crackling torches.

Caim put away his knives and checked his injuries. The cut down his arm had stopped bleeding, but his leg burned something fierce. He tried not to limp as he went over to the others. Malig had put a hand on Dray's shoulder, but Dray shook it off. With a turn of his head, Caim sent Malig over to help Egil get the mounts together. He stood beside Dray.

Caim hadn't gotten a clear view of what happened to Aemon, and now he wished he hadn't looked. The blond Eregoth lay in a ruin of burst organs and tissue, torn open from crotch to throat, his blood making a pool of red slush in the snow. His empty eyes stared up at the ebon sky.

'I'm sorry,' Caim said, then shut his mouth. What good were words? He recalled the night they had infiltrated the duke's keep in Liovard, how Aemon had been hurt and Dray refused to leave his brother's side.

'I'm fine. Let's get out of here.' Dray picked up his brother's spear. 'But we're taking Aemon with us.'

Caim frowned. The shadow warrior could return at any time, maybe with reinforcements. 'Mal. Egil. Get a rope and help him.'

As they rolled Aemon's body in a blanket and carried it to the animals, the stranger stepped around the pit, the empty brazier still dangling in his hands from a chain. He was taller than Malig and massively proportioned through the shoulders and chest. His shirt and pants were made from undyed wool, his boots battered and worn. Caim supposed the man deserved some gratitude for helping them, but he was too damned tired and sore to offer much beyond, 'Thank you.'

Footsteps crunching in the ice made Caim reach for his knives again, but he stayed his hand when he saw who it was. She looked like a lost waif wrapped up in a cloak. While the man had a pale complexion, her skin was the deep olive of the Southlands. With her chestnut hair and deep brown eyes, he pegged her as a Michaian, or maybe even Arnossi. Wherever she came from, she was a long way from home.

'We thank the gods you found us.' Her breath puffed in small clouds of steam as she stopped beside the giant. She was even shorter than Caim had thought at first glance. Standing beside him, she looked like a child.

Caim kept his hands by his sides, but his nerves were jumpy. 'Where did he go?'

'If you mean that man you fought, we do not know. I am Shikari.' She placed a hand on her companion's arm. 'And this is Hoek. We were taking shelter in that building when we heard noises.'

A short, braying cry rose, only to be cut short. Egil knelt beside the injured horse, now put out of its misery, while Dray and Malig loaded Aemon's corpse onto another steed.

Caim considered the strangers. 'You don't look like Northmen. What were you hiding from?'

The woman, Shikari, pulled her cloak tighter around her slim shoulders. 'Our masters.'

'You're slaves?'

She nodded. 'I am from Illmyn. Hoek comes from a village in Einar, to the south and east.'

'I know where Einar is.' Caim eyed the man. 'He doesn't talk much, does he?'

'Not at all, in fact. He's mute.'

The big man gazed impassively at Caim and said nothing, as if to prove her statement.

'How did you come to be a slave up in these parts?'

Her full lips, chapped from the cold, turned up in a fetching smile. 'We were both taken from our lands and brought here by the barbarians. When Hoek escaped, I came with him. I thought anything would be better than to live another day in bondage, but we don't know the land, so we stopped when we found this place. Now that you know about us, who are you?'

Caim introduced himself and gave the names of the others.

‘I suppose we should thank you, but I’m curious. How did you know to use fire against the shadow?’

Shikari was staring at him, hard enough that it might have made him uncomfortable in other circumstances. ‘I was not sure, but when Hoek took the coals from our fire it seemed like a good idea. Creatures of night must surely fear the light, no?’

Caim regarded the duo. Something about them bothered him. Two slaves out here alone, just happening to be in the right place to lend a hand when he and his crew were attacked. He didn’t like it. ‘We have to go. I suggest you take yourselves someplace else. That warrior could return anytime, and like as not he’ll bring friends.’

Egil came over, his knife back in its sheath. ‘You want I should butcher this animal? It’s a shame to leave all that meat to waste.’

The thought of eating anything killed by the shadows turned Caim’s stomach. ‘No, we don’t have time. Find us a trail out of here.’

As Caim turned to leave, Shikari reached out a hand like she wanted to snag his sleeve. ‘We should like to go with you, if you will permit. There is safety in staying together, I think.’

‘We’re going north. If you want to escape this land, that’s the wrong direction.’

‘We are willing to take that risk,’ she replied. ‘I do not know how much longer we can survive out here alone.’

Caim scanned the plaza. Everything was quiet now. The dark had closed around them, making even the nearest buildings look distant and aloof. It made him miss Kit all the more. ‘I suppose you can stay with us until we get to another town.’

The Eregoths were mounted up on the surviving horses. Dray held his brother’s spear balanced on a stirrup. His eyes scanned the broken ruins as if he expected the shadow warrior to return at any moment. *He’s got the right idea.*

Caim exhaled through gritted teeth as he hobbled over to

his mount. His leg was stiffening up. He turned to Shikari. 'Here. Can you ride? It's going to be tough keeping up on foot.'

'We are accustomed to walking,' she said.

Caim held out the reins. 'So am I. Get on.'

She did as he asked, although she was a little wobbly as she swung her leg over the saddle. At least she wore pants, which made for easier riding than a skirt. Caim and Hoek trailed her out of the plaza. His leg ached with every step, but he felt better keeping them both in his sight. Just in case.

As they marched through the ruins' crumbling streets, Caim wondered if Kit was nearby, maybe watching him. Punishing him for what he'd said. She would turn up eventually. If not tonight, then certainly tomorrow or the day after.

CHAPTER SIXTEEN

The wind tugged at Caim's cloak as he stood on the rocky plain. The morning was bitter and gusty. Snow floated in the breeze, and the clouds smudging the slate-gray sky promised more to come.

The cairn was just a pile of rocks. Not much of a grave for a friend, but the ground was too hard for digging. Malig and Dray stood on either side of the grave like sentinels, Dray leaning on Aemon's spear.

Caim shifted to ease his injured leg. Egil's stitching wasn't as good as Aemon's had been, but it would serve. Dray started humming, and Malig joined in. The dirge didn't have any words, but its heavy tones suited the gloomy morning. Caim shifted again. He was going to miss Aemon, but part of him just wanted to be back on the road.

What's wrong with me that I can't even mourn a friend?

Caim looked north, following the pulling sensation. It had returned not long after they left the ruins, and now he could tell the subtle difference between the two magnetisms. This one was the low droning tug he'd been following since Othir. The other had only been a mirage of some sort, possibly created by the shadow swordsman. It had been a cunning trap, and they probably would have been caught, or killed, if not for Shikari and her protector.

The two escaped slaves sat on a flat rock away from the funeral. Shikari had tried to engage Caim in conversation while they traveled, asking him where he came from and why he was here. Though her interest seemed genuine, he deflected her questions until she fell silent like her mute companion. The big Einarian deferred to her in everything, following her around like a lost child. When they stopped, he built a fire for her and gave her his cloak. She hadn't bothered to thank him. An odd pair.

'Our father died when we was just boys,' Dray said, breaking Caim out of his thoughts. 'Our ma took care of us the best she could. But she took sick when I was eleven. Aemon was just nine. She never got better. Just kept getting sicker and sicker. By the end she couldn't leave her bed.

'Aemon wouldn't leave her side. He fed her, washed her face when she got fevered, even slept beside her. One night I went in to see her. Aemon was asleep, and I thought she was, too, but when I went to leave, she opened her eyes. She told me she was dying and made me promise I would take care of Aemon as best I—' His voice caught.

'He was my little brother. But damn me if he wasn't always the one looking after me. Mal, you remember the time we broke the ice in the creek behind your house in the middle of winter and went swimming?'

'Yeah, I remember.'

'You fell in and I went in after you, and neither one of us could climb out. Fuck, that water was cold. If Aemon hadn't pulled us out . . .'

'He was too good for this world.' Malig looked up with a scowl. 'Right now Aemon's sitting at the right hand of Father Ell, hoisting a big cup of mead.'

Dray lifted the spear to the sky. The wind fluttered their hair and cloaks. A pebble rolled down the cairn.

'What are we doing here?' Malig asked. 'What's so damned important up here that Aemon had to die for it?'

They turned to Caim, and he looked down at the cairn. It was time. He owed them the truth. So he told them about the raiders in black who had attacked his father's estate, about

Othir and Levictus and his familial tie to Sybelle. He finished with how he had learned of Erebus. 'So I'm here to find out what happened to my mother.'

'Bugger me,' Malig grumbled. 'Between you and Dray, ain't there no end to the tragedy?'

'I never asked any of you to come.' Caim was finding it hard to talk above a whisper. His throat had closed up tight. 'You were always free to go back.'

'Back? Across all those miles and over the mountains? Are you fucking serious?'

Dray hadn't moved. He still stared down at his brother's grave, but his fingers were white around the shaft of the spear. 'What am I going to do now?'

'I understand if you want to go back to Eregoth,' Caim said. 'But I'm going to see this through.'

Dray let out a long breath that curled around his head. 'All right. But I want blood. I'm going to send Aemon to the afterlife on a river of it. That one you were fighting. He was part of what happened to my brother, wasn't he?'

'I suppose so.'

'I want him. I want to send him down to the Dark myself.' Dray lifted up Aemon's spear. 'On the end of this.'

Malig scowled at them both. 'That's it, huh? We're decided? Fine. So where in the name of all that's holy is this Erebus place?'

Caim looked to Egil, who squatted at the foot of the cairn. 'North, I'm guessing.'

The guide shook his head. 'No one goes there. It's not wise to—'

'To speak of it,' Caim finished for him. 'I know. But what do you know about it?'

Egil stood up, brushing his hands. 'Just what I've heard from others. It's far up past the Bear lands. That's where the dark lord keeps his court, in a city with walls a thousand feet high.'

While Malig started a long litany of curses, Caim gnawed on his bottom lip. Levictus had mentioned the Lords of Shadow – it seemed like years ago now. 'We can make our own way from here if you want to go back home.'

'I'll stay on, if it's all the same to you,' Egil replied.

Shikari walked over, with Hoek shadowing her footsteps. 'We would also like to accompany you.'

'Now we're taking on strays?' Malig asked.

'It won't be safe,' Caim told her. 'We'll find a place for you to stay. A village or a homestead.'

She stepped closer. 'I don't ask for myself, Caim. My sister was enslaved the same as me. While I was given to a barbarian chief, she was taken north. I believe she may be at this place you speak of.'

'If we find her, we'll—'

'How will you know her? No, I must come with you.'

Caim sighed, wanting to argue, but it was pointless. He nodded, and Malig's string of curses grew. Dray saw to his horse, but Aemon's spear never left his reach.

While the others prepared to leave, Caim looked back in the direction of the ruined city. Where was Kit? He cursed her for leaving, and then cursed himself for a fool. He had all but driven her away. Why couldn't he just tell her how he really felt?

Something moved on the plains. Caim tensed until a low, four-footed shape emerged. The wolf's eyes were amber coins in the dark, staring in their direction. All by itself.

Caim pulled up the collar of his cloak as he put his foot in the stirrup and swung onto his steed. The wind was picking up again.

CHAPTER SEVENTEEN

The salty wind stirred up a white froth across the ocean waves below the cliff. White birds cawed as they circled overhead. The sun was painful to the eyes as it sank beneath the horizon, but not so bright as to be blinding.

Balaam inhaled and let the smells fill him. There was something about the water, its vast expanse and unknowable depths, the rhythm of the waves. He closed his eyes and remembered his homeland, the many nights he had stood on the beach at his father's house in Drechensvelt Prefecture looking out over the midnight lakes.

The summoning beckoned him, pulling at the recesses of his brain. Balaam considered defying it as he took a last look over the endless blue waters. The fire that had engulfed his cloak was gone, but the shame of failure remained. He saw the scene again in his mind: the trap laid perfectly, his heart beating with anticipation as the scion entered the killing ground, the daemon released from its etheric prison in the pit. And then their duel. Balaam had run through every moment of the fight in his mind, studying every step, every blow, every breath. It had been a dance of combat perfection. Elegant, fierce, and honorable. Until they were interrupted.

His flaw was that he'd failed to account for outside interference. Now he wished he'd stayed to conclude the battle with the scion, even if it had meant his defeat. *Better to die than face this dishonor.*

The portal deposited him in a rough-hewn chamber far

beneath the citadel's foundations. He followed the tunnel around several sharp angles to its conclusion. His breath misted before him as he entered a colossal cavern. Carved from the rock, it stretched more than a hundred spans from end to end. Fingers of translucent ice cascaded down the cratered wails, reflecting the light of the eternal blue flame burning in the obsidian urn at the center. The fire gave off no heat, but Balaam hardly registered the cold of the subterranean cavern. His anger and shame kept him warm.

The Shadow Lord stood on the far side of the chamber. His shoulders were slumped, his back bent slightly as if under a heavy weight. Balaam kept a tight rein on his composure as he crossed the uneven floor. All at court knew the Master came down here often by himself. The rumors of what he did here were rife with ill intent, but few knew the truth. As Balaam passed the urn of fire, the far wall vanished into a well of nothingness. *No, not nothingness. More, and somehow also less.*

It was the original gateway that had brought them to this world. Embedded in the stone wall, it was black and impenetrable like a starless sky. Many thought the gateway had been lost, destroyed by the Shadow Lord, but Balaam and a few trusted others knew that their Master had hidden the gate in the earth and built his citadel above it. Yet what wrenched Balaam's insides was not the gateway, but the pitifully small figure stuck within it. He remembered Isabeth from the old days. The Master's daughter had been so full of life and breathtakingly beautiful, but the warped, stone-gray statue before him hardly resembled that girl. Save for the eyes. Even embedded in the flinty substance her flesh had been transformed into over these long years, they retained a spark of rebelliousness.

Dark things moved under the surface of the void. Balaam remained still, hardly daring to breathe, as an inky tendril emerged from the gateway and touched the Shadow Lord. Abraxus shuddered, his eyes closed tight as if lost in rapture, or agony. Moments passed. When the Master turned, he was no longer the ancient man who had presided over Lord Oriax's execution, but strong and hearty with the bearing of a younger man, though his gaze was slightly vacant as if he'd been staring into the void for hours. Perhaps he had.

'Sometimes I think it means to destroy me. But I will endure it as long as I must.'

Balaam folded his gloved hands behind his back. 'Master?'

Abraxus stepped closer to the gateway, until his face was mere inches from his daughter. The void's eldritch energies writhed and palpitated, as if excited by the Shadow Lord's presence. 'She was my prize, Balaam. My magnificent jewel. Do you have children?'

'No, Master.'

'A wise decision. This is where your father died. Did you know?'

'No, Master.'

'It was here. The traitors came while I was in my meditation. Your father slew them all. When I returned from the ethers, he was lying next to the sentinel flame.'

Balaam said nothing. There was nothing to say, but for an instant he imagined drawing his sword and opening his lord's throat, saw the black blood spill out on the floor. *I am a soldier. I live only to serve and die.* He held fast to that belief as he clutched his hands together. The Shadow Lord's daughter stared at him from the void.

Abraxus turned away from the gateway. 'Have you found him?'

Balaam gave the full account of his ambush, leaving out nothing. When he came to the part of his defeat, his stomach clenched and a cool sweat broke out across his brow, but he continued on and ended with his new plan to use teams of Northmen to track the scion.

Abraxus nodded. 'Yes, Balaam. Do as you see fit. My trust in you on this matter is complete. But I have an additional task for you.'

Balaam bowed his head. Any duty would be preferable to continuing this farce, even a transfer to a distant battlefield far from Erebus. *And far from Dorcas.*

Lord Malphas emerged from the shadows on the other side of the flames. The majordomo was dressed in an impeccable gray suit with a long jacket. 'One of your Talons has left Erebus without permission.' *They are mine again now?*

Lord Malphas held up a black helmet. 'Deumas, I believe her name was. She left this at the foot of the Master's throne.'

Balaam took the helm, turning it over in his hands. Yes, it belonged to Deumas. Her desertion was no great surprise.

'You are to find the traitor,' Malphas said. 'Eliminate her and bring us proof when you have finished.'

Jaws clenched tight, Balaam bowed to Abraxus. 'As you command, Master.'

The Shadow Lord placed a thin hand on his arm. 'You are my chosen, Balaam. My most loyal servant. Let none stop you, and we shall deal with the scion in good time. He will come to us like a slouching mongrel, but his power will crumble in the face of . . . in the face of . . .'

'In the face of your power, Master,' Malphas finished.

'Yes,' Abraxus said, his voice hollow. 'Perform the tasks I've put before you. That is all I require.'

Balaam bowed again as the Shadow Lord took a step and vanished, leaving them alone together in the cavern. The majordomo approached within arm's reach of the lady, gazing into her blank, frozen eyes. The gateway's surface was now as smooth as black glass. 'You knew her,' Malphas asked. 'Did you not?'

'I was raised in the Master's household from a young age. I knew his entire family.'

Lord Malphas faced him, his features smooth like a sheet of dusky granite. 'I forgot you were raised as a Talon. I've always wondered what it must be like to live a life of service, beholden entirely to another's will.'

Balaam clenched his fingers around the helmet to keep from throwing it at Malphas's face. Deumas had been more right than she knew. This one *was* a snake. Balaam tried to get hold of his tongue, but it slipped away from him. 'I doubt you could understand the honor that is found in the service of a great lord.'

Malphas's lips twitched as if unsure whether to smile or frown. 'Do not fail in the task you have been given, Talon. This defection by one of your own has caused distress in the court.'

'I will not fail.'

'Very good. Lest we begin to question even your fabled loyalty.'

The majordomo left. The eternal flame's harsh light cascaded across the Shadow Lord's trapped daughter, creating deep shadows in her eyes and in the hollow of her throat. Could she hear what they said? Did she know her son was in the wastes, possibly on his way here?

Balaam considered the helmet in his hand. Then he created his own portal and stepped away from the cavern.

CHAPTER EIGHTEEN

Caim watched his crew as they marched ahead of him. After just couple hours' sleep, everyone rode in silence, but they were wound tight. Though he'd been riding with Malig and Dray for weeks, he didn't know them well enough to recognize their breaking points. When they came, he was afraid it was going to be ugly.

'You look troubled.'

Shikari looked down from atop his horse. Though the temperature had dropped overnight and remained uncomfortably frigid, the former slave didn't complain. And Caim couldn't criticize her resilience; she and her protector kept up with the pace without faltering.

'Just thinking about what's ahead.'

She gazed northward, her eyes narrowed as if studying the darkness. 'Yes, Erebus. Aren't you afraid?'

The question caught Caim off guard. Fear wasn't the word he would use for his feelings. Resigned, maybe. 'Back at the ruins, you—'

'Sturmgaard,' Shikari said. 'That is what the Northmen call the place. It's very old. Older, perhaps, than anything else in the wastes.'

'You know a lot about this land. How long were you a slave?'

'Less than a year, but it felt like most of my life.'

Caim considered the path ahead. The tugging had

intensified. Was he getting close to his goal? 'Don't the Northmen brand their slaves?'

'Sometimes. I had the good fortune to be owned by a man who didn't want me blemished. Hoek, show Caim your mementos.'

The big slave pulled up his shirt to reveal several marks burned into his skin. The older ones were seared over, but Caim could make out an animal paw with three claws and a wolf's head under the scars.

'You don't trust easily, Caim,' Shikari said. 'In that way you are like the people of this empty land.'

'I've learned that things aren't always what they seem.'

'All that is gold does not glitter?' She laughed. It was more sultry than her petite frame would suggest.

'You were held by the Bear tribe?' When she nodded, Caim asked, 'What are they like?'

'They are a grim people. They never laugh and seldom cry.'

'Not even the children?'

'When they reach the age of three, every child is taken from their mother and given to the *asherjhag* – the priests. Those found worthy are given to the warrior's society or the women's hall to raise in the ways of the tribe.'

Caim didn't want to know what happened to the children found unworthy. 'We saw some of those priests. Do they hold much power in the Northman tribes, then?'

'Not even a chieftain will defy the *asherjhag*. They speak for the dark lord, and as such their word is law.'

Caim stepped carefully over a patch of ice. From what he'd learned from the Eregoths, the relationship between the priesthood and the Shadow Lord sounded suspiciously like the cult Sybelle had formed in Liovard. It sounded logical, to control the populace through a state religion. 'What do the Northmen say about this dark lord?' he asked.

'They speak of him as a god. According to the *asherjhag* he is the Prince of the Night who once ruled these wastes millennia ago. Their myths say he was banished to the outer darkness, but he has returned to bring endless night to the whole world.'

Not a pleasant image. But Caim could believe it. They'd heard plenty of tales about the other marchlands, stories of Northmen armies bent on conquest. It had almost happened in Eregoth – would have if Caedman and his men hadn't risen up in defiance. All of it led back to the wastes. To Erebus, the heart of the darkness.

A jackdaw called from the front of the party. Dray was pointing. Caim followed the pointing digit to a flicker of fire atop a low hill. It looked like a bonfire, or perhaps several fires. It was too far away to be sure. Caim felt unfriendly eyes upon them, but saw nothing in particular. The shadows remained quiet.

'You think it's a town?' Malig asked.

Caim called for Egil, and the guide came hustling back. 'A Bear tribe holding,' he explained.

'Swing clear of it,' Caim said.

Dray sawed on his horse's reins. 'We should go for a look.'

'The last thing we need is more trouble.'

Dray lifted his brother's spear. There were thin gouges carved into the shaft. 'If my brother's killer is up there, I'm not about to pass by without—'

Caim heard the high-pitched whine a moment before his brain registered the sound of the arrow's flight. He pulled Shikari down from the horse and dove to the ground, cushioning her from the fall. Malig's horse reared up. Caim thought the Eregoth had been hit, but then Egil rolled over from where he lay on the ground, a feathered shaft protruding from his chest. Everyone else was down on the ground or crouching behind their mount.

'How many are there?' Dray asked.

Malig attempted to string a bow, but the string snapped in his hands. Egil groaned as another arrow passed overhead.

Caim traced the flight to a snowbank about seventy paces north of their position. He gathered his legs under him. 'Stay here!'

'Wait!' Shikari called.

But Caim was already running. The hilts of his knives were burning cold through his gloves. He stayed low as he moved across the snow, hoping the shooters didn't have his night vision. Two men with short bows peered over the snowbank. Both wore a stuffed ursine head over their helmet. Bear tribesmen, just as Egil had warned. Caim was stalking toward them when a bright light lit up the wastes. A pillar of flames erupted from the vicinity of his crew. *What in the hells?*

The two archers looked right at Caim. He charged their position. An arrow sizzled past his head as he dove. His seax knife took the nearest archer in the throat, cutting straight through the meat of the Northman's neck to come out the other side. Caim ripped the knife free with a twist of his wrist and lunged across the falling Northman for his partner. The second archer hopped back, swinging his bow like a club. Caim took the blow on his shoulder and punched his *suete* knife into the man's thigh near the groin. The Northman stiffened as Caim tackled him to the ground. They thrashed for a couple moments until Caim knelt on the barbarian's chest, the point of his *suete* under the Northman's chin. 'How many are with you?'

The Northman glared up at Caim. His mouth was a flat line framed with bushy, reddish-brown curls. Caim applied more pressure, and a line of blood trickled down the man's hairy neck. 'I said—'

'Drepta mae, ter fridjen sekrburr!'

The Northman tried to punch him, and Caim drew his knife across the jugular. Steam rose from the bright red blood pouring onto the ground. Caim stared at it, feeling himself lean down. The blood called. If he just—

Caim wrenched himself away from the dying Northman.

The bloodlust lingered, taunting him. *This place is turning me into a gods-damned ghoul.*

Sickened, he turned away. The second archer was stone dead. Beyond the snowbank, flames rose from a clump of bushes where he'd left the others, and the sounds of combat rang across the plain.

Caim leapt over the bank and ran back, alert for arrows. He arrived to find Dray bashing a Northman across the face with the butt of his spear. Blood and teeth exploded from the barbarian's mouth as he collapsed. Dray reversed the weapon and drove it down, pinning his foe to the ground. Streaks of blood ran down Dray's face as he twisted the spear back and forth. A knife's throw away, Malig dueled with another Northman. Malig swung his axe like a thresher flailing grain. It was a losing strategy, for the Northman was cagily holding back, waiting for Malig to exhaust himself. Caim could foresee the end. Malig would keep swinging away until he made a mistake, stepping out of balance for a moment too long, and then the Northman would cut him down. Caim hefted his knives. He could throw the *suete* in a flicker of an eyelash, but would Malig thank him for interfering?

Caim tensed as Malig's foot slipped out from under him. The Northman moved quick as a cat, swinging his sword for the kill, but Malig planted on his 'slipped' foot, twisted away, and plowed the edge of his broadaxe into the Northman's side. Before the barbarian could recover, Malig's axe split his face from forehead to chin, splattering his brains across the snow.

'Bear tribe,' Dray said, kicking his dead foe. 'Could be more of them out there.'

Snow crunched as Hoek trudged up to them. Blood covered his hands and forearms up to his elbows. His face was a white mask, showing no thought or emotion. Shikari walked behind him.

'What happened back here?' Caim asked. The fire was dying

down, leaving behind charred stumps and a strong smell of spirits.

'She fucking threw away our last bottle of hooch,' Malig grumbled.

'A diversion,' Shikari said. 'While Hoek and I went to make sure there were no other enemies lurking.'

Dray jerked his spear from the corpse. 'And?'

'There was another man with a bow, but he is dead.'

Caim went over to Egil. The guide was unconscious, which was probably a blessing for him. His breathing was labored. Caim cut away the guide's clothing. The arrow was sunk deep. The steady stream of blood leaking from the wound was bright red. Tiny bubbles formed around the mouth of the entry site. The arrow would be damned difficult to get out without shredding Egil's lung. Pushing it all the way through was the safer option, but that wouldn't stop blood from filling his lungs and eventually drowning him.

Malig came over to them. 'He don't look good.'

'What are we going to do?' Dray asked.

Caim sat back on his heels, trying not to look at the blood or listen to the tiny voices chittering in his ears. Egil needed a chirurgeon, and the last inhabited town was days behind them. He'd never make it. Caim considered what he would want if he were the one dying. A quick knife to the brainstem to end it? 'Let me have some water.'

Dray went to his horse and came back with a sloshing water skin. Caim popped the cork and held the skin to Egil's mouth. Most of it poured down the guide's chin, but he swallowed a little. His chest rose and fell with little shudders.

'Get some blankets,' Caim said. 'We'll make a sling to carry him.'

'He's done for,' Malig muttered. 'We need to get away from here before more company shows up.'

'Just do it.'

Malig and Dray did as he told them. Then he led them in the direction of the fires on the hill.

'Caim!' Malig hissed from the back of the stretcher. 'You're going in the wrong direction!'

But Caim kept walking. With each step the settlement on the hill's summit became clearer. The bonfires were enclosed inside a stout wooden palisade. Caim approached from the south where there was a gate in the fence. It was closed, of course, and he saw several holes in the wooden ramparts, presumably to allow for arrow fire. He stopped a hundred paces from the wall. Singing and shouting – chanting maybe – and the rapid beat of drums could be heard from inside. A pair of bear skulls perched above the gate. Caim studied these things, searching for something to tell him if he was wrong or right. Would these people kill Egil out of hand?

'You sure about this, Caim?' Malig whispered as he set down his end of the burden.

'No, but it's his best chance. I'll take him from here.'

'I'll go,' Dray offered.

'No, I'll go alone. If anything happens, run hard.'

Malig gave a short laugh. 'You can count on that.'

Just then, Egil coughed and tried to sit up, only to fall back on the blanket sling with a moan. Caim hunched over him. 'We're here.'

'Hurts,' Egil whispered. 'Arrow?'

Caim reached out to stop him from moving. 'Through the lung. We can't do anything for you, but we can take you someplace nearby.'

Egil craned his head toward the fires, and then settled back on the litter. 'At least there's' – he gasped as a shudder shook his body – 'no feud between them and my people. Anymore.'

Caim bent down lower. 'We have to keep moving. What do you want? I can take you inside, or . . .'

Egil moved his hand down to his hunting knife. His fingers wrapped around the bone handle. 'I'll take the chance.'

Caim took up the end of the litter and dragged Egil as smoothly and quietly as he could. While the drums inside continued to pound, he set his burden down by the gate and paused at Egil's side. 'We'll try to stop on our way back.' *Do you really believe that? Don't insult him.*

But Egil nodded. 'I'll be all right. By the time you get back, I'll be married with a pack of little warriors running around.' He coughed and winced. 'Oh! Don't tell Jenna I said that.'

Caim squeezed the guide's shoulder and pressed a pouch into his hand. It held all the money he had left, a handful of copper coins with a few silver in the mix. Then he whistled three notes out loud and ran.

When he reached his companions, Dray and Malig were huddled together, discussing something. Shikari and her guardian crouched farther back. Caim looked back to the compound as the gate opened. Two men appeared with spears in hand. When they found Egil, they shouted in their harsh language, and the drums ceased. Caim gripped his knife hilts as more people appeared at the gate. Was he willing to risk his life if they harmed Egil? But his conviction was not tested as two burly men took up the litter and carried it inside. Egil was too far away to see the expression on his face. *At least now he's got a chance.*

Caim started down the hillside, and the others hustled to catch up. 'What are we going to do now?' Dray asked.

'We're going to die out here is what,' Malig grumbled. 'A thousand shit-suffering miles from home. We're almost out of victuals, and we don't even know where we're going without Egil—'

'I know,' Caim said with a calmness he hardly felt inside.

'How can you? The sky's as black as a witch's cunny. We got no guide, no map, nothing!'

Caim pointed along the invisible line that was pulling him north. 'That's the way. I can't tell you how far Erebus is, but it's in that direction.'

Malig snorted. 'Yeah? Well, I think we've been wasting our fucking time out here. Now Aemon's gone. Egil's probably dead. When's it going to be enough?'

Caim winced like he'd been punched to the jaw. 'I can't bring Dray's brother back and I can't heal Egil. And I can't promise any of us will survive this. I told you before. If you want to leave, then go.'

'Where are we supposed to go?' Malig said, too loudly. 'We're stuck in the middle of nowhere. You ever think about the trip back home when you were planning this shit, Caim? Or maybe you figured we'd be happy to just follow you anywhere and give no second thought about it?'

They reached the horses, and Caim took up his steed's frayed reins. 'I never claimed to have a grand scheme. All I've got is a cold trail and an itch in my brain that won't go away.'

'You and your fucking quest.' Malig spat on the ground, some of it catching in his beard as he yammered. 'You know what I think? I think you're batshit crazy. How about that? And we're crazy for following you. Your ma's dead and gone, but you can't face that.'

'Mal,' Dray said.

'No! He needs to hear this from somebody, because he sure as shit can't figure it out for himself. We've heard you, Caim. Talking to yourself when you think no one can hear. I've seen the way you look out into the dark like there's answers out there. You're on a death trip and you're dragging us to the grave with you.'

Caim sucked in a deep breath and turned around. Malig stared back with an angry frown. This was the moment. In his younger, wilder days this was when Caim would have drawn and attacked. Kill or be killed. The urge was still there, but he kept both hands at his sides. Malig wasn't saying anything the others weren't thinking. Maybe this was a fool's errand, but he'd come this far. 'I don't have any answers. But I'm going to keep following this feeling until I find out where it ends, or someone ends me. If you're coming along, you need to shut up and start riding.'

Caim mounted up and steered his steed to the north.

CHAPTER NINETEEN

The sun dipped in the west, its fading rays streaking the sky in hues of purple and blue. Josey rolled up the stiff parchment and tucked it into her fur-lined jacket. Hubert's latest letter was filled with ill news. Food shortages were causing protests in the streets of Othir – not violent so far, but it was only a matter of time. He had no evidence tying the Church to the demonstrations. In fact, he didn't mention the Holy Office at all, and that worried her not a little. News from the envoy to Mecantia wasn't good either. Talks to bring the free city back into the Nimean fold had failed. Hubert hadn't said, but Josey suspected Lady Philomena of sabotaging the summit. But she had more immediate worries. One of them was kicking inside her belly.

She placed a hand over her middle. *Easy, little one. This will be a long night for us both.*

The child inside her kicked again, but then quieted down. Josey's other worry was right before her. Sitting astride Lightning, Josey looked down from the hill she had chosen as a vantage point. Below, men moved with purpose, digging and building and hurrying. *This is where we'll make our stand.*

It didn't look like much to her. The field was little more than a half-drained swamp. Here, between tufts of scrub brush and stinkweed, was where her officers had chosen to meet the invaders. They had marched three long days to get here, pushing the soldiers hard, leaving a trail of supply wagons in their wake. The enemy was somewhere to the north of them. It wouldn't be long. Another courier had made it through the chaos in the north. If possible, his message was more disturbing than the previous one, telling of villages burned and civilians put to death. By all accounts, the enemy was moving at great speed, and Uthenorian standards had been seen among the horde, putting to rest the theory that this force came from Eregoth. It made her feel better knowing that Caim's people weren't involved.

Lord General Argentus rode up beside her and dipped his head in a nod. 'Your Majesty, I have finalized the order of battle with the regiment commanders.'

As Argentus outlined the positions to be held by the units of infantry, horse, archers, and reserve companies, it reminded Josey of a chessboard. She imagined the footmen were her pawns, the cavalry her knights, and the archers her praetors. Except this wasn't a game. When the fighting began, real people were going to die.

'Will they attack tonight?' she asked.

'Not likely, but we have plenty of pickets out to forewarn us of an advance. I expect them with the dawn.'

Josey fretted with the reins looped around her hand. 'What about treating with them? A diplomatic envoy to ascertain their intentions.'

The lord general's bushy eyebrows came together over the bridge of his nose. 'Majesty, I believe they made their intentions quite clear when they sacked Durenstile and invaded Nimean territory.'

Josey looked down at a group of men digging trenches in the twilight. Exhaustion showed in their every motion. 'Very good. I place my trust in you.'

'Majesty . . .' Argentus bowed his head. 'If this battle should go awry—'

'That will be all, Lord General.'

With a nod, Argentus rode back down to a cluster of officers in clean blue jackets at the bottom of the hill. Josey tried to look serene and in control, but her stomach was churning, and her heart beat so fiercely she started to perspire under her clothing. She didn't blame Argentus for his lack of confidence. She'd sent missives to every noble and freeholder within a week's march, pleading for men and arms to help in the fight, but none had answered. And part of her didn't want to be here either. She wanted to be north, looking for Caim, and that made her feel horrible. This was where she belonged.

'Looks like something's put a bee in the general's britches, lass.' Hirsch winked as he reached the top of the hill. His eyes were bright, even after the hellish march they'd endured. It was strange how after just a couple months she had come to trust the adept so much. He had an easy manner that calmed her worries.

'Nothing too damaging,' she answered. 'I asked about diplomatic solutions.'

Hirsch's eyebrows rose in an arch. 'I can see how that might get him a bit riled. You having second thoughts?'

'It's not easy to send men into battle, knowing some of them won't survive.'

'I imagine not, but doesn't seem like you've been given much choice in the matter.'

'I suppose they have a plan for you in this?'

'Aye. I'm to remain with you.'

That surprised Josey. She would have thought Argentus and his officers would have devised a better use for the adept. 'You've heard the reports. What do you make of these invaders from Uthenor?'

'Uthenorian mercenaries are notorious, both for their love of war and for their fickle nature. Duke Bregone of Leipterhas employed a company of them when he made his spectacularly unsuccessful bid for the throne of Firenna. Sadly for him, his rival had a deeper purse. The Uthenorians slit his throat and raided his treasury house.'

Josey considered that. If they could find a way to entice the invaders to leave without further bloodshed—

'However,' Hirsch continued, 'these men aren't mercenaries. I spoke with the messenger. The banners he describes belong to clan chieftains, not sellsword companies.'

A chill dripped down Josey's spine. 'So what does that mean? Are they likely to be less ferocious than mercenaries?'

'Just the opposite, lass. These warriors aren't fighting for gold and pillage. The clans of Uthenor have been at each other's throats for centuries. I don't know what's got them stirred up enough to fight together, but they'll be eager for blood.'

Josey stared at the battlefield, lost in her thoughts, as a tall man on horseback rode past, Brian had been sent by his father along with forty militiamen while Lord Therbold returned to his estates, hopefully to gather more troops and material.

Perhaps feeling her eyes on him, Brian looked up and lifted a gloved hand in greeting before he joined Argentus's gathering. *Stop mooning, silly girl. He's just a man. A very tall, handsome man. But still . . .*

As Josey chided herself, her baby gave such a kick that it almost knocked the wind out of her. Hirsch took her lead rein in hand as she bent forward over Lightning's neck. 'Lass? Are you ill?'

Josey pushed herself upright. 'No, I'm okay. It's just . . . the pace. It's been difficult.'

As she breathed through her mouth, deep and slow like Doctor Krav had instructed, a rider appeared on the northern side of the field. His horse left a trail of churned mud as he rode up to Lord General Argentus. The officers circled around him. A few seconds later, Argentus pointed left and right, and men scurried to do his bidding. Josey bit her lip. What was happening? Just as she was about to ride down and find out for herself, Brian started up the hill.

'Is it bad news?' Josey asked as he reined in beside her.

Brian's eyes were shadowed in the failing daylight. 'Several of our scouts have gone missing, but one returned.'

Josey was holding her breath. She knew what that meant. 'The invaders are close.'

'Yes. They'll be here shortly after sunset.'

Josey exhaled through her mouth. The spasm was subsiding. 'I will require a runner here with me. Two, if they can be spared. And I believe Master Hirsch could be more—'

Brian glanced at the adept. A look passed between them. 'Pardon me, Majesty,' Brian said. 'But perhaps you should retire to the camp before the fighting begins.'

Josey fought to keep her voice even. 'Is this Argentus's suggestion? Well, you may inform the lord general that I'll stay with my soldiers until the battle is through. Do you under—?'

She grimaced as another painful shudder racked her body. She placed both hands over her belly and bit her bottom lip to keep from crying out. Panic ran through her. Something was wrong.

Hirsch put a hand on her arm. 'Lass?'

Then she felt herself lifted down from the saddle. Brian's arms were around her. He smelled of leather and sweat. Bright golden motes swam before her eyes, but she saw Hirsch's face above her. Someone called for her physician. The pain was getting worse. Josey focused on her breathing – smooth and deep, in and out – as the world shrunk around her.

Josey held her breath as the listening horn's cold mouth passed over the bulge of her bare stomach, slowly back and forth and then up past her navel to the edge of the gown she held under her breasts. Goose pimples covered her arms and legs despite the heat of the three braziers in the tent. Looking down at her state of undress, she wondered why she wasn't blushing like a maiden. But, of course, it was just Doctor Krav. Still, she was quick to pull down her clothing when he turned around.

'Is everything all right?' she asked. 'With the baby?'

The doctor cleared his throat as he put his instruments away. He wore the same black suit – a coat and trousers with a white shirt, shoes polished to a bright sheen – as the day he had discovered her pregnancy. *How does he keep so clean on the road?* 'Doctor?'

'Yes,' he answered. 'The child appears healthy. A little underweight, but that is normal under such trying circumstances.'

He looked down his long nose at her in a way that made her feel guilty. Josey started working on the ties of her dress.

'But,' he continued, 'Your Majesty needs to slow down for the sake of the life you carry. Too much riding and exercise aren't good for you at this stage. I recommend bed rest for the majority of your day, with brief walks every three to four hours to circulate the blood. And you could do with a richer diet, as well.'

Horns sounded in the distance. Josey's heart thumped hard. Had the fighting begun? 'I will, Doctor, but right now I have a battle to fight, and I can't do that from my bed. Will my baby be all right if . . . ?' She didn't know how to ask it. How far could she push herself and still be safe? It seemed harsh, even cruel, but lives were at stake.

Doctor Krav regarded her for a span of several heartbeats, and then said, 'A little more activity should not be harmful, provided that you are careful and take numerous rests – whenever you can.'

'I will. I promise. Thank you.'

With a nod, the doctor exited her tent. Iola entered before the flap settled. 'Is everything all right, Majesty?'

'Yes, it's fine. Please have Lightning brought around for me.'

The girl bobbed a short curtsy and started to leave, but Josey stopped her. She thought of Doctor Krav's advice. 'Wait. Make that a wagon. And inform Captain Drathan I'll be returning to the battlefield.'

Iola paused at the door. 'Majesty, I couldn't help overhearing—'

Josey hadn't even considered her conversation with the doctor might be overheard. Of course, she should have. This was a military camp, not the palace. And even back in Othir she might have been more careful.

'I didn't mean to,' Iola said. 'But then he – the doctor – said something about the baby's heartbeat and I couldn't help myself. I'm too nosy. I know that, Majesty. If you wish to dismiss me, I will—'

Josey sighed. 'Nonsense. I'm sure my maids back home have been listening to my conversations since the day I moved into the palace.' This time she *did* blush, imagining what Margaret and Amelia might have heard on the night she allowed Caim to seduce her. Or had she seduced him? 'Please, just fetch the wagon and Captain Drathan.'

Josey sat back on the bed cushion. She was considering how she could balance her pregnancy and the coming war when the clatter of heavy wheels rolled up outside. She got up as Iola returned with a heavy coat in hand. Josey shrugged into it, thanking her, and went out. The cold struck her as soon as she passed through the door flap. The sun hid behind a bank of fluffy gray clouds. *Please let it rain. It might slow our enemies and give us more time to prepare.*

The wagon was built to carry freight, and there was no place else to sit except on the high bench seat beside the drover, a white-haired man with a thick mustache and bangs that hung down over his eyes. He also had unusually large ears. Josey allowed a guardsman to assist her into the seat. Once she was settled and her bodyguard in place, the drover got the vehicle under way. The ride was a bumpy nightmare, shaking Josey so hard her teeth chattered. *This is better for the baby than riding?*

By the time they reached the hilltop overlooking the field, Josey was eager to get away from the wooden torture device. She jumped down before her guards could assist. Brushing past their outreached hands, she climbed to the crest of the hill where Brian sat on horseback, alone.

Josey pursed her lips as she approached. She hadn't forgiven his earlier comments. *Of all the people here, I thought he would understand. He loves his subjects as I love them. Heavens, why did he have to ruin it?* She almost tripped as the thought wormed inside her skull. Ruin what? What was developing between them? Josey didn't know. *Or I am too afraid to dwell on it?*

Swallowing her thoughts, and finding them a bitter medicine, Josey walked up beside Brian. What she saw below made her forget him for a moment. The site had been transformed in the short time she was away. Instead of a few scattered pits, an entire trench had been carved into the ground across the southern end of the field, complete with waist-high earthworks and a fence of sharpened stakes. Three rope-driven siege engines stood behind the trench. They were crude compared to the clean lines of the scorpions guarding the walls of the imperial palace, but looked deadly nonetheless. The troops were assembled in columns as their officers went down the lines, making changes as required. It was starting to look like the plan Argentus had described to her. *Perhaps this will turn out better than I feared.*

Captain Drathan and his men fanned out around the hilltop. Brian dismounted when he saw Josey and made a small bow. 'Majesty, I apologize if I spoke poorly before.'

'You were out of line,' she answered, perhaps a bit too sharply. *But he deserves it.*

'Yes, I was. I hope this can make up for my lack of manners.'

He held up a dagger. Silver wire wrapped around its handle,

curling down to a wide guard. The wooden scabbard was almost as long as her forearm.

Is this a joke? 'A knife, Sir Brian?'

'When knights ride in tourney, it is customary to wear the token of their ladies. But I would not presume to ask for your favor. Instead, I give you my token to wear, if you will. For luck.'

He drew the dagger. The fading sunlight caught the blade's milky gray steel. 'This dagger was one of twelve forged at the order of King Guldrien of Aquidon and given to his Knights Brethren before they rode for the last time.'

Josey knew the story of King Guldrien and the Knights Brethren, how the doomed monarch and his loyal companions rode out to meet the might of the fledgling Nimean Empire, and died for their bravery. Afterward, Nimea had absorbed Aquidon and divided it into the provinces of . . .

Aquos and Farridon. Oh, dear gods. In an instant, Josey understood how she had mismanaged her dealings with Brian's father and Count Sarrow. All this time she had been treating them like just another pair of squabbling nobles, forgetting the history of these northern provinces. 'Brian, your father and the count don't care about water rights or boundaries, do they?'

Brian's eyes were splinters of blue steel as he sighed. 'Now that the empire is fraught with turmoil, they both dream of breaking away and restoring the old kingdom of Aquidon. Only they cannot agree which of them should rule. Forgive me, Majesty. Though I do not share my father's dream, I could not bring myself to betray him.'

Josey took the dagger, which was lighter than she anticipated. 'You didn't betray him. He is your lord and father.'

'He is a traitor.'

'I will consider what's to be done with him, but I still have every faith in you.' Josey sheathed the dagger with reverence. 'As for this, I will wear it proudly.'

'Then I will ride to battle with a glad—'

A horn blared, and Josey's throat closed up. Down below, soldiers rushed to their positions along the trench and officers shouted. She followed their pointing fingers across the field. At first she couldn't see anything in the gathering twilight. Then a line of shapes emerged from the dusk. Men and horses, they came by the scores and then the hundreds. Fingers of dread clutched Josey's insides as the invading host grew before her eyes. There had to be several thousand, at least. And she had what? Five hundred if she counted Therbold and Sarrow's militiamen?

'God's breath,' Brian whispered.

'Is there . . . ?' She was afraid to ask. 'Do we have any chance to win?'

She expected a bold statement of valor and bravado. Instead, Brian replied, 'I must get to my unit.'

He leapt to his horse and galloped down the hill. Josey held the dagger to her chest as the horde drew nearer. She tried to imagine what it must be like for her soldiers, standing shoulder to shoulder, watching the inexorable advance of your enemy. Wondering if you were going to live to see tomorrow. Josey wished she could slow down time, or speed it up.

'War is mostly waiting, followed by moments of blind terror.'

She looked over her shoulder as Hirsch slid down from his little mare. 'Is that supposed to be a warning, Master Hirsch? You should know by now that a few words aren't enough to frighten me away.'

The adept harrumphed. 'Indeed I do, lass. Even when those words are true. What's that?'

Josey held up the dagger Brian had given to her. 'It's nothing. Just a memento. For luck.'

The adept looked down over the crest of the hill. The enemy

was closer, and with every step their numbers seemed to swell, like a black tide washing over the field.

'Gods protect us,' she whispered.

Hirsch nodded as he drew his hood down over his eyes. 'Aye, lass. That about sums it up.'

CHAPTER TWENTY

Remnants of a nightmare sifted through Caim's head as he awoke. He had been running across an endless field, with ferocious creatures snapping at his heels. Kit was there, too, running with him. Or maybe it had been Josey.

He started to get up, until a sharp twinge ripped across his lower back. Caim sighed and took it slow. He had no idea what time it was. Without sun or moon to guide him, the hours blurred together. The campfire had burned down to a nest of red cinders. Dray and Malig were both asleep. Caim wanted to kick them awake. He'd told them before he closed his eyes to each take a watch, and wake him for the third spot. Caim looked around for Egil, but then remembered the guide's fate. Was he still alive?

'You sleep uneasily.' Shikari sat with her legs folded. She had been quiet on the trail yesterday, hardly speaking to anyone, not even her guardian. Caim glanced over at Hoek, sprawled out across the hard ground behind her. They didn't act like lovers, but the giant never left her side. 'A victim of restless dreams?'

Caim picked up a stick of firewood and fed it to the flames. 'I could do with a comfortable bed in a warm inn, if that's what you mean.'

'I understand. But it's not the cold that bothers you, is it? What do you plan to do when you reach Erebus?'

Caim had considered that. At night, when he lay down to sleep and the darkness surrounded him, he imagined what he might find in the north and how he could hope to pick up a trail gone cold for almost two decades. 'I won't know till I get there.'

'Your foe from the ruins will likely be there, too. Yes? And perhaps more like him. A great many enemies for three men to face alone.'

'Whatever point you're trying to make, just say it.'

'Only that we could be of assistance.'

'It's probably best if we drop you and your man off at the next spot of civilization.'

She favored him with a smile that showed off her perfect, small, white teeth. 'This far north? You aren't likely to find any civilization. Not until you come to your destination. And I see the hunger in your eyes.'

Caim shifted his weight. This woman had bothered him since the day they'd met. For an escaped slave stranded in the wastes, she was strikingly confident. 'What's that supposed to mean?'

'A power dwells inside you. It is in the way you move, the way you kill, in the violence of your sleep. I have seen it's like before. Some of the *asherjhag* are workers of miracles. When they call to the dark, the dark listens.'

Caim patted his back where his knives rested. 'My only tricks are with these.'

'I think not.' She tilted her head. Her hair gleamed with a rich luster even in the gloam. 'You feel the pull of unseen tides. If you listen hard enough, you will hear their whisper.'

Caim thought of the pulling. It was still there, tugging in the back of his head, so much a part of him now. North, it whispered to him. Always north. 'I don't know what you're talking about.'

'The power.' Shikari indicated the fire between them. 'The priests say it is like this flame. It must be fed or it will starve. You've been feeling ill of late, yes? Weaker?'

Caim gritted his teeth so hard the muscles in his jaws

threatened to pop. The woman's guesses hit too close to home. In his mind he saw himself hunched over her, his mouth pressed to her neck, sipping her blood. . . .

Caim got to his feet. 'Wake your friend. We leave as soon as we've eaten.'

His hands shook as he walked away, so hard he had to clench them into tight fists within his gloves. He wanted to gut someone and watch their life drain into the snow. *Stop it! Forget her. She doesn't know anything about me.* But as he gathered his gear and went to feed the horses, the woman's words followed him.

They broke their fast and got back on the trail. Caim went first, jolts of pain shooting through his lower back with every step of his horse. Without Egil, he wanted to keep an eye on the way ahead, and he wanted to stay clear of Shikari. He also avoided Malig and Dray, who had woken up in bad moods and looking like they hadn't slept much.

Time passed slowly as their pace ate up the miles. As he rode, Caim considered the wastes in all their vastness and imagined leaving the others behind. Not to be bothered by their talk and their suspicious looks. Where in the hells was Kit? Her disappearing act was wearing thin. The next time she turned up he would tell her not to bother. He didn't need her either. He didn't need anyone.

What's wrong with me?

Caim shook himself out of the melancholy. He missed Kit. He *wanted* her back. And the clansmen were his responsibility. As for the others, he wasn't sure yet. With a deep sigh, he let his gaze wander over a rise in the distance, a low hill perhaps. There was another to the east of it, and grim black humps along the horizon that hinted at more beyond. He was tracing a route toward them when he saw the pile of stones.

Malig cursed out loud when they got close enough for the lantern to shine on the altar. It was much like the one they had seen before, a stack of flat rocks set on top of each other, but this fane had been used recently. The trophies stuck on spears around the site weren't moldy skulls, but full heads with flesh still attached, although their eyeballs were gone. At least one had belonged to a woman. Caim would have expected carrion birds nearby, and swarms of flies, but there were none. Then a shadow oozed from an eye socket and down the face of one of the heads. All of a sudden he felt exposed, like there were a thousand invisible eyes watching him.

'A sad but common sight in the wastes,' Shikari said. 'The tribes believe that the corpses of their enemies are pleasing to their gods, and so they display them at shrines like this. These poor souls were likely captured alive, tortured over the course of several days, and then finally beheaded in the culmination of a ritual that includes the consuming of flesh and—'

'Why don't you shut the fuck up!' Dray shouted at her.

Hoek swiveled like a weathervane and stalked in Dray's direction. There was no malice on the big man's face, but his huge hands were closed into fists. Caim reached for his seax knife, but Shikari shouted before he could draw it. 'Halt!'

Hoek stopped, but continued to stare at Dray with a blank gaze. Dray lifted his spear, but Caim spurred his horse between them. 'Dray, go take the lead.'

With a dark look at Hoek, Dray put heels to horseflesh and galloped ahead. Hoek returned to Shikari's side, standing with his arms at his sides like nothing had happened. She, however, glared at Dray's departing back.

Caim turned his mount around. 'Let's go.'

Animals snorted and leather creaked, but the others remained quiet as they filed behind him. Malig complained about wanting a stout drink, a hot meal, and a friendly woman, preferably in that order. Caim empathized, but he didn't think they'd be getting any of those things any time soon.

The land rose before them, in broken ridges and craggy ravines, steadily toward the line of hills hunched against the horizon. As the miles passed, Caim let his chin fall to this chest. He was resting his eyes when a familiar voice tickled his ear.

'Wake up, sleepyhead.'

Caim opened one eye to glance at Kit. She floated beside him, smiling like nothing had happened. For a moment, he considered whether or not that was a good thing. He looked around, but Malig and Dray were riding together a hundred paces ahead, and Shikari and her bodyguard trailed even farther behind. They were as alone as they were likely going to be. 'You have a nice holiday?'

'Actually, I've been taking some time for myself. And I've decided to forgive you.'

He started to argue that she'd left him. He was the one who had been wronged. Then he remembered his words to her on the hill and closed his mouth. 'I'm sorry,' he mumbled.

She drifted closer and planted an electric kiss on his nose. 'I know. You haven't been able to sleep since I left.'

His ire returned. 'How long have you been watching us?'

'Not long.' She alighted on his lap. 'I know how you can make it up to me.'

He wasn't sure he wanted to know, but he asked, 'Yeah? How's that?'

'Turn around.'

He squinted at her. 'Why? What's happened?'

'Nothing yet.' She leaned closer until they were eye to eye. 'But you're about to—'

'Caim!'

He looked past Kit. Dray stood up in his stirrups, peering ahead.

'Don't,' Kit said.

But Caim kicked his heels and rode through her. After a few strides he felt bad and looked back, but all he saw were Hoek and Shikari hiking through the gloom. Kit was gone. Again. Caim gritted his teeth and tried to put her out of his mind.

As he pulled up to the Eregoths, Caim spotted a blanket of tiny lights in the distance, directly in their path. It looked to be a village, or a small town. Caim considered the landscape, and how long it would take them to go around. *But we're down to the last of our rations, and we've got no idea where we are.*

'Well? Malig asked.

'We'll check it out,' Caim replied.

'Is that wise?' Shikari asked as she and her companion caught up to them. 'Perhaps stealth would be the better choice of action.'

'I'm sick of sneaking about.' Dray peeled something off the point of his spear and flung it to the ground. 'I want to see what's ahead.'

'Fucking right,' Malig echoed.

Caim kneed his horse to a canter in the direction of the lights. He was ready, too. Their increased pace, with the wind in his face, quickened his blood and dragged him out of the lethargy. He half expected a legion of Northmen to descend upon them at any moment, but the snowy countryside was quiet. After a couple miles, the outlines of rooftops appeared in the gloom. Rectangular and blocky, they looked like tenements or the government buildings in Othir's forum, but without any of the finer architectural details. The roofs were broad-beamed like longhouses with shallow peaks.

Caim reined up beside a post driven into the earth, capped by a massive bleached skull. By its shape, he guessed it had come from a bear, but the size of it was incredible. In life, the beast must have stood more than twelve feet tall. A true monster.

'Bear tribe,' Dray said.

'Seems so.' Caim curled his fingers into fists inside his gloves. 'We'll get what we need and be gone.'

For once, the Eregoths didn't argue. Shikari listened without comment, her gaze on the hills to the north. That's where he needed to go, but he was worn out from the road. They all were.

Rusty shackles hung from a wooden archway that appeared to mark the town's entry. The chains rattled in the wind as Caim and his crew passed under. The settlement had no burg or outlying structures, not even a palisade. The streets were a morass of mud and slush flanked by tall buildings. They were all built of the same grainy, blue-black stone. The construction was crude, with rough edges and ill-fitting joints. Wooden cages lined some of the streets, with lean faces pressed between the slats. Some were almost empty, others packed so tight their occupants couldn't sit down. Burning torches on tall iron poles shone upon bodies encrusted with grime. Northmen prowled the cages with truncheons in hand.

'Maybe this was a bad idea,' Malig said.

Caim looked for public buildings, but the places they passed had no signs or placards. Besides the slaves and their keepers, there were few people in the street. No merchants or peddlers, no whores lingering in the alleys, no children playing. Caim wondered how Shikari and Hoek would hold up back in the company of their enslavers, but Hoek's expression could have been carved from marble for all the emotion it showed, and Shikari looked merely curious. He supposed there was little chance they would be seen by anyone who knew them.

Then he spotted a group of five men in rust-red robes striding down the street toward them. People gave them a wide berth, slaves and warriors alike. The leader of the group walked with a tall black staff topped with a stuffed white bear's head.

'This way,' Shikari said, going to the mouth of a wide alley.

Caim took another look at the advancing priests, and then waved for his crew to follow the woman. With Hoek by her side, Shikari led them to an intersection, glanced left and right, and then crossed over to another alley. Caim wondered if he should stop her, but the second side street opened into a rough oval. Crooked buildings lined the large, open space. Raucous laughter and shouting emerged from some of the doorways, along with the smells of cooking.

'We should get indoors,' Shikari said, her eyes on Caim. 'These are entertainment houses.'

He picked one establishment at random, and they followed a narrow lane behind the building to a courtyard. There were no stables, but twenty-odd horses were tied to posts driven into the ground. A lamp burned over a back door.

Caim let out a long breath as he dismounted. The muscles in his lower back were bunched up tight. As he stretched, Dray came over. Aemon's spear was in his hand. *He carries the damned thing around like a holy relic.* Caim took stock of the Eregoth, but apart from deep rings around his eyes and the tightness of his mouth, Dray didn't look much worse for wear.

'What are your plans?' Dray asked.

I wish I knew. 'Right now, I just want something warm in my stomach. Then we can talk about plans.'

Malig pushed past them on his way to the rear of the building, where a wide door stood open. Caim checked out the outer wall as he went inside. He'd first taken the material for soapstone because of its grainy black composition, but it felt denser than that. Granite maybe, but granite was difficult to quarry. If every building was made from the same stuff, the amount of labor that must have been required was staggering.

They entered through a mudroom with cloaks hanging from pegs. Inside the establishment, a dozen smoky lamps illuminated a huge room filled with drinking, gorging, shouting Northmen. Most of the shouting was directed at an earthen pit in the center of the floor where two men circled each other. The shouts lifted higher each time steel clashed. Caim maneuvered through the crowd, drawing looks from the other patrons, to a small table set against a side wall. While the others tried to find a wench or serving man, Caim observed the crowd. There were a few outlanders sprinkled among the

Northmen. Iron shackles hung from many belts in the establishment, along with an overabundance of weapons.

Though he couldn't see through the press, Caim guessed by the sudden rise in noise that the combat in the pit had ended. Cups were hoisted and knocked back as the Northmen drummed on their tables for more. Serving girls, some just children, in high-necked smocks and aprons filtered through the crowd carrying fistfuls of foaming tankards.

Caim didn't look at Shikari as she sat down next to him. He hadn't forgotten their strange conversation over breakfast, nor the fervent look in her eyes. The woman saw too damned much.

Malig and Dray reappeared with large mugs, but only for themselves.

'Thank the gods they have beer here!' Malig said as he took a long swallow. When Caim raised an eyebrow, he shrugged. 'The wench said she'd send over some more.'

'And food, I hope,' Caim said.

Malig set down his cup, foam dripping from his beard. 'So what are we going to do here, Caim? I mean, we don't exactly fit in.'

'On the contrary, I think we look the part down to our toenails.'

'What part?'

Caim ran a hand over his whiskered chin. He hadn't shaved in over a sennight. His clothes were worn and travel-stained. 'Slave-catchers, down on our luck.'

Dray raised one black eyebrow. 'I hope you're joking. We don't know the first thing about—'

'Slavka!'

Two northern women in brown leathers pushed through the crowd, each hoisting a foaming stein. Caim started to take them for barmaids until he saw the longaxe hanging from one's belt, and the other woman wore a pair of shortswords and at least five knives that he could see. Both had long hair that hung down in braids past their shoulders, one blonde and the other brunette. They might have been halfway fetching if not for the mannish garb, and the rune letters the brunette had tattooed around her left eye in blue ink.

The blonde axe-woman looked around the table and said something. Caim was about to shake his head to show he didn't understand when Shikari rattled off a phrase in northern.

The brunette made a deep noise that might have been a laugh. 'Eregoth? You far way from home.'

'We are,' Caim answered. 'Can we help you?'

'Mayhap,' the blonde answered, and winked at the other woman. 'You just arrive in Braelsalr?'

'Maybe. What of it?'

The blonde woman elbowed her comrade. 'Have you any to sell? We pay good.' She reached into her jerkin and shook something that made a metallic jingle.

'No,' Caim replied. 'They all died on the journey. We're just staying a few days to restock before we go out again.'

The Northwoman clucked her tongue. 'Poor luck. The next time you come in, you ask for Yersa and Grunhild. We pay you top coin, ya?'

Malig slammed his cup down on the table. 'What if we want more than your coin? What if we want a gander at what's inside those tight pants?'

Not now. Caim had been afraid one of them might do something foolhardy. The blonde Northwoman laughed and said something to her friend, but the brunette didn't so much as smile. 'Mayhap we cut off your little spear and make you eat.'

Her fingers tapped the pommel of one of her swords as she and her friend sauntered away. Caim leaned across the table, fighting the impulse to grab Malig by his face. 'What the fuck is your problem? This isn't the time.'

Malig belched and turned over his empty cup. 'I'm fine.'

'He's fine,' Dray echoed.

Caim rapped the tabletop with his forefinger. 'I have to go out for a look around, and I need to know that you can handle—'

'I said I'm fine. Go do what you have to do.'

The owner of the establishment finally arrived with two young girls who delivered beer and meat stew – Caim didn't inquire about its provenance – served in bread trenchers. Caim remembered then that he'd given the last of his money to Egil, but Dray had some coin. The owner jabbered at them cheerfully in his language, and Shikari replied. They carried on a short conversation, at the end of which the owner nodded several times and left.

'What was that about?' Caim asked as they ate. The stew was piping hot and so good he wanted to cry.

'I took it upon myself to procure a place to stay.' Shikari pushed her plate away, and Malig snatched it for himself. 'He only had one room open, but promised it was large enough for all of us.'

After they had finished, and Malig polished off a third cup of beer, they followed a serving girl with a lantern out the back door and across the courtyard to a smaller building. The inside was divided into a central common area and two private rooms. She led them to their door and handed over the lantern. When Malig asked her fee for staying the night, the girl left without giving any indication she'd understood his question.

Caim dropped his pack in a corner. The owner hadn't been lying. The room was large enough to sleep a dozen. Rope hammocks hung from wooden pegs on the walls. They looked inviting, but he was too anxious to sleep. While Dray kicked off his boots, Malig tried to maneuver himself into a hammock. Shikari picked a spot on the floor between two hanging beds and sat cross-legged, eyes closed, hands resting on her thighs. Hoek rested his bulk on an adjacent sling.

Malig produced a bottle from somewhere, and the astringent smell of spirits filled the room. 'You got a plan yet?'

Caim pulled up his hood. 'I'll be back soon. Don't go wandering off.'

'Why? You going to skip town without us?'

Caim left without answering. The courtyard was empty. Checking to make sure his knives were loose in their sheaths, he started off down the side street. He avoided the lights shining from windows. With this many Northmen packed together – the town was large enough to hold a thousand or more with ease – he might have expected fighting and carousing to be commonplace. He passed a few drunks wandering the streets, but no soldiers or constables. The town had an air of lawlessness, and yet despite that it was as quiet as the grave. He found himself treading lighter, as if afraid to disturb the stillness, as he worked his way around to the north end.

The tugging in his head was stronger again. He wanted to bash his forehead against the side of a building. *Kit, this would be the perfect time to come back.* But she didn't appear, and that compounded his irritation.

Beyond the buildings, Caim reentered the snowy tundra of the wastes. Distant lights twinkled to the northeast. Another town, perhaps, but smaller. He looked to the west and thought he could make out another settlement in that direction, but the tugging pulled him due north toward the hills outside of town. He followed.

Caim was so intent on his destination he almost stumbled into the path of a tragic procession. The crack of a whip made him stop as a double line of slaves approached. Backs bent, legs straining, they pulled a massive block of glossy black stone behind them. Caim hunkered down to watch. The slaves were a scrawny, unhealthy-looking bunch. Mostly men, but a few women as well, clad in dirty rags. While one team pulled, a second group of slaves kept the block moving on a series of log rollers, taking them from behind once the stone passed over and rushing them to the front to go under the block again. Northmen in long cloaks and tall helms coerced them with kicks and buffets.

Caim slipped away. The terrain became rougher underfoot as the foothills rose to chalky, gray cliffs littered with snow and scree. When the slope became too steep, he picked his way around until he found a chimney in the cliffs. There were enough cracks in the bedrock he could almost climb it like a ladder. A grand sight was revealed to him at the summit.

Massive black walls rose from the plateau atop the cliffs. Round towers more than a hundred feet tall studded the ramparts. From where he had climbed up, Caim saw the mammoth gatehouse, by itself as large as the palace in Othir. Beyond the walls rose the tops of Cyclopean towers. Not round, but not completely square either, they were constructed with sharp vertices and bowed lines unlike anything in the south. Caim thought back to the slaves he had seen below and the huge block they'd been dragging. He imagined other camps strung around the citadel, all providing slaves and material.

This had to be Erebus. He'd found it at long last. Some part of him had despaired of ever finding it, fearing it was a lie, one last torment inflicted by his aunt before her demise. But it was real.

A monstrous pyramid dominated the skyline, and a hollow feeling gnawed at Caim's insides as he recalled the vision he'd seen in Sybelle's sanctum.

He hovered before an enormous construction perched on the desolate plain. Its angular black walls were riddled with silver veins and pockets of polished crystal. Gargantuan towers rose like titanic fingers, topped with dagger-sharp spires.

Was his mother inside, a captive for all these years? Or was she long dead? He gazed up to the pointed apex.

Now what?

That was the question. He didn't have a clue what to do next. Caim started walking parallel to the walls as he considered how to gain entry. The ramparts looked thick enough to shrug off any siege weapon he'd ever seen, but there were flaws in any design.

Caim halted as a sudden pressure constricted inside his chest. He dropped to one knee and reached for his knives. Distant sounds reached his ears from the west, where a cortege of people climbed a stone road leading from the cliffs to the citadel gates. Eight men carried a palanquin covered by gauzy curtains, and a coffle of slaves trailed behind. When they neared the gatehouse, a horn blew from the high walls, and a troop of soldiers in black plate armor filed out.

Caim was about to move closer when the litter stopped. The curtains covering its interior opened, and a woman's face appeared. He took her for a shadow woman by her lustrous, dusky skin and deep black hair. She was slimmer than Sybelle had been, with sharper features and thin, arched eyebrows. When she gazed in his direction, Caim ground his teeth in frustration, knowing on some level that she had sensed his presence, just as he'd sensed her. He ducked down to create a lower profile and concentrated on hiding from her extramundane perception, pushing back against the pressure in his chest. It was an uncomfortable sensation, similar to scrubbing his skin with a stiff wire brush from the inside, but after several slow, deep breaths the constriction eased.

On the road, the woman looked about for another minute, and then let the curtain fall shut. The soldiers formed up and escorted the palanquin inside the citadel. The gates of the barbican closed behind the last slave in line, sealing the fortress.

Caim sighed through his teeth, weighing his next move. Continue on alone and cast the dice, or retreat and regroup. The stars were out, red specks scattered across the black sky like fiery embers stirred by a strong breeze. He got to his feet and headed back to the cliffs.

As he reached the top of the chimney and prepared to lever himself over the edge, Caim noticed something that made him stop in his tracks. The tugging in his head, which he had followed for more than three months and several hundred leagues, was gone.

CHAPTER TWENTY-ONE

Josey ducked under a low-hanging branch, its pallid twigs curled like claws in the dark. She was bone-tired, but every time her eyes closed she saw them again – the hacking swords and axes, the maimed soldiers writhing on the ground, the cacophony of screams that filled the air and went on and on like it would never end.

'Majesty,' Brian said in her ear. 'Are you all right?'

She nodded and tried not to think about his strong arm around her middle or the places her backside touched against as she rode before him in the same saddle. But those thoughts were comforting compared to the horrors that otherwise haunted her. She had always imagined two armies made a titanic crash when they met, but from her vantage on the hill she had heard only muted shouts and tinny clangs, the thwacks of the siege engines as they released their fury. The invaders had weathered the flights of arrows and missiles to pour over the earthworks like an army of ants, filling the trenches with the bodies of friend and foe alike. Josey thought it was going to end right then and there, but Argentus sent his reserves straight into the boiling heart of the fight, and the auxiliaries held the center.

But then a fiery explosion rocked the battlefield. Soldiers were hurtled into the air like dolls, their mutilated arms and legs flailing. Oily smoke wafted from the glowing crater where a platoon of her men had been standing a moment before. Josey looked to Hirsch, but the adept had his eyes pinched shut while he mumbled under his breath. She couldn't understand a word of it. She expected balls of fire from him in response, or lightning from the sky, not foreign mantras. Another explosion decimated a squadron of archers, and Josey searched for the source. Then she saw them advancing through enemy ranks, a company of horsemen in gleaming black armor. They surrounded a mighty figure of a man who could only be the enemy commander. He was clad from neck to heels in crimson plate and wore no helmet on his shaved pate. A bannerman rode behind him holding a standard – a black fist clutching a bolt of lightning on a bloodred field. The warlord lifted his arm, and yet another explosion tore through her troops.

Finally, Hirsch spoke. The adept looked exhausted, though he hadn't moved, but he yelled above the mayhem, 'Go, lass! We'll hold as long as we can!'

Josey shook her head, determined to remain to the end. Then a rider plunged through the cordon of her bodyguards. Splashed in grime and gore, Brian thrust his bloody sword back into its scabbard as he reached down for her. 'Majesty, we must flee!'

She hesitated, but then she thought of the life growing inside her and took Brian's hand. He swung her up before him, and they galloped down the back of the hill. Her last view at the battle had been of Captain Drathan trading swordstrokes with an Uthenorian warrior while Hirsch looked to the heavens.

Settling back into Brian's embrace, Josey blinked away the tears forming in her eyes. *I have to be strong.*

She wasn't exactly sure what direction they were going, and part of her didn't care. She was content to let him take control, just for a little while. Brian had found a forest near the battlefield, reasoning that the trees would hide their passage. From time to time she looked back at him as they rode. Brian looked older than before, his hair stiff with dried sweat and mud. Dirt encircled his eyes and ran across the bridge of his nose. Yet, even grimy and sweaty he was magnificent. *Stop staring!*

Josey forced herself to look straight ahead. 'Are we being pursued, Sir Brian?'

'Most likely, Majesty.'

'Were you hurt in the fighting?'

He lifted his left arm. Some blood had leaked through the mail sleeve. 'I'll be all right.'

That sounded just like Caim. Why couldn't men just admit when they were hurt? A little voice whispered in the back of her head. *They do it for us. Just like you pretend to be strong for your people even when you feel like crying.*

'Do you believe your father will have had any luck gathering more forces?' she asked.

'I don't hold much hope for it, Majesty. Even if my father sent out messengers as soon as he reached home, the nearest holdfast is three days away. I've been thinking on this.'

'And?'

'Perhaps it would be wiser to gather the realm's remaining forces in the south, ahead of the invaders. The northern provinces, I fear, are lost.'

Josey bit back on a sigh. She had been thinking the same thing, but had been afraid to tell Brian that she must abandon his home to the enemy. *But I swear we will take back every inch of ground.*

'Do you think any of our soldiers escaped?' she asked.

'Perhaps. The trumpets were calling retreat as we rode away, and the enemy didn't have much cavalry to give pursuit. If the gods are gracious, some on our side might have survived.'

Josey grabbed for the reins. 'We should go back. We could rally the—'

'Majesty.' Brian gently gathered the reins back from her. 'We cannot risk it. If you were captured, the war would be over.'

Josey huffed, but she knew he was right. They rode in silence for some time through the dark wood. Her mind wandered, wondering about her men, about Hirsch and Captain Drathan. About Caim . . . *He's fine. He left you, remember?*

Brian tugged their mount to a halt beside a shallow creek wending through the trees. A shelf of rock formed a small waterfall. Josey climbed down from the horse and stood, feeling a little useless, as Brian stripped the saddle and blanket from his steed, took off the bridle, and let the animal graze on the wild grass. While he inspected its hooves, she asked, 'What can I do?'

'Do you know how to hunt? I could go for a juicy venison steak right now, or maybe some roasted boar.'

Josey bit her lip as he teased her. 'No. But I can cook.'

It was a little lie, but she figured she had observed enough cooks in her lifetime to concoct something edible.

'No need for that.'

Brian opened the saddle bags he'd dropped on the ground and pulled out a wrapped package. Inside were long strips of jerky, the sort that soldiers ate on the march. He gave her one, and they sat down beside the stream.

'Sorry, Majesty,' he said. 'But we can't risk a fire.'

Josey studied the jerky. It was stiff and leathery. Then her stomach overruled her brain, and she took a bite. It was salty and took a bit of chewing to eat, but she finished it and made Brian share another one. Then she dipped her hands into the creek and drank the cold water. It was divine. When she was sated, Josey folded her legs and felt a host of burgeoning aches in her thighs and calves. 'So what do we do now?'

Brian leaned back from the water with dripping hands and face. He looked like a different man clean of the grime, his hair wet and pushed back . . .

'We'll rest and get an early start,' he said. 'If we keep moving southeast out of the invaders' path, we should avoid their scouts. Then, whatever you command.'

Josey liked that he deferred to her authority, but he wasn't passive like some of the men at her court who primped and simpered like exotic birds. 'What would you do?'

He sat cross-legged and took out his sword, and then began to run a small, flat stone across its edges. His eyes were dark in the night. 'I would ride to Othir.'

Part of her agreed with him, wanting to retreat behind the capital's strong walls, but she shook her head. 'It's too far. I won't surrender the entirety of the realm to these northerners. They would kill thousands.'

'Aye, but you would live to fight again. These Uthenorians may decide to go home after they've had their fill of plunder.'

'Master Hirsch didn't believe so. He said these men were different from the mercenaries of the north, that they were fighting for something other than gold.'

'Perhaps.'

He lapsed into silence for a few moments, and Josey leaned back on her elbows. A thousand things whirled about in her mind. How many soldiers had escaped the battle alive? Where was Hirsch? What were the invaders doing now? Would they wait for their wounded to recover, or keep marching? Was it going to rain tomorrow?

Brian cleared his throat. 'Majesty, I've been searching for a way to talk to you.'

'You are talking to me, Sir Brian.' She smiled, allowing herself to relax, just a little. A tickle formed in her belly and floated up into her chest, warming her despite the chill.

'Yes, but this is difficult. See, when I first saw you, I only saw the empress. But since then I've gotten to know you better. I don't know how courting is done in the south. And we haven't known each other long enough to . . .' He rapped his knuckles hard against a thigh plate. 'Light and Dark! I'm no good at this!'

Josey wrapped her arms around her knees. 'I think I know what you're trying to say, but first you should know something.' *Am I really going to tell him? Oh, heavens!* 'There has been someone else.'

He lowered his gaze and nodded several times. 'Of course. I should have—'

'But he's gone.'

Josey swallowed as Brian moved closer. A cold sweat broke out across her forehead. She lifted a hand to her brow to hide it, and almost hit Brian in the nose as he leaned forward, mouth opening. *He's going to kiss me! Is this what I want? Yes, I think so, but what about Caim and the baby?*

Josey was torn, unsure what to do. Whether to let it happen, regardless of the aftermath, or put a stop to it. She started to close her eyes, but Brian jumped to his feet in a rustle of steel scales. 'I'm sorry, Majesty. I did not mean to . . . I'm only a knight from a minor house.'

'That doesn't matter to me!' Josey blurted. Then, quieter, 'It doesn't. But there is something else you should know.'

She stood up and touched her stomach. Her heart was pounding in her throat. *What are you doing, Josey? You're going to scare him away. Maybe, but he should know the truth before he says anything else.*

Before she could speak, Josey heard a sound from the trees, like something moving through the brush. A deer perhaps. Brian looked past her, and then lifted his sword. Josey spun around as a dozen men in rustic garb emerged from the woods. They came from every direction, aiming spears and swords and arrows. Brian tried to intervene his body between her and the ambushers, but there were too many of them. Steel rang out as he batted aside a sword pointed in her direction.

'Majesty,' Brian whispered. 'Run when I attack.'

'No!' she hissed at him. There were too many for him. 'Don't be crazy.'

'Just run and don't look back.'

Josey grabbed Brian's shoulder with both hands, trying to stop him from launching a suicidal act in her honor. They got entangled, and somehow Brian ended up with one arm around her waist and the other holding his sword up out of her reach.

'Throw down your blade!'

One of the ambushers had stepped out front. He was young, maybe a year or two older than her. Like the others, he wore simple clothing, a shaggy cloak over a buckskin shirt and breeches. He had a short sword with a wide, curved blade, which he held down by his side.

'Do it,' Josey said, and extricated herself from her protector. She was tired. Tired of running, tired of fighting, tired of always being afraid. Though it stung to admit defeat, she wasn't willing to throw away her life, or Brian's, on a final act of bravado. 'Put down your weapon, sir.'

Brian frowned at her, but dropped his sword. However, when one of their assailants bent down to take the weapon, Brian slammed his knee upward, catching the man flush in the face and catapulting him back. Like a crack in a dam, the rest of the ambushers rushed in, and Brian vanished under a mob of punching fists and jabbing spear-butts. Josey cried for them to stop and pounded her fists on their backs, but the men ignored her. Too late she remembered Brian's dagger sheathed at her waist. When she reached for the handle, a firm hand closed around her wrist.

'That wouldn't be wise, milady.'

It was the youth who had called for them to disarm in the first place. He watched while his men pinioned Brian to the ground and bound him, but he didn't take the dagger from her. *Because I'm no threat, right? Just keep thinking that, little boy.*

Josey studied him, looking for a badge or device, but he wore nothing to show his allegiance.

'Who are you?' he asked.

Josey considered lying to pass herself off as some lesser

noble's daughter. Brian's sister, perhaps. With luck, they might both be ransomed. But remembering those who had so recently fallen, she couldn't dishonor them with a deception. 'I am Josephine, Empress of Nimea. And I would have the name of my captor.'

Quick glances passed between the ambushers. The young swordsman looked from her to Brian and back. 'Tell us your true name.'

Josey lifted her chin and straightened up to her full height. 'Josephine Frenig Corrinada, the first of my name, Empress of Nimea, Protector of Othir, Lady of Highavon. Now I ask you again, sir, for *your* name.'

The youth squinted. A faint crop of whiskers covered his chin. Dirt encrusted his neck and matted his long hair. His clothes looked like they had been slept in for days, if not weeks. His entire company, truth be told, was ragged, for all their bluster. He cleared his throat.

'I am Lord Keegan, high captain of the Free Clans of Eregoth.'

Josey rode with her head down in the dark, hands clasping the saddle horn. A grizzled woodsman with a bristly red beard held the reins of her steed. Brian strode beside her with his hands tied before him and a loop of rope around his neck. They had been traveling for two to three candle-marks, she guessed, deeper and deeper into a wood that proved more extensive than she first imagined. With every passing mile Josey became more and more confused. They should have met up with other enemy units by now, or even the main body. She found it hard to believe that the invaders could have outpaced them so swiftly, not with so many men on foot with all the wagons and such they would require to sustain their march. But if they weren't going to meet the warlord, then where?

The young leader, Keegan, walked somewhere at the head of the company. *Lord* Keegan, he had called himself, but Josey seriously doubted his claim to nobility. She considered calling for him so she could demand some answers, but before she could muster the will, lights appeared between the trees ahead. She smelled woodsmoke and cooking as the forest path opened into a wide clearing where a camp was laid out on the grass. She counted six fire pits and a dozen or so canopies lashed to tree trunks to make crude tents.

As the woodsmen filed into the campsite, Keegan approached her. Josey opened her mouth, but hesitated as he drew a long knife from his belt and stopped in front of Brian.

'I'm told southern knights value their honor above their lives,' the youth said. With a quick slash, he cut the rope binding Brian's hands. 'If you try to escape, well put that notion to the test.'

While Brian massaged his wrists, Keegan turned to Josey. 'Milady, we don't have much to offer, but there's hot food if you will please join me.'

With a look to Brian – who thankfully held his tongue – Josey dismounted. A familiar voice rang out through the trees.

'Majesty!'

Josey was almost bowled over as Iola ran up and embraced her in a fierce hug. Tears burst in the corners of Josey's eyes as the emotions she'd been holding in broke free. They hugged each other and sobbed for several minutes before Iola peeled herself away. Rubbing her wet cheeks with both hands, the girl made a formal curtsy. 'Majesty, we didn't think . . . I mean, we feared the . . . Oh! We're so happy to see you, Majesty!'

'We?'

Josey looked past Iola to see a group of people sitting on the ground. Her tears threatened to flow again when Captain Drathan stood up stiffly and made a firm salute. Behind him were Lieutenant Butus, with a fresh bandage around his neck, and Sergeant Trenor and so many other faces she'd thought she would never see again. Forgetting about her captors, she went over to them. There were at least two score of her people here. Doctor Krav was working on a wounded soldier by the light of a lantern.

'How is this possible?' Josey asked. 'How did you all survive?'

'We ran,' Iola said. 'When runners returned to the camp with news that the battle was going badly, we packed up the wounded in carts and started away.'

'It was Iola, Majesty.' Captain Drathan looked odd without his weapons. His left arm was held in a sling, and he had a few other scrapes, but otherwise he appeared hale and whole. 'She organized the retreat. Without her, many more would have perished.'

Iola blushed at his words, and Josey had to fight back a laugh born of relief. But her gaiety ended when she looked to the woodsmen roaming around the camp.

'They're not sure what to do with us,' a gruff voice said.

Josey turned and hugged its owner. 'Master Hirsch! I thought I'd lost you, too!'

The adept disengaged himself as politely as possible, hissing softly as he peeled away from her. Through several rents in his shabby coat she saw white dressings, spotted with blood in a few places. 'Oh, Hirsch! I'm sorry. Are you all right?'

'I'll live. At least a little longer.'

'Hirsch, what happened? Those explosions—'

'Aye, lass. Sorcery. A little surprise we weren't expecting.'

Josey's pulse thumped in her ears as she thought back to her experiences with Caim and his strange abilities. She lowered her voice. 'Hardly just a little surprise, Master Hirsch. The invaders destroyed my army, killed hundreds of our soldiers, and eradicated the only thing standing between them and Nimea's heartlands. As catastrophes go, I'd say this was a major one.'

A shadow passed over the adept's face as he bent down to the fire. 'The enemy commander was very strong in the Art.'

Josey knelt beside him. The heat felt wondrous on her hands and face. 'Stronger than you?'

'It's difficult to say. His sorcery had no structure, no internal logic that I could fathom.'

'But you can defeat him, right?'

'I don't know, lass. Perhaps I could devise a way, with time.'

Something we don't have.

Josey breathed into her hands as she looked around the camp. Woodsmen stood and sat wrapped in fur cloaks, looking cold and a little malnourished, and nothing like the fearsome troops that had routed her army.

Captain Drathan and Brian came over to the fire. 'Majesty,' Brian whispered. 'We have a plan. If we can get you onto my horse, your men and I will handle the guards and—'

'No,' she cut him off. 'No one else is going to risk their life for me.'

'Majesty!' Captain Drathan's mouth hung open. 'Your safety is our only priority. These men are dangerous.'

'These are the Eregoths my father feared,' Brian said. 'Savages more practiced at rape and pillage than warfare. There's no telling what they are capable of.'

Josey shook her head. 'I said no. Now swear to me you won't do anything without my permission.'

Captain Drathan frowned, but he jerked his chin up and down in a firm nod. Brian just looked at her. Josey stared back. 'Swear it, or leave my service now.'

'I swear,' Brian said, his lips drawn back in a thin line.

A guardsman hissed, and Josey stood up as Keegan approached with a few of his men. 'My lady,' the young man said. 'Will you come with me?'

Captain Drathan started to intercede, with Brian right behind him, but Josey held out a hand. 'No. It's all right.'

She followed the enemy leader away from the fire. A tall

man in rawhide pants and vest brought them steaming cups. Josey accepted without asking what it was. The smell rising from the steam was horrible, but she didn't care. Just wrapping her fingers around the hot cup was a blessing.

Keegan watched her while he took a sip. His nose was a trifle too thin and pointed at the end. The bristles of new beard growth hid a soft chin, lending him the look of a young wolf. The pink half-moon scar carved into his left cheek was recent. 'It's mulled mead.'

Josey nodded and took a sip. The drink was actually quite good with a strong taste of honey, and it warmed her insides.

'Your war leader made a mistake,' he said. 'Offering battle like that. You didn't have the numbers.'

'How astute.' Josey allowed herself to glare, just a little. 'You named yourself high captain of Eregoth, but the last I heard that land was ruled by a duke. Please don't tell me I've been captured by some upstart tribal chieftain's son with dreams of grandeur.'

The youth drained his cup and set it aside. 'Duke Erric is dead. Eregoth is free once more, no longer in thrall to the Eviskines, nor to her Nimean overlords of old.'

'Is that why you've invaded my country? To wreak vengeance on your old masters?'

Now it was his turn to frown. 'We're no invaders. We've come for the Thunder Lord.'

'Who?'

'The one who bears this symbol.' He dug into his jacket and pulled out a scrap of black cloth. A fist holding a lightning bolt was stitched into the fabric. 'He's a northern warlord named Talus. Some say he's a sorcerer, and I believe it, too, after what I've seen.'

Josey recalled the battle, the explosions tearing out huge chunks of the earth, littering the field with corpses and flying stones. 'What are you trying to tell me? That you've come all this way, trespassing on my country, to attack the northerners that just crushed my army with . . .' She gestured around the clearing. The Eregoths numbered fifty at most. 'Just these few?'

Keegan put away the bit of fabric. 'There's more of us around. We keep separated to make our camps harder to find.'

Josey fought the impulse to nod. It was smart thinking. An army, while stronger on the field, wasn't as nimble as a small raiding party like this. 'Why? Why risk your lives to help us?'

'We're not here to help you. We've come to avenge our dead. The Thunder Lord attacked our homes and killed our people.' He snapped his fingers. 'With his army and his magic, he took Liovard in a single night.'

Keegan pointed to the men around the camp. 'These, and a few patrols, are all that remain of my warriors. We escaped the slaughter and hid to lick our wounds. But we are good at lying low. When the Uthenorians left the city, we followed. All these leagues south we've been nipping at their heels. Striking at their flanks. Burning their supply wagons. We cannot meet the Thunder Lord in open battle, as you tried to do, but every time he swats at us, we melt away to come at him another way.'

Josey considered that. If she had more men and enough horses, they could do the same thing, but on a larger scale. Tears threatened to form as she thought of all the people who had died. *I should have known better. I should have overruled Argentus. Those men could still be alive today.*

He interrupted her thoughts. 'You are truly the Empress?'

Josey wiped her eyes with the back of her hand. 'Yes. For now, at least. I thought you were part of the invading army. Scouts, maybe. I don't know. But it doesn't matter. When this warlord – Talus – reaches Othir, it will be too late.'

Keegan's brow furrowed into thin creases. 'A man once told me I could trust the Empress of Nimea. He said she had a good heart.'

Josey wanted to laugh to dispel the pain in her chest. 'I'm sorry. I don't think I know anyone from Eregoth.'

'He wasn't from Eregoth. I mean, he was, but he hadn't lived there in a long time. But he came back to – well, I shouldn't be telling his business. But he was a good man despite his rather ill look—'

Hope fluttered in Josey's stomach as she listened to the youth's rambling explanation. She didn't dare to believe it, but perhaps. Just perhaps. 'What was his name?'

'Caim Du'Vartha.'

Josey stared for several breaths, unable to believe it.

'You know of him, my lady?'

She laughed and threw the contents of her cup into the fire. The liquid hissed and made a cloud of steam. She looked over to Drathan and Brian, who watched her with startled expressions. 'Caim's alive!' she shouted.

Josey moved around the fire pit and took Keegan's hand. 'He is, isn't he? Alive?'

His eyes had gone as wide as double-weight golden royals. 'Yes. Well, he was when I last saw. He left us after the battle. The first battle, that is.' He paused, and his voice thickened. 'He saved us, my lady. He saved us all.'

Josey wanted to sing. 'He's good at that. Please, tell me everything. Every detail!'

While the night fled and the sun rose from behind the trees, Josey listened to the tale of Caim's involvement in Eregoth's war of independence. The whole time, she wanted to pinch herself. Caim was alive.

'Where is he now?' she asked when Keegan had finished telling about the sacking of the duke's keep in Liovard.

'He went north the day after we won our freedom. Following some fool quest.' Keegan lifted his open hands. 'He could have been duke. He could have called himself a king for all we cared. But he left, and took three of my best warriors with him. He could be all the way into the northern wastes by now.'

Still chasing after his mother's ghost. Caim, if you get yourself killed before I can reach you, I'll . . . I'll . . . She laughed to herself. He was safe. She knew it in her heart. *Oh, gods. Or Holy Prophet. Whoever rules the heavens, I thank you for this.*

She tried to stifle her elation. What mattered now was the welfare of her people. And she had the inkling of an idea. 'Keegan, what if the invaders reach Othir?'

'It's a big city?'

'Yes. It's the largest city in Nimea, rivaling Taralon, Firenna, or even the city-states of Altaia. It has two sets of walls and several fortresses inside them.'

His eyes narrowed into slits as he stared into the fire. 'That will make things . . . difficult. It would be hard to reach the Thunder Lord if he were to take such a well-defended position. But we will still have our revenge.'

'What if there was a way to attack him now? With more force than you've been able to bring to bear?'

'You mean to join forces.'

Josey smiled. He wasn't as backward as he looked. She could see why Caim had left him in charge. 'Exactly. More of my soldiers may have survived the battle, and reinforcements are being assembled as we speak. If we combined our strength, we could give this Thunder Lord a real war.'

He shook his head. 'We are done with Nimean rulers and Nimean troubles. We will do this our way. Alone.'

'Keegan, listen to me. I understand how you and your people must feel—'

'No, my lady. I don't think you do. We have been slaves to your empire for four generations. We fought for our freedom, and won it, only to see it trampled by one of our own. Now that we are free again – truly free – we'll never go back to that life. We'd rather die to the last man.'

Josey stood up. All eyes in the camp turned to her. She took a breath and steadied her nerves, fully aware that the future of her nation might well depend on what she did here. 'I hereby pledge, as empress and sole ruler of Nimea, that if you and your warriors assist us in this time of need, henceforth Eregoth shall be a free and independent nation, subject to her own laws, creator of her own destiny, for now and all time. I so swear by my crown, and by all the emperors who have ruled before me.'

Keegan opened his mouth, and then closed it. Then he stood up with her. 'My father once told me only a fool turns down a piece of bread when he's starving. We'll fight with you, my lady. And we'll hold you to your end of the bargain when it's done.'

He ordered her soldiers freed and their weapons returned, and then he left to look to his own men. Josey stood by the fire, wrapped in her thoughts. *I hope I did the right thing. It felt right, but I wish Hubert were here.*

'That was smartly done, lass,' Hirsch said. 'Now, what are you planning to do with your new allies?'

'I'm going to use them to bleed the enemy, Master Hirsch. I'm going to bleed the invaders every step of the way until they leave our lands or fall dead on Othir's doorstep.'

She gazed over at Brian where he stood with a group of her bodyguards. *But what am I going to do with you, sir?*

CHAPTER TWENTY-TWO

The colorless void transformed into black granite ceiling and walls as Balaam emerged from the portal. Stale odors met him in the great room. A fire crackled in the stone hearth, but a chill lingered in the air.

He heard the pad of the servant girl's bare feet in the hall. She paused at the doorway, staring at him with her large, pale eyes. 'Send for your mistress,' he said.

Balaam collapsed into his chair facing the fireplace while he waited. His hands caressed its supple leather arms. He was hungry, but just the thought of feeding made him ill. He rubbed his hands together, feeling the grit in the creases of his skin, the tiny flakes of blood that broke into smaller and smaller fragments. Deumas had been a good soldier, a good comrade, until she tried to escape her fate. *None of us will leave this world alive.*

Would he be allowed to end his own life with honor? Or would he be fed to the gateway like the Master's daughter? The thought sickened him. That was no way for a warrior to die.

His wife entered the room, and for a moment Balaam saw her as he had the first time they met half a century ago, when he visited her father's estate as part of his Master's entourage. She had been a maiden in the first blush of womanhood. She was still a young woman, still lovely, but something had changed. It was her eyes, he decided. They had lost their luster, dulled from all the lotus pollen, or perhaps because of him. It could not be easy to be wed to a killer.

'You're back,' she said. Her tone was even duller than her eyes. She could have been talking to a slave, or a wall.

'I've come to see you.' Balaam stopped before he added the words 'one last time.' He wasn't sure why he spared her that. He wanted to tell her about the failure he'd suffered, and the price he might be forced to pay, but instead he leaned back in the chair and watched the shadows ooze along the stones.

Dorcas came closer, but stopped at the edge of a low table. Platinum cubes of differing sizes were arranged artfully on the black lacquer finish. 'You look tired.'

Silence grew in the space between them until he couldn't stand it any longer. 'I have been given a mission, and it's possible I won't be coming back.'

'That's foolish talk. You'll be back. You always come back.'

'I have provided for you.' It was easier now that he'd said that much. The rest was just details. 'Go to Catolus in Hveifeld and tell him to—'

'No.' She came around the table. The folds of her long turquoise gown moved, showing the flatness of her stomach, the lean length of her legs against the fabric. 'Balaam, stop it.'

'He is holding money for you. When I'm gone—'

'No!' She stood just outside the reach of his arm now. Her eyes were red and swollen, but alive like he hadn't seen in so long. *Ah, Dorcas. Would that we could have seen this day coming and lived our lives another way.*

'If you're afraid, don't go, Balaam. Give up your post. You've done enough.'

He released a long breath and felt his chest collapse. Couldn't she see how he longed to do just that? 'It is my duty.'

'Your duty.' She scoffed, making it sound obscene. 'What of your duty to me? All those promises you made when you asked for my hand. Were they all lies?'

'No.' He lowered his head into his hands. 'But I was naïve. I'm lost, Dorcas. Everything I've done, my whole life, is wasted.'

She touched his shoulder, as lightly as a bird settling on a branch. He smelled the acrid bite of the lotus pollen on her breath. It should have infuriated him, but he was too tired to fight. 'Nonsense. You have me.'

'I let her go, Dorcas.'

'Who? The scion?'

Balaam slammed his fist onto the chair arm, making her jump. 'No! Deumas fled. I found her in a dingy roadhouse in Illmyn. I could have ended it then. I could have done my duty. But I let her go.'

His wife knelt beside him. 'Balaam, you must go to court and explain. You cannot be blamed for someone else's cowardice. You must convince the Master.'

Balaam stood up and stepped closer to the hearth, away from her. 'There will be no forgiveness. I will face the consequences for my failure. You must leave Erebus.'

'Leave? Where would I go? This is my home.'

He thought back to the seas of the Shadowlands. The quiet roar of the waves lapping against the black sands. 'If I wanted to leave, would you come with me?'

Dorcas stood up, too, her drawn eyebrows pinched together. There was something in her gaze, something he hadn't seen in a long time. Concern. *She's frightened. She finally sees what lies ahead for us.*

Then she smiled. 'Were you following me today? I thought I felt your presence earlier when I went out.'

'No, I only just return—' He turned to her. 'Where did this happen?'

'Just outside the citadel. I thought it might have been you following me. Balaam, what has you so upset?'

Balaam seized her by the arms. 'Tell me exactly where. What time did this happen?'

'The gates! Right outside the gates! Stop, you're hurting me!'

It was him. It had to be. The scion has come to Erebus.

When his wife had given him all the details she could remember, few as they were, he released her, and she ran from the room. From the doorway, her servant girl watched with a cold stare before following her mistress. A door slammed.

Balaam ignored the sobs and condemnations echoing from his wife's chamber. This could be his redemption, but he had to act swiftly. First, he had to eliminate all other possibilities. There were few Shadowfolk dwelling in Erebus. He had to question them. He had to be sure. There would be no second chance.

He went to a window and pushed back the shade. The citadel below was black except for the torches of a sentry patrol on the lower ward. Where was the scion hiding? Where would he go? Balaam considered what he would do if their roles were reversed.

He looked to the darkened hallway that led to his wife's suite. Then he left.

CHAPTER TWENTY-THREE

The wind tousled Kit's hair as she gazed across the crystal-blue waters. The sun stood in its customary spot, somewhere between midmorning and noon, never wavering.

She didn't know how long she'd been standing here on the edge of the surf. Thoughts flew around and around in her head, all weighed and pondered and dissected a hundred times over. But in the end, she knew what she wanted. What she needed. With a cleansing sigh, she walked up the beach and climbed the stone path to her grandmother's house.

'Do you think these heliconias are getting too much shade?' Her grandmother stood up from a bed of lush red and orange flowers.

Kit paused under the arbor leading to the garden. 'Ealdmoder, I've come back to ask you how I can become human.'

The old woman put aside her pruning shears. 'Yes, I thought you might. I'm sorry, Kitrine. I love you with all my heart, but I refuse to help you throw away your life.'

Kit bit her bottom lip as a seed of anger opened inside her. 'But you don't know.'

'Kitrine Alessa Diamuntaria. I *do* know about love, and I know more than a little about mortals. They are savages who live short, meaningless lives filled with misery and despair. They know nothing of beauty or the harmony of the *kwa* that ties all things together.'

'You don't know *him*,' Kit said, as respectfully as she could manage. 'You don't know what it's like to be close to someone, to watch over them and protect them, but not be able to express your love. You don't know what it's like to die inside every time you try to touch him and fail.'

'Child, child. Shedding your immortal essence isn't like changing your clothes. Once done, it can never be taken back. You will never be able to see your family again, never see the land of your birth. You will be mortal to the end of your days, however long or few they may be. Do you understand?'

Tears tickled the comers of Kit's eyes as she nodded. She had dreamt of this for so long. She and Caim would finally be together. That was worth anything, even the prospect of growing old and facing the long sleep of death. 'Yes, Ealdmoder.'

Her grandmother looked at her with eyes as gray and serene as the sea. 'I wonder if you do. If you truly seek mortality, go into the garden and you will find it.'

Kit wanted to run into her grandmother's arms one last time, but she remained still, afraid to ruin this opportunity. Her grandmother gave a sad nod, and then turned and walked back inside the house. When the door closed, Kit faced the garden. She remembered playing in it as a child, but it seemed larger and more forbidding today. *This is what I must do to be with Caim.*

Taking a deep breath, she stepped onto the path.

A cool breeze rustled through the trees and wrapped around her as she entered the garden, raising goose bumps on her arms. Kit walked past rows of plants and flowering bushes. Their open blossoms followed her as she wondered where she was supposed to go. Would she know mortality when she found it? Following the curve of the path, she came to a crossway. She turned left on a whim and kept going until she arrived at another crossing and chose the right-hand track. It was getting darker as a bank of storm clouds tumbled across the sky. Kit turned another corner and another, until she lost all sense of direction. Finally, she stopped in the middle of the path. She turned in a circle to figure out where she was going, but it was hopeless. She couldn't see beyond the wall of vegetation.

Kit was about to try to retrace her steps when she heard a sound that sent chills down her backbone. She held her breath and listened. She started to exhale as the only thing she heard was the wind, but then it came again, an ominous crackle in the bushes. Kit whirled around, and stopped when she faced a mass of scarlet flowers. Two yellow eyes watched her from the shadows at the base of the plants. Kit shuddered when a sleek, black head elongated into the light. She couldn't help herself. She ran.

Kit raced blindly through the garden maze, pushing through hedges, trampling flowers, knowing that Death stalked in her wake. She jumped to get a glimpse of her grandmother's house, and finally found it. *But it's so far away!*

She was darting through a bed of daffodils when she realized what she was doing. Stopping in the soft loam and turning around took every ounce of her willpower. She had to face this. This was what she wanted. *Right?*

But the fear returned like a vise around her throat when the serpent slid into view. The creature was as thick as her wrist and very long, extending more than twice her height before it drew in its coils. Kit swallowed. She was shaking while sweat ran down her back. The serpent's eyes were enthralling, cold and incredibly deep at the same time. She didn't want to look away. A strange languor had infiltrated her limbs. *It will be all right. I'll have Caim, and he's all I need.*

Yet even as she tried to comfort herself, another part of her brain was screaming and thrashing about like a wild bird trapped in a cage. The serpent's lower jaw yawned as it approached. Kit took a deep breath as Death touched her foot and crawled up her leg, its raspy scales caressing her calf. Her thigh. Her hip. She couldn't control her shaking. *I love you, Caim. I love y—*

When the fangs pierced her flesh, they hardly hurt at all.

CHAPTER TWENTY-FOUR

Caim ducked out of the path of a slave coffle, hardly sparing a glance for the shackled men and women marching past to the crack of whips.

He was tired. Not just in body, but in his spirit. The citadel loomed in his mind, titanic and impregnable. How many shadow people lived inside? Too many for him to overcome. He needed an army, but all he had were Dray and Malig and two escaped slaves.

Caim turned a corner and pressed his back to a wall. He almost reached for the shadows, but caught himself in time as a group of Northmen priests in dirty red robes passed by. The few people on the street, slaves and warriors alike, made way for them.

Once the priests were out of sight, Caim crossed the street and slipped into a narrow alley between two squat tenements. A quick jaunt down a zigzag brought him to the courtyard at the rear of the tavern where he'd left his crew. He only hoped they had managed to stay out of trouble.

A candle was lit in the foyer, with a tin plate to catch the drippings. Caim went to the door of their room and lifted the latch. It was pitch-black inside. He squinted, but his eyes didn't adjust to the gloom. A smell like seared grass met his nose. He reached down with his right hand as he stepped over the threshold. He expected to feel the presence of shadows, but they were strangely absent. There was no sound either. Then something slid across the floor. Hard leather. A boot. Caim eased the seax knife free of its sheath as he maneuvered sideways around where he guessed the noise had originated.

Caim started to take a step forward, but he was jerked backward by an arm across his windpipe. He grabbed for the arm out of instinct as his feet left the ground, but the limb was insanely powerful, its muscles and tendons as hard as petrified oak. White spots appeared before his vision before he remembered his knife. Caim stabbed behind him, aiming for the midsection, but the point of his knife rebounded off something solid. While the white spots grew and pulsed, Caim reversed the grip and plunged the knife over his shoulder. The arm around his neck loosened, and Caim kicked backward and thrashed his head back and forth until he was free. As soon as his heels hit the floor, he spun around and drew his *suete* knife. He could make out the outline of a big man, so big he first thought it was Malig, but then a chill touched his ankle and the gloom lifted.

Hoek stood before him. Blood ran in a thick stream from a puncture in his cheek, but the wound didn't seem to slow the big man as he shambled forward. Caim ducked under outstretched hands and lunged with both knives. He wanted to inflict nonlethal wounds, but found himself aiming for the bowels and groin anyway. His knives pierced woolen garments, but stopped when they hit the flesh underneath like they'd struck plate armor without the accompanying clang. Caim didn't have time to recover before Hoek barreled into him. Powerful fingers gouged into his face and shoulder. Caim slashed his way free, but again Hoek didn't stop, as if the pain didn't register. Caim threw himself to the side. He rolled to his feet beside a hammock and saw Dray lying in the rope sling. Malig was in another hammock. Both men stared up at the ceiling as if drugged.

Caim shouted, 'What's wrong with you two? Get up!'

A light blossomed in the far corner. He risked a glance over his shoulder to the corner where Shikari stood, smiling as she held a twisting flame in her hand. She had changed into a rust-red . . . *Oh, shit.*

Shikari wore an *asherjhag* robe. A black medallion hung around her neck on a long cord. Caim squinted. The medallion was shaped like a tower with square battlements. He'd seen that design before.

The breath left Caim's lungs as Hoek grabbed him by the head and threw him to the floor. A huge boot rose into the air, and Caim rolled aside before it connected with his skull. Shadows appeared along the low ceiling. Their tiny voices echoed in his head, making it hard to concentrate. Then Hoek was upon him again. Caim slashed at everything that came at him – hands, wrists, and kneecaps – until Hoek staggered back, bleeding from half a hundred slices. The big man's mouth gaped as if he suddenly understood what he was doing, but then his features slackened, and he charged again.

Caim braced himself. His knives trembled in his grip. He was on the edge of losing control. The smell of blood in the room was overpowering. The shadows urged him to let go, to give in to the killing lust. Hoek closed within three steps.

Two.

One.

Caim unleashed the shadows. They dropped from the ceiling, inundating Hoek in a night-black deluge. His arms churned as if trying to swim from the shadows, until his legs gave out and he collapsed on the floor to the sound of soft chittering. Through the swarm of darknesses, Caim could see the big man's arms changing color from pale white to black and gray. He pushed the shadows away with his thoughts. They resisted at first, but then oozed away at his insistent command. Where Hoek had lain was now a horrid, mottled creature, roughly man-shaped, but with longer arms and plate-sized hands with curled talons. Knobby lumps covered the thing's bald skull. For reasons he couldn't discern, Caim was reminded of the shadow serpent that had attacked him in his apartment in Othir. The Shadow had caught up to him again.

Caim stared across the room at Shikari, still with the flames dancing in her hands. Her eyes shined with the fiery light. 'You escaped my trap in Jarnflein,' she said. 'But I knew I would find you again, scion. My rewards shall be boundless when I bring you before the Master's throne.'

Not alive, you won't. Caim pushed off from the wall toward her, knives extended—

—and leapt back as an axe swept across his peripheral vision. The blade struck the wall just above his shoulder in a shower of wooden splinters.

'No!' Shikari shouted. 'I need him alive!'

Caim turned and slashed with his knives, but pulled up as Malig's bearded face reflected in the firelight. He dove under Malig's arm and circled around behind him. 'Mal, what the fuck has gotten into—?'

Caim hissed as a pack of shadows adhered to his torso, sinking through his jacket and shirt to cleave to his skin with frigid claws. Before he could react, a spear thrust from out of the gloom. The point struck him below the nipple, but deflected from the layer of shadows instead of piercing his lung. Dray followed up with a low counter-thrust, but Caim batted the spear away. What in the hells was going on? Malig and Dray were crazy, sure, but not *this* crazy. Caim blocked Dray's next thrust and got in close, but instead of burying his knives in his companion's heart, he cracked him in the forehead with a pommel butt. Dray didn't even blink, but swung his spear across his body and forced Caim to leap back. Malig recovered his broadaxe and lumbered at him again.

The Eregoths came at him side by side. By the firelight, their eyes were black as squid ink. Caim retreated until his heels hit the wall behind him. His companions came on with silent intensity, aiming stroke after stroke that he deflected or evaded. They moved slowly, like they were swimming through oil, but he had nowhere to go. Behind them, Shikari hummed a strange, hypnotic song while the flames twisted in her palms, looking almost like two small people as she manipulated them back and forth. Every time she turned her wrist, the Eregoths lurched forward.

Caim twisted sideways to avoid a stab from Dray as Malig chopped down with a two-handed swing. A gap opened between them, and Caim lunged through it. Before he could take three steps, a wall of orange flames burst from the floor in front of him. Caim jumped back from the hellish heat. Dray and Malig turned with jerky motions and were once again attacking him. Caim ducked under an axe stroke aimed at his neck, pivoted on his heel, and threw.

The seax knife spun pommel over tip through the flaming curtain and struck with a wet thud. The flames evaporated in puffs of smoke from Shikari's hands as she looked down at the steel protruding between her breasts. A slithering sensation ran through Caim, like an invisible line between him and the sorceress. As Shikari collapsed to the floorboards, a burst of energy exploded inside him. It happened so fast he hardly understood what had occurred. As the strange vitality surged through his body, Caim lifted his *suete* against the next attack from the Eregoths, but they were standing motionless, weapons hanging limp in their hands.

With effort, Caim took a deep breath and exhaled through his nose. Dray groaned. Malig shuddered and snorted as if he'd been plunged into an icy lake. But their eyes had cleared of the black film.

'What the—?' Dray started to ask, but his voice was hoarse.

Caim grabbed them both and shoved them toward the door. Once the Eregoths were out, Caim darted back inside the burning room. The curtain of flames had spread to the walls and ceiling, feeding on the stone as if it were kindling. He started to form a portal for a short hop through the fire, but then recalled the shadow-jumping he'd seen the shadow swordsman do during their brief duel. Without knowing exactly what to do, Caim concentrated on being on the other side of the room. Nothing happened except that the fire burned closer and sweat dripped down his face from the intense heat. He almost gave up, but then a sharp pain pinched behind his eyes. His stomach twisted upside down, and he landed on his feet, standing over Shikari's body.

She was still smiling. Blood covered her chest, drenching her amulet. The black tower stared up at Caim, the same icon that had been etched into Soloroth's armor. He yanked his knife from her corpse, grabbed their gear, and used the new energy coursing through him to make a proper portal.

Smoke seeped through the seams of the stone walls as Caim emerged from the house. Dray was bent over in the courtyard, coughing. Malig watched the spreading fire with a dull stare. His beard was singed at the bottom.

Caim wiped his hand down his face, and it came away black with soot. His neck and shoulder ached from where Hoek, or whatever he was, had gouged him.

'What happened?' Dray asked when he could breathe.

Malig shook his head. 'I had this gods-awful dream. I was lying abed, and someone was talking in my head, but I couldn't move. Then I saw Caim.'

Dray squinted at Caim. 'I heard the voice, too. I wanted to kill you.'

Caim saddled his horse. 'It's over. Let's move.'

'Where are we going?' Malig asked.

'I've got a plan, of sorts. But you might not like it.'

Malig grunted. 'What a sheep-fucking surprise.'

Caim sat by the window of his new room, looking out over the town at the pale cliffs in the distance. After the fire they'd found another boardinghouse, but he hadn't been able to sleep. The influx of energy buzzed inside him.

He flexed his wrists as he watched the dingy gray of twilight slip into full night. His hands had finally stopped shaking, but the feelings inside him remained. He tried not to think about the thing Hoek had turned into and what it meant, or how he would have killed Malig and Dray if his knife-throw hadn't ended Shikari's sorcery. His focus was on the upcoming mission. *Kit, if you can hear me, come back. I need you more than ever.*

The truth of that had sunk in these past couple days. She was the only person who understood him. She would know what to do, would know if he was just throwing his life away on a hopeless dream. *I'll listen to you, Kit. Just please come back.*

There was a knock at the door. Dray peered in. 'You ready?'

Caim pulled on his cloak and checked his knives. Malig waited in the hallway. Both men carried heavy sacks that smelled of oil and paraffin. Without speaking, they went downstairs and out the back. He'd told them his plan before they retired. Neither of them liked it, but they had as much at stake in this mission as he did. 'My brother's shade must be avenged,' Dray had said. Whether it was true or nor, he couldn't say no after bringing them this far. They were all damned in this together.

Few people on the street paid them any mind. Caim peered into every nook and shadow, glanced down every alley as they made their way through the maze of stone buildings until they reached the plains. The hills glimmered in the dusk like they were coated in Stardust. Caim concentrated on his core, where his powers originated, and suppressed them like he had before. It was more difficult because the new energy inside him wanted to burst free, but he felt better when the sensations subsided. He couldn't say why, except that the citadel unnerved him less with his powers masked.

'Saronna's dugs,' Malig swore when they reached the top of

the cliffs. 'My da used to tell stories about giants who built castles in the north. I think he must have been right.'

'Keep your mind on the job,' Caim said.

The outer ramparts rose to the sky like a colossal black wave poised over them. Red lanterns shone at the front of the gatehouse. Caim led them east around the curve of the wall, searching for a flaw in the design, but the walls were solid, the massive towers all sloped and positioned to provide enfilading fire. By the time they had hiked nearly a third of the way around the citadel without finding anything they could exploit, Caim halted. Motioning for his crew to stay put, and praying they obeyed for once, he crept forward to a span of the wall where the curvature appeared to form a blind spot where neither of the two nearest towers could view it directly. A quick inspection confirmed his suspicion. Perhaps there had been a gate planned for this section, or an imperfection in the bedrock called for a different configuration. Whatever the reason, he didn't waste time. He hissed for the others to come.

While Dray and Malig uncoiled ropes from their satchels, Caim tied one end to the back of his belt. Then he found his first handholds and started up. The curtain wall was too high for a grapnel, but the gaps between the massive stones were wide enough to provide good purchase. He wedged his fingers into these seams and hoisted himself up, foot by foot. His arms and shoulders began to burn from the exertion, but then he settled into a comfortable rhythm. Scaling the bartizan at the summit was the hardest part. Caim had to dangle by his arms as he searched for the holds around and over the stone projection. He crawled through a crenel and dropped into a crouch on the other side of the battlements. The allure running along the top of the wall was clear in either direction. Caim untied the rope from his belt, secured it around a pointed merlon, and gave a firm tug.

While he waited, Caim studied the citadel from his perch. Erebus was built in three tiers stacked atop each other. The lowest tier – and the broadest – featured long buildings with few windows. The middle ward was divided into neat estates behind low walls. Lofty towers stretched above the walls, straight and smooth, capped with sharp points. All the buildings were built from the same black granite as the slaver town but polished so that every surface gleamed with a silky shine. But he saw no people, no lights in any of the windows, and heard no noise. From his vantage, Caim could have been the only living thing in the citadel.

Wide stairways led to the highest tier. Caim's gaze climbed the smooth, slanting walls of the pyramid that dominated the citadel, and the vision he'd seen in Sybelle's sanctum rushed back to him.

The vantage slowed as it approached a massive structure at the center of the cyclopean city, a pyramidal building of the same black stone. A window yawned in the side of the structure, and Caim's perspective halted before a narrow balcony. A man wrapped in a loose cloak stood looking over the city. Shadows cloaked his face, but his eyes shone with the dark majesty of a new moon. Caim forced himself to meet those haunted eyes without flinching. There was something about him . . .

Now he was here, gazing upon this place that he had half hoped would turn out to be a figment of a warped imagination. Thoughts rolled through his head, of his father and mother, and the old anger resurfaced.

Caim turned as Dray's head appeared over the battlements. The black-haired Eregoth pulled himself over the top with a sigh, Aemon's spear lashed to his back.

'Fuck me,' Dray said, looking down at the citadel.

When Malig was up, Caim dropped the rope over the inside of the wall and ushered them along. Once they were several fathoms down, Caim started his descent. By the time he reached the ground, Dray and Malig had hidden themselves in the shadow of a building across from the wall. Caim joined them, rolling his shoulders to ease their ache.

'It's damned eerie in here,' Malig grumbled. 'Feels like we're in a barrow field.'

'Fucking dark, too,' Dray said.

'We can't risk a light,' Caim said. 'So stay close.'

The streets were paved in long bricks of black stone like finely polished onyx, fitted together so closely the seams were almost invisible. It was like walking on a river of glass. There was no refuse in the alleys, no night soil or manure piled in the doorways. Instead of the usual sounds of a city, there was only the mournful howl of the wind through empty streets. Yet as they made their way through the benighted avenues, something lurked on the periphery of Caim's senses. After a few minutes of listening, he heard them. Shadows. Lots of them. But they stayed away.

Caim and his crew crossed a boulevard lined with statues of tall men and women in long robes. Each sculpture pointed up to the pyramid at the top of the city. They found a stairway to the second tier between two wrought-iron gates. From there they made their way through a forest of towers. Caim could tell Dray and Malig were trying to be quiet, but every sound they made echoed off the stone walls and made him wince.

They were moving parallel to the boulevard, searching for a way up to the top tier, when Malig hissed under his breath. Caim stopped and listened. The tromp of boots echoed from behind them. Caim beckoned the Eregoths over a short iron fence into a side street and pushed them against a wall. The sounds grew louder until a troop of soldiers – Northmen in black armor – marched past. The brands lighting their way were painfully bright in the darkness. Caim held his breath until they tromped out of sight.

Malig sighed. 'I'm getting too old for this shit.'

Caim tapped his crew on their chests and went back into the

street. They followed the soldiers at a slower pace. While they crept along, Caim racked his brain to formulate a plan. His goal had been simply to reach the pyramid where the vision hinted his mother might be kept, but the closer they got, the less confident he became. He needed an edge. Normally he could rely on his skills and the shadows, but he didn't think they would be enough this time. Then he recalled the woman in the palanquin. Like pouring grain whiskey on a fire, the energy flared up inside him, and a new pulling took hold of him. It pointed upward to the heights of the city, but a few points west of the pyramid.

He stopped in the street and considered this new development. He had already followed his powers to one ambush, and lost a good man in the bargain. Did he dare trust it again? *What other choice do I have?*

'You all right?' Malig asked.

Caim nodded and started off in the direction of the new pull. They climbed two long staircases, past a row of impressive manors – all apparently vacant and unused – and over a small bridge spanning an empty channel. With every street they passed, the pull grew more precise, leading Caim like a mariner's compass, until it brought him to a small palace. There was no other way to describe it. The main structure was three stories tall with broad, angular windows. Two round towers protruded above the roof. Stone arches covered a breezeway leading to the back. The pull was dragging Caim straight to it.

They found a side alley about a hundred paces down the avenue from the palace. Once Dray and Malig were situated inside, Caim asked if they had everything they needed.

'Sure. We know the plan.' Malig took the bottles from his pack and set them in a row against one wall of the alleyway. Each bottle had a length of cloth wadding extending from its corked mouth. 'How long are we going to have to wait?'

Caim looked to the sky. It was past evening and well into true night. 'Not long. When I give the all-clear signal—'

Malig waved him away. 'We know, we know.'

Caim spared a last glance at Dray, who stood with his spear, looking out over the forlorn city. 'You all set, Dray?'

The Eregoth nodded, but maintained his vigil. *He's wound too tight. He'll snap if the pressure gets any greater.* But Caim didn't have any other choice, except to terminate the mission. *No, it's now or never.*

He left them and slipped down the avenue toward the manor. There was no sign of activity inside the palace, but as Caim approached he began to feel a dull ache in his chest, the same feeling he got whenever a shadow warrior was near. Checking his knives, he stole across the avenue, leapt, and pulled himself over the high wall.

He made no noise crossing the lawn of crushed black-and-white stone. When he reached the corner of the main building, he searched for the best way up. He planned to scale the palace and start a search from the top – his usual routine. Keeping tight control over the energy inside him, and hoping that was enough to cloak his presence from anyone nearby, Caim scaled the breezeway and jumped to catch the sill of a window on the top floor beneath the sloped roof. There was no hinge or slide; the window was sealed shut by design. Cursing through his teeth, Caim glanced around at the other windows on this side of the house. They were all the same. *That makes things more difficult.*

Faced with the options of either abandoning the plan or trying something unconventional, he listened for several heartbeats. He hadn't seen any sentry patrols on this tier, but noise carried in this citadel. When he didn't hear anything except the sound of his own breathing, Caim took a deep breath and kicked the window dead center with the heel of his boot. The glass shattered, and Caim had to resist the impulse to jerk his foot back. He drew a knife and knocked out the remaining shards, and then slipped inside.

He landed in a hallway with one closed door on the left side; the corridor turned to the right about fourteen paces from the window. Caim's boots crunched on broken glass as he went to the closed door. He turned the handle and looked into a modest-sized bedroom. There was a plain bed, low to the floor, next to a narrow wall cabinet, a basin on a wooden table, and a porcelain chamber pot. The pulling beckoned him deeper into the palace. He approached the end of the hall with quick steps, then continued around the corner for another six paces before turning to the left; two more closed doors entered into the hall. Caim checked them and found a bedchamber, also vacant, and a storage closet with shelves of linens and a waste bin. He went around the next corner, feeling the sands of time fall quickly through the hourglass in his head. Ahead were double doors of fine hardwood. If they were locked or – gods forbid – barred from the other side, he would have a hard time getting through.

Not if I use the shadows. He toyed with the idea, but using his powers might advertise his presence. Caim put a hand on the latch of the left-side door and pushed.

He entered into what had to be the master bedchamber due to its massive four-poster bed in lustrous hardwood with matching armoire and a lady's vanity. His gaze was drawn to the bed, where a woman with long, black hair reclined on the coverlet. In three long steps he was across the room and beside the bed. The woman wore a modest ivory gown that contrasted with her dusky complexion. Her eyes were closed.

Caim pricked the hollow of her neck with his seax knife. Her eyelashes fluttered open, and she started to roll over until he increased the pressure. 'Don't move,' he whispered.

The woman stiffened, but made no move to escape. Caim took that as a good sign as he considered how to proceed. He was reasonably sure this was the same woman he had seen in the palanquin. That indicated she was someone important. A noble, perhaps. 'Is there anyone else in the house?'

The woman nodded, firmly, but just once. Her hands shook a little, though. Caim didn't feel any other presences. 'Sit up.' When she complied, he asked, 'How many more people? Where are they?'

The woman held up one finger with a long, tapered nail and pointed down at the floor.

'A guard?'

She shook her head and made a rubbing motion as if she was wiping a flat surface, maybe cleaning something. When he guessed a servant, she nodded.

Caim nodded to himself. That made things a little easier, if she was telling the truth. He missed Kit in the worst way. He could really use her talents right now. 'All right. I'm going to remove my knife. If you scream or call out—'

The woman shook her head. A flowery perfume lingered in the air. Caim pulled the seax back. 'Who are you?'

She touched the spot where he had pricked her. 'My name is Dorcas. I live here.'

'Alone? I mean, with just your servant?'

She started to nod, but then shook her head. 'My husband lives here as well, but he is away.'

Caim jerked his head toward the pyramid above them. 'What is that big building above us? A temple?'

'No, not . . . exactly.' Her thin eyebrows almost – but not quite – touched over the bridge of her delicate nose. Everything about her was delicate. Refined. 'You are not from the wastes.'

Caim extended his knife to within an inch of her throat. 'Just answer my questions. Is that where the Lords of Shadow reside?'

'There is only one Shadow Lord, our liege and master. I do not know who you are, but you have placed yourself in great danger by coming here. Nothing happens in Erebus without the Master's knowledge. If you are a spy from the south—'

Caim pressed his knife back against her neck to shut her up. 'How many warriors does this Shadow Lord keep with him? Not Northmen, I mean people like you.'

'People like . . . ? Oh.' The woman leaned forward, heedless of the knife, which forced Caim to pull it back. 'You are the one talked about. The scion.'

'Who was talking about me? Your husband? And what—?' He tried to hold back, but the question burst out. 'What is this scion talk? Who do they think I am?'

'You are the one they have been waiting for.'

Caim was so intent on her answer he almost didn't register the sharp sensation tingling behind his breastbone. A shadow presence, but it wasn't the woman. It came from—

Black holes opened around the room. Without stopping to think, Caim ripped open a portal of his own and jumped through it.

He gasped as he landed in the street. His insides were on fire. He stumbled into the wall of a round tower and reached out to hold himself up. He was a few streets over from the woman's palace. Caim pushed off from the tower and ran down the avenue as fast as he could manage.

The pain had lessened by the time he reached the alley where he'd left Dray and Malig, but he felt the pulses of multiple shadow presences. As he came up to the mouth of the alley, an object about the size and shape of a wine bottle flew out, trailing a wisp of bright flame. Caim ducked and covered his head as the explosion assaulted his ears. Shards of light pierced his eyelids, and glass tinkled on the pavestones. Dray or Malig had thrown one of their oil flasks. That meant—

Caim rushed around the corner into the alley and came face-to-face with a man a little taller than him, encased in dull black leather, with a black visored helm. Caim bent backward to avoid the dagger point racing toward his left eye and parried the thrust of a second dagger by pure instinct. Caim started to counterattack with a high riposte, but drew back as another barrage of agony seized his chest. The shadow warrior shifted from side to side as he advanced, his black armor absorbing the light of the flaming oil. Over his opponent's shoulder, Caim saw Dray was holding off another shadow warrior while Malig worked at lighting the taper of another flask. A portal opened at the rear of the alley, and a third shadow warrior emerged holding a polearm with a black, curved blade.

Caim's wrists stung as he deflected another pair of dagger attacks. He didn't know if he could hold off three shadow warriors. He backpedaled to create more room to maneuver and couldn't suppress a grunt as another sudden pain pierced his chest. A quick glance over his shoulder revealed the arrival of a fourth shadow warrior. Caim's blood cooled when he recognized the newcomer's sword. This was the one he'd fought at the ruins, the one who had nearly killed him. Caim ignored the agony that ripped through him and reached out to the shadows. They were all around the alleyway, on the rooftops of the towers above, creeping along the pavement, and he needed them if he was going to have any chance to win.

But they did not answer.

Caim tensed as a cold sweat formed on his face. The swordsman drew his blade with a whisper-quiet slither of metal dragged over wood. The dagger fighter spun into a lightning-quick rhythm of alternating high and low attacks. Caim sucked in a deep breath and focused his powers. The alleyway shifted, and he arrived at a spot behind the swordsman. Caim lunged, and he was forced to duck as a flaming flask whipped past his head to explode in a fireball on the other side of the street, but the swordsman was gone.

Caim braced himself to meet both attackers, but the dagger fighter backed away and took a defensive posture. The shadow warriors in the alley fell back as well, leaving Malig fumbling with another flask. Dray gulped for air as he hunched over his spear. Caim glanced about. This was just like Liovard all over again, only worse. *This is going to end messy, probably with us lying in pools of blood.*

But the prospect of death didn't bother him so much as knowing he had come so close to his goal only to fall.

The swordsman appeared half a dozen paces away. He spoke in stilted Nimean. 'Put down your weapons.'

Caim measured the distance between himself and the dagger fighter. With a turn of luck, he might take that warrior out so he could focus on the swordsman. He looked for the shadows, but they still held back. *What do you want from me?*

He thought he was strong enough to perform another shadow-jump. Escape wasn't an option. Caim prepared himself to leap beside the dagger fighter for a surprise attack. He'd only get one chance.

Just as Caim was about to make his move, a slender shape appeared in front of him. He almost slashed her across the throat and belly before he recognized it was Kit. He had just enough time to register that she was completely naked before she fell into his arms. Caim's mouth hung open as he caught her, but no words emerged. A storm of emotions rocked his brain at the sight and the *feel* of her. *Gods below, she's human!*

She looked up at him from under droopy eyelids and smiled. 'Caim.'

He froze, looking around. The dagger fighter shifted. Malig looked over and did a double-take.

Caim stepped back, cradling Kit. Her hair smelled of wildflowers and sunshine. Her body fit perfectly against him, making him keenly aware of her nudity. How was this possible? And why in the name of all that was holy did she choose *now* to display this talent? But whatever the answers, her arrival changed everything. He had to get her out of here. Shutting away the shame of leaving his crew, Caim focused on creating a portal to a spot far away to the south. *I'll return if I can. If not, die well, my friends.*

Caim staggered backward as his balance twisted upside down. He grabbed Kit tighter to keep from dropping her. The portal never formed, but a piercing pain cut across his temples. The seax made a dull chime as it bounced on the hard pavestones, followed by his *suete* knife.

The shadow warriors darted at them, ripping Kit from his grasp and knocking him to the ground. The dagger fighter bound his wrists together with a thin cord while the spearman did the same to Kit, but she appeared to be only semi-conscious. It was then that Caim spotted the blood on her chest and the two small puncture marks over her heart.

The swordsman walked over and picked up Caim's knives; he slid the *suete* through his belt, but held up the seax a moment before tucking it away. Malig wore an evil scowl as he was marched out of the alley with his hands likewise bound, but Dray remained where he was, holding his brother's spear. The shadow warrior said something, and Dray took a step. Caim saw the torsion begin in the Eregoth's hips, propelling him around as he drove the spear. The shadow warrior stepped away, but too slow as the spear's tip pierced his right eye and sheared through the brain until it exploded from the back of his skull. Dray recovered from the thrust and started to turn, but jerked to a halt in the space between two steps. The point of a black blade emerged from Dray's neck, and a line of blood bubbled down into his collar as he crumpled to the ground. The swordsman stood behind him.

Malig yelled and struggled until his captor slammed him onto the ground and gave him several sharp kicks to the head. Caim flexed his muscles, but did not react. He could see by the way Dray lay on the stones that he was beyond help. The swordsman flicked the blood from his weapon and returned it to its scabbard. His visor gave no indication whether or not he felt anything for the life he'd taken.

A gateway formed in the middle of the avenue. The shadow warriors carried Kit through and dragged Malig by his heels. Caim was hauled upright with a dagger point pricking at the base of his skull. Back in the alleyway, a mass of shadows covered the bodies of Dray and the dead warrior. Caim sighed as he was shoved into the portal's inky depths, and the street fell out from under his feet.

CHAPTER TWENTY-FIVE

The message was short.

Her Majesty, Empress Josephine I,

Regiments from the southern garrisons have begun to gather. I can send two thousand foot militia under the command of Knight-Major Pontias Vitario within the sennight. I pray they will find you safe and in good position to repel the enemy.

There are many other things to relate, but they can wait. Something has happened.

The word 'happened' had been scratched out, and then repeated.

Your old friend from the Vine paid me a visit this past night. He was quite distraught to find you gone from the palace and in the north. Pardon me, but I told him as much of your recent activities as I was able. Still, the information did not satisfy the gentleman, as he left in quite a rush. His present whereabouts are unknown.

Hubert's signature was scrawled across the bottom.

Rain dripped on the parchment as Josey rolled it up. Her heart hadn't stopped pounding since receiving it. The 'old friend' had to be Caim. After all the hoping and praying, she knew for certain he was alive. Josey shivered against the cold and fought to get ahold of her thoughts, which were flying off in wild directions. If Caim was coming for her, he would have arrived long before Hubert's messenger. That meant he'd been delayed, or he wasn't coming, and she couldn't think of many things that could delay Caim.

They rode through a forest of denuded aspens and oaks, a foretaste of the larger forests they would encounter in the south. The sun was coming up over a chain of low hills, streaking the sky with orange and gold. It was four days since the battle, and three since she'd been captured by the Eregoths. Now Keegan's band rode with her. The men of the northern marches were excellent scouts and foragers. In addition, her cadre had increased to nearly two hundred as they found survivors from the battle and picked up new men on their dash south.

Lightning whinnied. Josey patted his neck as she smiled at Iola riding beside her on a small gray pony. According to Captain Drathan, the girl had saved Lightning, too, riding him as she led the wagons and baggage carts to safety.

'Are you cold, Majesty?' Iola asked.

'No, just thankful.'

The girl smiled back, and then glanced ahead. *Looking for a certain officer of my bodyguard, I'll wager.* Josey followed Iola's gaze through the woods. Every morning she sent small mixed groups of her soldiers and Eregoths to harry the invaders, and every evening she waited to hear the casualty reports. Although this new straregy of striking the enemy and fleeing before they could respond was safer, her forces were so few that each loss felt like a spike driving through her heart. She put a hand over her stomach. The bump was hard as old wood under the four layers of clothing she was wearing. *We'll stop soon, little one. Sleep a little longer.*

The pregnancy hadn't bothered her much during this long march, but she worried just the same. Doctor Krav had warned her about extensive riding, but there was no time for weakness. She had to press onward.

Brian pulled up beside her. They had been riding through most of the night, but if he was as tired as she was, he didn't show it. He was cleanshaven, his long hair tied back in a queue. 'We should stop soon,' he said.

'Yes. The men must be tired.'

Josey looked away as the words she really wanted to say formed on the tip of her tongue. *I like you. No, I care for you. Deeply. Heavens, I sound so stupid. He must think I'm a complete featherbrain.*

She still had his dagger strapped to her belt under her cloak, but now in the light of Hubert's letter it seemed . . . inappropriate. She carried Caim's child in her womb. She had no business flirting with this knight. Yet, when he looked at her . . .

'These men would not complain if their legs were falling off,' Brian said. 'They would die for you. As would I.'

'Brian, I want to say . . . Well, it's just that you have been very—'

Three horsemen rode back through the lines. Drathan and the Eregoth captain had their heads bent together in conversation, and it looked like Keegan was doing most of the talking. Hirsch rode a few steps behind them. The brim of his hat was pulled down low over weary eyes. The adept had insisted on traveling with the scouts, hardly ever stopping, as they searched for a location to make their next, and possibly last, stand. She hoped he found someplace soon, before they all dropped from exhaustion. Hirsch opened his mouth to speak, but Josey beat him to it.

'When was the last time you slept, Master Adept?'

'Yesterday. Or maybe the day before. How are you faring?'

He didn't glance at her stomach, but Josey knew what he meant. 'What have you found?' she asked.

Captain Drathan gestured to the trees. 'Beyond this wood,

the hills of the east and west come together in a valley, Majesty. If the invaders keep coming in this direction, they'll have to pass through that funnel, or travel many leagues to go around.'

'We will make sure the enemy comes this way,' Keegan said.

'How can you be sure?' Josey asked.

Keegan dug a hard roll out of a saddlebag. 'Our men prick them at every turn. By now, they'll be eager to crush us and be rid of the nuisance. So we just need to bait the trap. The Thunder Lord came straight at us at Liovard, sent his men in waves until our defenses crumbled. Same as he did to you. He will keep driving straight south until he takes your capital. Or until he's stopped.'

'So we can force him to give battle, but that's not enough. His forces outnumber ours.'

'By ten to one,' Brian said. 'At the least.'

Hirsch patted the neck of his tired steed. 'The valley ahead is the best place we've found. There's a stream that would make a good obstacle to blunt their advance. And the land south is generally flat.'

So we can make a swift escape. 'What about their sorcery, Master Hirsch? Can you defend us from it?'

'That remains to be seen, lass.'

Josey clamped down on a sigh threatening to erupt from her chest. If this was their best chance to stop the enemy, then so be it. 'All right. That's where we will set up to meet them. I want lookouts posted in every direction for five miles.'

Keegan raised an eyebrow, but he left with Captain Drathan to relay her orders. She had been worried that the high captain, being a northerner, might hold her sex against her. Yet so far he had been content to follow her lead. And Captain Drathan said he learned fast.

Hirsch departed, too, but Brian remained at her side. Josey could tell by his expression that he wanted to continue their conversation, but she didn't trust herself not to say the wrong thing. Her face grew warm just thinking about it, and then a sharp pressure pushed against her stomach. Josey dropped a hand to her middle without thinking. Was that a kick? She felt for it again, but nothing happened.

'Majesty, do you wish to stop?'

He sounded so sincere, Josey had to smile. She was about to answer when a horn bellowed to the south. It wasn't the one used by her scouts or the Eregoths. Had the enemy found a way ahead of them?

Before she could react, Brian had slammed his helmet onto his head and was galloping away. He drew his sword and slipped his other arm through the straps of his shield as he guided his steed with his knees. Several of her bodyguard rode up to surround her. She looked around and found an officer, 'Lieutenant Hillmund, find out what's happening!'

He dashed off with a salute. Lightning stamped his hooves while Josey waited. Part of her wanted to rush ahead, but she reminded herself that she was an empress, not a soldier. Still, it was maddening to just sit here. Her impulse to know had almost overridden her better sense when a group of men on horseback rode out of the trees. She didn't see any blood on them, and their weapons were in their sheaths. She saw Hirsch and Brian with Captain Drathan, but the others were unfamiliar. Then she spotted a face she hadn't thought she'd see for months, if ever again. He smiled when their gazes met, his large white teeth shining in the gathering daylight. His hair was a little longer than it had been at court, brushing past his shoulders in silky black waves. He shook his reins and cantered ahead of the group.

'Your Majesty!' he called as he approached. 'We meet again.'

Josey swallowed. 'Lieutenant Walthom. This is a surprise.'

She hadn't seen Walthom since she sent him and his cavalry unit to root out brigands in western Nimea.

'Please, call me Dimas.' He tapped a pair of silver strips on his collar. 'And I am a major now. Twice promoted on the battlefield for valor.'

The rest of the party caught up. Captain Drathan came to her left side, and Brian to her right. 'How is Lord Du'Quendel?' she asked.

Major Walthom reached into his tunic. 'He sends his regards and wishes he could be here, as well. But his infantry could not keep up with my light horse.' He pulled out a scroll and attempted to hand it to her, but Brian passed it to her. Josey couldn't help but notice the look he gave Walthom. It was almost possessive.

Walthom frowned, but covered it with a fresh smile for her. 'If I may say so, Majesty, you are a glowing vision after a long and difficult journey. We came as soon as we heard of the marchlanders' advance across the border. And your yeomen have been telling me about your unfortunate contact with these invaders.'

'Yes. Many were lost.'

Walthom placed a hand over his heart. 'But now I am here, and we shall avenge our fallen brothers. These barbarians will taste the temper of our steel before we send them down to hell!'

Josey had no idea what that even meant, but she nodded. 'How many men did you bring, Major?'

'Two hundred of the empire's finest cavalry!'

'And how far behind are the footmen?'

Walthom raised an eyebrow. 'A sennight. Perhaps a few days more. But my light horse are more than capable of crushing these band—'

'That's too long,' Brian said. 'We can stall for two or three days at most.'

'We could still make for Othir, Majesty,' Captain Drathan said.

Major Walthom grasped the polished handle of his sword.

'Now see here. I did not ride all this way just to turn tail and run. Majesty, we have come to fight.'

Josey considered. Even with the addition of the cavalry, they didn't have near enough soldiers to match the invaders. But if they fled they would cede half of the empire, and possibly more.

'Majesty?'

'Ah, Major.' Hirsch cleared his throat. 'Perhaps you would be so good as to inspect the site for the coming battle.'

'Yes.' Walthom smiled at Josey and extended his hand. 'I must go, my empress, but I shall return.'

Brian pushed between her and Walthom. 'Come, sir. The enemy approaches.'

The major allowed the officers to steer him away with good grace. As they rode away, Brian looked back. Josey mouthed, 'Thank you.'

He winked as they passed under the trees.

CHAPTER TWENTY-SIX

Caim awoke to blinding light in his eyes. He blinked and squinted up at the three yellow globes on the ceiling. He sat on the floor in a tiny cell with his back against a wall; the room was so narrow he might have been able to touch the sides if his hands weren't shackled above his head. From the numbness in his hands, he guessed he had been here for some time. His head felt stuffed with wool. A sour taste lingered on his tongue. He shut his eyes, but the light intruded through the lids.

He remembered entering the shadow woman's house, and the fight in the alleyway. Then he'd been hit with back-to-back shocks. To finally have Kit real and tangible, to hold her in his arms, and then have her snatched away by his enemies was like a vise squeezing his brain. And Dray . . .

He tried to swallow, but his mouth was too dry. The cell wasn't especially cold, but he had a chill and a soreness in his chest. The only exit was a large iron door. There were no windows, no way of knowing where this cell was located, whether it was day or night. Caim shifted to ease his shoulder muscles, but there was no comfortable position. He looked up at the gray ceiling and noticed something else. There were no shadows. Not a single one anywhere. He was tempted to call for them just to see if any would appear, but the ache in his chest gave him pause. After killing the sorceress he had felt so powerful, so full of life, but that vigor was gone, replaced by emptiness.

Caim was examining his shackles when the cell door rattled. Light-headedness took hold of him as he turned his head, but it cleared as the door swung open, crashing against the inside wall, and four men entered. All wore black plate armor; two carried halberds with polished blades, and the other two had swords at their hips.

The sight of the armor took Caim back to his father's estate. He could imagine them carrying his mother away. He let out a slow breath that burned his throat. The soldiers didn't speak as the two swordsmen came over and unlocked his fetters. Caim had a brief thought of resisting as they hauled him to his feet, but his legs buckled under his full weight and would have dumped him onto the floor if the soldiers hadn't caught him under his armpits. They dragged him out of the cell, the halberdiers following behind.

Two shadow warriors awaited in the hall. Caim's hands itched to have his knives back again. Without a word, he was steered down the corridor, and the warriors fell in behind.

Dim lamps were set high on the stone walls. Caim clenched and unclenched his fingers as the circulation returned. The soldiers carried him past other cell doors. Were they taking him to the Lord of Shadow? Caim smiled at the thought of being dragged into a majestic setting like the Grand Hall in Othir. He was dirty and disheveled, and he smelled gods-awful.

Caim was yanked to a halt as his captors stopped before a broad iron door. With a knock it opened. As they maneuvered him inside, Caim got a good look at what awaited, and his stomach dropped. The room was small and dirty, lit by a brilliant globe hanging from the ceiling. A heavy wooden chair was bolted to the center of the cruddy floor. Restraint straps hung from its arms and legs. A table sat against the left wall with an assortment of sharp instruments. He tried to stand up on his own, but the soldiers manhandled him inside like he was a child.

The door closed behind him with a deafening clang.

Caim straightened out his left leg slowly – ever so slowly – and released a long groan as the tendrils of pain eased around his knee. *At least I should be grateful it's not broken.*

He wasn't so sure about other parts. He opened his eyes and forced himself to look. Naked except for his breeches, he made for a gruesome sight in the brilliance of the globes above his cell. His knees looked like joints of meat from a butcher's shop. Half of his toes were burst open, nearly black with blood. Ribbons of skin hung from the back of his right hand; his fingers curled like bony claws crusted with blood. His pinky finger stuck out straight from the middle knuckle. His wrist was swollen and ringed with purple bruises. He tried to move it, and stopped when the pain became too much.

He couldn't say how long the torture had gone on. The Northmen worked with quiet efficiency, applying the various instruments to him in turns. There were no questions asked, no demands made. Just pain.

Afterward Caim was dragged back to his cell. Funny how he had come to think of this little room as *his*, taking ownership because he had nothing else to call his own. Nothing except a sliver of pride, and he suspected they would eventually take that, too.

Caim stared up at the lights. He was exhausted, but they wouldn't let him sleep. He stared until his eyes ached and forced him to blink. Where were Kit and Malig? Were they even still alive? He tried not to think of that, but then his mind turned to Dray, devoured by shadows. And Aemon buried in a cold grave on the wastes. Their blood was on his hands as surely as if he'd killed them himself. And for what? He'd failed in his grand quest, no closer to the truth about his mother than he had been back in Othir.

As he gazed into the lights, finding solace in the pain, a sensation intruded on his thoughts. It was mild at first, like an irritation on the fringe of his perception, but it grew with the passing minutes, transforming into a pleasant feeling that diminished the pain of his injuries. There was a presence behind this feeling, just beyond his awareness, but it comforted him. *Kit, is that you?*

Caim's stomach clenched as the cell door rattled. He wanted to roll up into a ball, but forced himself to sit up. Four guards entered the cell. Caim couldn't tell if they were the same ones who had fetched him before or another quartet; they never talked or lifted their steely visors.

They unlocked his shackles and carried him out. Caim tried to work up a little moisture, but his mouth was drier than sand. He couldn't help shivering as they approached the door to the torture chamber. He didn't know how much more he could take. Yet the soldiers passed by the heinous door without stopping. Caim held his breath, expecting them to turn around at any moment, but they kept going, pulling him along. He focused on moving his feet, keeping up with the soldiers' pace. It wasn't easy. He felt pathetically weak.

They passed through an archway and down another hall with more doors. Faint sounds issued from behind some. Moans like the lamentations of the damned. How long before he started to make those same noises? How long would it be before he was beyond hope, crippled in mind and body? Used up and useless.

The corridor ended at a wide doorway framed in large black stones. On the other side was a longer hall. The air was a little less stale. Instead of cell doors, side passages branched off at regular intervals. Caim tried to estimate how far they'd walked, but he had trouble making his brain function properly. *Come on. Snap out of it. This is routine stuff. How far since the last intersection?* He tried to remember. Twenty-three paces. Another pair of side tunnels arrived at the thirtieth step. He was still counting when the soldiers opened another door and ushered him inside. Caim tensed as they entered a long chamber with a high ceiling. It was as large as the Grand Hall in the Luccian Palace, but darker and gloomier, devoid of windows. Every surface was polished to a rich, black luster.

Caim thought the room was empty until a figure separated from the penumbral shadows cloaking the wall. The swordsman wasn't wearing his helmet, but Caim recognized his armor and weapon. The warrior's features were leaner than he imagined, with the same dusky hue as Sybelle's.

Caim flexed his fingers, wanting to hold his knives one last time before they finished him. Maybe he could goad this one into a duel. *Better to die on my feet facing my enemy than on my knees waiting for the axe.*

The swordsman tossed a sleeveless gray tunic to the guards, and they put it on Caim none too gently. By the time they were done, the garment was stained with blood from his hand. The swordsman walked away, and the guards dragged Caim after him.

They passed through a set of double doors made of dense, black wood, down another passageway and up a series of staircases that switched back on themselves several times. Caim gritted his teeth as cramps developed in his legs, but he walked under his own power, determined not to be dragged to his own execution. He lost count of the number of steps somewhere around five hundred, but finally they reached another hall. But it was only a foyer. More soldiers stood at attention at the far end. The blades of their poleaxes glimmered in the faint light, but did not move as the swordsman passed between them and pushed open a pair of massive bronze doors. Caim's breath caught in his throat as he stepped into a much larger chamber, and a powerful aura washed over him. It bound his limbs with invisible tethers and stole his wits like a hammer blow to the forehead.

The chamber was magnificent, with great chandeliers of leaded glass. Thick pillars of black granite rose like charred fingers to the vaulted ceiling a hundred and fifty feet above his head. Accents of gold and obsidian adorned the walls. A great basalt throne, almost godlike in stature, rested upon a raised platform at the far end of the chamber. A man sat in the throne. He wore a wine-colored surcoat over deep gray robes, devoid of accessories or diadem, but Caim knew him for the monarch of Erebus. His head was shaved, his shoulders broad. But it was his eyes that drew Caim's attention. Flat, black, emotionless. They were like holes cut in a mask, revealing a vast power within.

A crowd of people turned as Caim entered. He took them for gentry by their fine garb and jewels. Caim recognized the lady, Dorcas, from the palace, though she did not look in his direction. The others were shadow folk, too, but they numbered no more than a score. Caim struggled to shake off his captors. He wanted to face this creature standing on his own feet, but the soldiers held him easily. Then a moan echoed through the hall. Ten Northmen were spiked to a wooden framework erected against the left-hand wall. Blood dribbled from the wounds at their wrists and ankles and the dozens of cuts covering their hairy torsos. Three weren't moving, but at least half were still alive, their chests rising and falling in shuddering breaths.

Caim's bare feet shuffled across the cool flagstones as he was shoved forward. The anger of years past blazed inside him, suffusing his face with its fever. These were the people behind the attack on his father's estate. The aura of malevolence increased as he approached the tall dais, like an army of biting ants was crawling all over his body.

Caim was stopped a dozen paces from the steps of the dais, where a pair of shadow warriors stood guard. A sharp blow to the back of his legs knocked him to his knees. He struggled to stay upright until the blade of a halberd forced his face down to the floor.

'Finally, the feared scion.' The voice reverberated through the hall. 'Does he have a name?'

'Caim, Master,' the swordsman answered with a clipped accent. 'Caim of the House Du'Vartha.'

'Du'Vartha?'

'He took his human father's name, Master.'

'I see.'

Caim relaxed his muscles as the blade lifted from his neck. He had to conserve his energy and be ready for any opportunity. He straightened up to a kneeling posture, both hands on his thighs. The Shadow Lord's face was lean and taut, especially around his eyes, like the skin had been stretched too far. 'Do you know who I am, boy?'

Caim worked his tongue around his mouth. 'Where are the others?'

A hard blow struck the back of Caim's head, and he dropped onto his hands. He sucked at the inside of his bottom lip as he sat up again.

'I am Abraxus of the House Thargelia. I am told that you are my eldest daughter's child. That you have come all this way from the Southlands to kill me. Is this true?'

'Where are Kit and Malig?'

Armor clinked as the soldiers shifted behind him, but the Shadow Lord lifted a finger. 'Who are these he speaks of?'

A throat cleared on the dais, and a slim shadow man in a crimson brocade robe appeared beside the throne. Caim recognized him as the silent observer at his torture sessions. 'Great Lord,' the official said, 'the scion was captured with two mortals. A male and a female. Nothing of interest. They appear to have been his companions.'

Nothing of interest? Through his pain-haze, Caim eyed the swordsman, who had seen Kit appear from thin air. But while

Caim waited for the man to speak up, the Shadow Lord waved his hand. 'Then deal with them, Lord Malphas. Now you, Caim, tell this court why you have striven so hard against your own kind, who only wish to dwell in this realm in peace.'

Caim almost choked on his tongue. Peace? He wished he had enough saliva to spit. 'You know nothing of peace. You're all a pack of conquering, slave-making monsters. Everywhere you go, people suffer.'

'We are alone in this hostile world, surrounded by enemies. We must conquer or perish. That is the law of survival.'

'Where is my mother?'

The Shadow Lord frowned. 'Ah, yes. Isabeth. She is here, of course. But she cared nothing for you. How could she? You are a mongrel. A mistake.'

Caim exhaled until his lungs were empty. His gaze locked on the Shadow Lord's eyes. Ignoring his injuries and pains, he delved deep inside himself looking for any scrap of energy. He found a vein of power, far below where he'd ever searched before. In his mind, it pulsed like a white-hot wire. He tried to grab hold of it and aim it toward the throne, but it was like trying to catch a greased serpent, writhing out of his mental grasp. Finally, with beads of sweat dripping down his face, he had to give up.

The Shadow Lord shook his head. 'This one is no blood of mine.'

At a signal from the robed official, the soldiers hauled Caim to his feet and marched him out of the hall. None of the nailed Northmen moved as he passed. Perhaps they were all finally dead.

Caim held his composure until the doors slammed shut behind him, and then he let his chin drop to his chest.

CHAPTER TWENTY-SEVEN

The boom of the closing doors sent a tremor through the floor stones as Balaam watched the scion depart from the hall. The assembly whispered among themselves. Their words traveled through the hall. 'The grandson . . . heir to the black throne . . . dishonored death . . .'

Balaam glanced around. There were so few of his kind left in the citadel, less than a score, but they had become strangers to him. Even the others of his clan were like odd creatures in a menagerie, and he was locked inside with them.

Malphas cleared the chamber with a command while the Master sat silently and gazed at the doors at the end of the hall. Balaam stood with his hands clasped behind his back. When they were alone, Abraxus sighed. He looked fatigued. 'He is strong. Stronger than I had reason to anticipate, considering his mixed lineage.'

'He is an untrained abomination,' Malphas said. 'Forgive me, my lord, but that is all the more reason to execute him immediately. So that his deviancy and the threat he poses to your empire will die with him.'

The Shadow Lord gazed down from the throne. 'What is your opinion?'

Balaam considered his words carefully. There was something in Malphas's expression he did not like, something predatory. *Is this what we have become? We surround ourselves with slaves and servants, but are we all just tools like this scion, to be used and discarded?* 'He is dangerous, Master.'

Lord Malphas began to nod in agreement, until Balaam continued, 'But I counsel you not to slay him out of hand.'

Malphas sniffed, but the Shadow Lord asked, 'Why not? Do you believe he could be one of us?'

'No, Master.' Balaam groped for some reason to defend the scion's life. *What shall I say? He fights well, and with honor, which is more than I can say of everyone in your court.* 'But he may be the last of your line. With one of your daughters departed, and the other—'

Abraxus waved his hand. 'I will not be swayed by the virtue of blood alone. Are you sure he cannot be convinced to join our conquest?'

'Quite sure,' Malphas said before Balaam could reply. 'I attended his interrogation personally. Believe me, my lord. There is nothing of your greatness in him.'

Balaam considered challenging those words. He had tested the scion in personal combat. He knew the man's mettle better than anyone else in Erebus. But then he thought of Dorcas. If he crossed Malphas and lost, who would care for her? 'Master, I do not agree.'

Malphas stepped to the edge of the dais platform, where he towered over Balaam. 'The court is grateful for your efforts in capturing this enemy, but be mindful of your station, Talon.'

Balaam felt the muscles in his arms and legs contract as cool detachment filled him. His gloves creaked. But Abraxus stood up. 'Prepare the scion for execution. Tomorrow at the high diurn.'

Malphas bowed. 'Yes, Master. I shall see to it myself.'

Balaam lowered his head and kept it down until Abraxus had departed. When he looked up, Malphas was gone as well. Taking a deep breath, Balaam turned toward the doors. Why did he care if the scion was put to death? The man was nothing to him. But then he recalled the execution of Lord Oriax.

This is not the empire we once knew.

Balaam pulled the hood of his cloak down over his eyes as he opened a portal to a place far away.

CHAPTER TWENTY-EIGHT

Kit muttered one of Caim's favorite curses as her hand slipped.

She sat, naked as the day she was born – the humiliation of *that* was something she would not soon forget – trying to pick the lock of the golden cage in which she'd been placed. The room around her was large and fancy, but with hardly any furniture except for her cage. Her hand shook as she bent the copper wire and jammed it back into the lock.

She didn't remember much of her sojourn back to her grandmother's retreat. She had been in the garden, running from . . . something. She vaguely recalled a pair of yellow eyes, and then a sharp pain in her chest. The next thing she knew, she was falling into Caim's arms, and he caught her!

Kit sighed as she relived the memory. Touching Caim, being held by him, had affected her more than she thought it would. But then she had been pried from his arms and . . . and . . . darkness. She awoke here, caged up like an animal, being pawed by an old shadow man with large, black eyes. She had nearly spit in his face when he told her that she was his slave, but she didn't. Because he, Lord Malphas, had known at once what she was, or what she'd been. The way he looked at her, devouring her with hungry eyes, made that abundantly clear. So she remained quiet and demure until he left.

For a while she sat in the cage and stewed, but then her anger turned to motion as she searched everything she could reach through the bars, which wasn't much. But the leg of a decorative table had yielded a short length of pliable wire. Picking a lock had always looked easy whenever Caim did it; just push in the tool and move it around until the lock popped open. Yet she'd been working on it for the past candlemark with nothing to show for her efforts except cramped fingers and fraying nerves. With a sob, she tossed down the wire and buried her face in her hands.

She could only imagine what Caim was going through, all alone without her. Had she made the wrong choice becoming human? If she were still Fae, she could find him in a heartbeat. Now she was locked away with two hundred and twenty-seven paces of stone ceilings and corridors between them.

Kit choked back her anguish as she realized she could feel Caim's presence. She looked down at the floor. That's where he was, exactly two hundred and twenty-seven paces away. Best of all, she knew he was alive, knew it down deep in her newly solid bones.

Rejuvenated by this knowledge, Kit took up the wire and started on the lock again. Once she was free, she would track down Caim, break him out, and they could flee. She blew a stray strand of hair from her eyes and squinted down into the lock. *Just hang on, darling. I'll find you.*

Kit was jiggering the wire back and forth in the lock when footsteps echoed outside the room. She snatched out the wire and slipped it under her leg as her new 'master' entered. Kit watched Lord Malphas take off his outer robe, and a burly Northwoman came to take it away. Then the shadow man looked at Kit until she squirmed. She had stared into the eyes of snakes and wolves and some really big monster fish that prowled the seas, but this man's look disturbed her. It wasn't lust for her naked body, which she could have handled. It felt like he was peeling off her skin with his eyes.

'*Jai asta raelano, mei hai?*' he asked. You're a long way from home, aren't you?

Kit's breath left her lungs. Her native language sounded foul coming from his mouth. She sat in her gilded prison and shivered, glad for once for the bars between them. After a few minutes, he went to another wing of the suite and left her alone.

Kit let out the breath she'd been holding. Forcing her hands to be steady, she took out the wire and got back to work. On her next try, something clicked. With one eye on the doorway, Kit lifted the latch.

The door of the cage swung open.

Kit waited with one hand on the bars, listening for any nearby movement, but all was quiet. Telling herself to be brave like Caim, she slipped out of the cage and went to the front door. She could have cried with joy when the latch opened. The hallway outside was empty. Kit thought for a moment. If she left now, there was no turning back. Her absence would be noted and a search was likely to ensue. How fast could she get to Caim? She had no way of knowing.

With a deep breath to calm her nerves, Kit grabbed a yellow silk duvet from the back of a chair and wrapped it around her shoulders. She could do this.

She stepped through the door, pulled it closed behind her, and hurried down the cold stone corridor.

CHAPTER TWENTY-NINE

'Armenis of Freehold. Dalros Vicencho. Fur – Furio Three-Finger. That duelist from Mecantia with a lisp.'

The names echoed back to Caim as he dredged them up from his memories and spoke them aloud. A list of all the men he'd killed. Some he didn't have names for, but he remembered exactly how they'd looked when they died. So much blood. *I'm a killer. It's the only thing I've ever been good at.*

Shackled once more to the wall, he stared up at the lights. He was tired down to his bones, but he couldn't sleep. *I'll be dead soon. Then I can sleep forever.*

'Chiel – No, what was his name? Chellish the Mad. Yes. Edric Klapsur.'

Caim looked up to the shackles holding his wrists to the wall. Blood had run down from his right hand and formed a crust around that cuff. He tugged, but it was too tight and the metal didn't have any play. And even if he managed to slip out of the stocks, where would he go? The door was solid iron – he'd seen that in his comings and goings – and locked from the outside. They'd taken everything except his smallclothes. *Well, old boy, I think this might be the end.*

How would they do it? Beheading? Draw and quarter? That seemed a little extravagant for the quiet man sitting in the black throne. *Maybe they'll send someone down here to slice my throat and be done with it.*

He was about to resume his list of names when he caught a flicker of movement in the far corner of his cell. Had the lights dimmed? Though no shadows existed anywhere in the tiny room, he couldn't see into that corner. It was just a grayish haze.

It's him. He had been waiting for the swordsman to return since the audience with the Shadow Lord. He wasn't sure why, but something in the warrior's gaze had made Caim think that they shared some kind of connection. *Yes, we're both killers. We know our own.* 'You just going to stand there and look at me?'

When there was no answer from the misty corner, Caim yanked at his shackles and cursed. 'You want to cut my throat? Then do it already!'

Caim fought his bonds and shouted until he was breathless, slumped against the wall, but his efforts evoked no reply. With a grunt, he looked down at the floor and kept his gaze there while the blood throbbed in his eardrums. After a few minutes he looked up. The haze was gone. He was alone again. *Or maybe I'm going fucking crazy down here.*

The cell door rattled. Caim took a deep breath. *If they let me free, even for a moment, I'll damned well take one of them with me.* He clenched both hands into fists, not caring about the pain. The soldiers were fully armored, but he might be able to get his fingers inside one of their visors. Take out an eye. Pluck a dagger from a sheath and plunge it under a gorget. He let out the breath, and almost choked when the door swung open.

'Caim?'

This isn't real. He tried to swallow, but his throat had closed up. *I've gone mad. It can't be.*

A wan face peered into the cell. Her eyes widened as she entered. 'Caim!'

Then she was draped across him. He buried his face in her hair, afraid to believe it was really her. Then he noticed the bloody knife in her hand. 'Kit? What happened? Did they hurt you?'

She planted a kiss on his mouth. Her lips were hungry, her

tongue darting out to caress his, and for a moment he forgot all about his captivity, the time they'd been apart, everything. The moment could have lasted forever, as far as he was concerned. When she pulled away, he kept his eyes closed. Then he felt her fumbling with his shackles. Caim opened his eyes and found himself staring at her chest, and not minding at all.

'I'm fine,' she said, sorting through a ring of keys. 'But you look pretty rough.'

Caim advised her to try the small iron key he had seen his captors use. 'Where did you get that knife?'

The lock holding his right wrist clicked open, and Kit moved to the other one. 'I stole it from a mess hall not too far from here.'

Caim sighed as his hands were released and pinpricks raced into his extremities. His right hand began to ooze. 'And the blood?'

Kit handed him the knife, hilt first. 'Here. We need to get moving. Can you walk?'

'I can try.' Getting to his feet took a painful effort even with Kit's help. His legs wobbled, both knees screaming out as they took his full weight. But once he got up, he felt a little better. The returning sensation caused his right hand to throb. 'So are you going to tell me?'

'Tell you what?' she asked.

Caim looked her up and down. She wore a short yellow smock that hung a few inches below her bottom. It was a shapeless rag, but she made it look damned good. 'You're real.'

She smacked him in the arm – his good arm. 'I was always real, dummy. You just couldn't feel me before.'

'And I'm not complaining, but—'

'It's a long story. But I promise I'll tell you everything once we get out of this place.'

'Is this something you did purposely, Kit? Why would you—?'

'For you. All right?' She pushed a strand of silver hair out of her eyes. It was such a Kit gesture that he wanted to kiss her again. 'I couldn't bear to see you go back to that mud-woman.'

'Josey?'

'I saw you go back to the palace. I heard everything. I just . . . I wanted a chance with you. A real chance.'

He pulled her close. She resisted for a moment, but then melted into him. 'I love you, too,' he whispered.

Caim finally released her, and they went to the cell door. The hallway was clear.

'Why haven't you used your shadow friends to escape?' Kit asked as she led him the opposite way from the torture chamber.

They passed other doors, and Caim wondered who was behind them. 'I tried, but I don't think they'll obey me here. Something's changed. Do you know where Malig is being held?'

She led the way down another corridor. This one had a brighter light at its end, some forty or so paces away. 'Changed how?'

'They don't come all the time when I call. And even when they do, it's different. Like they've gone wild.'

'They were always wild, Caim.' Kit paused and forced him to halt with her. He hissed as his wounded hand brushed against the wall. 'But what you said reminds me of . . .'

'What?' When she didn't answer right away, he pressed, 'What, Kit?'

'Your mother.'

'What about her?'

Kit started walking again. 'When she was in the south with you and your father, she hardly used her powers at all. I didn't pay much attention to it. To tell you the truth, I was actually glad about it. Being around the shadows has never been too comfortable for me. And I suspect your father felt the same way. But she got headaches sometimes and would take to bed for days at a time. Now that I think of it, she hadn't been, you know, *feeding* since she left the north. Maybe that relates to your problems.'

Caim remembered how the shadows had fed on the dying, the way they sucked at the blood. Whenever he killed lately, he'd felt like he wanted to drink with them. 'They're hungry.'

He meant it as a whisper, but Kit smacked him in the stomach. 'That's got to be it! Just feed the shadows more, and then they'll respond to you again.'

'No.'

'Why not? What's the difference between feeding them and just killing for money? This will actually be better. It'll be for a higher purpose.'

'No, Kit.' He would have pushed away from her if he didn't think he would fall on his face. And she smelled so damned good. 'You don't know what it's like, watching them feed. Knowing you made it possible. It makes me feel like a monster. I won't do it again.'

'Listen. There's a guard room just a few floors above—'

'I won't do it.'

'Even if it means dying? Without seeing your mother again, or the sun, or even that damned mud-woman?'

Caim swore under his breath. She wasn't fighting fair. But before he could muster an answer, she said, 'Caim, you can't defeat these people without your full strength. You have to know that.'

You think I don't? Every time he closed his eyes, he saw his failures again. Aemon's death. Dray's, too. He hadn't been strong enough to protect them. And now Kit was here, in the flesh, and she was the one carrying him. But if he gave in to his shadow side, would he lose what was left of his human soul? Kas's voice echoed in his head.

Caim, you've been walking a line between light and dark your whole life. Maybe it's time to choose a side and stick with it.

Kit stopped again and put a hand on his chest. 'You can have my blood.'

'Kit! No!' He shoved past her, hobbling down the corridor. Up ahead, the light had grown brighter.

With a loud huff, Kit caught up to him and slipped her head under his arm again. The corridor entered a small room. Caim dimly remembered passing through here when he was first brought to the prison. Three gaolers had been playing stones at the table in the center. There was only one man here now, lying facedown on the floor in a pool of blood. Kit tugged on Caim's arm without meeting his gaze. 'This way.'

Impressed, he followed her through to another small room. This was where they had stripped and searched him. Besides the archway he had originally entered, there were two doors. Holding the knife low, Caim eased open one of them and found a long storage room. Bundles of clothing, shoes, and other personal effects were piled on shelves and hanging on hooks, all kinds of clothing from peasant rags to fine silks and dainty caps. Caim found his gear on the floor, including his belt with the *suete* knife still in its sheath, but the seax knife was missing. He looked around while he pulled on his pants, but there was no sign of it.

'We have to get going,' Kit whispered. 'More guards could be coming anytime.'

Caim stepped out, pulling his jacket over his injured hand with care. 'You didn't time their rotations?'

She huffed and glared at him. 'No. But if I'm not rescuing you correctly, I can just take you back to your cell to rot some more.'

'You're doing wonderfully.' He held up his belt. 'Would you mind?'

Kit buckled it around his waist while he held his hand over his head. The flayed skin was oozing again, but they didn't have time to bind it. He considered shoving the hand into a glove, but didn't think Kit would appreciate having to carry him if he passed out. Caim hissed as he pushed his damaged feet into his boots. The he slipped the butcher's knife through his belt and drew his *suete* with his good hand. Kit looked like she wanted to cry.

'You all right?' he asked.

She brushed a hand over her eyes. 'I'm fine. I just want to get out of here.'

Through the archway was a short corridor leading to a staircase that ran both up and down. Kit started up the steps with Caim holding her arm. He was feeling a little stronger, but after waiting so long to touch her, he didn't want to let go.

They ascended one floor, and Caim expected Kit to keep going – his cell was several levels below the street level – but she led him through an open doorway. Seeing more rows of wooden cell doors, he realized why. 'Malig's down this way?'

Kit nodded as she pulled out the ring of keys. 'I think this is where they keep most of the prisoners.'

Thankfully, one master key opened all the locks, so they were spared from having to find the right fit for each door. Kit stood behind Caim as he peered into the cells. The first couple were empty, though they smelled awful. Then Caim pushed open the heavy door to the third cell, and light spilled into the dim room. Malig sat against the far wall with his legs drawn up. He was bare-chested. His torso and arms were matted with thick brown hair. 'Dray?' he asked. 'That you?'

Caim swallowed. *What kind of nightmares was the man having to think his dead friend was here for him?* 'It's Caim, Mal. And I've brought a friend.'

Malig climbed to his feet. Large bruises glared purple and black on his arms and a few spots on his torso through the hair, but otherwise he didn't appear to have been harmed. Physically, at least.

Malig walked out of the cell, his long hair trailing across his shoulders. 'You're the last damned person I expected to see, Caim. Who's this?'

'This is Kit. A friend of mine.'

With a wink at Caim, Kit extended her hand. 'Nice to finally meet you in the flesh, Malig.'

Caim resisted the urge to smack her on the bottom. 'We're getting out of here.'

'That sounds good to me,' Malig said.

'You know where they stowed your gear?'

'I've got no fucking idea. But just put a sword in my hands. Or a good axe. They won't take me alive next time.'

'I'd rather there wasn't a next time.' Caim turned to Kit. 'Which way?'

'We should go back to the stairs,' she said. 'They're the fastest way out of the building, but there's more guard rooms on the floors above.'

'Perfect,' Malig said with a grim smile. 'Dray wanted to send Aemon off to heaven on a river of blood. I say we open the floodgates.'

Caim stayed by Kit's side as they made their way back to the stairs. All was quiet aside from the slap of their footsteps, and yet his stomach was clenched tight. It would only take one outcry, one alert guardsman, to ruin their chances. The guard-room on the next floor was empty. Malig found a long cloak to throw around his shoulders and a rack of swords. He tried a couple, swinging them around, and settled on a hand-and-a-half bastard sword with a wide blade.

Caim glanced back in the direction of the stairs. He didn't know which way to go from here. The shadow warriors had used a portal to transport him down to the dungeons. If he had his full strength back, that might have been an option now. Kit's offer echoed in his mind. *You can have my blood.*

He crammed it back with all his other problems. He needed to focus. 'Where do we go from here?'

Kit pointed to a door on the other side of the room. 'I think that will take us out to a lower level of the city.'

'Fuck leaving.' Malig struck his newfound sword against the stone floor so that the steel rang. 'Let's go reap a slaughter on these pigs. For Dray and Aemon.'

'No.' Caim knew what he had to do, but enough people had died for his cause already. 'Mal, you're taking Kit out of the citadel. Once you're back in town, find horses or steal them, and ride south—'

Kit leveled a finger at him. 'No, Caim! I'm not leaving without you. We both go, or we both stay.'

'I have to complete what I started.'

'Fine,' she said. 'Then I'm coming with you.'

'You're not Fae anymore.'

Malig frowned at Kit. 'What?'

'I don't know how you managed it,' Caim continued, 'but I won't let you put yourself at risk for me anymore.'

'You don't get to decide that,' she responded.

'No need to argue,' Malig said. 'We'll all go look for some blood to spill.'

Caim stepped closer to Kit. Her eyes were huge pools of violet water threatening to overspill. 'I can't lose you,' he whispered. 'Please go. If I can, I'll find you after . . .'

'No you won't. But if I can't stop you, then remember this.' She rose up on her tiptoes and kissed him with her open mouth. Warm, coppery liquid spilled onto his tongue. Caim tried to pull back, but she pressed herself harder against him. His efforts to break away lessened as a buzz stirred inside him. It began in his stomach and flowed outward through his entire body, filling him with a pure, white-hot energy. It cleansed away his exhaustion and pain. Even his hand ceased to bother him. When he opened his eyes, the world had changed. The walls of the room pulsed with life – tiny darknesses oozed down the surfaces and greeted him with soft chitters. Finally, he pushed her away.

'What did you—?'

Kit wiped her bloody lips with the back of her hand. 'Call it a wedding gift. Now go kick some ass.'

Wedding gift?

Caim looked to Malig, and the Eregoth snorted. 'Don't look to me for another kiss. And don't worry either. I'll get your girlfriend out of here. You sure you're going to be all right alone?'

'I'll manage.'

Kit gestured back to the stairwell. 'Those go most of the way up. After that, I don't know. And there will be guards.'

Caim nodded. 'I understand. Better get going.'

Malig peered out the other door. 'Looks good. Come on, girlie.'

Kit stopped on the threshold. 'Be careful, Caim.'

'I will.'

Malig saluted with his sword. 'I got her, boss. Go get some.'

As the door closed behind them, Caim called to the shadows. They flew to him like old times, adhering themselves to his skin, their tiny claws nipping at his flesh. The worst was his flensed hand, but the shadows wrapped around it almost gently, enclosing it in a wriggling second skin.

Caim pulled a glove over his newly mended hand. His pulse pumped hard and steady through his veins. A bead of sweat ran down the side of his face, along his jaw, and wavered on his chin. It fell, and he was gone before it hit the floor.

CHAPTER THIRTY

Caim climbed the tall steps of the staircase. Lamplight at each landing cast long shadows across the walls and ceiling. His knees ached a little, but the exercise felt good after being cooped up in the cell.

Windows studded the outer walls at each landing. Beyond their stone casements, the night sky rippled like a sheet of black silk. A moon would have been fitting, big and red like a spot of blood, but there was none. The citadel spread out beneath him in a darkly shining panorama. A great, dead city.

Caim ascended level after level, past empty halls gathering dust, until he reached the top landing. He inched open the door. The room beyond was empty. He entered what was either a long chamber or a wide corridor. A stone table was set against the left-hand wall with two clay jars. The air was dry and carried a faint scent of ordure, or maybe it was his imagination. In any case, he was alone. The tugging sensation reawakened in his head, coming from overhead and slightly north. *Toward the apex.*

He padded around to a bend to discover a door. The brass handle was corroded with verdigris. He lifted the latch and pushed it open. A low creak filled his ears as he peered through the gap. A hallway extended on the other side. The iron cressets on the walls were empty.

Caim advanced with every sense straining to its fullest. He passed an open archway leading into another room, square and deep with a high ceiling. A stone seat sat facing the doorway, flanked by a pair of cold braziers atop small caryatid pillars. He came across other rooms, some empty, others with a few pieces of furniture, but all of them dark. There was no color, no texture save smooth stone. A thick layer of dust covered their floors.

The hallway terminated in an archway. As Caim started toward it, the tromp of marching boots echoed down the hall, and a flicker of torchlight appeared ahead. Caim pressed himself against a wall, drawing the shadows around him. They chittered as they clung to him, and a spasm rippled through his chest. Not painful so much as jarring, like a jab to the breastbone. The feeling subsided just as two Northmen in black plate armor marched through the archway. One held a halberd across his chest, the other an oil-soaked torch.

Caim waited until the soldiers passed by, and then he emerged behind them. The torch-bearer's gasp was like air rushing from a bellows as the point of the *suete* knife punched through the mail webbing under his armpit. At the same time, the butcher's knife thrust between the gap of the halberdier's helmet rim and the collar of his backplate. Caim shoved hard with a foot stomp and pulled his knives loose as the Northmen toppled. The torch guttered on the floor and went out.

Shadows descended on the dying men, and through them Caim tasted the dwindling life forces, felt their energy flowing into his bloodstream. His heart beat strong and a trifle too fast, as if intoxicated by the power. Caim breathed through his nose until the rush abated.

The small chamber beyond the archway had a vaulted ceiling and four branching corridors, but no soldiers down any of them. He chose the north hallway and found more stairs at its end. This staircase had no landings, but kept rising around a central newel column as thick as a wagon wheel. Caim climbed with both knives ready. The stairs ended at a door made of black stone instead of wood. There was no handle or latch, but a circle had been carved into the center, two handbreadths across. Caim studied the door. It was well set into its frame. A slab of this size would have to weigh at least fifty stone.

Caim started to reach for the circle, but stopped his hand just before it touched the stone. Something tickled the nape of his neck. A part of him whispered that if Kit were still an ethereal Fae, this is where she would appear to tell him he was about to stumble into a bad situation. *No, she'd appear right after I stepped into it.*

Caim released the energies seething inside him to form a new portal. Its opaque surface undulated and shimmered in the dark. *No balls, no glory.*

Gritting his teeth, he walked through.

Caim blinked as he stepped into an empty chamber. There were no furnishings or personal effects. The four walls slanted inward to form a point two spans above his head. A window pierced each wall. He looked around. This was the apex of the pyramid, which he'd seen in his vision. His mother had to be here, but there was nowhere for anyone to hide.

Then he felt something, a texture to the air that reminded him of . . . home. Not Othir, but his real home in Eregoth. His father's estate. For a moment he could almost smell his old room, the sunshiny scent of his favorite blanket, the beeswax polished into the wooden chair where his mother had held him and rocked him to sleep.

The images were dispelled by a burst of pain flaring in his chest. Caim crouched against the wall as a figure in black armor stepped out of the shadows. The swordsman had one hand on the long hilt of his sword, which was still in its scabbard. His visor was up. Caim shifted to a forward stance as the swordsman took something from his belt and held it up. The seax knife. He moved his arm, and Caim tensed, but the knife sailed in a gentle arc between them. Caim dropped the butcher's knife and caught the seax by the hilt.

The swordsman did not move, did not draw his sword. 'The

Master foresaw this. You and I here at this moment. I doubted, but here we are.'

Caim gripped his knives tight, feeling every ridge and whorl in the hilts as he advanced. 'And now one of us will die.'

'That is unfortunate. I have come to regret the need to eliminate you.' The warrior retreated a pace, arms by his sides. 'We are both killers. Predators. Unfit for this world.'

Caim tried to ignore the words, but they slipped past his guard and struck home. He'd thought much the same himself. *Would the world be a better place if I'd never been born?* 'If you're trying to make it sound like we're the same, save your breath.'

The swordsman's eyebrows rose. His lean features were more haggard than at their last meeting. Black stubble shadowed his jaw. 'The same? Hardly. You kill for yourself, for profit, for desire. I kill for a cause to which I have devoted my entire life.'

Caim recalled some words he'd said to Josey on a rooftop overlooking her dead foster father's mansion. *Why is it that if a lord or a king sends you to kill a man, it's somehow noble? But if you do this for yourself, it's murder. Explain that to me.*

Caim let the memory slide from his thoughts as he lunged. The swordsman's hands flashed, and his weapon appeared, slashing across the intervening space between them. Caim beat aside the sword and lunged with a stop-thrust that was likewise deflected.

Caim stayed low, knees flexed to carry him in any direction. The sword tried to cut off his approach routes, but he fought with every trick at his disposal, fueled by the cold fury bubbling inside his gut. As they traded cuts and parries, he alternated between pressing his opponent and falling back to draw him in.

'You believe I am evil,' the swordsman said as he circled away. 'And perhaps I am. But are you without sin? Have you not killed to defend your beliefs? I accept what I am. Do you?'

Caim felt his lips curl back in a snarl as he lunged again. Just before their weapons met, he channeled his powers and made a short shadow-hop. There was a moment of resistance, as if a skin had formed in the air to prevent him passage, but he pushed through it.

He reappeared behind and to the side of his foe. As the swordsman spun, with an upward slash that cut through thin air, Caim attacked low and fast. The black sword deflected the seax knife, but the *suete* stabbed deep into the tendon under the kneecap.

The swordsman jerked his wounded leg back and made a circular disengaging slash between them as he retreated a few steps. Caim hung back. The wound was crippling. The pain must have been extreme, but the swordsman settled into an off-balance stance and waited, as still as a pillar of ice.

Caim drew in a deep breath. His fury remained, unabated, but this victory gave him no joy. His opponent hadn't fought with passion or pride, or even fear. *He's a pawn, like me. His master points, and he follows orders.*

Caim lowered his knives, even though he wanted to cut open the man's throat and let him bleed out on the floor. The swordsman stood up as straight as he was able, favoring his injured leg, and let his blade droop. 'Your mother, Lady Isabeth, is held in the caverns beneath the citadel, deep underground. But none can pass the wards without the Master's leave.'

'So if I find him . . . ,' Caim said.

'You will find the way to her. But this is a trap. The Master is waiting for you.'

Caim pointed with his seax knife. 'Why are you telling me this?'

'My name is Balaam. I have no house save my Master's and I am the last of my line, but I still have my honor.' The swordsman opened a portal beside him. 'And there is one thing more. They have your woman.'

A tremor wriggled down Caim's spine. 'Kit?'

The swordsman gestured, and a cool touch caressed Caim's calf. A picture formed in his mind. The grand audience chamber, draped in darkness.

Caim blinked, but the swordsman was gone. Could he trust him? *There's only one way to find out.*

Caim squeezed his fingers around his knife hilts. The power thrummed inside him like a second heartbeat. He fed his rage into it, feeling the inferno grow higher and hotter. Then he opened his own portal.

CHAPTER THIRTY-ONE

Kit brushed the hair out of her eyes as she turned the corner. The building looked simple from the outside, just four walls and a point at the top, but inside it was a warren of passages and halls, most of them empty. She had started off trying to be quiet, until the clang and clatter of Malig lumbering in her tracks with his huge sword made her give it up as useless.

Seeing that the corridor ran due south, toward what she hoped was the way out, Kit started down it. With every step she thought of Caim. She shouldn't have let him go on alone. She had become human to help him, but then he'd sent her away when he needed her most. *It's just like him. He never listens.*

The corridor widened into a long, high chamber. Arcades ran along either side, topped with balconies overlooking the room. Kit wondered what the place was meant for. It looked like a ballroom or a theater. There were a few doors to choose from, although none of them seemed to head in the right direction.

'You got any idea where you're going, lass?' Malig asked.

'Of course.' The bit of hair fell over her eyes again. She licked her palm and pasted it back behind her ear. 'A little.'

'Let me take the lead, then. Maybe I'll find us some action.'

'I don't *want* any action, you oaf. I just want' – she almost said 'Caim,' but amended it to – 'to get out of here.'

'And when we get out? What then?'

'Caim said—'

'Caim won't be there,' Malig said. 'You got any idea how far it is back to Eregoth? We won't make it. Well, I might. But a little thing like you? Never in a hundred years.'

Kit blinked back the tears that had been hovering in the corners of her eyes since they'd left Caim. 'I know! All right? So shut up and let me think.'

He watched her closely while she considered the options, which made her self-conscious. Just to get moving, she selected the southernmost door in the right-hand wall, but as she headed in that direction, a cold draft blew down the back of her smock. Kit stopped, shivering, and looked up. Two black eyes peered from behind a black visor on the balcony above. The chill took root in her stomach and seized her legs. The face vanished, and then something moved in the far left corner of the chamber. Kit looked, but saw nothing. Only darkness and shadows . . .

'What's the problem?' Malig said as she backed into him. 'I almost cut off your—'

He shoved her aside with a hairy hand, and Kit fell to her knees as a slender figure dressed in black stepped out of the shadows under the balcony. A short spear rested on his shoulder.

Malig pointed his new sword at the man. 'I remember you, boyo. But you don't have your brothers around to protect you, huh?'

Shadows swirled about the room, and another figure in black appeared. And then a third behind them. 'Mal . . . ,' *Kit said.*

But he'd seen them, too. The Eregoth looked around as he hefted his borrowed weapon. 'Run along, little girl, while I entertain these rotten pricks.'

Kit started to say that she wouldn't leave him, but her words turned to a gasp as a warrior darted in close and slashed Malig across the middle of his back with a hooked knife. Malig swung and missed as his enemy drifted away. Kit climbed to her feet. She didn't have a weapon, not even a knife anymore. *Thank you very much, Caim!*

She stepped away from the melee. Malig was turning faster now, trying to keep all three warriors in view, but they were too elusive. Just watching, Kit lost sight of them as they dipped and wove in a swift circle. Malig's sword would have sliced any of them in half if he connected, but he never came close. Inch by inch, foot by foot, they tightened the ring around him. Kit backed away until she touched the wall. She was under the balcony, hidden in the darkness, but she knew the warriors would see her as clear as day when they finished with Malig. They ignored her for the moment. She was no threat to them. *Just a mud-woman. Just a pretty face.*

Spotting a torch in a holder above her head, Kit reached up on her tiptoes for the unlit brand. It was little more than a short wooden stick topped with a wad of pitch-soaked cloth, but it had some heft. *If I only had a flame . . .*

Kit jerked back as a tall shadow loomed over her. Behind the warrior, Malig knelt on one knee with long ribbons of blood running down his side and back. He continued to swing at the other two warriors, but it was over. *We're done for.*

Kit swung the torch with both hands. She put all of her rage and hopelessness into the attack, all of her love for Caim and her wishes for a future with him. The warrior caught the torch with his hand and wrenched it from her grasp. In his other hand, a wicked knife pointed toward her.

CHAPTER THIRTY-TWO

Rays of crimson light slanted down from the throne chamber's vaulted ceiling as Caim leapt out of the portal. The light shone on a person curled up in the center of the floor, but left the walls and periphery swathed in deep shadow.

Caim froze when he saw the silver hair. Kit lay on her side, her arms and legs sprawled lifelessly on the black stones. Knowing it was a trap, and damning it anyway, Caim ran over to her side. He shook her gently, but there was no response. He pressed his fingers into the groove of her neck and released the breath he'd been holding when he found a faint pulse. The skin around her eyes was purple.

As Caim reached to lift her eyelids, a sharp pain pierced his chest. He rose to his feet as the darkness lifted from the room, revealing a crowd of people around him. Their dusky faces watched him, impassive. Four shadow warriors stood at the foot of the dais, black steel weapons in their hands, but his attention was focused on the throne's occupant. The Shadow Lord's face was hidden within a deep cowl, but his presence overshadowed the court like a great black bird of destruction.

Caim's hands sweated inside his gloves. The energy inside him wanted release. It wanted blood. The shadows crawling along the walls hissed and snapped. He moved between Kit and the throne, and stopped a dozen steps from the dais. *A short throw. Just a flick of my wrist.*

'Caim.' The Shadow Lord's voice rang out through the

chamber, and the shadows on the ceiling rustled. 'We are come to preside over your execution.'

The shadow warriors spread out into a semicircular formation in front of him. Caim didn't react, his gaze still on their liege.

'However.' The Shadow Lord gestured to the floor in front of the dais. 'I will stay your death if you would bow before me now and claim your rightful place as the defender of your people.'

Caim wanted to laugh, but it came out in a rumbling growl. 'Whenever people start offering me things, I know they're either trying to stab me in the back, or they're afraid. That's what happened with Sybelle and your other stooges in Othir. None of them understood that all I ever wanted was to be left alone.'

The Shadow Lord opened one hand, and the air beside his throne split open. The swirling vapors resolved into a picture of a woman. At first sight of her profile, Caim took her for his aunt. She had the same narrow nose and full lips, but her features were stony gray, frozen in a horrified rictus. Caim was ready to ignore the image as a statue, though fantastically lifelike, when he noticed the eyes. They were deep and black, boring into him from across the distance.

A tumult of emotions punched through Caim's chest like a spear. For a moment he was a young boy again, sitting on her knee as she sang to him. Words he hadn't understood, and didn't understand now, tickled his ears. A harsh roar scattered the lullaby. Caim looked past his mother's image to a huge black gateway poised behind her. In its unfathomable depths, darkness strove against itself and roiled in eternal combat. He knew its destination at once. *The Other Side. The Realm of Shadow.*

The window vanished, swallowed back into the air as the Shadow Lord closed his fist. 'I think you want more than that, my son. What do the mortals of this world offer you? Nothing but a life of skulking and murder, without purpose, without honor. Here, with your people, is where you belong.'

'Where was that?' Caim asked, taking a step toward the dais. 'What have you done to her?'

The Shadow Lord pulled back his hood. His skin appeared duller, perhaps even looser, than it had before in the audience hall. His eyelids drooped a little. 'I did what was necessary to protect my people. When we first came to this world, there were some who believed we would eventually return to the Other Side. I could not allow that false hope to exist, so I hid the gateway and made it seem as if it were lost forever.'

Murmurs whispered through the hall. The warriors, though, stood as still as eidolons.

The Shadow Lord stood up from his throne. 'We have endured all these years because of my efforts and sacrifices. I even gave my own daughters for this cause! Who dares question me?'

The voices fell silent, but Caim still could feel the tension. He tightened his grip on his knives. Only nine steps separated them. A leap and a long lunge. In less time than it took draw breath, he could plant his knives in the adversary's chest. *My mother's father. Blood of my blood.* 'Is she dead?' he asked.

The Shadow Lord shook his head, and a pained look crossed his face. 'No, she is as you saw her, trapped between our two worlds. I could not destroy the gateway, but I have been able to keep it sealed so that its influence would not interfere with my plans. But keeping it at bay has been difficult. I needed another source of energy, and Isabeth provided that source.'

Caim didn't see the attack coming. The Shadow Lord didn't move, but the air around Caim filled with darkness. Icy fangs tore into his flesh from all directions, ripping into his chest and back, his legs and arms, and across his face. Caim lashed out with his knives, but they encountered nothing. Hissing as an attack slashed across his forehead, he lost his patience and tried to open a portal, only to have it collapse before it fully formed. Something was blocking him. *Not something. Someone.*

Blood dripping down his face, he pushed outward with the energy pulsing inside him, and bit by bit the oppressive blackness retreated. When it cleared, Caim didn't have time to brace himself as terrible agony ripped up his spine. It spun him around and shoved him to the floor.

The Shadow Lord descended the dais steps. 'When I first heard of your existence, I considered exterminating you. Sybelle could have snuffed out your life the night she retrieved your mother, but I withheld my judgment. I wanted to see what would become of you. But I am not impressed.'

Caim started to get up, but a swarm of shadows rained from the ceiling. He could feel their hunger as they sped toward him. Caim reached out to the incoming creatures, and the shadows collided with a bulwark of solid air, sliding down the bubble to the floor where they milled around in circles. On one knee, Caim wrenched himself around and threw. The shadow warriors tried to move in front of their lord, but they were a step too late. The seax knife flew past them, only to halt in midair. The blade shimmered in the ruddy light, six inches from the Shadow Lord's chest.

Caim started to get up, but a massive unseen force shoved down on his shoulders and drove him onto his hands and knees.

The Shadow Lord gestured, and the knife fell to the floor. 'Pathetic. And to think I might have chosen you as my successor. You were a mistake.'

Caim's left elbow buckled, slamming his forehead to the floor. Images flashed through his mind. Of sitting in his mother's lap while his father spun tales in front of a log fire. Of Josey lying beside him on her big feather bed. Of Kit laughing at his misfortunes. He turned his face. She was so close, yet just beyond his reach. Caim groaned as the air was squeezed from his lungs. The power was beyond anything he had ever encountered, stronger than ten Sybelles. Part of him wanted to give up, let it crush him and be done, but another part clung to every tortured breath. As he had done against the black cloud, he pushed back with his will. The pressure above him eased for a moment, and Caim took advantage of the respite to dredge up all his strength. He pushed and thrust himself up to a kneeling position. New strength surged through his veins as he met the Shadow Lord's hooded gaze. *He's a man, the same as you. If he can bleed, he can die.*

'You're going to tell me,' Caim said as he got one foot under him, 'where she is.'

Before the Shadow Lord answered, a faint pop reached Caim's ears, and the shadow swordsman, Balaam, appeared beside him. The force pressing down on Caim vanished at once. Swaying slightly, he struggled to his feet. He gripped his *suete* knife tight, ready for anything.

'Enach ir thune panthador.' Balaam took off his helmet and tossed it on the floor at the foot of the dais. 'I renounce my service to you and your house, Abraxus Thargelia. From this moment forward, I am my own man.'

The Shadow Lord frowned. 'If that is your choice . . .'

Balaam flew back as if he'd been slammed by a stone from a catapult. Caim turned, expecting to see the swordsman splattered against a wall, but he lay a few paces behind Kit, flattened to the floor. Caim reacted by instinct, channeling his power into a tight punch. A lance of pure darkness shot across the chamber. The Shadow Lord staggered back and folded his arms across his chest.

The majordomo opened a portal and jumped through. At the same time, a face in the crowd disappeared, and then another. The Shadow Lord looked around as his court abandoned him in twos and threes. Then he stepped into a patch of shadows beside his throne and vanished.

But not everyone departed. Caim braced himself as the

shadow warriors advanced on silent footsteps. When they got within three paces, Caim attacked. He charged in fast, knife held high, and then dipped down in a slide. The lead shadow warrior spun his spear around as he retreated, but Caim's momentum carried him past the warrior's guard. He punched up, and links of black mail burst apart as the *suete*'s point drove deep into the warrior's diaphragm.

Caim jumped over the body, flinging shadows behind him as he snatched up his fallen seax knife from the dais steps. The three remaining warriors batted the darknesses aside and rushed toward him. Caim parried a curved sickle from his left, feinted, and darted back with a high-low attack that met a pair of black daggers. The seax gave off blue sparks as it rebounded from the dusky metal. As Caim pressed with a series of quick strikes, the sickle-fighter slipped behind him. Caim focused his powers and hopped to the opposite side of the chamber. Before his enemies could track him, he beckoned to the thousands of shadows lurking along the walls and high ceiling. Their voices chittered as he wrapped his mind around them. When he released his hold, they flew.

The warriors vanished and appeared around him. At the same instant, the storm struck. The shadow warriors were hurtled back as a whirlwind of darkness tore through them. The sickle fighter slammed into a wall; the collision made a satisfying crackle of breaking bones. The other two disappeared into portals.

Caim released the shadows, and the whirlwind dispersed. He was battered and torn, leaking blood from several places, but still alive. He jumped back as the dagger fighter appeared to his left and prepared to meet the shadow warrior knife-to-knife, but black steel flashed, and the dagger fighter collapsed to his knees, blood running in spurts down his side as his severed right arm and most of the shoulder joint fell to the floor. Balaam stood behind him, sword held in a low two-handed grip.

The last shadow warrior arrived behind Balaam and swung a short-hafted poleaxe of black steel at his back. Balaam stepped out of the weapon's path as smooth as a dancer and took off the warrior's head.

Stomach clenched, Caim ignored the deaths and ran over to Kit. Her eyes fluttered when he touched her face. 'Can you hear me?' he asked.

'Yeah, But you're a little fuzzy.'

She tried to sit up, but he held her down with a gentle hand. 'Take it easy. How do you feel?'

'Like I got run over by a pack of mules in steel shoes. What happened?'

'I was going to ask you the same thing. I thought you and Malig were leaving—'

Kit put a hand to her mouth. 'Oh, Caim! Malig! He's . . . We ran into trouble, and he . . .'

Caim took her in his arms and let her sob into his chest. Balaam walked over, cleaning his weapon. 'You,' Caim called out. 'Why did you come back?'

Balaam dropped the cloth – a ripped cape – he'd been using, but kept his sword in hand. 'I have served Lord Abraxus for most of my life. My honor demanded that I leave his service in person.' The ghost of a smile haunted his mouth. 'And I had debts of my own to pay.'

But then his face smoothed. 'There are caverns below Erebus. That is where your mother is held.' Balaam pointed, and the outline of a circle glowed beside the throne where the Shadow Lord had disappeared. 'That is the way.'

Caim looked down to Kit. She had stopped crying and seemed content to rest against him. *I should take her away and forget about all this.* And yet, he couldn't leave without knowing. 'Can you take her out of here?'

Balaam observed them for a long heartbeat. 'I must see to my own affairs, but I can take her.'

Kit placed a hand on his chest. 'No, I won't leave you again.'

He wanted to kiss her, but instead lifted her in his arms. 'I'll be right behind you.'

She smacked him in the chest. 'Liar.'

'Isn't that why you love me?'

Kit smiled and planted a peck on his chin instead. 'Hurry then.'

Caim handed her to Balaam, who held her awkwardly. Caim started to turn away, but the swordsman stopped him.

'Wait. Take this.'

Balaam held out his sword. The black steel shimmered.

'I . . .' Caim recalled his father's sword, and how wielding it had made him feel. 'I can't accept that.'

Balaam tossed the sword, and Caim caught it by the hilt. He braced himself for a flood of bloodlust, but felt nothing special. It was just a sword, though extremely light and well-balanced. The edge looked sharp enough to shave with. He sheathed his seax knife.

'Be careful,' Kit said, her eyes closing.

Caim stepped back from them and opened a portal in the spot of the glowing marker. Raising the black sword to Balaam in a salute, he stepped through.

CHAPTER THIRTY-THREE

White mist hovered above the plain, obscuring everything beyond the stream, which was swift and turbulent from the recent rain.

Sitting astride Lightning, Josey looked across the valley floor. The soldiers were set before her. Their helmets and the points of their spears reflected the dull morning light. Damp flags hung limp in the hands of the standard-bearers. The ranks were drawn up differently than last time. Lord General Argentus had been an old-school strategist who followed the traditional methods – infantry had to be deployed a certain way, with archers placed just so, and the pikemen thusly – but Colonel Klovus and Brian were more flexible. The troops were not so spread out as before, but the steep hills on either side of the field protected their flanks. They had no siege weapons this time, and few archers, but a platoon of cross-bowmen had survived the last confrontation. They were placed on the slopes of each hill. Josey hoped it was a good tactic, but the troops looked woefully exposed on the bare tors. A priest moved among the men, touching their foreheads as he prayed. His white cloak billowed behind him in the breeze.

Lightning stamped on the soft ground, and she leaned forward. 'Easy, boy. It's all right.'

He calmed down, but Josey's stomach was turning cart-wheels. *I wish someone would tell me that everything is going to be all right.* She touched her belly. Again last night, her officers had urged her to quit the battle and flee south. Josey knew their concern was genuine, especially Brian's, but she couldn't leave now. It was her decision to give battle; she owed it to the men risking their lives to stand with them. And if she should fall, she knew Hubert would defend the realm.

In the early light of dawn, Brian had stood with her, outlining his plans, but she had interrupted with a question. 'What is this place?'

She saw pieces of stone, too regular to be natural formations, jutting from the ground at the base of their hill.

'It's the Valley of Seven Arrows,' he replied, gazing with her.

The name sounded familiar, but she couldn't place it.

'This is where King Guldrien and his Knights Brethren made their last stand.'

Josey looked down into the valley again with new eyes as fragments of the epic poem floated through her mind. ' "And anon they stood shoulder to shoulder against the tyrant's charge," ' she quoted.

' "Each was pierced through the heart with deathly steel and fell down at his feet," ' Brian finished.

'This is a place of honor.'

He smiled. 'Not everyone would see it that way.'

Josey was shaken from her thoughts as a clarion call resounded across the field. It looked as if High Captain Keegan had been correct; the invaders were coming straight at them. *Heaven help us.*

The Uthenorians arrived in a great, roiling tide. Like before, they followed no order of battle. Spearmen marched beside men carrying huge axes and swords, even a few wielding hammers on long handles. Their numbers appeared even greater than last time, if that was possible. As Hirsch had said, there was little cover in the valley. The only true obstacle was the creek, but the water was just waist high. The first enemy units plunged into the cold waters without pause. They were halfway across when the vanguard bunched up. Their shouts echoed in the rising mists as blood swirled in the water. It had been Brian's suggestion to plant sharpened stakes in the streambed. An officer called out, and a flight of arrows and bolts sailed high, falling on the enemy. Men collapsed and were dragged away by the swift current, but the reprieve was short-lived as the mass of soldiers surged onward to the shore. The missiles from her troops continued to fall, but they were pitifully meager compared to the number of enemies approaching. As the invaders gained the southern bank, they drove ahead.

Brian commanded the center of the battle line where the bulk of her infantry was concentrated. He rode back and forth through the ranks, exhorting them to stand firm. The troops readied their weapons. Less than a hundred yards separated the two armies.

Just as Josey wondered where Hirsch was, the adept rode up. His pants and boots were caked with mud. Leaves and dirt were smeared across his oversized jacket. If possible, his hat looked even sadder and floppier than before.

He handed her a slim package wrapped in burlap. 'Here, lass. I thought you might be missing this.'

Josey handled the pouch gingerly. 'What did you do to it?'

'Just a little something in case things take a turn for the worst. But keep it out of sight and hope we won't need it.'

She slid it into a pocket in her riding jacket. 'Yes. Let's hope.'

The enemy rolled toward them like a front of storm clouds, vast and unstoppable. When they came within throwing range, javelins and flying blades flew between the armies. Josey was heartened to see her soldiers get the better of the volley, but her joy was fleeting as the first elements of the two forces clashed. Her soldiers locked shields and dug in their heels, but they couldn't hold back the tide. Holes appeared in her front line and widened to gaping rents through which the enemy poured in. Everywhere Josey looked, her soldiers were falling back, except for the center where Brian stood firm inside a knot of stubborn pikemen. Yet, when he got down from his steed – or was knocked down – that section gave way as well. A sick feeling bubbled in Josey's stomach. She flinched at the screams of the dying and wounded. This was her fault. She wrapped the reins tighter around her hands.

But then a standard waved back and forth through the rising mists. It bore the green eagle of House Therbold on a golden field. The fighting cleared for a moment, and Josey saw Brian on his feet, waving the standard amid a cluster of her soldiers. To her amazement, they held for a moment against the grinding invader force surrounding them. The moment extended to a full minute, and then another. Bodies piled up around the standard, both enemy and ally alike, but Brian did not falter. Josey's heart pounded. Pain squeezed her fingers, and she looked down to see her hands bound up in loops of Lightning's reins, so tight it cut off her circulation.

Lightning took a couple steps as she unwound her hands, but Hirsch caught hold of the lead. 'Not yet, lass.'

Josey swallowed her tears. Brian's men held out, but they were isolated in a sea of gray and black. She looked to the eastern hills where the mists were thinning, and saw only a few scrub trees. *Where are they?*

Then a sound like distant thunder echoed over the field. Josey held her breath as she saw them: Walthom's light horse charging down the hill. The morning light gleamed on their shields and lances, pennons fluttering in the breeze. The crash of steel and splintering wood as they struck the invading force resounded across the battlefield. Walthom's cavalry pierced deep into the enemy's flank, trampling bodies as they went.

But the Uthenorians' numbers were too great. Enemy units turned to meet the new threat, more and more with the passing minutes, until Walthom's momentum was blunted. Josey looked to the west and almost missed the charge of the Eregoths.

High Captain Keegan rode at the tip of the wedge as his

men crashed into the enemy from the opposite direction. There was no order or pageantry about the rise and fall of their swords and axes as they clove deep into the invading host. It was slaughter in its purest sense.

The breath she'd been holding whistled through Josey's teeth as the two opposite forces crushed the enemy flanks and rolled them back. The crossbowmen renewed their barrage on the enemy. If the center held just a little longer . . .

'Is there anyone we can send to reinforce Sir Brian's position?' she asked Hirsch.

He opened his mouth, but a loud explosion scattered his words. A plume of black smoke rose from the battlefield amid rows of soldiers in shredded armor. Josey stood up in the stirrups, her heart thudding in her throat, but there was no sign of Brian. His banner had vanished in the oily cloud. A roar like the ending of the world broke over the valley, and the daylight fled under the rising pall.

'Down!'

Hirsch snatched her down by the arm, but she had already seen it. Him. The enemy warlord had crossed the stream. His bodyguard cleared the way before him. Those few soldiers who had held their positions at the front line were smashed aside like cloth dolls, and the warlord rode through their blood.

'Can you help them?' Josey asked Hirsch.

But the adept's eyes were closed. His lips moved to a low sound like the purr of a bullfrog.

'Master Hirsch?' she asked.

'Shhhhh.' He put a finger to his lips. 'He's getting close.'

Yes, I can see that! And if we don't stop him, all the schemes and tactics in the world won't save us. The warlord waved his gauntleted hand, and another explosion rocked the battlefield, this time closer to her position.

Remaining still while the explosions walked closer and closer like the footsteps of an invisible giant was the hardest thing Josey had ever done. She wanted to kick her heels into

Lightning's sides until the field was far behind. *I need to do this. For all who have died today for me, I can at least show that much courage.*

She watched the approaching death with her chin held high. From across the sea of clashing arms, the warlord faced in her direction with his hand out, one finger pointing as if in accusation. The debris from the next explosion showered down on Josey's head. She wanted to shake Hirsch as he continued his mantra, but kept her hands locked on the reins, afraid she might scream if she didn't have something to hold onto. Then the adept took off without a word on his nimble steed, leaping over the smoking crater and out of her sight.

Josey held back for a moment, and then shook the reins. Lightning took off like his namesake. She bent down over his muscled neck, his mane flying in her face, and wondered what in the name of the gods she was doing. But she knew one thing: if her army was destroyed this day, she would go down with her men. She freed one hand to press against her belly. *Forgive me, little one. It's not fair. I love you more than you can know, but I must do this.*

She didn't wipe away her tears this time, but let them run down her cheeks as she plunged into the fray.

CHAPTER THIRTY-FOUR

Caim emerged from the portal with his knees bent and sword extended, ready to meet an attack. But nothing happened.

He was surrounded by the rough walls of a cavern, their slopes clad in cascades of white crystal up to an unseen ceiling. The floor was uneven. Stark blue light shone from a low, uneven archway ahead of him. Caim stole through the arch toward the eerie light, and paused at the entrance to a cavern even longer and broader than the throne chamber above. The light came from the center of the floor, where a rich, azure flame rose from a stone urn, throwing deep shadows across the walls and ceiling.

The Shadow Lord stood with his back to the entrance. He looked smaller, bent and crooked like an old man. Caim focused on an imaginary spot between his enemy's shoulders as he started across the cavern. But halfway to the flaming urn he stopped, his gaze drawn to the wall beyond the Shadow Lord where a cave mouth yawned. A cold dread settled over Caim as he realized it was no cave, but the gateway he had seen in the vision. Utterly black, massive in proportion, it sucked in all the light around it. As soon as he saw it, Caim felt a sharp pang in his head. This was the source of the pulling. All this time he'd been thinking it was his . . .

Caim spotted a slim figure immersed in the gateway. She wasn't moving, and at first Caim thought she might be unconscious, but then her eyes sought him out from across the cavern, the same black eyes as from his childhood memories.

Mother!

Caim couldn't stop from taking another step, but the Shadow Lord's cool voice brought him to a halt.

'We aren't the first people of the Shadow to find this world.'

Abraxus turned, looking nothing like the imposing dark lord he'd been before. His robes hung loose on his frame now, his complexion a dingy sallow pocked with brown spots. 'The tribes of these wastes have a myth of an immortal tyrant who ruled over them centuries ago. When my family and I arrived here, it was simple enough to assume the role of this eldritch despot returned to life. Few as we were, we succeeded in subjugating the local peoples and began the construction of this city. It was to be a monument to a new empire, a new world.'

Caim took a step, hefting the black sword. 'What have you done to my mother?'

The Shadow Lord lifted his hand, and a shudder went through the cavern. Shards of crystal and stone shattered on the floor. Caim thought he saw his mother's eyes shift, but it might have been a trick of the light.

The Shadow Lord sighed, or perhaps it was a stifled groan. 'Isabeth was my last hope for a new chance for our people. My shining jewel. And look what this world has done to her.'

Caim ground his teeth together. 'The world didn't do this to her. The world didn't send soldiers to my father's home to kill him and steal my mother away. *You* did those things.'

'All to ensure the survival of our people. When we crossed over into this world, the rift we created remained open.' The Shadow Lord shuffled a step closer to the void, and to Caim's mother. 'At first this was desirable. Despite your brilliant sun, we grew in strength and power, strong enough to scorch the sky and begin to make this world more hospitable to our needs. But we also noticed changes in the Shadow. Minor incongruities at first, but they grew to the point where it became obvious the Shadow would not stop until it had devoured this entire world, just as it consumed our homeland.'

The Shadow Lord shook his head as if talking to someone else. 'Once I realized the danger, I held the gateway sealed for as long as I could, but as the years passed it became more difficult, more insidious in its ways to defeat me. My daughter did not always agree with my methods, but even when she ran off with that . . . with the man who was to become your father, I always believed she would return. She understood that the gateway to the Other Side needed to be controlled.'

Caim gazed at his mother, trapped in the maw of the portal. The vibrancy had been leeched out of her. Even worse, she still lived. 'You're trying to tell me she volunteered for this? Go to hell. Release her now. Undo whatever you've done.'

'That I cannot do.' The Shadow Lord, his grandfather, waved him back with a veiny hand. The tendons on the back of his neck stood out as if they could barely hold up his head. 'Even if I wanted to, the rift will not release her now.'

'So you lured me north for what? To take my mother's place?'

'No, my son. I never wanted you to be a part of this. But I fear it no longer matters what either of us want. The choice is before us.'

The Shadow Lord reached out his hand toward the void, his fingers splayed as if they were plunging into a vat of filth. Lines of dark energy flowed from the Shadow Lord's hand, into the gateway, and the black void was pushed back. Just a few inches, but it allowed Caim to see more of his mother. She was hunched in her frozen pose. Her eyes stared at him with silent intensity.

Caim ran toward the Shadow Lord's turned back. He didn't care about choices or old myths. He was going to end this here and—

The shadows swarmed to him. At first he thought they were

attacking, until they folded around him in a protective cocoon. A moment later the gateway expanded, pulsing like an open heart, and a tide of spectral energy burst through the cavern. Caim was batted across the floor to land against the wall where he had entered. His skin was ice-cold where the shadows bit into him; he felt them shivering.

As he struggled to his feet, Caim looked across the cavern. The Shadow Lord stood rigid, back arched, with the point of a black knife protruding from his back.

The Shadow Lord collapsed, and Lord Malphas appeared behind him in the wavering azure light, blood dripping from his belt dagger. Caim shook as a mélange of emotions coursed through him. He had intended to kill his grandfather to save his mother, but to see another standing over the Shadow Lord's corpse, with a cool smile on his lips, fanned the flames of his rage. Caim called, and the shadows coalesced around Malphas in a swirling storm. The cacophony of a thousand chittering voices filled the cavern. Yet just as fast as the storm formed, it flew apart, the shadows shrieking as they were hurtled away to gouge deep ravines in the cavern's walls. Caim threw an arm over his face. Lord Malphas stood in the now-empty space. His eyes were flat black discs within their puckered lids.

'You'll forgive us,' the majordomo said, 'if we disregard the speech making and proceed with killing you.'

Caim only had a moment to react before an avalanche of gleaming black shards flew at him. Without knowing what he was doing, he reached out with his powers, and the shards shattered in puffs of dust. But they came thicker and faster, until Caim felt his protection being chipped away. He braced himself and twisted the direction of his mental shield, pushing the torrent up and away toward the ceiling. Bits of rock and dust rained down on him, but Caim was moving, maintaining his barrier as he maneuvered around the flaming urn. *If I can just get within reach of him . . .*

A massive buffet sent him tumbling across the floor. His sheath of shadows fluttered, some of them peeling off and falling away. His entire torso felt like one big bruise. Caim didn't see the next attack coming, but he rolled away as an unseen force gathered above his head. He opened a portal and dove through. As he emerged, the air sizzled as Malphas hurled a bolt of black fire. Caim twisted away, but the dark flames followed him. The floor slipped out from under his feet. Falling, Caim raised his arms to protect his face, and his sword hand was enveloped in icy cold. The chill passed up his arm, numbing his burning flesh. When he lifted his hand, the fire was gone. His glove and the sleeve of his jacket on his right arm had been burned away – nothing but tattered black scraps remained. He'd lost some hair underneath, too, but the skin of his hand and arm were unharmed.

Lord Malphas stood beside the chromatic flames, ebon sparks raining from his fingers. A section of the cavern wall sloughed off and crumbled to the floor. The gateway writhed and wriggled as if agitated by the combat. Once again, Caim's mother had slipped deeper into its black embrace.

'Is that it?' Caim climbed to his feet. He grimaced as the words passed his lips, but he couldn't help himself. 'I've crossed half the world to find this place, and this.' He used his *suete* to scrape some pieces of burned leather from his shoulder. 'This is the best you can do?'

Lord Malphas turned to the gateway. The void pulsed again, and Caim braced himself for another burst of dark energy. Instead, something emerged from the blackness. It was a hand, as black as the gateway itself, followed by an arm and shoulder. Caim swallowed a curse as a man-shaped thing slunk out of the gateway, slipping past his mother, to stand on the cavern floor. Its face twisted into a visage that he remembered from a long time ago.

Dalros Vicencho.

With a whining growl, the merchant's doppelganger

lurched toward Caim with a black dagger in its hand. Caim set himself to meet the threat, but more shapes were emerging from the gateway. Like the Dalros shade, they took on the resemblances of people he'd known. Duke Reinard of Ostergoth. Liram Kornfelsh. Even Edric Klapsur, one of the men he'd killed in Freehold when he was little more than a boy. A cold finger scratched down Caim's spine when he realized they weren't just men he'd known. They were men he had killed, all returned like revenants from the grave.

Caim was jarred from his horror by a sweeping strike from Dalros. Caim blocked the dagger with his sword and stepped in close to drive his *suete* knife into the creature's paunchy stomach. The knife sunk in easily, but the doppelganger didn't react like a man who'd been stabbed. Instead, it grabbed for his face with its other hand. Caim jumped back, and narrowly missed being spitted on Duke Reinard's black rapier. Caim knocked the thin sword aside, and ducked a clubbing from the duke's young, dead son. *Robert?*

The cavern drew dark as the murderous shades surrounded Caim. He tried to keep them at bay, deflecting their attacks and staying a step ahead of them, but they were so many. Sooner or later he would miss a block, and then it would be all over. Beyond their sooty shoulders, Lord Malphas watched with a look of cool satisfaction.

Gritting his teeth in frustration, Caim abandoned his defensive posture and lashed out. The shade of Melbin Westering, second-rate loan shark, paid no mind to the *suete* knife that stabbed into his thigh, but one slash of the black sword separated the moneylender's head from his shoulders and he collapsed in a pool of black ooze. A small tingle ran up the hilt of the sword, and Caim smiled.

The shades fell one by one, sloshing their liquefied remains on the cavern floor. When the last one had been dispatched, Caim stood alone. Panting and covered in ooze, but alive.

Standing before the gateway, Lord Malphas no longer

smiled. His eyes bulged like he'd eaten something rotten. Caim shook the gore from his weapons and started to advance, but hesitated when the shadow noble staggered. A wet cracking sound echoed through the cave, and a drop of black ichor dripped from Malphas's left eye.

Caim imagined a spot beside the nobleman, but something went wrong when he tried to shadow-jump. The floor dropped out from under his feet. He landed hard on his tailbone and rolled over, biting back the pain. Malphas loomed over him, ribbons of shadow shooting out from his hands like long, black whips.

Caim lunged, though his tortured muscles cried out in agony. His black sword pierced Malphas's stomach and sunk half the length of the blade. Caim started to relax, until he looked into his enemy's eyes. They showed no pain or fear of death, only infinite contempt.

With a jerk of his arms, Lord Malphas looped his tentacles around Caim in an iron embrace. Caim shouted aloud as the ebon cords sliced through his protective layer of shadows and into his flesh. Blood poured down his legs.

A rapturous hiss echoed from Malphas's open mouth. Caim watched, horrified, as the skin peeled away from the noble's face and neck, revealing a rippling blackness underneath.

CHAPTER THIRTY-FIVE

A curtain of smoke swept over Josey, making her eyes water and filling her lungs when she tried to breathe. Coughing into her sleeve, she tried to find her battle standards. Harsh shouts and pain-filled cries echoed from all directions. A wobbling arrow flew perilously close as she looked around, reminding her that she wore no armor or helm.

This is foolish. I can't make any difference here. True, she had no weapons save for a pair of knives, and she wasn't likely to turn the tide with her skill at arms. But she had a voice.

'Nimea!' she shouted. 'To me!'

Her voice was swallowed by the raucous din and the smoke, but Josey stood up in her stirrups. 'Nimea to your empress! Nimea to me!'

There was no answering call. But then a soldier in Nimean livery limped toward her through the mists. Another pikeman stumbled after him, followed by a trio of crossbowmen in scale-mail hauberks. As more soldiers appeared, they formed a ring around her. One of her bodyguards emerged from the smoke, holding the side of his head where blood leaked down in a steady trickle. Josey leaned down as he clutched her stirrup strap. His ear had been torn away, along with a goodly portion of the skin along that side of his head.

Josey looked to the nearest men. 'Help him!'

'Majesty,' the bodyguard said. He was having trouble catching his breath. 'Captain . . . Drathan. Must get you . . . away!'

'No. My place is here with you. We'll fight.'

Lightning reared up as an explosion rocked the ground. Josey couldn't see where it landed, but chunks of sod rained down on her little squad. She started to tell the bodyguard to seek assistance for his ear when a horn sounded nearby. Foreign voices rose beyond the veil of smoke. As Josey pulled her steed under control, there was a sound like a stick striking a tree. Then a flood of enemies emerged from the haze, screaming like demons.

Josey fought to keep her seat as her ring of defenders was driven back. A volley of arrows peppered the front rank of pikemen, and Josey almost swallowed her tongue. Alone atop her steed, dressed in a sky-blue riding jacket, she couldn't have made a more obvious target. Yet she rejected the urge to hug Lightning's neck. Her soldiers fought like heroes. Invaders fell around them, their bodies piling up in the bloody mire. When one of her men collapsed, another stepped into the gap. They suffered horrible wounds and kept battling, returning blow for blow. Josey forced herself to watch the carnage while she shouted orders. The pikemen stayed at the front. Her crossbowmen fired point-blank into the sea of enemies, cocking and loading their heavy weapons as fast as they were able. Stenches of death and blood swirled above the battlefield. They crept into Josey's throat and brought tears to her eyes, but she clutched to the hope that they could hold out, that the invaders would exhaust themselves and draw back. She was turning to her right flank when a turbulent wave of air crashed over her. She spun around in the saddle as Lightning floundered. Josey clung to the stallion's mane with both hands as he righted himself.

The world had fallen silent. Men opened their mouths, apparently shouting as they fought and died, but she heard nothing. Through the haze and Lightning's flying mane, a huge warrior in black armor strode into view. His greatsword sliced into the side of a pikeman and almost cut the man in half. More black-armored fighters charged from out of the mist. Her soldiers struggled, but they were too few. And the northerners were too fierce, battering her soldiers with massive hammers, swords, and axes. Josey looked around for reinforcements to fill the gap, but her voice failed her as the enemy commander emerged from the horde on his tall black horse.

Talus. Keegan had called him the Thunder Lord. He looked even more fearsome up close. His crimson armor made him look like a primal god of war bathed in blood. Trails of shadowy smoke rose from his eyes, which burned like smoldering coals in their cavernous sockets. Her soldiers fell back as he crashed into their faltering lines. Some turned and tried to flee, but there was nowhere to go. They were cut down from behind as the warlord's steed trampled over their bodies.

Josey didn't know what to do. All of a sudden the will to resist seemed too much effort. Where were her defenders? Where was Captain Drathan? Where was Brian? *I wanted him to be my savior. But he's gone, just like Caim.*

The Thunder Lord drew a sword from a scabbard by his side. The blade was black as midnight. Etched designs ran up its sides like tongues of fire. Josey drew Brian's dagger and held it close to her breast as she imagined her head tumbling to the ground. Would it hurt much?

A Word resonated from the warlord's mouth. Josey felt Lightning thrash like he was trying to run in four different directions. Then she was falling. A sharp pain impaled her hip as she struck the ground. She had landed on a shield half-submerged in the mud. Its metal boss was wedged under her side. Josey found it hard to take a deep breath as agony like she'd never felt rippled through her pelvis. Lightning had bolted off, and she'd lost Brian's dagger. With one hand clutching her stomach, she looked up.

The Thunder Lord had cut a swathe through her soldiers. The iron-bound hooves of his warhorse pawed at the ground as if it wanted to crush her into the earth. His black sword rose up, blocking out the hazy sunlight. This was it. Her final moment. Josey tried to swallow, but her throat would not work. She braced herself to receive the blow, but then a flood of scintillating light burst before her eyes. She blinked through the radiance to see a man on a white horse plunge between her and the warlord. Josey almost choked on a joyful sob as Hirsch pushed the Thunder Lord back with beams of blazing light flung from his hands.

The adept's sudden appearance reminded Josey of what he had given her before the battle. She reached into her jacket pocket, but couldn't find it. Frantic, she tore off her cloak and the jacket and searched it again. Her fingers found a hard edge in a different pocket. Josey ripped the fabric open, and the box fell out. She opened it with trembling fingers. Her signet ring was nestled inside on a bed of white muslin. The carbuncle jewel shone like a miniature sun, too bright to look at directly. Hirsch had required a gemstone to fashion his magic, and the signet was the largest one she had. Josey reached for the ring, expecting it to be hot, but the smooth metal was cool to the touch.

Josey stood up on wobbly legs as Hirsch's hands flashed again. *Maybe I won't have to use it if Master Hirsch can—*

The earth shook, and a harsh wind crashed over her. Through squinting eyelids Josey saw Hirsch slumped over, holding up his right arm. It took her a moment to realize his hand was gone, severed below the elbow, with a river of blood streaming from the raw stump. The adept swayed in his saddle. The Thunder Lord's sword smoked as it rose again. Josey bit her tongue and threw.

The glowing signet sailed like a leaf. Josey's chest was clenched too tight to breathe. Hirsch pitched forward as the black sword started to fall. Then the ring struck the Thunder Lord in his armored shoulder. An instant later, Josey was lifted off the ground and thrown back. Her hip shrieked at the rough treatment, and various hard surfaces battered her head, neck, and elbows as the world spun over and over. Tremendous heat surged over her and filled her nose with a choking, acrid stench.

She came to rest, partly curled up, on the ground. Josey opened her eyes to the lead-gray sky. She couldn't feel any part of her body for several long heartbeats. When sensation resumed, it was filled with jagged pains. It seemed to take hours for her hands to find her stomach, but she felt better when she touched the bump under her clothes. All her worries fell away, leaving her calm in the midst of the battlefield. She attempted to sit up and regretted it as everything hurt. Then she looked around.

All her men were down. Sorrow stabbed her heart until she saw them, friend and foe alike, getting up with blood running from their noses and ears. Yet there was no sign of Master Hirsch or the Thunder Lord. Josey had managed to rise to her knees when she saw part of a torso and a pair of legs clad in mutilated remnants of crimson armor, half buried in the mud. There was nothing left of his head and upper body. Josey looked away as fresh nausea ripped through her stomach. *It's over. My people are saved.*

Then she saw Hirsch's torn brown jacket and she crawled over to him, ignoring the fierce pains in her knees and hip. The adept had lost his hat. His eyes were closed. Half his beard and mustache had been singed away. Josey peeled back his jacket and almost cried. Ripping off his shirt, she shouted for help and then wrapped it around the stump of his right arm, but Hirsch reached up with his remaining hand to stay her.

'He's dead?' His voice was wan and labored.

Josey nodded as a tear ran down the side of her nose. 'Your trick worked. Blew him straight to hell.'

'Not a . . .' Hirsch coughed, and his entire body quaked. The grimace of agony on his face made Josey want to wail. 'Not a trick. Good, clean magic.'

She laughed through the tears. 'Don't talk. We'll find a

physician and you'll be back to your old self again in no time at all.'

'Don't lie to me, lass.' The next cough almost lifted him off the ground. When it left him, he sighed. 'Done a lot of things I regret. I earned the name Red-Hand . . . a thousand times over. Death is the least I deserve.'

'Don't say that.' She couldn't swallow. 'You saved me. You saved us all.'

He looked at her with a crooked smile. 'I'm glad I came to your palace that day. Maybe that makes up for some of the other. Maybe.'

A rush of emotions ripped through Josey as she watched his chest rise and fall. Rise and fall. Rise and . . .

She willed herself not to cry. She wanted to be home, back in Othir, with her sorrows behind, but the fighting continued. Her soldiers made a human barricade around her, but how long could that last? A patch of blue on the ground caught her eye. Josey reached over Hirsch and pulled a sheet of fabric from the dirt. It was her imperial standard, the golden griffon on a cerulean field, attached to a broken pole. Josey stood up, trying not to groan as her hip protested, and raised the banner. With her other hand she drew her stiletto and brandished it to the sky. Then she shouted at the top of her lungs.

'Nimea!'

She screamed it again, pouring out all of her sorrow and frustration. Some of her troops glanced over their shoulders, and then they surged forward as if buoyed by her cries. A tall man pushed through their lines, and Josey pointed her knife at him until she recognized his face. Brian looked like a gift from heaven, despite the covering of dirt and blood. He lifted his visor, and Josey smiled, more relieved than she had any right to be. Then he took up her rallying cry and rejoined the fight.

Josey couldn't see much beyond the circle of her defenders, but later she would hear accounts that the invaders had lost the will to fight after their commander fell by her hand. Or possibly his sorcery held some sway over them that evaporated with his demise. Her army, bolstered by the light cavalry and Keegan's fighters, pushed the Uthenorians back to the stream. Small groups of invaders peeled off and tried to ford the channel to safety, many of them drowning. Others tried to scale the hills, and most of them were cut down by crossbow fire. Before long these defections triggered a full rout.

And so the second battle for the Valley of Seven Arrows ended.

As the sun touched the tops of the western hills, Josey and Brian stood among the dead and dying and looked out over the incredible carnage. Flocks of ravens and other carrion birds covered the valley floor, taking their due as soldiers and camp followers separated the living from the dead. To the north, her cavalry was pursuing the surviving invaders. She couldn't believe it was over.

'Majesty.'

Josey turned to see a soldier holding Lightning's reins. It was her bodyguard with the missing ear, his head now wrapped in a crude dressing.

'I found him wandering a ways back. He's yours, isn't he?'

She nodded, unable to stop the tears this time. 'Yes, he is. Thank you . . .'

'Prett, Your Majesty. Sergeant Nikodemus Prett.'

'Thank you, Sergeant Prett.'

Josey hugged the stallion's neck, wanting to burrow into his soft mane. She looked around for something to use to mount up, and Brian went to one knee beside her. Settling into the saddle, Josey turned Lightning south and let him carry her back toward the camp. Brian walked by her side.

They exchanged no words, only an occasional glance. The sky threatened rain.

CHAPTER THIRTY-SIX

'You cannot fight the Shadow.'

The black eyes of the thing that inhabited Lord Malphas bore down on Caim. 'We are everywhere. We *see* everything. We know your deepest fears. Submit or we will destroy you.'

Caim bent down to the floor, weighed down by the black tendrils and the awful truth of those words. He wasn't strong enough to win against this enemy. His knives were useless, and the shadows wouldn't hurt one of their own.

He has been corrupted by the Shadow.

Caim lifted his head as the words formed in his mind. The voice was soft and feminine, and after a moment he recognized its source. *Mother?*

Malphas has succumbed to the power of the Shadow, but he is not invulnerable, my son. You must seek the strength that dwells within.

Caim closed his eyes and shut out the pain. How could he kill the majordomo without his powers or his weapons? Then something glimmered in the darkness behind his eyelids. It glowed like a spark in his mind, growing brighter as he concentrated on it. He remembered the surge of energy Kit had given him with her kiss, and a soothing warmth suffused his chest, flowing outward to his limbs.

Caim shifted his arms under the coils. His first step was getting free. Focusing on the spark, he climbed to one knee, and then the other. The shadow tentacles constricted around his thighs and calves, making movement difficult, but he gathered his legs under him.

'You *must* submit,' Malphas hissed.

Caim strained with his arms, forcing them upward. The black tendrils squeezed tighter, digging deeper into his skin, but he didn't stop. He pushed back with his mind, and the coils stretched inch by painful inch. Malphas growled as the tentacles snapped apart. Caim gathered his strength and leapt, not for his weapons on the floor, but toward Malphas with his hands extended. He unleashed every iota of power he had left. The spark blazed like a tiny sun in his imagination. Caim squinted as shards of white light appeared in his hands. About the length of his forearm, they looked like nothing so much as knives carved from pure starlight. He plunged them both into the nobleman's chest.

Malphas's lips parted in a silent howl as oily smoke issued from the wounds. His hands clawed at Caim's back and shoulders. Caim held on and pushed to drive the blades of light deeper. The black of Malphas's eyes lightened to milky white as his throes lessened in their violence. Finally, without an utterance, Lord Malphas toppled over.

Caim let out a long breath. His hands shook as the shards of light vanished, leaving behind ghostly afterimages. He looked around for his grandfather's body, but all he found was an inky blot on the floor. The shadows had already covered Malphas's corpse, devouring it in the same fashion.

Caim bent down to pick up his weapons, and gasped as something lifted him off his feet and hurled him back.

He landed on his hands and knees, hunched over as every muscle in his body twitched, contracting and releasing too fast to control. His vision dimmed as a dark pulse sucked most of the light from the cavern and a grinding agony sliced through his chest.

Caim!

His mother's voice cut through the pain. Caim looked up,

fearing Malphas had arisen anew to rejoin the fight, but the assault had come from the other side of the cavern. The gateway was twisting, its surface lapping at his mother as if it meant to consume the rest of her.

He stood up and took a wobbly step. The pain in his chest soared higher, but he kept advancing toward the gateway, step by step. The portal loomed incredibly huge before him, drawing his gaze into its impenetrable depths. There were shapes in the darkness, a row of tall spindly things that might have been leafless trees. They lined a pathway into a dim landscape. The longer he stared, the clearer the picture became. He saw wide plains dotted with black seas, and a distant horizon hedged with soaring mountains. Silver lightning flashed on their peaks. Caim shifted as whispers crooned in his ears.

The Lord of Shadow is dead. Take up his mantle and all will bow before you.

Caim put his hands to his temples, wanting to block out the voice. It wasn't his mother now. The Shadow could fulfill all his dreams. His mother? Returned to him with a word. The power to control nations? In the palm of his hand. Infinity lapped before him, greater than anything he could imagine if he would just embrace . . .

Caim halted his hand inches from the gate's surface. Was this what it meant to be a son of the Shadow? The longing. The corruption. Blood for power and to hell with anyone else? He forced his hand back down to his side. He'd tasted that dish, and he had no appetite for it.

Caim stumbled back as another pulse exploded from the gateway. It hammered at him in a series of waves, each stronger than the last. He forced his eyes open. A pair of black eyes stared back at him. His mother had sunk deeper into the void. Only her face and one hand were visible. Caim fought through the pain to reach for her. A heavy rock fell from the ceiling and shattered less than ten paces from him. With a yell, Caim jumped across the final distance. His fingers closed around her wrist. Her skin was as cool as stone, but still pliable. He pulled, gently at first, but then with both hands when she didn't move. The muscles in his arms and shoulders bulged under his shredded jacket; his legs strained. Then he heard her.

Caim, you must help me. As long as the gateway stands open, this world is in danger from the Shadow.

He leaned back, still holding onto her. 'How can I free you?'

You cannot, my son. I am too far gone.

Caim's chest ached like he'd been run through with a spear as he flailed through the vicious tide of his emotions.

You must let me go and seal the way behind me. Nothing else will stop the powers of the Other Side from entering.

'But I – Mother, I can't leave you. I refuse. There has to be another way!'

Caim, I chose my path a long time ago. For a while I was your mother, and those days were the happiest of my life. But I had a duty to this world.

Caim struggled with her words. The anger that had lain dormant inside him for so long flared up. 'So you left me? I was just a child. Why didn't you bring me with you?'

You've seen Erebus, Caim. I knew what it would have made of you. By leaving you, I had a small hope that you would enjoy a life of freedom, the kind of freedom I never had. I'm so sorry. Even though I had to leave, I never stopped loving you.

Caim felt the rage drain out of him. All this time he'd been holding onto the belief that his mother had been forced to leave him. The truth was crueler, and yet it was the decision he would have made. 'What must I do?'

An impulse flashed through his head, and he saw how the gateway was tearing her apart, piece by piece, down to her very essence. She was almost gone, and when she eventually succumbed the Shadow would flood through unfettered. Everything in this world would die.

Caim, if you love me and honor the sacrifice your father made, you will do this.

He closed his eyes and sought the spark inside him again. It was there, blazing bright. He reached for it . . .

And stumbled as a powerful force shoved him back, breaking his grip on his mother's arm. Even as he lunged for her hand, she sank beneath the rippling surface. The last thing he saw were her fingertips disappearing into the blackness.

Tears stung his eyes. Part of him wanted to dive in after her, but he had a task – a task no one else could do. Caim held out his hands and unleashed his powers. Crisscrossing lines of bright energy appeared across the face of the gateway. As he bent them to the pattern his mother had shown him, the darkness reached out and snarled around his arms and neck with a freezing touch. Caim leaned away as he strove to finish his labor. His injured toes pinched inside his boots as they dug for traction. Cold sweat formed on his face and under his shirt. He tried not to think about his mother, but memories from his childhood flashed through his mind. He saw her standing in the fields surrounding their home, her simple, homespun dress blowing in the breeze, long hair rustling. She was looking at the setting sun with one hand shading her eyes. She looked so peaceful.

Caim fought with all his remaining strength. Torment scalded his nerves as tissue stretched and separated, but he refused to give up. Then the last line was set in place, and the pattern blazed like a star with a thousand points. The gateway seethed, its ripples becoming choppy waves, but they remained confined by the matrix of lines.

Caim retreated until the cool rim of the urn dug into his back. The air of the cavern had turned dry and fetid. He found his weapons on the dusty floor. The gateway, churning and wriggling only moments ago, had become flat and docile. Its black edges were turning gray, the same color as the cavern walls, and he knew with certainty that his mother was gone. He had come all this way to find out what happened to her, and now he knew. She had sacrificed herself for him once. And now she'd done it again.

Caim, if you love me and honor the sacrifice your father made, you will do this.

The crash of shattering stone jarred Caim from his grief. The ceiling creaked as more rocks showered the cavern floor. He didn't know if he had enough strength to form a portal as he reached for his powers. The air rushed from his lungs as he found not a spark, but a gushing wellspring of energy. It wasn't exactly bright, but it wasn't completely of the Shadow either. It felt like a combination of both.

When the portal snapped open beside him, he thought of Kit and stumbled into the void.

CHAPTER THIRTY-SEVEN

Vibrations ran through the ground as Caim stepped onto the plateau outside the citadel. Over the great walls, the black pyramid trembled, and then disappeared in a thunderous collapse that shook the hills.

Caim turned with the black sword raised as a big shape shifted behind him, but he relaxed when he saw it was Malig, bloodied and bandaged, sitting on a low boulder. Kit lay at his feet, wrapped in a dingy fur cloak. Caim looked around as he went to her. There was a texture to the air, both familiar and elusive at the same time.

'Took your time,' Malig said.

Caim grunted. 'You look like I feel.'

'Yeah, I ran into some trouble. Not even sure how I got here, to tell you the truth. Thought I'd lost your girlfriend, too, but I see she made it out all right.'

Caim nodded. Were any of them going to be all right, ever again?

'Anyways,' Malig said. 'I figured you be along sooner or later. No sense in starting back home alone.'

Caim brushed a strand of silver hair out of Kit's eyes. She looked better, just tired. The bruising around her eyes had subsided. To have her, alive and human . . . it was more than he'd ever dreamt could be true. Yet something remained between them, and he had to deal with it if their relationship was going any further.

'I need a favor,' he said.

'Not another fucking quest, I hope?'

'Just keep watch over her until I get back.'

Malig shrugged. 'Fine. Just don't take too long. I still don't like this place.'

That makes two of us.

Caim walked away before he changed his mind. He'd put this off long enough. He navigated a path down through the foothills. Once he was well away from Kit and Malig, he slipped into a gap between two tall boulders. Not sure how to bend his powers to what he wanted to do, he closed his eyes and listened to his breathing. It was steady, but his heartbeat thumped loud in his eardrums. He set the sword against a rock and he reached under his shirt. The golden pendant was warm as he slipped his fingers around it and jerked, snapping the cord. He held it up. The key turned slowly on its tether. The power coursed through him, strong and intoxicating. There was no pain as the portal opened before him. At least, not physical pain.

Caim stepped out onto soft carpet. The night wind whispered against heavy fabric. Outside, a horse whickered.

Instead of a grand hall lit with candles and oil lamps, he was inside a dark pavilion held up by two stout poles jammed in the ground. It was cold, too, despite the miniature cast-iron stove resting beside a large table.

Caim was beginning to think he'd come to the wrong place when he noticed the cot on the other side of the tent. The long, black hair on the pillow gave her away. Watching Josey, Caim realized he'd missed her. It seemed like he hadn't seen her in years. So much had happened since Othir. *I've changed.*

He peered out the tent flap. Soldiers lounged around campfires in the field outside. Four men in heavy plate armor stood at attention just a few steps from the tent. Caim let the flap fall back and turned to the table, which was covered in maps and sheaves of papers. He scanned a report from Hubert about Mecantia. Something about succession. The tent, the maps, the army. *She's changed, too. She is truly an empress now. How does Her Highness remember the hired killer who helped her secure the throne? As a hero, or a convenient accident?*

Wood creaked as she sat up. For a moment she couldn't see him through the jumble of her hair, and Caim took that time to study the girl he'd rescued from a High Town mansion. She looked a little older, more mature, but that could have been the silk nightgown with pearls sewn into the collar. 'Iola?'

Caim stepped into the firelight. 'It's me.'

He wasn't sure what he had expected. Recriminations? Kisses? Hurling teacups? But there was only silence. Then she asked, 'What are you doing here?'

'I, uh . . .' He sighed, not sure how to boil down the last few months into a simple explanation. 'I wanted to see you.'

'You don't look so good,' she said.

'It must be true. Everybody says so.'

'Did you just arrive? I was about to ask how you got inside here without being announced.' She smiled. 'But I remember how good you are at breaking into guarded places.'

'Where are we?'

'How couldn't you know wh—?'

'Never mind. Have you crossed into Eregoth yet?'

'No. Have you seen Keegan?'

'You've met Keegan? Hagan's son Keegan?'

She stood up, holding a blanket over her body. 'Of course. He's the reason we won.'

'Won what?'

By the time she'd finished her tale of assassination attempts, battles, and the new alliance between Nimea and the 'high captain' of Eregoth, Caim was speechless. He never would have suspected it. *No, that's not true. I saw her greatness, that day at the cemetery in Othir. She was born to be empress.* And Keegan had proved himself worthy again. While it was painful to know that death had come to so many in Eregoth, Keegan was the man to rebuild the war-ravaged country. He'd have to tell Malig.

She walked around the stove. 'What of your quest? Did you find . . . ?'

'My mother?' Caim paused as the pain of losing her, still fresh, ripped through him. 'Yes, I found her. But she's gone.'

'I'm sorry.'

He nodded.

'And what about you?' Josey asked. 'Are you back now? To stay, I mean?'

Caim held out the key pendant. 'No. I came back to give you this.'

Josey took it from his hand. For a moment their fingers touched. Then she threw herself into his arms. She was warm and soft, not the scrawny girl he'd left behind, but even as he held her Caim didn't feel the same ardor that had swept over him before. He loved her, and would always love her, but she wasn't the one he wanted.

'I'm sorry.' It sounded pathetic, but he didn't know what else to say. He could hardly tell her about Kit. 'I can't imagine what you've been through, but I know I'm not the one to share it with.'

Caim started to reach for her shoulders to push her back, but Josey broke the embrace first. 'Caim, there's something you should—' She shook her head. 'Just know that I'm fine. I always knew I couldn't hold you, but I'll always love you. I hope you're happy.'

'You know me. When am I ever happy? Is it all right if I check up on you once in a while?'

'Anytime you want. But use the door next time. All right?'

Caim looked at her, trying to etch this moment into his memory as he stepped back into the shadows. Her eyes glistened, but she didn't cry. He gave her a nod, and then he departed.

The portal snapped shut between them.

CHAPTER THIRTY-EIGHT

Josey stared at the spot where Caim had disappeared and wondered if she'd dreamt it all. Then she squeezed the key pendant in her hand.

An animal bleated outside the tent, and in that moment, in the darkness, Josey felt his absence fully for the first time. She could still smell his sweat, his dyed leathers, the faint metallic scent of his knives, the oil of his unwashed hair. She had held out hope that he would return for so long, but the hope had grown fainter with the passing days. Until now. He was her friend, her first lover, and now he was gone.

Josey caressed her belly. Why hadn't she said anything about the child? Caim deserved to know he was going to be a father. *Why? So I can make him stay with me? Is that what I want? No, this isn't Caim's child. It's mine.*

But a memory bubbled up through her brain, of a moment she'd shared with Hirsch before the final battle. 'You remember you asked me about my magic?' he had asked.

'Yes,' she answered, her mind focused on the oncoming fight.

'Well, one of my gifts is the ability to sense the power in others.'

She wasn't in the mood for cryptic talk. 'What are you talking about?'

The adept leaned closer, until the brim of his hat almost touched her forehead. 'The child, lass. He'll be strong in the Art. Damned strong.'

Strong like his father.

Fingernails scratched at the tent flap as Iola peeked inside. 'Majesty, is everything all right? The guards heard voices.'

'Come in. Please.' Josey dropped her hand from her stomach. 'I was just talking to myself.'

Iola ducked inside with a smile. 'They say one shouldn't do that, Majesty. Or you're likely to go mad.'

'I feel like I'm already there. Come sit with me.'

They sat on the cot that served as Josey's bed. *Heavens, I miss that big feather mattress back in the palace.* But she didn't want to think about creature comforts. She had a big decision to make. 'How is your father?'

Colonel Klovus had been injured in the battle and had lost an arm.

'Well, Majesty. He is resting. The doctor believes he will recover his full health, except for his . . .'

Josey put a hand over the girl's trembling fingers. 'He'll live, and that's the important thing. Iola, have you ever been in love?'

The girl blushed and looked down at the comforter beneath them. 'Majesty, I'm just a maid. I haven't any suitors . . . yet.'

'You don't need suitors to be in love. Now tell me true, have you ever loved?'

Iola nodded, and her face grew solemn. 'I think so, Majesty.'

'Josey. You must call me by my name when we're alone. Or else, how can we be friends? And I want to be your friend very much.'

'As you say. Josey.' Iola's smile returned. 'I am in love. I think maybe.'

Josey leaned closer. 'It's Captain Drathan, isn't it?'

'Yes, Your Majes – Josey. He's so . . . everything!'

Josey thought back to all the things she and Drathan had been through. She agreed. She couldn't think of a better match. 'Then you must tell him.'

'I couldn't!' Iola slapped a hand over her mouth as the cry escaped.

They both giggled, and Josey felt the tears she'd spared Caim begin to appear. It was so nice to laugh.

'I cannot, Josey. He doesn't even see me. I'm just Your Majesty's servant.'

'No, you are much more than that. You are my confidante and lady-in-waiting.'

Iola's eyes grew wide in the dim light. 'I am?'

'Yes. And as an honored member of my court, you deserve the respect of your rank. Do you think your father would look favorably on a man like Captain Drathan?'

'I think so. Both my sisters wed soldiers, and he gave them his blessing.'

'Then we shall see to it.' Josey noticed the interior of the tent had lightened. Dawn was approaching. She fought back a yawn. 'As soon as we return to Othir.'

Once the words were said, Josey realized she had made up her mind. She'd done the right thing, for her people, for Caim, and for herself and her baby. Yes, Caim was the father, and perhaps the day would come when she would tell him, but he had his own destiny. Hers was to serve her nation and raise the heir to the throne.

'Majesty. I mean, Josey. May I ask? Are you in love?'

Iola couldn't hide a brief glimpse down, toward Josey's growing middle. Josey clasped her hand tighter. 'Perhaps.'

'Is that why you were talking to yourself before I entered?'

Josey looked to the corner where Caim had vanished. It was empty now, its shadows fleeing as daylight grew stronger.

The tent flap rustled, and a voice called from outside. 'Majesty, a message has arrived. From the capital.'

Josey stood up, adjusting her gown, which seemed tighter and less concealing than it had before. 'Enter.'

Iola curtsied as Brian ducked under the low doorway. 'I'll go see if the cooks have made Your Majesty's breakfast.'

Brian made room for the girl to scurry out, and Josey took the moment to run her hands through her hair. *Good gods, why didn't I make him wait until I had at least cleaned my teeth?*

Brian stood there, looking at her. Just like he had looked at her at the creek. Then, as now, they had been alone. Then, as now, her heart had beat in her throat. He was so . . . everything.

Brian seemed to suddenly remember the message in his hand. He stepped forward and extended it, but his eyes never broke contact with hers. 'Majesty.'

Josey took the letter, stained with mud on one side, but didn't open it. She should say something, but no words came to mind. *What about 'I love you'? He'd probably think I was a fool, or worse. But you won't ever know if you don't take a chance.*

He saved her by speaking first. 'I'll be going back to Othir with your party, Majesty. If it pleases you.'

Pleases me? What did he mean by that? Calm down, Josey. He's just trying to be courtly. 'Your father's idea, Sir Brian?'

'Not likely. He'll birth a calf when he finds out, but I'm going anyway. I want to see those southern lands you told me about. And if I'm to be lord of Aquos someday, I'll need to know how things are done at court. I don't want to be a poor country boy all my life.'

That made her laugh. *Twice in one morning. It must be a good day.* 'Well, I'll be glad for the company. I've decided we'll be leaving today. For the south, that is.'

'Calling an end to your northern excursion so soon?'

His smirk was insolent, and made her heart beat harder. She decided right then to release the hold she'd kept over her feelings since the day Caim left her standing in the cemetery. 'Yes. I think I've found what I was searching for.'

Josey opened the message. Brian said something else, but she didn't hear him as she read. 'Brian, could you assemble my commanders here? Right away, please.'

'That sounds serious.' Major Walthom entered with a horseman's rolling gait. 'Bad news, Majesty?'

Josey tamped down her irritation. The major had accounted himself with valor. Between that and her dearth of good officers, there was the possibility she would have to promote him again before they reached Othir, as much as it galled her.

Josey didn't want to explain the contents of the message twice, but seeing how Brian was glaring at Walthom, she gave in. 'Yes. The lord regent writes that the governors of Mecantia have voted to join the kingdom of Arnos in a new crusade against Akeshia. And they have severed all trade and diplomatic agreements with the empire because of our failure to' – she looked down at the letter— ' "eradicate the threat of the godless heathens of the east." '

Major Walthom sat down on her undergarment trunk. 'That's prickly.'

'And decidedly poor timing,' Captain Drathan said as he walked in. His left leg was bandaged from his thigh to the top of his boot, but he refused to walk with a crutch despite the army physicians' advice. 'This smells of diplomatic sabotage.'

Josey had been toying with the same thought. 'Philomena.'

Drathan nodded, but Brian asked, 'An enemy of the throne?'

'Yes,' Josey answered. 'Well, not exactly.' But before she could launch into an explanation, another man entered her tent.

'Empress, I thought you'd like to know . . .' High Captain Keegan took a look around and stopped. 'Oh, sorry. Your Highn – er, Majesty. I didn't know you were having a meet. I could come back—'

'It's quite all right, my lord.' Josey forced herself to smile. *After all, if I'm going to keep my promise and grant Eregoth permanent autonomy, we must remain on friendly terms.* 'You were saying?'

Keegan cleared his throat. 'Ah, the Uthenorian survivors are fleeing north in good order. My band is going to follow after them, if that's all right. To make sure they don't get into any mischief.'

Josey rolled up the message. 'That's excellent, my lord. I have decided we shall start back south today, but before we left I wanted to speak with you about what assistance the empire can lend your country to rebuild.'

Two more of her officers had arrived, and a quartermaster with the list of their remaining supplies, which were depressingly scarce. Brian talked with Keegan about the Eregoths' return trip home while Captain Drathan grilled the junior officers about their preparations for departure, and Major Walthom looked around for a drink. But there was one face missing. Josey's eyes misted as she imagined Hirsch standing at the table, scratching his beard as he listened to the others. She'd only known him for a couple months, but he had become such an important figure in her life since she took the throne. *I would be dead if not for him.*

Josey wiped her eyes as Iola returned with a covered bowl. It was boiled oats, but Josey was too hungry to complain. While she ate, Iola herded everyone out of the tent and started rooting through the trunks. The girl pulled out a black gown with a high neck and long sleeves, but Josey stopped her and pointed. 'No, that one, I think.' *Hirsch always preferred her in lighter colors.*

'Majesty?'

Josey nodded, and together they manhandled her into a flowing yellow kirtle with small green flowers that was only slightly muddied. When she was ready, Josey stepped outside the tent. A cool wind caressed her hair and pressed the material of the dress taut against her belly. Closing her eyes, she enjoyed the sun on her face. Someone cheered, and the hurrah was picked up by other voices, until a multitude called her name. Josey looked across the camp to a lone hill. A yew tree stood atop the bald tor, its leaves shining like gold in the early light.

An honor guard stood ready on either side of the elmwood casket. Captain Drathan and Brian stood at the front of the procession, looking to her.

Iola clasped her hand. 'Shall we, Majesty?'

Josey took a deep breath. A trumpet called as the honor guard took up their cargo and began the slow march to the hill.

Josey smiled. 'Yes. Let's say good-bye to our friend.'

CHAPTER THIRTY-NINE

The rising sun warmed his back through the heavy cloak. Balaam resisted the impulse to pull up his hood. He'd have to get used to the sunlight.

He shifted his weight. His knee was stiff from where the scion had left his mark, but it would heal. Balaam focused on what lay ahead.

The waves beat recklessly against the shore below, where a team of men wrestled large casks onto the waist of the tall sailing ship. She was beautiful and sleek, like a great wooden mare riding on the sea. Turquoise waters stretched into the morning's gray mist, slowly burning off with the advent of dawn. Balaam took a deep breath of the briny sea air and held it. *I am my own man.*

He had dreamt of this day all his life, even before he understood what his spirit wanted. Freedom. It was the sweetest smell in any world.

He hefted the haversack slung to his shoulder. Inside it was everything he owned: spare clothing, an extra pair of boots, a pouch of metal coins. His belt was empty, with not even a knife to weigh him down. He had left his *kalishi* sword behind in Erebus. A difficult decision, but he felt freer for it. He was tired of living by the blade. Perhaps one day he would find a place to settle, take up a peaceful profession, but for now he just wanted to see this world with new eyes.

Balaam took his gaze off the sea and looked over his shoulder. Dorcas stood behind him, with her burgundy cloak draped over her arm and her hair flying free. He reached out, and she gave him an uncertain smile as she took his hand. She was nervous. *But so am I. We're both trying something new. To trust again.*

He returned the smile and nodded, and then led her down to the shore where their ship awaited.

CHAPTER FORTY

Caim stepped softly as he arrived back on the wastes. Kit, still wrapped in the cloak, sat beside a small fire made from broken sticks. She was beyond beautiful. The sight of her calmed him. She was the only person in the world he trusted completely. She knew all of his secrets, but she loved him anyway.

She looked up, and then jumped to her feet, dropping the cloak as she ran to him so quick it was like her feet never touched the ground. But she was real when she crashed into his arms, and the kiss she planted on his lips seized his heart in a vise-grip.

'Can't you two wait until I'm gone?'

Malig dropped a pair of crude burlap sacks beside the fire. His stolen sword hung over his shoulder by a rope. 'Looting already?' Caim asked.

The big man shrugged as he squatted beside the fire. 'Just trying to make something good out of this shit-storm you served up. There's lots of good stuff sitting around here, and I figure nobody's coming back for it.'

'There's been fighting in Eregoth.' Caim told Malig what he'd learned from Josey about the invasion. 'Are you still going back?'

Malig nodded. 'I've had enough of these wastes. I'll go back home and maybe find a wench. Settle down and have a pack of whelps. What about you two? Back to Nimea?'

'Not on your life,' Kit growled.

Caim laughed, 'I guess not. But it's a long walk back to Liovard for one man alone.'

'I was thinking about that.' Malig spat into the fire. 'You get around pretty quick, vanishing in one place and appearing in another. Can you send me back?'

Caim fought back a smile. He never thought he'd see the day when one of his northern countrymen would even acknowledge his powers, much less request their use. 'I think so. Do you want to go to Liovard?'

'Sure. It's as good a place as any to start out. You know, Caim. You could come back with me. I'm sure Keegan would like having you around.'

Caim was tempted. He could imagine clearing the land around his father's estate, trying to rebuild the manor house. Raise some horses, or cattle maybe. But then the ache in his chest reminded him of all that he'd been through, and all that he'd lost. And there were his powers, only half-understood and never far beneath the surface. Being around ordinary people didn't seem wise. 'Thanks anyway. You ready now?'

'Sure enough.' Malig looked around. 'I got to hand it to you, Caim. You took us all the way to the edge of the world.'

Kit hugged the man around his middle. 'Be good, you big ox.'

Malig chuckled and patted her on the head. When they separated, he picked up the sacks and squared his shoulders. 'All right. Make with the magic before I lose my nerve.'

Caim opened the portal on the other side of the campfire. 'Safe journey. Until we meet again.'

Malig stepped up to the black oval. 'You think it's all right to leave Aemon buried out there? In the wastes, I mean. Seems awful far from home. And Dray. We don't even know where those bastards put his body.'

'They are together,' Kit said. 'And at peace.'

Caim didn't know if Kit had some special knowledge, or if she was just trying to offer comfort, but Malig seemed to accept it. With a firm nod, he took a breath and jumped into the portal. Caim let it close behind him.

'Caim, look.'

He followed her gaze as streaks of cobalt appeared in the slate-gray sky. The blue turned to orange and then to a shimmering glow of pale gold as the sun broke over the horizon. Caim put his arm around Kit, and they watched the dawn sweep away the darkness for the first time in decades.

'So,' he said. 'Now what?'

She slipped her arms around his neck. 'We can go anywhere?'

'Anywhere you want.'

Kit trailed her fingertips across the tops of his ears and planted a kiss on his chin. 'Surprise me.'

The portal opened behind Caim with hardly any effort. Kit laughed and let go of him, and he watched the rising sun for another moment. Light was returning to these wastes, but some darkness remained inside of him. He didn't see any shadows, but he felt them nearby. Watching him. Hungering.

Then Kit pulled him by the hand, with the sunlight flashing in her eyes, toward the portal and their future, and Caim forgot his worries.

ACKNOWLEDGMENTS

As always in a novel such as this, there are too many people to thank properly, but I want to acknowledge:

Lou Anders, my editor and art director, for guiding me through this project from start to finish. I hope it's everything you envisioned.

The staff at Pyr and Prometheus Books for all their help and expertise.

My agent, Eddie Schneider, for keeping me (semi-)sane in a business that seems to get crazier by the day.

And a special thank you to Jenny, Fred, Charlie, Jeff, and Chris for their wit and wisdom.

ABOUT THE AUTHOR

Jon Sprunk is the author of *Shadow's Son, Shadow's Lure,* and now *Shadow's Master.* This Shadow saga has been published in seven languages worldwide. An avid adventurer in his spare time, Jon lives in central Pennsylvania with his family. Visit him online at www.jonsprunk.com or www.facebook.com/JonSprunkAuthor/.